Spirits of the Rock

Book 3

by

Jan Hawkins

Dedicated to the Mothers

Spirits of the Rock

THE DREAMING SERIES

Book 3

By Jan Hawkins

About Jan Hawkins

Australian Author, Jan Hawkins, was raised in the Australian bush on the outskirts of Sydney on the Georges River. Now residing in Queensland, she spent 20 years in education at secondary level in the IT field. Her love of computers pales in comparison to her love of the Australian bush and Jan now has quite a portfolio of photographs. She is passionate about the history of her country and a strong desire to discover and experience new places fuels her desire to travel extensively throughout the land. Along the way she relishes being able to listen to people and to share and enjoy the adventure she calls life.

Sprits of the Rock is the third in a series of four books which introduce the spiritual culture of the First Australians. The third book in The Dreaming Series continues to explore the characters' and their lives, their loves and the balance of the world in which we all live. It's a blending of modern culture with the ancient spiritual culture of our indigenous Australians. Learn of the Spirit Creatures of the Dreamtime and about the men and women who are so much part of The Dreaming.

Two-Fellow Level 'gether

Missus boy and my little boy two fellow grow up 'gether
Level play in mud all day longa the rainy weather;
Two-fellow chase em dog all-time, fight and climb em tree,
Listen hard when my man tell stories longa to we.

That little white kid him likem me, properly nice one boy,
My old man go bush all day, cut em out boomerang toy;
Two-fellow play-play all the day, one fellow black one white,
Two fellow same when play at game, two-fellow level fight.

And my old man him say to me, 'must be someone mad,
Whitefellow think him all time good, blackfellow all time bad;
But kiddie him no more think that way, two-fellow level play,
Whitefellow talk-talk one-fellow God, two-fellowlevel pray.

'Blackfellow all day help 'em white, somebody must be fool.
Whitefellow boy go different kind whenever him go to school;
"Can't understand," my old man say, "somewhere somebody mad."
But I no more listen, me only see, two kid happy and glad.

So I talk, 'old man, listen here, no more growl-growl white,
All-about must live him way, which one say him right?'
Kiddie him play-play every day, kiddie him no more fool.
Two-fellow level understand when two-fellow level school.

An Australian Poem
Unknown Author
Drawn from 'Tales From the Aborigines'
By Bill Harney (1895-1962) – First edition Oct 1959

LAND OF THE RAINBOW SERPENT

Ngaire:

Life carries us along on so many different paths that it's a wonder that we don't often lose our way. I had never thought I could return to this place, never imagined being here without him and yet here I was and I had enjoyed the journey, the small reminders and the beauty of this place. It had been a long journey for me but now I could feel life opening up with the fervour of a new breeze in my world.

Returning here… spending time here on my own since the death of my man had bought me a great deal and I was glad that I had found the courage to return to this place. That he had prepared the way for me in his own time, made being here all the more poignant. My friend Yoonda had been right to advise me to return and I was glad I had listened to her wisdom in the end.

The cooler air of the night still clung to the earth as I waited for the full dawn, but around the campfire the warmth of the fire was like a cocoon as I stirred the embers, encouraging them to life; encouraging them to catch the fresh wood. The movement lent a pungent smell and taste to the air as the fire slowly came to life along with the new day.

I loved this camp. There were many happy memories here for me; memories that were precious and I would always consider this place to be one of peace, good times and gentle discoveries.

The sounds of the bush about me were welcome. I loved to listen to the song of the morning, this was a Spirit place and here I felt safe. This land of the Rainbow Serpent was somewhere I felt I had links with even though the serpent wasn't of my Lore. I belonged to the Wandjin, the Spirit people of the skies but the gifts here in this land had been many.

As I thought again of the cache of plants, seeds and lichens which I had collected here, many more than I had thought to find, I knew that it was truly a bountiful land here in the Channel Country in the Gulf area of Far North Queensland. I particularly loved the old Lawn Hill Station that was now preserved for everyone to enjoy.

Sweeping my long hair carelessly back from my eyes and tucking it behind my ears out of the way, I contemplated the beautiful gorge and its welcome flow of water as I watched the flickering fire spring back to a tenuous life. Once the sun had warmed the air I would go for a swim I decided. It was safe here, it was a place where the wallabies came to drink and I had become accustomed once again to the movements of the wildlife.

Later I would climb back up onto the plateau once more as there were places I still wanted to search. I wondered again at the thread of campfire smoke I had seen yesterday, wondered if the campers had moved on and what had been their business in the secluded tablelands.

It was a surprise to see the wispy string of smoke, announcing another campfire. It had been too fine a stream to be other than a campfire and that it was high on the drier tablelands rather than nestled into one of the gorges was also unusual. Not that there were many people who made their way into the remoter reaches of the old Lawn Hill Cattle Station.

One of the things I like most about Far North Queensland was the lack of population in that it was so far away from the Eastern coastal fringe. Here in the Gulf country I could find myself living in a world seemingly inhabited only by the animals of the land, rarely stumbling across another human for weeks on end. Boodjamulla is a beautiful and remote location. A place of yesteryear, one of the oldest places on earth and a fitting home for the Serpent. It was a place where Namarrgon, the Spirit man of lightening also raged across the heavens in his season and where the Creator Spirits protected their lands.

It had been that very reality, the primitive land which had bought me here. I knew the forests, the ancient bush of the country of the Rainbow Serpent held many treasures and as a healer there was much to attract me. Many mysteries and gifts were to be found in the green shadows and red and sandy earth of the bush country. There were medicines and bush herbs which would be difficult if not impossible to find anywhere else, clays and pigments that had a great value for my people. I was content to spend my time here and as I glanced over at Tango curled up close to the fire, his dappled blue-black coat only just now catching the moving play of light, I smiled at the query in his eyes.

He was my companion, my guard and he worried over me like a parent worrying over an errant child. But it was his very presence that gave me my sense of security. He was also my best friend and as I stretched to ruffle the hair about his ears in a loving gesture, he nuzzled his nose into my hand and then returned to his place.

It was his nature to protect and many times I had been offered a price for his services, others knowing I would not contemplate his sale. As a blue cattle dog, he was a valuable and faithful dog. Though his pedigree was chequered, it was his intelligence, his spirit which commanded his value for me. With Tango at my side I was secure in my world, knowing that there was nothing and no one who could harm me or even threaten me without facing the wrath of my closest friend.

We had been in this area now for many weeks and the camp had a settled feel about it which I enjoyed but I knew the bush would claim back its own very quickly once I left. It would leave only the skeleton of a camp to be reborn in another visit and that time would come in the next weeks when I would step back into my life.

I planned on leaving before the full flush of summer arrived but now it was still the dry season before the rains. The days were beautiful and full of the static of fire in the air, a static building before the season of flooding storms. Though the night was no longer as cool as it had been, the shifting winds still reached up into this gorge. This was relieved by the warm touch of the day and I was now waiting on the sun to reach up into the gorge. It bought with it the promise of the summer heat and rains.

In the coming wet, I knew the whole character of the land would change. The humid heat and the torrential rains of the wet season could hold anyone captive for months with their flood waters turning the land into mire and a spaghetti of creeks. I needed to be away well before then. I had perhaps four to five weeks before this season began its inevitable progress across the land. It would transform this world from its dry slumber into a shallow sea with the torrential rains making much of the land impassable by any vehicle.

As I tidied the camp an hour later, preparing for my trek back up onto the plateau, I contemplated the character of the plants which I sought. I knew that often there were more efficient remedies available but the old people preferred the gentler cures of traditional medicines. I could use both together taking the values from each, more often than not, to not only treat my people effectively but also treat their spirits, knowing that they held to the old ways as well as the new. The old cures were an invaluable tool and I followed the ways of the old people as well as newer cures learnt with my medical experience as a nurse.

The tablelands were dryer than the forests of the gorge and they offered their own flora and fauna. Vehicle access was nonexistent so I climbed onto the tablelands when I had a need to collect more specimens and to forage. My little vehicle, though sturdy was beyond the demands of crossing this terrain and it remained down in the shadow of the gorge near its mouth. Here I was equipped with my back pack and sturdy gear required for trekking in this region and as I whistled up Tango yet again from his own adventures, I headed out into the bush away from the shelter of the gorge and up onto the tablelands ahead.

I enjoyed the explorations of the morning, finding plants of interest and testing bush fruits as the warmer, moister conditions steadily coaxed the bush back to a vibrant life. This was a careful process of selecting the bush medicines I would need and adding their bark, fruits and leaves to my small cache for the medical kit. There were plants to be tested, others to be hoarded, collected for my store of remedies.

 It was the scent of smoke lingering around the bush which first alerted me to the presence of others and Tango, more alert and curious than I, was soon following the trail left by them. I could have whistled him up but I refrained from announcing my presence to unknown ears and as I followed him carefully, I hung back to better judge the situation.

Being a woman alone in a remote location it didn't pay to announce my presence unnecessarily and while I felt no fear, I wasn't overly curious either. I had been looking out for myself for many years. I knew my land and my world intimately and I moved comfortably across the land generally unfettered but this was because I not only knew how to look out for myself but with Tango's protective presence I felt secure. My man had taught me how to become one with this land.

Tango was settled up ahead, hanging back from the camp. He knew where to stop and wait for me and he would not announce his presence either. The first thing I realized was there were no other dogs in the camp; I would have heard them by now acknowledging Tango's presence even if they couldn't see him. These people were neither shooters nor hunters, nor was it an Aboriginal camp as all would usually have had dogs with them.

They couldn't be travellers or campers, this part of the plateau was beyond the reach of their vehicles and I was curious to see just who was in the camp. As I approached quietly I realized it was a small camp, I could smell and see evidence of a struggling camp fire. Whoever had set up the camp had not taken care and I at first suspected that the camp was in fact empty for the time. With an untended fire dangerously left to the bush and the variant mood of the breeze. It was a stupid thing to do on the edge of this dry part of the season, when even the grass was brittle and could easily leap to a fiery life hampered little by what new growth was still struggling. At least that was something I could remedy.

As I stepped forward with a signal for Tango to proceed into the camp I paused as I realized it wasn't as abandoned as I had thought. Across from the rough campfire I recognized the shape under a dusty camp blanket as Tango too bounded towards the form to investigate, his keener senses making him more aware.

I waited, I knew to be cautious. If I needed him to return I knew I would only need to click my fingers and he would obey. The figure under the blanket was still and I wondered what kept them so quiet. Tango saw the figure as no threat whoever it was, he was more curious than wary. Seeing this I moved closer in towards the struggling fire recognizing what looked to be the lanky form of a man who was now restless under Tango's persistent attention; his nose travelling the length of the blanket and then satisfied he sat, looking across to me expectantly.

His behaviour was unusual and more curious now myself at the man sleeping at such an odd hour of the day, I approached carefully. If it had been alcohol which Tango could smell, my dog wouldn't be sitting there. He would have growled as he had no love of liquor, equating it with violence as he did. For a moment I wondered what it was that kept Tango at the man's side.

He was tall and his feet were edging out from beneath the blanket as well as the dark, thick crop of hair which hinted at an Aboriginal heritage. His breathing was somewhat laboured I realized as I approached and this bought me to his side more quickly. The man was obviously in some distress or possibly ill.

Pulling the blanket back carefully I recognized the ill-favoured flush of his skin in its dank blanket of body oil and sweat. In a moment I was measuring the heart beat at his throat while he stirred with a weak moan under the chill touch of my fingers. I had my water canteen to his lips quickly as I struggled to help him sip at the precious water. The odour of fevered skin enveloping me along with the pungent smell of infection.

He was disinterested in my presence, something which triggered alarm. He was lacking curiosity and I knew immediately his state wasn't good and as I dropped my back pack, I looked around to find what was in camp that I could use. My thoughts raced as I registered a lack of equipment. A small pack had been dumped nearby, its contents obviously scarce and scattered.

There was also an empty canteen thrown aside, its cap hanging loose and as I pulled the blanket carefully away from him while I eased his head back to the earth, my eye ran over his limbs looking for clues as to what had bought about his distress.

His arms appeared sound under the brushed cotton fabric of his shirt and I guessed it had been some weeks since the shirt had been washed. This was no normal tourist, he was a man of the bush but it was the deep red stain of dried blood at his thigh, high on his leg and it halted the path of my eyes.

A ragged gash had been opened in his leg, something which had also torn at the fabric and the blood spoke of the depth of the wound, it was a horrible mess. Immediately reaching for my pack I emptied the contents and moved around to better access his leg. I covered his upper torso to prevent the chill touching him and then exposed his injured leg. Under my touch he stirred restlessly as I cut back the canvas fabric of his trousers with my small bandaging scissors. They seemed woefully inadequate against the heavier fabric and I moved carefully to try and clean the wound a little, using the water from my canteen and a small cloth from my pack, wishing all the time that I had my larger medical kit.

When I released the rough bandaging from high on his thigh which had helped in putting pressure on the wound, I realized that the bandage was something he had obviously fashioned to stem the loss of blood and was the torn end tail of his shirt. I was pleased to see only a relatively small amount of leakage of blood from the wound. The bandage had not been too tight and the spill was soon stilled with finger pressure though he winced at the pain of it. Working steadily I inspected and cleaned what I could of the wound.

Using the small scissors from my bandaging kit, I cut away the leg of his trousers completely and tore a rag from the fabric. With the scarce water left in my canteen I was better able to manage the ooze of infection and clear the dust and debris which was still part of the deep tear in his leg though the bleeding began again and I was grateful for the few bandages I had.

The man stirred restlessly and often, obviously feeling the pain of my attentions but he remained in the half world of fever. More than anything I knew I would need more equipment than I had with me. Moving him at the moment wasn't an option I entertained but I would need to return to my camp and this before the nightfall. When the wound was as clean as I could manage I made sure it was covered carefully and then turned my attention to the grey ash of the fire.

The gash was deep, obviously a wound from an animal and it was my guess it was a wild pig or boar, maybe a buffalo, they were the only horned or tusked animals capable of gouging a person in such a fashion. I wondered for scarcely a moment where his main camp was located. This was obviously not it but there was no evidence it was nearby either, perhaps he was travelling. The supplies in his pack, if its size was anything to go by were lamentably low and more than anything he would need food and water. Plans to do something about this began to form in my mind.

At some time during the night previous he must have attempted to tend the fire, the wood was now mostly ash so I searched for timber nearby to feed the flame. Each time the man stirred I tried to get him to drink but after the first initial thirst had been quenched his interest seemed only to be to sleep. The fever had taken its hold and still held him in its grip.

I had everything I needed back at my camp and as I mentally packed my medical kit with the things I would need from there, I tried to make him as comfortable as I could. The smoke from the rekindled fire would lead me back to the spot and I had a good idea of where we were located.

In under half an hour I had readied the camp and the man for my departure knowing Tango would also lead me back to this place if I left my pack here. It wasn't long before I had set out again leaving what was left of the canteen of water infused with what herbs I could find which would help. I left this within the man's reach if he stirred.

The return trip back into the gorge was quicker than I had thought. I collected my much larger medical pack and a few necessities for the night and checking that the kit had all I needed, I also replenished my water supply and I was soon back up on the plateau. Although I was weary with my need for haste, with Tango at my heel egging me on it seemed much easier and it was barely dusk as I once more approached the man's camp. I knew it was going to be a long evening, if not a long night but I was thankful for my training and that I had with me the things I would need.

Within an hour of arriving back I had the wound cleaned again properly and dressed adequately though I recognized the signs of infection. My patient was restless in his confused state and more than once I needed to hold his leg steady as he struggled against my not always tender ministrations. Regardless, I made good use of the penicillin and the few wound clips I had with me to attempt to contain the worst of the damage. Binding it only with a loose dressing would allow better management and I considered if there was really any more I could do at the moment.

I knew he was growing stronger over the following hours once his fever peaked and then began to subside, it was a good sign. It was the greater ease of his breathing which reassured me the most through the long hours that followed.

In the next few days I could stitch the wound but for now the clips and penicillin powder would suffice helping the infection to subside. I watched him carefully as his temperature began to return to a more normal range soon after what I guessed was about midnight.

Once I was satisfied he was in as good a position as I could make him and he was settled on top of his own grotty blanket with mine now spread over him for warmth, I quietly set about preparing a light soup. This would be a supplement to the pain killers I had used to help control the fever, and the natural antibiotics I had laced his water with as I waited for more signs of improvement.

It had been simple to build a rough shelter over the man, a gunya of brush and sticks would provide a light shelter during the early morning and it would leave scarce evidence once we left camp. There was comfort to be found in such a simple shelter, comfort we would welcome against the light blanket of cold which still hung over the land at night, along with shelter from the variable movement of the wind. As the deep night settled in around us I also began to wonder how long he had been in the state I had found him.

Most bushmen would have built such a shelter but that he hadn't, told me more about his movements than his intent. Perhaps he had been trying to reach a main camp and maybe there were others who were now looking for him. I once more had reason to be glad of Tango's presence and so I settled to the night sounds knowing I had now done all that I could and that Tango would keep a careful watch.

It was only then that I allowed my curiosity its free rein as I sat curled beside my dog by the steady burning fire and watched the dark stranger across from me. He looked only to be in his early twenties, a similar age to me, perhaps a little older though his beard was lacking the thickness of an older man. What he was doing out here without the company of mates and with so little evident equipment I could only guess at.

Tango and I enjoyed some of the light meal and the rest I set aside for the stranger. When he stirred I could feed him the nourishing liquid and I kept it warm by the side of the fire. I also began to add layers of clothing myself, as I became aware of the arrival of the fast cooling early hours of the morning.

I considered the resting shape under the blankets, noting his ease and I decided that he wasn't an unattractive man. His features were strong and well formed though it was difficult to see the manner of the man he was without the animation of expression. He obviously had some bush skills, his hands were broad and weathered, he was accustomed to practical labour but his clothing was more like that which would be worn by someone who had the opportunity to change more often than a man of a tribe would. It was his shoes which I had noted the most, they were relatively new, it was likely they had been bought only recently though they had been well used. He had done a great deal of walking and it was all a puzzle to amuse me I decided.

As I spread a light weather tarp I had bought with me over him, offering a warmer covering than only the blanket would provide, I measured his temperature feeling the strain of the long night reach me. I was pleased to feel the more moderate heat of his body though he was still suffering with a fine layer of beaded sweat. His breathing too had become more moderate, the drugs were working well. I signalled Tango to his side, calling him with a look and a hand signal. I was satisfied to see him curl into the strangers' body as I settled myself on a corner of the tarp before the fire and enjoyed a strong cup of tea in the light of the flames. The early morning hours in this season were often cool and a shared heat would keep us all more comfortable.

Before I settled myself down I relaxed watching the flame. When I knew I could sleep without fear or worry I moved to the shelter of the blanket myself. I was careful not to disturb him too much, shifting my body into the steady heat of his on the outer edge which didn't benefit from the fire, settling in the most practical manner to monitor him.

It was perhaps around the small hours that I felt him stir. Tango's sharp movement alerted me and quickly I sat up to check on the man. He lay there perfectly still, a moment frozen in time and confusion as well as discomfit as he took in the presence of Tango curled still at one side of him and my own patient curiosity at his other side.

"Hi," I said softly. "How do you feel? You were pretty sick when we got here."

The man just frowned, then testing his voice carefully a dry sound escaped unexpectedly and I reached in response for the canteen.

"Here, drink this. If you can sit up I have some soup, it's likely still warm, it will do you better." Supporting him carefully as he stretched his neck to the canteen of water I watched as he drank deeply, then wiped his mouth, his eyes curious as he again tested his voice.

"Who... where am I?"

"You are where we found you, I couldn't move you. I found you about lunch time yesterday. It was about twelve hours ago now. I know something of nursing, which is lucky for you I think."

The man went to sit up further and then with a groan relaxed back onto the small pack I was using as a pillow for him. I continued, "You are still pretty crook, I wouldn't be moving around much if I was you," I suggested. Setting the canteen aside I climbed carefully out from under the blanket to retrieve the billy of soup still warm from near the dying embers of the fire. "If you can drink this though, it will help with your strength, you will be pretty weak. I don't know when you ate last?"

His eyes caught mine the depth in his glance surprising me as I again moved back to him with the light billy of soup. Carefully he propped himself up with studied precision and a grimace when his movement reached his leg, then he reached for the billy I held. That he sniffed it first made me smile, but he was obviously satisfied as he put it to his lips drinking the warm liquid readily, giving scant pause before he neared the bottom of the billy of watery soup.

For a long moment he waited silent, his eyes running over my features carefully as he frowned then he tried to once more sit up higher. He was halted unexpectedly by a low growl from Tango who was still curled into his side, but who was also now paying avid attention to the animated stranger.

"I wouldn't move too quickly if I were you, Tango obviously thinks you need to stay where you are," I said softly with a confident smile. "My dog is very serious about people doing what he thinks they should and I won't call him off until I know you're harmless."

He relaxed back onto the support of the pack with due consideration, setting the billy aside carelessly. "I don't think I could move if I wanted to, I just wanted to see how the leg was," he answered a little coarse of voice; obviously taking my warning serious.

"It's been dressed but it's infected. I can stitch it for you when the infection subsides a bit but for the moment I would leave it as it is. I can show you now if you like, but it would be better to wait till daylight. Are you hurt anywhere else?"

"No. Just where the boar got at me," he explained. "Is your dog going to stay there all night?" he added carefully nodding to Tango still curled into his side who I knew was watching while listening to every inflection of my voice.

"Yes, I think so. I'm sorry if you don't like it but he is helping to keep you warm and your temp even."

The stranger considered me again, after his eyes left Tango. "I'm Andrew, by the way," he said haltingly, introducing himself. "I'm glad you came along though maybe I don't sound it… I'm sorry. I'm just a bit groggy, sort of fuzzy for some reason."

I could see he was struggling with his explanation and knew it would be some hours before he was fully lucid.

"It's probably the fever." Reaching for my bag I tipped out a couple of tablets from a bottle readily. "Here take these, they won't help with the foggy feeling you have but they will keep your temperature under control. You still have a fever but it's subsiding."

"Thanks."

Andrew took the tablets from my proffered hand and as I reached for the canteen, I found it unnecessary as he popped the tablets easily into his mouth and swallowed them without any trouble. When I offered the canteen anyway, he did reach for it then and followed the tablets with a swig of water, when satisfied he handed the canteen back.

"That water tastes off," he said surprised.

"It has bush medicines in it they will help with your fever."

"You didn't say who you were," he added after a moment as he eased himself back. "I know your dog better than you."

His smile reassured me that he had to be feeling better. "I'm Ngaire, it's spelt funny but has a silent G. I'm here on a bush study. My interest is related to my medical training," I explained easily. "Tango is my companion and as I have explained he can be overly protective at times which is not a bad thing."

"You're on your own? That is a bit risky isn't it?"

"I often travel on my own it's something I am accustomed to. Tango as I have said is more than just a dog. I'm stronger than I look," I reassured him with total confidence. "You also are on your own, or is there someone off getting help?"

"No, I'm alone. I'm listening to the country."

Andrew's steady look complemented his explanation. I knew what that could mean and I wondered for a short moment what his ceremony was about. He obviously was past the initiation of manhood which he would have been a participant in perhaps around a decade or more ago but I also knew there would be no explanation coming. This was men's business.

"Where are you from?" I asked curious.

"Wollumbin country, near Nimbin, it's in the Northern Rivers Region of New South Wales. How about yourself?"

"You're a long way from home. I'm from the west, sunset way. I grew up around the Kimberley's and the Top End, though my father was an Islander, a Maori."

I watched as Andrew nodded, his attention span was growing shorter and I knew it wouldn't be long until he slipped into sleep again as he was struggling to stay attentive.

"So we meet in the strangest of places," he added absently. Tango eased his head up then stretched out into Andrew's side happily. "Shhh... boy," he said softly, his hand seeking the warm coat of my dog. "I'm not going to hurt her... it's OK," he said with a whisper as he slipped back into sleep.

After watching them quietly for a moment I tidied up about me, smiling at his assumption that he would be given the opportunity to hurt me. I knew he would never have that chance with Tango or I. The two of them lay together seemingly the best of friends as they both drifted back into rest companionably.

Then feeling the weariness of the long day and most of the night myself, I turned back to the fire and banked it carefully. Once satisfied and very conscious of not disturbing Andrew, I slipped under the weather tarp and blanket that covered him and stretched out along his side again realizing he was once more beyond knowing I was there. It was warm here and I didn't want to steal the warmth of my blanket too much. I knew what Tango could do and I was confident of his protection as I slept.

I had no hesitation in sharing my warmth with Andrew plus it would be easier to monitor his own temperature, I would be more readily aware if his fever returned. It wasn't long before I slipped into sleep myself with the sounds of the night moving peacefully around me.

BACK FROM THE SHADOWS

Andrew:

I woke to the movement of the dog. The pressure of his presence against my leg had become uncomfortable but the sudden movement triggered actual pain which speared through my upper leg making me suddenly tense.

It was a moment before I realized I also had been enjoying the comfort of her body heat curled into my other side. It surprised me, that she was there and I lost the awareness of my pain in my confusion, while I readily acknowledged the mutt I hadn't expected the woman to be here.

The dog settled again and I felt the ease of my muscles at his stillness. His name was Tango I recalled, as I thought over the memories of the midnight discussion and I struggled to recall her name. All I could remember was that she had said the G in her name was silent. For the life of me I couldn't remember what her name was though I knew she had told me. I debated the possibilities; Caree or Clarey... neither sounded familiar.

Once more I felt the pain in my upper leg as I moved, but that I could feel anything at all was a relief. I had thought at one point I was facing death when I realized that the wound had become infected before I had the opportunity to reach any settlement or town. As I contemplated the turn of events I knew that the arrival of the girl at my side had been my salvation and it amazed me that she had even found me at all. That I couldn't even remember her name was an irritation not worthy of the flood of gratitude I felt.

Carefully I tried to shuffle my position only to hear the responding deep throated growl of the dog and that stilled me. I didn't know how this mutt was going to react to anything I did, I knew I had been warned but that told me little other than to be wary. Once more I felt the discomfort of my body and I knew I would have to move soon.

The girl at my side suddenly stirred as I drew a deep breath and I watched as she blinked at the brightness of the morning. It was well after the dawn and the morning bush sounds filled the air around us announcing the move from the dawn into the day.

"Hi," I offered carefully as I watched her prop herself up on her elbows, collecting her own thoughts.

"Morning. How do you feel?"

I considered how to answer her question as I took in her features. She had a confidence about her eyes which was uncommon in someone her age, which had me wondering just how old she was. Perhaps she was older than she looked. She was an attractive woman, her skin a deep honey and I remembered she had said her father was a Maori and I recognized this in the rounded shape of her facial features.

Her dark hair scattered around her shoulders in a curtain of disarray escaping from a loose plait, it was long and looked like heavy silk which held my attention. I watched as she suddenly sat up, swept it into a tail and using a band from her wrist to hold it she bound the tresses firmly back into a tail which lay down her back leaving it slowly to unravel again from the plat. It was an extraordinary length, unusual in today's women and for a moment I wondered what it would feel like slipping between my fingers.

She was shapely; I wouldn't have described her as slender but as womanly. I could see this even from her back and that I had the company of such a woman, so unexpectedly in so remote a location kept my interest in her movement.

"I feel alive, which is an improvement on yesterday." I answered ruefully realizing she was waiting for an answer. "But I need to get up. Your dog...?"

Without ado she stood in a single graceful movement as she spoke. I felt the distraction of interest, but my body was more demanding of my attention. I struggled to divide my interest and my own needs, struggled to control the bite of pain which demanded my attention also. Time wasn't a commodity I felt I had in this moment.

"Tango," she called softly.

Immediately the dog sprung to its feet completely ignoring me and as she stepped carefully over me and moved towards the fire, the dog followed to dance at her heel.

As I eased myself up carefully I felt my head swim and I fought it trying to steady myself. The pain in my leg held me still though, as I swore softly without thought.

"Maybe getting up is not such a good idea," the girl warned. "I could get you an empty container or something you could use, I'm sure there is something around."

Surprised I caught her glance as her eyes searched the camp, she obviously knew what my concern was and then I remembered that she had said she was a nurse or had some sort of medical experience.

"No thanks, I need to move," I answered self consciously as I swept the blanket aside realizing it was obviously hers, I also realized I was missing most of the leg of my pants but that was the least of my worries. The movement to prepare to stand was excruciating but I fought to ignore it which seemed to add to my discomfit. Perhaps it was the tenseness of my muscles so I tried to relax

"Let me help you there," she said quickly as she moved to my side not waiting for a response.

Her support was a godsend but it left me aching for relief from the act of standing and moving. I made it as far as the first spindly bush, a few scarce steps and I knew this was as far as I was going to get. Gripping the branches of a bush for support I released her impatiently.

"I'm sorry, I can't go any further. Could you just go," I said tersely as I fumbled with my pants.

"Sure, no need to be so uncomfortable."

I didn't have the patience to answer and with blessed relief moments later, my conscience returned. Struggling to return to the blanket, it was a relief when I carefully eased my aching body back onto the blanket while she consciously ignored me. Then when I took the opportunity to check my injury, the girl arrived wordlessly at my side with the canteen and tablets.

The paracetamol I recognized, but at the others I frowned.

"They are painkillers and antibiotics, part of my kit," she explained handing them to me. Turning back to the campfire she left these in my hand and busied herself with arranging the billy.

"Thanks," I knew my behaviour might appear churlish. It wasn't that I was meaning to be so it was just that her behaviour was a constant surprise. She seemed to easily anticipate my needs, something I didn't expect.

What scattered my wits, aside from the pain of my leg and my aching head was the more I looked at her, the more I could see how attractive she was. The way she moved and the casual grace of her step demanded attention. The unconscious swing of the long rope that was her hair which she had carelessly woven firmly back into a plait was equally distracting. I had spent way too much time on my own I recognized easily.

My eyes weren't the only eyes that followed her, Tango, the dog who sat attentively and leisurely near the fire was watching her every move. He seemed to totally ignore me though I knew better as I could feel his acute awareness. Struggling with my wits I eased my body back and again turned my attention to my wound, the main source of my discomfit.

I picked at the dressing, trying to ease it back from the dried and bloodied mess but within moments she was by my side again. Pushing my fingers aside almost absently, she lay a warm and wet cloth over the dressing, a piece of cloth from the missing leg of my pants I realized. She left it there, allowing the warm water to soak into the gauze.

"Give the water a chance to soften the gauze," she explained softly. "It might sting a bit as it has some antiseptic in it."

I was relieved to lie back, to let go of my concerns for the moment. This woman was more competent than I in this I realized and it was something of a relief. The dizziness was becoming a problem for me and I could feel the beads of sweat against my skin. It was wonderful to allow her to take control. She asked nothing of me other than for me to allow her to work steadily and I could manage that I knew.

As I struggled still to recall her name she attended to my dressing. Her touch was soft and incredibly gentle as she worked the dressing from its hold. When I felt the release of the gauze I lifted my head up curious. I didn't recognize the angry gash of a day or two ago, the one I despaired of ever seeing healed as I had steadily sunk into discomfit and pain. She had obviously dressed the wound at some point that I had been little aware of.

Surprised I saw where she had used wound clips to hold some of the torn skin together in places and as I watched she tended to the raised angry skin gorged with infection. Trying desperately not to complain at the pain I felt, fighting to set it aside, I disentangled it from my senses knowing the wound was an inevitable result of my own stupidity. I should have shown more care in this terrain that I was passing through and I knew I should have been more aware of what risks and dangers were around me.

There was no excuse for my lack of awaremess and I didn't look forward to explaining my inevitable scar to Taipan and the guys when I got home.

This accident was effectively going to put an end to my time up here I knew. The wet season was approaching and I would run out of time but I had at least gained an incredible amount of knowledge in my training. My mentor had left me weeks ago and I knew my awareness of the land had been finely honed in my time spent with him and on my own.

Sean would find some amusement in the fact that I had failed to prevent the boar from attacking me, after all I was supposed to be learning how to control and influence the animals and creatures around me. I would find it hard to explain to him that I had been totally taken by surprise. It was such a dumb mistake for me to make. I should have made camp earlier than I had and I would have been less distracted with weariness.

I knew I could now continue my training anywhere, even here, now; and I looked over to the mutt wondering how much I could influence his behaviour with what I had been taught. But first I had to heal, that was going to be my focus. This woman at my side now tending to my wound, would be enough of a distraction to my senses and I wondered how long our paths would travel together. If only I could remember her name I would find conversation easier to start.

"I haven't thanked you," I said conscious suddenly of her care, her presence and the fortune which had caused our paths to cross as I watched her tend to the wound despite the discomfit it caused. I had managed to separate my awareness from the pain and it helped a great deal.

Her flashing glance caught mine as she then turned back to her ministrations. "That's OK. I'm just glad you weren't dead when I found you."

Surprised at her candid comment I grimaced, "Yeah well... that was a real possibility."

"Yes it was. We will have to move you soon, we need more water. As it's I'll have to get down into the gorge again today to replenish the supply, I have nearly used it all. Did you have a base camp somewhere?"

"No, I left the Cooktown region some time ago and had been making my way west." Surprised she turned to me as I continued answering the unspoken question in her eyes. "I have been in the bush for a few months now, I left some friends a while or so ago. I travel light."

My words sat between us as she turned back to redressing the wound and I wondered how much she understood. The woman gave nothing away and I was beginning to find it frustrating. Cooktown was hundreds of kilometres east across the Gulf country and yet she asked no questions, displaying no more than idle curiosity. Her interest was purely in my wound it seemed.

"My camp is down in the gorge, perhaps we can move there in a day or so when you're stronger. Then I can get you out to a base hospital, I have a vehicle near camp at the head of the gorge," she said as she began to apply a covering to the wound.

"Is that necessary? You seem to be coping well. I should be mobile given a week, perhaps if I can just hook a lift to Mount Isa I can make my way from there back into Cooktown way."

"Your confidence in me is flattering, thank you. But you will need stitches and unless we get this infection under control you may need more attention than I can give you."

"I have total confidence in your ability. Can you do stitches?" I asked. I didn't want to attend a base hospital if I could at all avoid it. That would take days out of my time and I considered it something of a waste.

"I can, but I have no anaesthetic."

For a moment I considered the prospect, "I'll manage."

"Let's see how you cope first." Laying the last of the tape to hold the gauze dressing she began to gather together her kit.

Breakfast was more welcome than I could have ever imagined and as I watched her move about the camp I began to appreciate her presence more and more. It had been a solitary few weeks since I had left the other men. I was pleased for my solitude to end. I was ready to return back to the Community and for a moment I wondered how Sean and Jenna had fared in these past months.

It had been a difficult year so far, though it was looking to improve for them. I knew that Sean had every intention of staying close to Jenna for the time being as she grew more independent of the Community and I smiled at the memory of the challenging minx she was becoming. They would have been back in Brisbane for some time now and Jen would be back well into her studies.

When the small camp was in impeccable order the woman set about putting her pack to order, taking some items out and setting them aside she came over once finished. She had repacked my own small back pack adding items from her own; she now left it near where I was stretched out.

"I'll be back after lunch Andrew, I need to check my fish trap," she remarked and flicking her fingers at Tango, she turned to leave.

I was struck with the quandary of my situation. If I could recall her name I would have furthered the conversation but my thoughts were incapable of being tamed and I could think of nothing to delay her departure. So, I watched her leave and then reached for the canteen she had left nearby. My weariness got the better of me in the end and I fell into a restless sleep nursing the still dull throb of my leg.

When I again stirred to movement around the camp, the sun had moved fully across the sky. I gave myself a few moments to test my senses, then, slowly I eased myself up relieved that the dizziness that had kept me on my back had largely passed. The woman was back and was moving about the fire. She noted my alertness as I sat up slowly and then with a small satisfied smile she turned back to the fire busying herself with the billy.

I'd never been in camp with a woman who was so self contained that they didn't require conversation and I found it disconcerting, particularly in an attractive woman. I struggled with what to say, wondering how I could engage her attention in some way.

"How did the fishing go?" I ventured carefully, testing my leg gingerly as I moved it, ignoring the discomfit and debating whether to attempt to join her at the fire.

Immediately she looked up at my movement frowning. "We have fish for dinner. I've made something of a stew with a few things I've collected."

Standing, she moved over towards me carrying the billy. "I've warmed some water here, you need to wash. You smell."

Surprised I watched as she sank down beside me and looked at me expectantly waiting. It took a moment before I realized for what she was waiting.

"You want me to strip?"

"Can you think of any other way to wash?" she countered with candour. It was a simple statement, not a question and as I began to unbutton my shirt I wondered what she would make of my markings.

"You don't have to do this, I can do this," I offered with an uncertain deference.

"Yes you can. I'll do your back and your leg, I need you clean Andrew. Tomorrow you can wash in the gorge before we stitch the worst of your wound. But for the moment sleeping beside you is not pleasant."

"Oh. Sorry about that," Smiling, trying to entice a smile in return as I pulled off my shirt I waited to see what she would say, if anything. The scarring across my torso was barely healed and although it was still somewhat raw, it was no longer troublesome. It ran into a deep V form across my chest muscles and had been patterned to produce a raised hatching in two marked rows.

The woman frowned and carefully reached out to run her finger along the freshly healed raw skin deep in the V, where the thinness of my skin tissues had made healing more prolonged.

"This has given you trouble?" she said softly. "You're a Shaman?" Her look was direct, serious and as I nodded my head she continued, "You're not long out of ceremony." Then suddenly her expression changed as she continued. "Sorry. That's obvious."

Collecting the billy she quickly moved behind me and I felt the warm water suddenly sweep across my shoulders as she went about cleaning the skin of my back. The heat and wet cloth felt incredibly good as I eased my muscles into the heat of the cloth.

"It's OK." I said, looking for anything to say. I didn't want her to act in anymore a remote a fashion than she already did. "I really appreciate everything you've done and are doing. I owe you a debt."

"You owe me nothing," she countered softly spoken. "I only do what's asked of me by right. You would understand this I think Andrew."

I watched as she came around to my leg and as previously, she laid the wet cloth over the gauze of the wound, sitting back to wait as the warm water softened the stiffness of the dressing.

"You make it hard to talk to you," I said wanting to put a chink in what I was beginning to think was a natural defence.

Without pause, I watched as she dipped another cloth torn from the missing leg of my trousers into the warm water and sitting back handed it to me and then once more wet down the cloth over the dressing and applied scant pressure to the wound, encouraging it to soften as I winced. I distracted myself by using the cloth she handed me to wash down my upper body.

"What would you want to talk to me about?" she asked dispassionately.

"I'd like to know more about you."

"Why?"

I shook my head confused at her reticence. "Why do you think?"

I meant to tease her, but immediately I could see that it was ill received as her eyes met mine. Her look was steady but then to further confound me she smiled.

"Take off your pants," she said suddenly. "You really do need a good wash Andrew. I need to find some bush honey and I have an idea where there is a hive. I'll be back in a short while and I'll redress your wound."

Climbing to her feet she flicked her fingers and immediately her dog jumped up from where he had been sitting at leisure, now fully attentive. I watched as they moved off together, still at a loss as to how I seemed to be making such a hash of this.

However, I didn't wish to aggravate the situation any more than it appeared I was doing, so carefully and somewhat gingerly I worked what was left of my trousers down over my leg and washed as best I could. Then taking to the remaining leg with my knife from my pack I ripped away the other leg of my pants so the length of the legs matched making shorts of my trousers, it would help with the need for cloths. When I had finished washing I hauled my pants back on and gingerly worked at the dampened cloth over the wound as I waited for her to return. I wasn't sure why she would need honey for the fish stew still cooking off to the side of the camp fire and I was half convinced it was a ruse she had used to allow me privacy.

True to her word, she was back well within an hour and had in a plastic bag, a small handful of bush honeycomb, dripping with the delicious bush honey that pooled in the bag, her mutt still at her heels. I was stretched out under the shade of the gunya still with the wet cloth over my wound as it worked to soften the scabbing and I mulled over the possibilities of her name which still escaped me.

I had debated simply asking her, but given the time we had spent together it seemed somewhat ignorant on my part though I had been unable to come up with anything which seemed probable. My latest guess had been along the rhymes of Narrel or Neralie, but I couldn't see how a G could be silent in either spelling.

Quietly, she collected the now empty billy and before long she had heated more water and returned to my side to inspect the condition of the gauze. It wasn't long before she had worked it from my wound and went about washing and cleaning the area with whatever mix she had steeped in the billy which stung like the blazes and kept me silent as I concentrated on minimising the pain.

Finally she sat back satisfied. "I'm sorry that hurt so much, but I need this as clear as I can get it if I'm going to stitch it tomorrow."

Gingerly I sat up relieved that the worst was over. I surveyed the wound myself carefully. "I don't know if I'm looking forward to that," I added grimacing.

"We could head into Mount Isa or Camooweal Base Hospital. They would do it there very well."

"No. I have confidence in you. Besides I'm not ready to head into civilization yet."

For some reason, she smiled and then sitting back took up the honeycomb, carefully opening the bag she dipped in her finger and surprised me by reaching over and spreading the sticky honey carefully over my chest where the hatch scars were most raw, deep on my chest bone.

Surprised I caught her eyes in question.

"It's an antiseptic, and aides in healing. It will be most powerful on your leg, helping to prevent the scabbing reoccurring and it will help prepare the skin for stitching."

I watched fascinated as she carefully poured some of the golden liquid contained in the comb over the angry gash and then gently smoothed it along the wound with her finger. The sting was only slight and easily controlled. Carefully she worked around and over the wound clips.

"It's clearing nicely," she added. "We will have to be careful as we move you across country tomorrow. It isn't too far to go, dropping down into the gorge might be more difficult but the ready access to the water will make it much easier to manage the wound and the question of infection, not to mention the convenience of the camp. My car is near also, so we can get to Camooweal if you change your mind or the infection flares. I'm running low on supplies, this is the last of the gauze which is a bit of a problem if all doesn't go well but I'll wash the other cloth and we can use that to bind the wound when we are ready. It will do for the time being."

Surprised again, I considered what she had said. "That is the most you have ever said, I was beginning to think you didn't like me much. I couldn't work out how I'd upset you?"

As she wiped the honey from her fingers in a damp cloth she considered me. "You didn't upset me."

Shaking my head at my inability to understand her I added, again carefully. "I'm glad to hear it."

"Andrew, I'm sorry. I'm not used to being around men, I'm unused to their ways. I was raised by my mothers."

"You don't have a man in your life? No father? Husband?"

"Yes. I have a son but that is different. He does as he is told usually," she said candidly. Then standing she moved back over towards the fire emptying the billy and refilling it, setting it to the side of the fire to heat, she seemed completely indifferent to my surprised expression.

Easing myself back, stretching out on the blanket I watched as she busied herself around the fire, checking and tending the fish stew the smell of which had become a rich promise about the camp.

That she was a mother and had a son stayed with me. Somehow I saw her in a different light. She looked different although I knew it was only my perception that was different. What had become of her son's father? Surely he wouldn't have left her on her own with the child so early in their relationship, as it could only have been a couple of years. The child could be no older than a few years at the most I figured.

"I didn't imagine you with a child." I said into the silence of the camp, attracting her glance again as she moved over to pet her mutt who was settled back in his favourite spot near the fire not far from her.

"He is back at home. I miss him."

"How old is he?"

For the first time I noticed the animation in her eyes as she thought of the child. "He's four."

"Four! You must have been a baby..." discretion stopped me, though she didn't seem insulted by my ill considered words.

"Would you like some food, the fish is ready?" Not waiting for an answer she moved to the fire, took up my pannier and filling it bought back to me.

"I'm sorry, I didn't mean to imply anything by that," I added taking the hot stew carefully as I sat up.

"I'm not offended. I was very young, my husband worried over just what you're thinking. I could never really understand why."

"Is he with the boy?"

For a moment she was quiet, as she too settled and took up her own pannier of stew. "No. He isn't with us now," she added softly. "My boy is waiting for me in Katherine and I'll be heading back there soon. Do you have kids?"

"No." I answered, surprised at the very thought. "Geezus, I wouldn't know what to do with kids."

With a small playful smile she turned back to her meal, sipping carefully as she continued. "Tell me about yourself? You said you live near Nimbin, that's in New South Wales isn't it?"

"Yes... Northern Rivers, I live with my family there in a Community, some of the Bundjalung mob."

"Initiation has bought you up here?" she added watching me carefully, curious I could see.

"Yes."

"My husband was like you, a Shaman," she explained in the same soft voice she used when she required no comment.

Quietly I digested this along with my dinner. That explained a lot, he had likely been much older I guessed. She seemed so young and yet so competent in everything she did. She even moved quietly over the ground in a way that was natural to her and I guessed she had spent a great deal of time in the bush.

"It must have been difficult for you, being so young," I said after a moment, knowing the ways of the tribal Shaman were not easy. I had met a few of the older Shaman over the past months and many were strong and powerful men though I had not met any of their women. Those not living within a Community were solitary men, their ways unbending but their freedoms considerable.

"No. It wasn't difficult. My husband was very kind and I was very happy. He taught me a great deal. Tango was his gift to me, to help me when he no longer could. I think sometimes he is still with me in the manner in which Tango will take care. He is very like my husband in many ways."

I looked across at the dog with a new respect as I watched her smile across at the mutt and the confident response in the dogs fleeting glance. To say this knowledge rattled me would be sound, suddenly I felt the presence of the man as his shadow crossed between us and it was a powerful thing. The women of the Shaman knew more about their husbands Lore than most and this in itself made them stronger women.

Women like Gran back in the Community and like Aine was becoming. You never crossed such women as these, they knew much that was secret and they drew their strengths from this.

As night fell, I tried to be more a part of the small camp and managed to persuade the dog to notice me. He had stayed clear of me at first but as the woman moved about the camp, she helped by largely ignoring him, her glance only fleetingly finding us as I tried to gain the trust of the dog.

Tango in turn studied me. He wasn't about to be part of any game and I often thought he was amusing himself at my expense. I had never had to work so hard at maintaining any animal's attention. It was a new and frustrating experience for me.

An easy way with animals had always been a part of my skill; it was something which Sean and I shared, something we had played about with even as children but this animal was like no other that I had ever come across.

After more than an hour I had managed to coax the mutt close enough to be almost companionable but when the woman set aside a bowl of now cooled stew and simply flicked her fingers, Tango immediately disdained my company and almost bounded to her feet. I consoled myself that he must have been hungry though I felt he had truly just been marking time and I was some type of entertainment for him which could easily be discarded.

While the mutt wolfed down the meal, she bought over a hot steeped tea and handing it to me, joined me, sitting on the edge of the blanket.

"He likes you," she said suddenly, nodding to the dog still busy with his meal.

I chuckled, feeling that she was being more friendly than sincere. "I have my doubts."

Sipping the hot tea I watched as she considered her dog. "He does like you. Normally he will have nothing to do with anyone else except me."

"What about your son?"

"Oh that is different. Tango adores Jem, he treats him like a puppy and shadows him everywhere when he's with us. They are inseparable. When Jem is around it's the only time Tango willingly leaves my side."

The night sounds of the bush moved around us quietly as we sat before the fire and it wasn't long before Tango joined us, though I had the feeling he made it very clear for me just who it was he was joining as he settled nearby.

I felt the weariness of the day begin to envelope me and it wasn't long before I was stretching out along the dusty blanket under the shelter of the gunya again. I couldn't believe how easily I was tiring and guessed it had something to do with the added exertions of the afternoon. Hopefully tomorrow I would be up-to the move down into the gorge and I pondered the prospect as I drifted off.

I knew it was a dream, but it was comfortable so I was enjoying the experience. I was with friends and the travelling was pleasant and companionable but I felt the presence of others, older, surer company almost that with a parental interest. It was a secure and comforting experience.

Those I travelled amongst had been teasing me about my leg, it was healed but I was more than conscious of the reality of the finely lined scar even though it gave me no grief and I recognized Taipan and a few of the others, even young Tom. We were a hunting party, though I wasn't sure what it was we had hunted. It was different, an odd sensation that the quarry we had tracked wasn't for food and it confused me but success and satisfaction were feelings we shared. I enjoyed the feeling and I knew part of me wanted a return to simpler times.

It was a river we were on and there was an awareness of a serpent which again confused me. I couldn't understand why we would be hunting a serpent but we were and it was important.

I felt the warmth on my chest, a faint tickle. The moisture relieving my skin and I wanted to spread the sensation but it was more contained and I wondered how I could spread it about me as I enjoyed the feeling. It bought to mind the touch of a woman, which was now part of my dream, though I knew there were no women in the hunting party, they had remained back at the house with the kids. I couldn't think who the kids were but yet I did feel the presence of women and children?

As the warmth travelled up over my chest in small even movements I stirred. I could feel it and it was with the conscious realization of movement about me that I came back to the noise of the night.

I must have tensed as I opened my eyes and noticed her. She was there, tucked into my side but she was awake and watching me, moistening her lips as though tasting my mood she looked like she belonged in my dream.

"Your chest is still sticky," she said softly as she watched me curious. "I was just cleaning it a bit." Her voice was like a whisper and as I listened, I moved towards her carefully to taste her lips as she still flicked her tongue over them, the thought of a shared sweetness tempting.

Her lips were sweet and warm, deliciously so and as I savoured the taste of her I felt the need to venture more. This wasn't a dream I realized slowly when the discomfit of my movement shifted to actual pain and surprised I broke off from kissing her.

As my head swam strangely I stretched back, struggling to still the movement. I wasn't sure if this was a dream or was I in something of a strange reality but then it became lost to me anyway. It was a carefree moment in my dream and I had enjoyed it intensely.

Once again it was late into the morning when I woke. For the moment I was content to simply lie still. The lethargy of my body wasn't normal and I knew I should have been recovering my senses by now.

I was alone in camp but I could hear movement about me, sticks snapping, it wasn't long before she returned to camp and with difficulty I sat up, sitting still as my head swam and then settled. I took a moment to wonder about my dreams, my chest was no longer sticky but maybe it had been a dream, maybe my sweat had dealt with the honey. I couldn't be sure and I couldn't think how to resolve the question and I even began to wonder about the honey, had I really felt it?

"Morning," I called, still struggling to gather my wits.

"Hi. I have found you a crutch of a sort; you should try using it a bit. It will help with moving you."

Watching as she moved over to me, I noticed her dog drop to a space beside the fire seemingly disinterested. The crutch was a dry branch, but it was strong and clean, it looked able to take my weight and as I levered myself up she handed it to me. It was a good height and the top, while not entirely comfortable, fitted neatly as a Y brace under my arm.

"It's good. Thanks." My head once again began to swim and I dropped back to the ground heavily, wincing.

"You need something to eat, the tea hasn't worked off yet."

"Tea?"

"Yes. It will make you sleepy, it's a bush draught. You have been drinking it for the last two days to help you heal and keep you quiet. It has sedative value but I think it might be best if you move about now. We can head down the gorge once you feel strong enough this morning."

"You drugged me?"

She nodded, quite unrepentant then turned back to the fire. She filled my mug with what was obviously breakfast while I took in the reality. I wasn't quite sure whether to be angry or thankful. I had slept well and felt better for it but I wasn't keen on the means to the end.

"It will wear off this morning and there's no need to have more, your temperature is under control."

As she handed me the mug, I frowned suspiciously and looked up at her, wondering if there was anything else in my food she wasn't telling me.

"At some point you have to decide to trust my judgement. You have no need to eat or drink what I give you but you'll feel better for it. The choice is yours, you can leave at anytime." she added softly with a small grin, turning back to the fire and taking up the walking stick I had dropped to the side she began to bind some of the leg cloth from my trousers around the top creating a softer pad for comfort of use.

It was then I realized that I had to trust her, she was right. I had no reason not to and every reason to do so. I wouldn't get very far as I was.

The soup was good and was a variation on the evening meal but with different flavours added which changed its character. It also seemed to be thick with some kind of cress that had a peppery taste and the long bush yam's I easily recognized.

"I don't mean to appear ungrateful but I'm not used to having decisions taken for me."

"Well, there should hopefully be no need for me to help you sleep anymore. Though I will need to use something to dull your senses when we come to stitching you up, I trust you won't mind that so much?" Laying the crutch to the side of me she finished off her own soup as she watched me steadily waiting for the obvious answer.

"I have some stuff with me. We could use that unless you would rather something else," I offered.

"I noticed you had some pituri in your pack. It will help you. I am happy to use that as you'll be familiar with it," she agreed turning away to attend to the camp.

Surprised that she even knew what it was in my pack, aside from having any knowledge of any gear I carried, it was a moment before I realized it made sense to have searched my scant gear. I would have to stop thinking of her as an antagonist. She was far from that and I was being stupid thinking that way. I wondered for a moment where she had gained knowledge and recognition of pituri in its prepared form. Then I remembered her husband and I realized as a healer herself, she would have been privy to such things. It left me wondering what else she knew of men's Lore.

Just before lunch time we were underway. The bush camp was dissembled and aside from the small stone ring that marked the fire pit there was nothing to say we had been there. The walk across the tablelands and down into the gorge became slow and painful after the initial good start. My injury began to bleed with the constant rhythmic movement of my leg and I took to almost hopping using the crutch to ease the discomfort of it. I didn't want to stop as this would have meant further delay to stitching the wound, further risk of infection and a need to set up a second camp.

It wasn't until we reached the head of the escarpment that she noted the bleeding and the discomfit it was causing me as I tried hard not to delay us but it was Tango, the dog which bought our trek to a halt temporarily.

It was mid afternoon, our pace had been by necessity slow and although the nights were still cold, the days under the sun could be exhausting under the chequered shade of the escarpment. When we stopped to rest Tango willingly approached me, something which was in itself remarkable and as I eased myself onto the dry ground overlooking the deep gorge he settled down by my leg, watching the woman expectantly.

Immediately she came over to investigate, it was like watching a silent conversation between the two of them.

"You should have said that your wound was giving you trouble," she scolded as she peeled back the rough bandage, inspecting the damage. "I have no more dressing clips, we will need to find something else to serve. The sooner we get into camp the better off it will be I think."

"Is it far down the gorge?"

"No, I have a canoe. Once we have dropped into the gorge we can get to the camp by the river. Getting down the escarpment will be difficult for you though, we will rest here for a moment. Do you have much water left?"

My canteen was still half full as I hadn't been bothered to drink much despite the relentless sun. I had been more intent on keeping up the slow pace she had set.

As I handed my canteen to her, she checked the contents, frowned and handed it back. "Drink some, I don't want to be dealing with dehydration. Once we are in the gorge, water will not be an issue."

She was right, dropping into the gorge down the escarpment was more trying on my legs and injury than the entire trek had been and I couldn't describe the relief I felt as we finally reached the base of the escarpment.

The canoe was a two man affair and Tango went straight to where it was tethered at the bush by the small bank. It didn't take much to drag it down to the water, it was a light, hardened plastic build, the type which was so commonly used by commercial groups and we were soon settled into the two seats, Tango happily in between us as she took the back and I eased myself into the front rider's spot, aware that she would be doing most of the work controlling the thing. I knew I was too exhausted to be of much help.

The gorge here was beautiful; the breeze riding up through between sheer cliff faces was refreshing and the birds welcome song so very different from the tablelands. I wasn't sure if the salt water crocodiles lived in the fresh water of the gorge though there were scant breeding banks available. I would have been surprised if the more docile fresh water crocks were absent. I knew, that while these animals, the 'freshies' were easy to get along with, you didn't test the cunning of the 'saltie'. They would kill you quickly as they were one of the lands most ancient and efficient predatory hunters and their numbers had been growing since there had been moves to protect them from slaughter by hunters.

About forty-five minutes later we edged the canoe into a shallow side gorge and as soon as she banked the craft Tango bounded off the thing and headed directly into the bush down what looked to be a small path, leaving me to struggle from the seat. As I gained my footing, it was short work for her to haul the craft higher up onto the bank. Something she had done many times before, I realized.

"It's not far from here, just up behind the bush line."

The small gorge was well guarded by the deep escarpment cliffs. It would be a sheltered spot I realized, the only apparent access way by the river and I was curious to reach the camp.

"Have you been here in camp long?" I asked as she led the way along the light track, between the pandanus and light bush.

"About eight weeks. We would come here every year, my husband and I. Arriving mid winter and staying until the full heat of summer kicked in or until the wet arrived. The camp is high enough to survive the wet season mostly but it doesn't pay to stay around once the monsoons arrive."

The camp when we arrived into it was well set up which surprised me. Obviously it had been used for many years and I wondered just how many years. The coloured sandstone escarpment walls provided shelter and were not so high as to trap heat allowing the campsite a breeze, shaded by the rich bush growth of pandanus palms and grasses running along the gorge.

The only permanent structure was a large shelter consisting only of a roof made of sheets of paper bark roped to the frame, built without walls there was a large square platform of a few split logs and old saplings covered by woven grass mats raised slightly off the ground and located centrally under the roof shade. I recognized a strapped camp bedroll, a swag, the rough platform was where obviously she slept. The bedding was the type which when unrolled opened out to a padded bed base, which sat atop the canvas ground sheet. Over this was a sturdy green mosquito net suspended from the roof structure and now draped around the swag helping to stop unwelcome visitors setting up residence in the bedding. It all looked as comfortable as I knew it would be.

Low table benches of rough saplings and woven mats, arranged in groups ran along three sides of the shelter nestling into the encroaching bush, one of these was obviously used as a kitchen utility area while the other two held an assortment of books, now under plastic sheeting and there was reference material also protected momentarily from the effects of weather, as well as big plastic storage barrels under the benches, the type with spring seal cap lids. There were a number of old camp chairs, some of the canvas variety, others being bush stools strung with canvas or cloth tucked around the benches. It looked like rather than move chairs from one place to the other she had set up a number of work areas, each with its accompanying chair or bush stool.

The fourth side opened onto a well established camp fire pit and small lower level workbench, complimented by a pile of firewood stacked neatly, already pre-cut and ready to use. Obviously there was a chainsaw around somewhere though there appeared to be no other equipment of value, I guessed there was a cache nearby.

"You had better settle down on the platform. I'll take a look at the wound as soon as possible. I will need to get the fire started and there are a few things I need to collect. If I leave you with an antiseptic bath can you clean the wound? You'll have to have a good soak in the river tomorrow as we are going to run out of light soon. It shouldn't take me long to get what I need and I would like to stitch the wound before dark."

"Yeah sure. I can manage that, thanks."

I watched as she built up the campfire, bringing it to life competently and then after leaving me with a bowl of warm antiseptic water and cloth, she headed off to collect whatever it was she needed.

The camp was well equipped, I couldn't imagine what it was that she would find in the small bush nestled in the gorge but it was obvious she knew just what she needed and she was soon back with a silk scarf folded into a wooden bush bowl she had taken with her, now handled carefully as she laid it aside.

I had exposed the wound and the bleeding had eased to almost nothing, the honey had minimized the scabbing making it easier to manage and as she inspected the wound she seemed satisfied. I watched as she bought over a bulky medical kit and then reached for my back pack, taking the pituri I had stored in a small tin container from the side pocket she handed it to me.

"We have about an hour before sunset, it should be enough time to allow this to work and then I can stitch up your wound. You ready for this?"

I nodded, slipping a pituri plug into my mouth and easing myself back onto my elbows, chewing steadily. I was sufficiently familiar with the effects of the chewy plug, something I had used over the last few months with the Elders who had seen to my training and initiation. When I had prepared the plant plug, I had no idea that it would be used for this purpose and I knew it would dull the senses and allow the ease of passage into the Dreaming.

I didn't know however as to how much it would affect me physically with pain management though she seemed confident that it was the most effective drug we had available to us. Confidently I waited for the effects to set in and I was aware of my passage as I began to slip away from conscious awareness. Easing myself back, allowing the drug to take effect, I schooled my mind to follow the path I was familiar with for meditation. Something I understood would help me as I travelled the familiar path letting go of my reality.

THE PASSAGE TO ENLIGHTENMENT

Andrew:

As my mind eased along the Dreaming paths I was still aware of the discomfit of my leg. I knew what was happening and could isolate the pain, directing my thoughts away from the knowledge of her work, though sharp consciousness intruded. I struggled to disassociate myself and my mind from the awareness, the pain and instead became aware of other things.

I couldn't reach my Dreaming however, I was constantly pulled back by pain which was delivered in shards and I instead became aware of the shifts of light dancing around me, aware of other forms, those with the fibre of life but without substance. I heard the songs, soft rhythms which were warm and which soothed me as I struggled to alienate the pain I felt. I could feel the pressure of her sitting on my leg, holding it still and as uncomfortable as that was, it was a welcome distraction, something else on which to focus.

Then a spiralling pain took over and I drifted, lost.

It was a strange reality that captured me in those moments as I came to consciousness, I knew I wasn't alone as I could feel his power... immediately I submitted. I was familiar with this sensation, I had felt it before with the strength of the 'Clever Men' and I knew not to fight, if I didn't fight then I would learn, I would be taught things I could use.

Though I couldn't see my companions, I could feel them. Seeing came in time and with familiarity but there was an odd awareness of smoke about me. This wasn't mist, the moist soft mist of the Dreaming, but the harsh smoke of death which warned me I was entering another world. That I was with another Shaman, whose strength I could feel and it calmed me. I could feel no threat but I could feel the loneliness of death sit about me.

As we moved through the smoke we arrived at a place of light, the glistening of water reflected on the stone of a cavern. It was a beautiful place, calm and strong. I recognized this place but I knew I had never been here, this told me it was a world which would mean a great deal to me... a place of the Spirit. It was a large dark pool of sheltered water, which was on the move and in constant slow motion towards a broad rim over which it flowed continually, a secret place. It was cold although I couldn't feel it, but the light which was cast over it was life itself.

This was a ceremony, there was something going on here and as I felt the burn in my gut I knew it was an initiation, I could feel the sudden emptiness within me and then the weight of the stones, it was like a rebirth. I had been warned of this, I had heard the stories of the Shaman when I had first discovered the substance of the earth lights on my fingers. My time was here and I had only to submit to it. My Spirit people were claiming me and I was choosing to be of their world. Nothing else mattered and as I travelled through the experience I recognized the presence of the mutt, I felt his heat curled into mine.

When I woke a lifetime later it was dark, the promise of a sky brilliant with a million stars met me. I knew I was still on the platform, beneath the mosquito netting which helped explain the unusual dullness of the stars which was what confused me at first. I knew they should be brilliant. As I shifted, turning my head towards the camp fire, immediately she joined me pushing the netting aside.

"Here, drink this it will help, you have been very restless," as she held the pannikin to my lips I tried to ease myself up, my gut tense and tender still, my leg reminding me of its ordeal.

The drink was warm, rich with flavours and I knew it was some kind of soup.

"Thanks." I could feel the fresh discomfit of my gut and I wondered at it, wondered if the soup would make me ill. But I finished the drink slowly, then I gingerly sat up and moved my leg towards the light cast from the camp fire. The movement was painful but the sight was reassuring. I could see the line of the gash where it was weeping still through what appeared to be some sort of covering.

As I frowned she answered one of my unspoken questions. The other questions which remained were not the business of women, they would remain unspoken.

"It's a bush dressing, cobweb, it will help heal and bind the wound. I'm pleased with the stitches, they have held well though I think you will always have a bit of a scar to show, I would have preferred to stitch it earlier."

"Spider web?"

"Yes. It's a good sound dressing."

"You constantly bloody amaze me you know," I said quietly as I dealt with my discomfit. "I'm sure they didn't teach you that at nursing!"

"No, I learnt that from my mother." she said smiling back at me.

I hadn't seen that smile so often that I missed it, but when it shone out it was the most endearing of things. Amazed again, I watched as it transformed her eyes to soft dark pools. Breathing steadily I tried to figure how much she would tell me of herself, I had guessed it wouldn't be much for some reason, but I recognised a burning curiosity.

"You can't have got much sleep?" Looking up to the heavens again I gauged the time to be late, she knew what I was doing and I wasn't at all surprised when she climbed to her feet, reached for her own bed roll and opened it out nearby, stretching the mosquito netting also, though as far enough away from me as was possible in the cocoon of the netting. I would have been able to reach her had I wanted to, though Tango was settled at my side sharing my bedding and he sat confidently between us.

"Now I know you are OK, I'll turn in. I would offer you a draught of something to ease you back into sleep but I don't think you would take it?"

"I would take it," I said after a moment's hesitation. Aware of the discomfit of my wound, the sting of any movement, plus I felt this was perhaps an opportunity to make amends for questioning her skill and judgement earlier.

When she bought it to me in the canteen I was more settled, easing my leg having stretched it carefully, she watched as I took a long drink, trusting her.

"I can give you other tools to heal and manage the pain if you will allow it," she said softly. The light in her eyes was fascinating and I wasn't at all sure what she was talking about but I think I would have agreed to anything. Though I was tired, I knew that sleeping was going to be an uncomfortable struggle, something I wasn't looking forward to.

"Anything that will help," I said gingerly, wincing as I tried to sit up and straighten up more. "What do you have in that arsenal of yours?"

"Be still," she said softly and then settling herself on her knees at the edge of the bedding facing me she stretched her hands to my chest, very gently running her fingers down over my body and drifting them across the plane of my belly having gently crossed the newly healed scars. Her hand reminded me of the delicate discomfit I felt earlier in my gut. Immediately though I felt my senses react, my body responded to her touch. A purely sexual reaction which she must have understood I reasoned as I caught my breath in surprise trying to tame my response.

"If I had oil, it would be easier," she added smiling.

Reaching up she then put her hands either side of my face and soothed the skin with her thumbs between my brow sweeping across my forehead with a firm gentle pressure.

I reached for her, moving to draw her to me but as quickly she left off. She stood swiftly evading my reach and stepped back. It was Tango's low growl though that stilled my instinctive movement.

"No," shaking her head she frowned. "You should be still."

Moving back to the edge of the bedding she sat, just out of my reach as frustrated I frowned not understanding her.

"Take the energy you feel, the body's force now moving through you and empty your mind. You need to redirect that inward. It will feed your immune responses. This is what I meant," she explained on a small mischievous smile, expecting me to understand.

"That is not going to help me sleep now," I countered.

"Maybe, but it will help you heal. The draught will help you sleep," she countered back.

I considered her. "You weren't ..ahh... suggesting a more effective way to distract me? That too will help me sleep," I challenged her softly, even somewhat hopefully, a smile playing around my mouth at the possible invitation I knew I would be more than pleased to accept despite my body's complaints.

One thing was certain, I was decidedly distracted. I couldn't believe just how distracted I had become at the suggestion filling my thoughts. The suggestion put there by her actions, her gentle touch. I was now wide awake, my body tingling still where her fingers had ventured.

"Turn that energy inward Andrew."

Climbing to her feet she moved over to her bedding and with a flick of her fingers Tango joined her there, waiting as she climbed under the covers and then he coiled into her belly as she lay watching me. As they both watched me carefully.

There was no fear in her, no hesitancy. She had total faith that I would not attempt to join her and she was right. The dog watched me carefully and I wasn't about to get into a tangle with that mutt.

"This does not feel entirely fair," I commented with some irony. "They didn't teach you that in nursing either I bet."

"No. They didn't. That I learnt from my Dreaming, it's our Lore."

I frowned, "You said your husband was a Shaman, did he teach you that?"

"Is this helping you?"

Helping me? I considered the suggestion and realized that it was calming me, it was definitely distracting me. For a moment I closed my eyes and struggled to do as she had suggested, drawing the energy of my body back in on itself. It wasn't easy, so I eased myself back into the blanket and adjusting the covers carefully I took a moment to settle. Still trying to use the sexual energy she had fired to work for me rather than against me.

It was working in other ways, I was calming down and I did feel better for the whole exercise. I was definitely distracted from my injury, which I knew for certain.

"It does work. In some strange way, it helps," I said softly after an eternity. Then I wondered if she was even listening as it occurred to me she may well have fallen asleep. I turned to her and she was still awake, her eyes still on me. Though I noticed Tango looked to have settled in for the night, still coiled into her belly.

"I know it works," she answered, then she smiled across at me.

"I could think of improvements," I suggested hopefully.

Her chuckle was a gentle promise I thought. But this idea was destroyed when she shook her head despite the smile.

"Where is it you come from?" I added. Curious now, the clarity of the night giving the bush about us a sense of confidences shared, even friendships forged.

"The Northern Territory, I did tell you before but you might not have heard. I am a woman of the Wandjina, a healer as I mentioned. Katherine is where I am staying at the moment with my mother."

I felt the drift of my thoughts and recognized that the draught I had drunk was working subtly. "I have a friend whose father is from the Wandjin People, she would love to meet you I think."

"She would? Why?"

"She wants to know her father's people. Her Dreaming is different from the Serpents and it confuses her. She has no one to talk to who understands the ways of the Wandjina" My thoughts felt as weighted as my body and it was difficult not to drift, to lose myself in the pleasures fired by my imagination, which swept along my body. I closed my eyes to better feel the sweet sweep of energy trying still to harness it. Only now slightly aware of the discomfort of my wound I was distracted instead by the pleasures of my mind.

"Is she known by the name Mindindi? I have a Spirit friend known by that name and I have been looking for her. An old Shaman drew her to me a while ago now. He said I would meet her one day soon."

"No. She is Jenna, she is with the Bama people." I frowned, something escaped my thoughts but these thoughts were too heavy to surface and I felt the drift into other worlds. This was like a conversation in the Dreaming I realized, and I felt I could confide any thought and it would be understood. It was comforting.

But I knew there were few conversations in the Dreaming, I would know these things, there was only knowledge, but strangely it felt like that. This was when I entered the Dreaming paths again, lost to the soft whispers of the night; this was where the adventure began. I could feel the tide of time sweep past drawing me with it.

FRIENDSHIPS OF THE SPIRIT

Ngaire:

I loved the light of the morning, though now it had mellowed out to the richer depth of the day. Talking about Mindindi last night had been a mistake. I should have said nothing as it bought to mind the painful time when I had lost my husband, the fear and the loneliness.

I had fled to Yoonda's, an old friend who had known my man. Her father was an old friend of his and therefore I knew I would be welcome by both Yoonda and her father, George, an Elder amongst the desert Shaman. At the time I hadn't known what to do, how to deal with my loss although it was to be expected it was still a shock at the time. I was afraid to be without his guidance, his warmth. I had been so very young at the time I realized now.

I knew my man had passed to the world of the Spirit Men and as a woman he was beyond my reach, I could not call him. George would know how he fared; he was a strong Shaman and a man of the Spirit. They had welcomed me. Yoonda had taken me and little Jem into her care until I'd become stronger. It was George who had bought her to me, a Spirit friend in whom I could find a companion, find comfort in our shared spirit.

He had said little about Mindindi only that she was in life as a sister, who would know exactly how I felt. Our fates were entwined though we had never met, and one day I would know her. For now though we often met in the Dreaming and when we had the opportunity to come together our friendship, our spirit links, had grown. Even now, I wondered where she was, wondered about her and what her life was like.

I don't know why I had thought that Andrew's friend might be Mindindi, I guess I was just hopeful that it was time to meet her. Then for a moment I wondered what my man would make of my impatience. He had spent so long trying to teach me patience yet still I struggled with it, and the thought made me smile.

Restlessly I spread my hair about my shoulders again, rearranging it as I waited for the sun to dry the dark curling strands. The water had been chill this morning, but I had enjoyed it none the less. I found I broke my bathing into two parts, one was for my body the second part for my hair and it wasn't usual for these things to come together. Because they had today, it was taking longer but I was enjoying the respite.

Still wearing the sarong I had tied about me as I had washed my hair, I felt its warmth as it too dried in the morning sun. Andrew would be awake soon I was sure, I had taken more time than I had first thought but I hoped he would remain under the shelter until I returned. Today he too would need to bathe and I wondered absently how he would manage. I had no plans to help him this time, though perhaps I should.

Taking up the brush I began to untangle the now warm and dry strands of hair working up from the very tips of its length. They were drier in part, though still damp around my scalp. It seemed sometimes that this took forever but it gave me time to think about things. As I remembered how Jem liked so much to play with my hair, even hang off its length like a rope, I chuckled. I missed him. It would be nice to get back soon.

"Hi, I wondered where you were?"

Surprised I looked up and caught the look in Andrew's eyes before he hooded them quickly. That look made me smile as I remembered what my husband had told me of younger men, they were impatient and lacked subtlety, though I found Andrew more subtle than others had been.

"I wanted to wash without disturbing you. You should wash too; your hair is full of dust and quite greasy."

"Looks that bad hey?"

I grinned as he settled on the rock in front of me. He tested his hair absently as he set aside the crutch from yesterday, leaning it against the rock. He had his shirt carelessly about him this morning and I figured he had just stretched it over his shoulders and arms for the sake of warmth. He seemed to no longer care about the scar's which rode across his chest and I was pleased for this.

"How is your leg feeling?"

"A little sore but much better, I seem to be able to move it about without as much discomfit."

I nodded, "It's the security of the stitches. We should soak it now it's settled. You could use some more honey on the gash it will help it heal."

"Soak it? Hmm... Is the water cold?" he asked, looking hopelessly optimistic and I laughed as I recognized the familiar optimism of four year old Jem.

"It's freezing! But it's soft, you're a big boy," I chided. "I'll do you a deal, you wash and I'll shampoo your hair after for you. I think you need more than a wetting for your hair and we can do that up here, it will keep the soap out of the water."

"That sounds like a good deal," he chuckled and then thinking better of it he looked out over the flow of the gorge and considered it. "I guess it doesn't warm up too much does it?"

Shrugging off his shirt he glanced across at me, I figured he was wondering if I was going to stay.

Instead I stood. Flicking my fingers at Tango nearby, he came to heel then I smiled in answer to the question in his eyes. "I'm going up to tidy the camp, yell when you're washed and ready."

"Will the spider web be OK?"

"No. But let what will, wash off. It's already part of the healing wound." I turned as he moved to unbutton his shortened trousers then I added, "It might pay to give those a bath too."

"Yeah," he grinned back. "I might just do that. Do you mind if I use your towel?"

Nodding at the towel still drying in the sun near where I had been sitting he waited for my answer.

"Yes, that's OK." Turning back to continue up the path with Tango at my heel, I didn't look back though I was curious enough to be tempted to see how he managed getting into the water. It was strange having Andrew up and about, something I hadn't given much thought to I realized as I reached the camp fire and set about tending and banking the fire while my hair dried in the sun, warming me through.

I busied myself around camp until I heard his cooee. Then collecting the heated billy from the fireside I made my way back to the small sandy beach. He was waiting there, sitting back on the rock resting his leg, my towel strung and tucked carefully about his hips, his shorts drying on the rock nearby.

Taking up the wide bowl of still soapy water from when I had washed my own hair I emptied it into the sand and went to gather more from the river. Adding the billy of steaming water, made the water warm and settling the basin on the rock, I used the billy to begin by pouring water over his head.

He wasn't expecting it, I guess he figured I would just soap up his damp hair and he jumped surprised as he felt the warm water pour over him.

"You're going to soak the towel," he warned with a splutter as the water drained over his face unexpectedly, he laughed none the less.

"It will dry," was my only comment.

"Tell me when you are gunna do that again OK."

"OK," I said with a smile as I poured a liberal amount of shampoo into my palm. "You're going to have to get lower, can you move down a bit."

Tossing me a glance over his shoulder he grinned. "Hang on." Moving across to a lower boulder which was half buried in the sand he gingerly eased his leg then looked up. "Howz this?"

He looked less comfortable, lower to the ground but it put his head at a good height so I just nodded agreement, smiled and shifted up behind him again. The basin was still within reach and his position was much more comfortable for me.

Sweeping the palm full of shampoo into his hair I eased it around, then began to massage it in, leaving off and adding small amounts of warm water where I thought it was needed.

Andrew responded immediately to my touch. I was used to doing this, it was something I had done often and I knew how to use the heavy pressure of my finger tips to ease the skin, the nerves and tensions of the scalp. I was surprised when he moaned softly appreciating the firm pressure through his hair and across his scalp, my fingers finding less tension as he relaxed into my touch.

As the suds began to build in his locks I gently used the pressure to tilt his head back and added more warm water to run through his hair in a warm wash and then I began again to build up the suds as the bubbles drained down his back. His hair was thick, with a strong curl. It was easy to hold the suds and I used the building bubbles to massage into his lower skull with the deep pressure of my thumbs, running them up behind his ears firmly and into his scalp.

"God that feels good. Now I know why women spend so much time in the hairdressers," he said softly, appreciating the pressure of my fingers, his eyes closed. "Don't stop," he added as he stretched the muscles of his neck gently and I shifted my thumbs down to ease the tautness of the stretched muscles.

"Washing," I warned leaving off suddenly and then I quickly emptied the billy full of warm water over his head.

Andrew gasped, and as he spluttered I followed the first billy with a second, drenching him this time as he had moved forward. I couldn't help the giggle that escaped and as he swung to me surprised, still spluttering as I shrugged. I was enjoying teasing him like this, it was almost a game.

"I warned you." I said defending myself though I knew he recognized the mischief in my eyes.

I could see he wasn't quite sure about what to do and as he swept his hand across his face, his glance fell to Tango who recognizing a game, was now paying attention, then Andrew's eyes returned to me full of reluctant indecision.

"You still have bubbles in your hair. Do you want me to rinse it out?" I offered further indicating the bowl of still remaining water, my eyes dancing at the thoughts I could see reflected in his glance.

"You don't play fair," he said eventually, settling himself slowly back onto the rock. He threw me a challenging glance exasperation oozing out of every one of his muscles.

"Well don't move forward and you won't end up wearing it all."

Andrew laughed in what was almost a tacit surrender as he held his head back now, letting the wash sweep down his back, no longer caring where it spilt or ran and I combed my fingers through his hair absently, helping the water to drain freely.

"There you go, finished!" I announced satisfied. "I do have another towel up in camp or you can wear your wet shorts," I added as I began to collect up the shampoo and bowls. "Then..." I said suddenly, turning back to him as he climbed to his feet and reached for the crutch. "I could lend you one of my sarongs till your things are dry."

"A sarong? I wouldn't know how to wear it."

"It's just like a towel, only you tie it to the side of your hip for men. It might be easier to manage than your wet shorts and you can tie it on the side of your injury."

"Let me think about it till I make it to camp."

I felt his eyes run over me, following the line of how I now wore my own sarong knotted neatly about my neck, bringing the fullness to the front my modesty protected in its folds. I was confident in how I was wearing it. I usually wore sarongs in camp if I was planning on remaining all day as I found they were more comfortable than clothes in the tropic regions and during the day, when the summer heat was beginning to build they were much cooler than closer fitting clothes.

"I'll be changing into shorts up in camp myself I just didn't want to get soaked. But you might find a sarong more convenient," I offered as I headed up, not waiting for him.

By the time he reached the camp, I was already changed into my camp shorts and a simple singlet top. I smiled as he came through the camp, still wearing the wet towel and carrying his own shorts.

"I might try that sarong, if you can show me how to secure it."

Without a word I gathered one of the simple lengths of fabric I kept in the plastic storage barrels and handed it to him then I stood back. "Just tie it around your waist. You can use a single or a double knot, with the single knot you tuck it around. It really is very secure.

Setting his crutch aside he swept the sarong around his waist and then gripping it with one hand, pulled away the short wet camp towel from his hips struggling somewhat but managing and then glancing at me, waiting for comment he tied the sarong firmly leaving the opening to run down the side of his injured leg.

"That's it," I approved. "See how you go. You had better sit down and I can do something about your leg."

As I examined his wound moments later I was pleased to see he was managing the sarong well and learning some of the disadvantages of being a male and wearing such a garment. He managed it however and I knew he would find it more comfortable despite its inherent problems.

Soothing the honey over his now clean gash I was happy with his progress, it was healing well, but after so much activity I could see it was wearing, in his expression and his strength.

Lunch was a simple affair and as I collected his pannier I noticed his weariness, yet he was reluctant to stretch out while wearing the sarong.

"You need some sleep. Don't worry about the sarong, turn that sexual energy inward and use it to work on healing. You'll become used to the freedoms you feel."

Andrew looked up at me and smiled. "I should have known you knew what was going on. Sorry..." shrugging he wasn't sure how to go on as he appologized. "It's just bloody inconvenient at the moment."

Moving over to the one old chair which had a worn cushion, I picked it up, walked back, handed it to him and kept moving towards the camp fire to sort out the stores on the table taking the opportunity to plan a few meals.

I had to smile as I glanced back, to see him now stretched out on the platform where he had been sitting. He had a pillow under his head as he tried to rest, clearly weary from his exertions and the weight of the cushion over his hips giving him a certain confident reassurance.

Camping was getting interesting I decided, presenting problems I had never really considered. I had not had these problems camping with my husband, but then it had never really been an issue that was a problem. Our relationship had been easy and in part playful despite the disparity in our ages. I guessed it was really as I had been told, that younger men have less control and are more easily aroused. It was an oddity that was somewhat entertaining I decided and I smiled as I went about planning the next few meals.

There was plenty to keep me busy around camp. I still had a store of plant specimens to sort which I preferred to do before I left the area. My catalogues were extensive and very valuable to me as a reference though it was time to start packing them away carefully again I realized. I also needed to do a final check on what remedies I had stock of and what I still needed though I knew I could restock on the less traditional medicines in Mount Isa before I headed back across the dry Barkly Tablelands, travelling through the heart of Australia and on into Katherine in the Territory. It was a road trip that I would allow a few days to complete, enjoying the travelling as I passed through the landscape.

Glancing around, recognizing the now soft snore coming from the platform I wondered what Andrew's plans would be. I would need to begin packing up camp too, that would take some days I realized, as it would be perhaps at least a year, maybe two before I returned to this area.

There was much to be cleared and stowed in the small dugout we had fashioned years ago to protect the camp gear until I returned. I would miss the help of my man, but maybe Andrew could help and it would be wise to give him some activity to entertain him. I would discuss it with him later I decided.

It wasn't wise to leave him without mental or physical resources, he would want to create some for himself if I didn't find something to keep him occupied. I didn't want to be the focus of any entertainments he may plan for himself and that thought too made me smile.

For a moment I considered him, stretched out on the platform, snoring softly, my smile softened with the path of my thoughts. I had no need of another man in my life, one who would only complicate my world though if I was to choose someone it might just be someone like Andrew. I wouldn't want him about me all the time; it wasn't something I would choose anymore. Taking a man into my life bought added responsibilities, the need to care for him, plan his meals daily and work my life around his and the demands of living together as a couple. This was something I no longer wanted. Jem was the only companion I really wanted around and there were already enough demands on my time.

Andrew though, he made me smile, bought humour to my day and had a way about him that was comfortable to be around. As a young Shaman, he too would have much to attend to which would only be hampered by the presence of a woman. Maybe we could simply be friends and as a description sprang to mind of such a friendship I considered it.

It was very modern, then as old as time itself. I knew I missed the warmth and company of a man around, though at other times I was pleased for the independence of having no mate. The presence of Tango was company enough at times and looking over at my furred companion I suddenly climbed to my feet. It was time we had a game, just the two of us. Tango would enjoy the exercise and so would I.

Giving a soft whistle, I swept my hair into a loose bind to help contain it. It was the type of whistle I reserved only for play and Tango immediately rose and eagerly went to retrieve a toy, usually a stick. Any stick I knew; he was hard on my heel when as we headed down the path, both of us happy for the chance to play on the small beach strip. As I broke into a light run Tango bounded around me, now full of promise and energy and I settled into the game we would play for a few short hours with obvious pleasure as the afternoon light moved around us.

It was a time for companionship and leisure, it was something we both enjoyed a great deal and it was good to let the concerns of looking out for Andrew drop away and immerse myself back into my life, one which was my concern alone.

LIFE AT PLAY

Andrew:

The camp was empty, I was alone but I could hear her and her dog nearby. Though Tango had rarely barked, he was barking now and it was a sound of fevered pleasure I realized. They were playing I guessed.

Easing myself up I knew I felt better for the rest, my leg felt good and moving it was much easier. I guess it had something to do with the soaking and as I ran my hand through my disordered hair I recognized the sense of clean and knew my hair would be a riot of locks, which I particularly hated. I hadn't had it cut in months and my beard was getting more unruly as well I realized as my hand made a sweep over my chin.

I badly needed to shave but I wasn't too keen on using the embers of a stick as the old Shaman did, those who I had spent some considerable weeks with. I had a razor somewhere in my pack but I hadn't seen a mirror around the camp which I considered unusual when I thought about it. Shaving hadn't been a priority in the past weeks but now it was something I wanted to do.

Digging out the razor in the side pocket where I kept my scant grooming and first aid supplies I soon found what I wanted, along with soap and set about as best I could in bringing my appearance to order. It felt good to feel less like a bushie and more civilised I realized as I ran my hand around a clean shaven chin. There was little I could do about my hair so after attempting to give it a cursory comb through I decided to leave it. I didn't have to look at myself anyway so it wasn't a problem. A little more length and I would be able to confine it with a tie. I debated the merits of just hacking it off, or leaving it to grow that extra length and decided on leaving it. It required less effort and I remembered how good it had felt having her wash it for me.

That brought to mind that I still didn't know her name. It was becoming a shaming reality and glancing around I wondered if there was anything that could give me a clue. She had plenty of books in camp, maybe I would be able to find something in these which would help me. Not knowing what to call her was annoying, there had to be something around I hoped.

I had all but given up trying to guess when I had realized how awkward it would be if I guessed wrong after all this time. As I walked along the rough line of tables, running my eyes along the scattered text I could see nothing until I came to the very end table and saw this stuff was all hand written, a log or record of some kind.

Picking up the book she had obviously been working in most recently I flicked it closed, disappointed to find it had no front cover reference and as my eyes ran down the neat script I then carefully returned it to its open state. A lot of it was Latin, I figured it was a catalogue of some sort, or reference to botanical stuff, so I left it. I didn't much like the sense of intruding I was feeling, so instead I wandered over to the bench near to the fire.

The fire was banked, ready to be built up for cooking and there was an array of items on the table. Obviously tonight's dinner, some sort of pasta I guessed. Then a thought occurred to me. I was good at pasta, it was an easy dish. I usually just made some type of sauce, added any type of meat or fish and anything else by way of vegetables to a sauce and then the cooked pasta. I could do this for her, it would be some way of repaying or rather helping out around the camp and there were only a few hours of light left.

The dried pasta was easy, ready to go in the water that had been set aside, but as I studied the contents of the cans and realized some of the dried herbs she obviously planned to use and I knew then that the sauce for me was going to be a hit or miss affair. Then I smiled, wasn't it always. So I set to work.

Dinner was ready when she appeared, emerging from the track into the camp with the dog. All I needed to do was to cook the pasta in the heated water and as her eyes swept over the pots and the bubbling sauce I had created, her smile was worth every effort and doubt I had entertained.

"I thought you might like a break from cooking."

"Wow. I'm impressed," she said surprised as she dipped her finger into the tomato based sauce as it balanced on the rocks beside the fire, and tested its flavours. "Very impressed...! I was just coming up to start. It's so nice to see it done already. Thank you!"

I grinned happily. "It's nice to do something for you for a change, even if it's for us," I added ruefully. "I can manage pasta, but don't ask for anything more complicated. It helped that you had it laid out already."

"You've lost the beard too. You look particularly civilised even in the sarong."

Again I laughed at her expression as I carefully stretched to my height, pleased for her approval. God if only I could remember her name this would be so much easier I thought ruefully.

"Yeah, I'm getting used to it. It's quite comfortable surprisingly. I don't know how it will go with my shirt but I am about to find out. It's getting chilly, sunset won't be long," I said it cheekily, as though this too was something I had arranged for her.

I watched as she smiled up at me, the smile lighting her eyes. Reaching for the pasta she obviously was intent on adding it to the now boiling water so I wandered over giving care to my movement as I retrieved my flannelette shirt. I only had two with me, one to wear and one to wash. The one in my pack was clean, I could wash the one I had been wearing for the last week or so tomorrow, it was well overdue I realized. I had decided on leaving my other gear, my second pair of trousers for civilisation. I knew a sarong wouldn't cut it in Mount Isa and torn off shorts would be equally questionable in a strong outback mining town.

Dinner was a great success; I had done myself proud and was overly pleased. She even seemed to enjoy it and there was nothing left for Tango who generally got the leftovers as well as his biscuits I realized, as he had waited with expectation. Tonight the mutt would have to do with biscuits alone I thought as I watched him, his dinner obviously lacking while she tidied the bench and I finished off the last of the meal. He wasn't the only one who was hungry.

As she settled back down again sometime later, the camp chores complete, I enjoyed watching as she unbound her hair and taking up a brush began to put it to order with rhythmic strokes. In the dark of the night, the firelight made glints in the dark tresses, something I found fascinating as I watched her. I was tempted to ask if she wanted help, but it seemed such a brash thing to suggest.

There was no need for conversation though I could think of a dozen other questions. I had never camped with someone who was so content with the noisy silence of the night. For some reason I wanted to engage her, find out more about her and as I struggled for a topic of conversation she might like, she suddenly beat me to it.

"You seem to be moving around easier, your leg is not too sore?"

"Yeah... but it's not as uncomfortable as it was. I need to move about to exercise it I think."

She nodded.

"Did you have any plans about breaking camp?" I asked, curious.

"Soon, I need to put most of this into storage. There is a dug out nearby that I'll use. I won't be back this way for a while, maybe a year or more and most of this is stored till then."

"I can give you a hand with that if you tell me what you want to do." Looking around I realized that most of the benches would collapse. It helped that everything seemed to have a box or container of some kind. It was a well thought-out camp.

"What do you leave?"

"Just the platform and the back bench doesn't pack away, it stays. The roof gives some protection but we need to repair the paperbark roofing every time we're back. We..., I will do that before I set up camp again."

I noted the 'we', obviously she meant her husband and as I glanced across at her I realized her thoughts were likely with him as she continued to draw the brush through her hair. She flicked some aside and sweeping the curtain about with a movement of her head to reach other sections, her face became quietly sombre.

How did I get to this point in conversation I wondered, kicking myself mentally, though after a moment's hesitation I thought of something, "Do you mind if others use the camp occasionally?"

Looking up, she shook her head, "It would be nice to see repairs done when I get here. It happens occasionally but not often. There is another dugout a little further from ours, though I have never met them."

"I wouldn't use your gear I could manage with my own gear. It would be handy though. I will be back this way again sometime I don't doubt."

"You would be welcome. Maybe we could start packing up tomorrow. I have some work to do first but if you start it will be all the more easier. We can take a few days and then head out to Mount Isa. You could be on a plane by the end of the week, back to Cairns."

Back to Cairns? The thought stuck like a mouthful caught in my throat. As I drew a steady breath I realized that it was a sane plan.

"What are your plans?" I asked hesitantly. Not wanting to seem as though once more I was being intrusive. Though she didn't know about my exploration of her books I realized.

"I'm going to Katherine. Jem is there waiting for me, it has been too long and I'm missing him." Her expression was soft at the thought of him and for a scarce moment I envied him that tender look about her.

"Well civilization in Cairns isn't missing me much," I added with a grin.

"Will you travel home?" she asked softly, "Back to Nimbin?"

I shrugged. "I need to pick up some work. The bank account is looking like a disaster. I have the chance of a job out of Brisbane but nothing is settled and it will be fly-in, fly-out if I go ahead with it. I haven't decided anything yet. It's on the rigs, the season won't start for a few months. I do my next round and training when I get back so it's relatively new to me. I have another offer starting January or February. They are working out the contract and should get back to me over the Christmas."

Quite suddenly, she left off brushing her hair and putting the brush aside absently, stretched. I could see she was tired, her voice had been getting softer but when she stretched her arms over her head I couldn't but notice the womanly shape of her. Her loose hair had in part acted like a curtain about her but now, her hair was tossed back. Watching her stretching quietly was a pleasure and I felt my immediate reaction to her; I also swore that the dog knew it too.

Almost carelessly she swung her hair back and with quick deft movements plaited it in a loose fashion, securing it absently and flicking it out of sight.

Soon after, she turned in for the night, well before I. Leaving me to the fire and the company of Tango, who was still curled across from the fire where she had sat. After saying goodnight she obviously hadn't expected him to join her though she glanced his way and took a moment to pet him. I found it strange that the mutt stayed with me, but didn't question it. Perhaps it was the exercise of the afternoon, or maybe the mutt was beginning to trust me then on second thoughts I considered it something of a dim idea.

It was a good opportunity for me to make a friend of the dog though so I spent quite a lot of time trying to do just that. I thought I was getting somewhere when he allowed me to join him by the fire. He was more responsive but the suggestions I made to him were never acted on. He just seemed to tolerate me and if anything amused himself at my expense I thought, but I was amused by the mutt's reactions.

When I finally decided to turn in and stood to bank the fire for the night, he knew immediately I had made the decision and left me to join her on the platform, curling into her side protectively as he had before. It wasn't until I had finished with the fire that I realized he had known my intent, it came to me slowly. I had said nothing, but he had known I was headed to bed; he had preceded me in a simple action. The dog somehow had understood and the realization left me wondering just what kind of mind link we had or how damn smart the dog was.

Mind linking with animals was a skill I nurtured and it often gave me a measure of control over them. It was a skill that I was continuing to practice. With this mutt, it seemed to be reversed. Then I wondered if he was indeed controlling me, I didn't like the idea at all but I knew it was within the bounds of possibility. An interesting concept I could sleep on and as I settled for the night I wondered what sort of training the animal had received. The thought stayed with me as I allowed the ease of the night to settle my mind.

The next day I got into the job of starting to pack up the camp. I left her to continue with whatever it was she was doing at the table with the catalogues. It had been explained to me how the packing was organized. There were two boxes which were taken with her, most containing texts and catalogues and plant samples as well as a duffle bag of clothing and personal items. The rest which were more sealed barrels it seemed and were packed away, then stored in the dugout.

It didn't take long to prepare the dugout, sheltered under the cliff face rock we scooped out the sandy soil which had made its way into the hole leaving a big enough store for the containers which at the moment were supports for the benches. These once packed would be later buried again. It was an ingenious setup and she pointed out where the other dugout was located. Once sealed, they were indistinguishable almost from the surrounding bush and high enough to miss most of the monsoon river heights. Even if the camp was inundated in the wet, little damage would be done. Most everything was sealed in water tight containers of some sort and what wasn't, wouldn't suffer for the drenching.

Packing up camp was merely packing the plastic barrels and stowing them systematically. I noticed that provision was made even for the storage of dry and canned foods which would make bringing in stores and replenishing them a much simpler task. Something undertaken each time the camp was used, I could see.

The books and catalogues I left for her to sort and by the second day, she had most of these packed along with other tasks she had undertaken. As she began to sort her gear into the duffle bag it dawned on me that we would likely be breaking camp the next day and it was with regret that I considered that reality. Though it was a good two day run over rough roads to reach Mount Isa I knew, which meant we would be likely camping out overnight somewhere along the track.

That afternoon, as we sat around the campfire having finished our light lunch, she set out our final plans for the camp breakup and I realized she had done this a number of times. It had been a pleasant few days, our conversations had evolved to an easy banter and I would miss this as much as I would miss her company. As she looked over the last of the packing and I waited her suggestions, I felt a keen sense of loss which unsettled me

"I will need to take the books down to the car this arvo'." Indicating the two crates she went on, "I can take them down in the canoe and be back within an hour or two at the most, the car is parked down at the head of the gorge. Could you give me a hand getting the boxes to the river?"

My leg was much stronger and only gave me the odd twinge but I had enjoyed her attention to the wound and as the healing was well underway now, I was missing this small part of our relationship. As she no longer needed to check and dress the wound as much as she had previous, it had become almost like her slow withdrawal from me as the gash was healing. My injury had been something we had shared and now with her suggestion that I help in other ways doing things she would find difficult to undertake herself, I recognized again the sense of companionship. I knew the crates were heavy but the weight wasn't an issue and I was glad to help. I doubted she could manage them otherwise without using some sort of slide.

"Yeah sure, no worries. How will you manage them at the other end?"

"The car's not far from the water and I'll park it down as close as I can, it shouldn't be too hard. If I have trouble I will just unpack the crates and move them piecemeal."

"When did you want to head out?"

"Tomorrow, getting to Mount Isa will take two days, depending on how bad the tracks are. We can take the last of our things down in the morning."

Looking around I considered the camp. The finality I felt annoyed me for some reason. I had enjoyed my time here, her company and even the company of the dog, who seemed less wary of me now. I knew I had time up my sleeve before I needed to be back in Brisbane and I wondered for a moment what she would make of an alternative suggestion. If I didn't say something soon, there would be no opportunity later I felt.

"It will be strange getting back. You know, I don't have to be in Brissy till Christmas, I can defer my training block. I was wondering if you would like company into Katherine. It's a long way to travel on your own."

I knew what I was suggesting wasn't a simple car trip with a companion and so did she as her eyes softened, the smile which played around her lips had nothing to do with the car trip. I answered her smile with a playful grin of my own and waited for her to consider the possibilities.

"Andrew... I like you, I really do," her smile was playful but I didn't much like the way she had begun. "But I'm not looking for a relationship with anyone. You have to understand that I really don't want any more commitments in my life. I have absolutely no plans to partner up with anyone, now or in the near future."

I considered her words and then shrugged on a smile. "Nor do I, there is a lot going on in my life and these last few months, in many ways have offered me a lot more. I don't think I could sustain a relationship twenty-four seven. But God knows; I'm tempted to try... with you," I added softly. "But if that isn't what you want then maybe we can consider something else that might work for us. Maybe we could even just try and see how it goes."

I watched the indecision move across her eyes, the little smile that played around her mouth and I grew hopeful. It wasn't such an outrageous thought, we were adults and mature enough to enjoy a relationship that just might be other than platonic. Thinking quickly I tried to find something that would explain how I felt without swamping her.

"You're really beautiful, I would hate to lose contact..." stopping myself, suddenly I realized how selfish that sounded. "I don't know how many times I have wanted to kiss you in the last few days," I added with an almost apologetic note to my words. "It might help to have someone you can call on. I could be that, it would be a way I could thank you for everything you have done, it wouldn't be just a physical thing," I grinned suddenly, then realizing what I was saying; "I mean it doesn't have to be physical at all... friend's maybe?"

This wasn't coming out right I thought suddenly to myself, it sounded almost a clumsy attempt and I was beginning to regret my rash words, I could have planned this better.

I was silenced though as I watched her climb to her feet and move around towards me. Quickly I stood as she reached me, realizing that she was coming to join me and as she reached up I thrilled with her hand gently fluttering about my neck testing the skin. I knew what this was about, the acceptance in her eyes was clear and as the delight rushed through me, I reached out to hold her and draw her to me.

Her lips were soft, sweet with all the promise I had imagined and after an initial kiss I wanted more. The thrill of holding her at last swept through my body but this time I gathered her to me and she was so deliciously warm, vibrant, my senses slipped into overdrive way too quickly as the scent of her skin enveloped me.

At the sound of the dogs whimper, she broke off and pulled away suddenly, immediately looking for him. I could have killed that mutt at that moment, but I buried the urge just as quickly as I carefully released her.

"Tango, come on baby. It's OK," she said softly reaching for the dog, calling him to her and he immediately came as she knelt down to him. "Sit," she said tapping the ground lightly with her fingers and the dog obeyed quickly squatting at our feet a devoted quandary in every nervous twitch.

I was tempted to squat down with her but I waited to see what she would do.

"It's OK," she said again softly, nuzzling his neck and as she signalled, I did squat down, slowly. "Andrew is not going to hurt me you silly goose."

Her smile as she looked up at me in that moment sent a thrill through me and then I too reached towards the dog but merely held my hand for his nose instead of petting him. My scent would be different, taking on the scent of pheromones in the warm rush of blood and I wanted the dog to get used to that.

He whimpered obviously confused, looking for her reassurance and she cooed softly in response nuzzling him affectionately.

"He isn't used to me being physical with anyone, not a grown man anyway," she explained as her glance shifted between us. "He has been taught to be wary of men. I think he is not quite sure what to do. It's not something he has been taught to deal with."

I grinned as I realized I liked her description of our relationship. "Who trained him?" I asked thoughtlessly and then, seeing her expression change I knew the answer.

For a moment she paused, as though the dog and her were in conversation, without having actually any word said between them, then she answered with an inflection in her voice I had not heard before. It was way too sad.

"My husband, he trained him to look after me when he left us."

"Sorry, I didn't mean to intrude..."

"He was a good man, he thought of everything in some ways."

Nodding, I didn't want to add to the emotional depth in her eyes. "Maybe Tango will get used to me. I would like to give him the opportunity to try."

Smiling she sat backcross legged settling on the ground and petting the mutt as she reassured him. "I don't think you should come to Katherine with me. I can travel fine with Tango and I'm not ready for you to meet Jem." She shook her head gently at the thought, "Maybe we should just see how it works out."

"Yeah sure."

Those two simple words, I marvelled at them as later I watched her manoeuvre the canoe out into the gentle flow of the river a half hour later, laden as it was with the crates of books and Tango, looking extraordinarily happy about me remaining on the bank. He had her company to himself and I'm sure he knew I would have loved to be in his seat at this moment.

An hour or two, it was enough time to tidy up the camp and rustle up dinner. I felt like a school kid planning a hot date and the thought ran along my nerves tightening them, then for a moment I wondered how she felt.

It would be an hour or so before dusk when she got back, and until that time it was going to be a long couple of hours. But tonight, tonight I had plans. I wanted this to work and the thought that she could become part of my life so simply, so easily we could shift into a relationship that could be not only a friendship but be everything else beside was something I had never envisioned and I loved the idea.

The job waiting for me in Brisbane, flying out to the rigs when it meant being gone for weeks on end and then flying back into wherever home was in the weeks in between contracts, wasn't good for relationships in general. This however could really work and the reservations I had were vanishing. It didn't mean a degree of loneliness. I would have the time to train as I had planned. She loved the bush life and the thought of bringing her into my life really left my body humming.

I couldn't describe how high my spirits were running as I moved around the camp preparing dinner and for the night ahead. My relationships with women were generally of little substance, more physically satisfying than emotionally deep. Though I understood a sense of envy that I had for the ties between Sean and Jenna, I had never experienced the same draw to any one woman and I had never really wanted to experience it before. Though what I was feeling with this woman was something entirely different and I was struggling to understand it.

Sean had been attracted to Jen from the very start, theirs had been a friendship which had grown, matured and which now drove him. Everything he did was done with thoughts to their relationship and that in some ways scared the hell out of me. I wasn't sure if I even wanted that type of commitment. There was something about this woman which was so very different but then maybe it was just the thrill of the chase, the edge of the unknown, the thrill of promise and as I bought her to my mind's eye I knew that thrill which moved through me.

She was beautiful, desirable and in some ways so different to other women I had known. This woman was strong and independent, she had no real need for me but the warmth I had felt when I had held her to me was a need that was strong and she had felt the same desire I was sure. Between us this was going to happen and we both welcomed it.

Images flicked through my mind, images of promise about how we were going to come together and how I could make the experience really something. I wanted to please her, it wasn't just about my needs I knew and for some reason this was important to me. The thought was distracting and I left off, knowing where that could lead; but the promise still lingered tormenting me. I wanted her, needed her and that I recognized her need outside the moment also, was new to me. This woman was unlike any other I had known. She was very much a woman, not a girl and my body thrilled to the thought.

A NEW BEGINNING

Ngaire:

Paddling back was a much longer business than I had anticipated, I had not factored in that I would have no one else paddling. We had always either gone tandem or I had stayed back at the camp and continued to break camp in preparation for leaving the same day. Of course it wasn't the same this time and I had forgotten to consider this.

Thinking of Andrew waiting back at the camp gave me a small flood of pleasure. There was something about embarking on a new type of relationship with him, in this place, that seemed fitting and I was looking forward to the evening and everything it promised. I knew I was physically attracted to him, more for the mischief and depth of his eyes than for other things. But in those other things there certainly was nothing to complain about, and I wondered what kind of lover he would be.

My husband had been mostly a loving man and he had been kind though at times impatient with my youth, I had known this. My mothers and aunts had often commented on his patience with me. He had always been aware of the disparity in our ages and had taken care in showing me much about myself and I knew that was generous of him. He had not been a demanding lover, but his ways were gentle and he had been a patient lover. Our time together had been much more than a physical union. We had been the best of friends and he had often teased me about what he considered to be the rashness and impatience of youth. The impatience with which I had dealt with many things and that memory now made me smile.

I felt as though I was fourteen again and it was how I had felt when my mothers had bought me to my husband's camp. Only this time I wasn't afraid, I looked forward to the intimacies we would share and the companionship we hopefully would find. I had missed these things and I was seeking a way to bring them into my life without added demands reaching other parts of my life. That I had made the choice this time, instead of my family, was the only thing that concerned me but at some time I had to make my own choices, I was no longer a child but a woman. This was what I had wanted, it was time to move on with my life and it was the way it should be I knew.

Andrew was waiting on the beach for my return and as I pulled into the shallower water, he came out to help control the canoe, dragging it up onto the sand before I even moved to climb out.

"You were longer than you said... I wondered if you had trouble?"

"Sorry. The flow was stronger than I remembered." He looked concerned, but his ready smile soon appeared as he moved to help me up from the shifting craft, lifting me high and setting me down so unexpectedly that I squealed surprised, something which startled both me as well as Tango.

Immediately Tango flew to the sand near me and growled setting his weight back on his haunches, his hair rigid along his back as he faced off at Andrew who startled, stepped back.

"Al-loe!" I said firmly, knowing that command would freeze his action. Tango sat back conflicted and whimpered softly, clearly not wanting to stop while Andrew had spread his hands in a submissive stance. Both of them waiting for me to indicate what I wanted of them.

Bending and flicking my fingers bought Tango to heel and I squatted down to feel the agitation in his shoulders as I tried to soothe him.

"It's OK sweetie. I was just playing really... "

Andrew squatted slowly at my side, but sat back from Tango. He didn't offer his hand this time and I was pleased. I wasn't too sure Tango would attempt to take it off him if he took a mind to.

"Maybe we should tie him up tonight." he said, his thoughts running along lines I had not yet considered. I knew he thought he was helping and I tried to reason away my initial reaction to his suggestion but failed. There was nothing that would induce me to constrain Tango in such a fashion I knew.

"No. Tango is never anchored, he wouldn't understand it. At the most I will put him on a lead and that won't achieve much now. He will have to adjust. I will just have to be careful about how I react."

Standing slowly, soothing Tango as I moved I held out my hand to Andrew. Tango was watching carefully as I did so and his agitation was immediate, but he was willing to allow Andrew this.

Andrew on the other hand understood what I was doing and while carefully taking my hand turned us towards the camp and speaking in a studied monotone continued.

"OK, I can see what you're doing. Do you think he will? It could be an interesting night, I've put together some dinner by the way. Didn't do anything for Tango, never actually gave him a thought or I would have done something special to bribe him. Is he open for bribes? We could of course find him a girl to play with, know any around here? That might distract him..."

Breaking into a giggle at his running monolog I glanced down at Tango following at my heel and realized he was accepting of the calmness of our progress up the beach.

"This is smart of you," I offered quietly. "I think he has decided to let you stay around."

"Well that's a plus. After all, I cooked dinner for us."

As we arrived into camp I could see that he had indeed been busy. The place looked incredibly tidy if somewhat bare. He had left the kitchen table out and this was set out with the basic plates and cutlery. That it was set out at all was remarkable, usually we simply ate around the fire.

"It's only pasta, but I hope you enjoy it. I don't know what I would call it but it tastes OK." Moving to the fire he moved the water into the flame and then taking up the spoon from the warming sauce offered me a taste.

It was good, creamy and thick with reconstituted vegetables and what looked to be finely diced tinned ham.

"Hmm... You have used herbs, it tastes really nice."

His grin was appreciative as was his glance as I moved over to the camp chairs by the table instead of perching on one of the logs as we always had done. He soon joined me, bent on ignoring Tango who shadowed my every move and settled at my feet by my chair.

The meal was everything it promised to be and we talked about how he found the prospect of his work off shore and the expectations he had for his future with the drilling group. He was interested to hear about my work as an assistant nurse and I couldn't avoid talking about Jem and his small world in Katherine where he lived with some of my mothers and aunts.

It was well into the evening when he rose and set quietly about banking the fire for the night and as he finished he simply turned and held out his hand, pulling me easily into the circle of his arms when I reached him. I could feel the firm length of him heat my own body, feel the promise of his desire for me. He was taller than I was accustomed to and again I had the sense of being bought into a world I didn't know. Though I did know exactly what we were doing, the knowledge in our eyes was as sweet as a promise and I was glad that we had finally arrived at this point.

His mouth was firm, persuasive, as carefully he pulled the tie from the base of my hair and gently began to untangle the weave of my hair. As he threaded his fingers through the long length I felt him test its weight, watched him gather its scent, the bush scent of acacia which I used as a rinse. It was a bright, healthy scent that I enjoyed about me.

"I love your hair, it's so much part of you," he said softly. "I wanted to brush it for you but I didn't know how to ask or if you would be offended. It smells like freedom."

I bit my lip softly, I knew my eyes clouded over with my memories and I saw his frown and realized he was following my thoughts.

"I'm going to cut it off." I said quietly. "I should have done so before this but it's very hard for me to do. It's part of letting go and it's time I did let go."

Andrew continued to frown as he thought about what I had said and I wondered if he understood the tradition. I couldn't have explained it to him without destroying my peace and as such I had no intention of even trying at this time.

Tangling his fingers through my hair, he strained them through the length carefully again, once more considering the weight. Then he sighed and bought my lips slowly back to his as he released my hair and gathered me into his heat again. After a moment he shifted a finger lightly under my chin, tipped my head up to the star light as he searched the thoughts in my eyes.

He accepted my decision to cut my hair I realized and he wasn't even going to argue the issue. I felt a growing appreciation in that he would allow me my own decisions without rancour.

Our passion began as a gentle flow as he drew me towards the camp bed. I'm not sure if it was because of the presence of Tango, who had settled quite happily on the platform with us, still not far from my feet. But as the tide built quickly I lost the thread of listening for him, though Andrew tried to quieten me more than once, half teasing, half tormented, it served to make me laugh more than I perhaps should have at the thrill of his touch, the tickle of his light whiskers and the trace of his lips.

He was a patient, playful lover and while his impatience emerged as we came together, he had taken care to ensure that the pleasure belonged to both of us and wasn't just his. I understood the difference and appreciated his care more than I could say. I would have hated it to be otherwise I knew, although I would have accepted it in part, at least for the time. That I had no need too, made curling into his warmth that much more pleasurable.

As our bodies joined and became one I was lost to the height of it. His strength, his gentleness and then his vigour swamped me in a way I was unused to. I don't know if it was the difference between age and experience but it surprised me and I felt power in his lack of control as our passions overwhelmed us. I recognized the differences between a playmate and a mentor and stretched my own knowledge to coax him. It was something I don't think he was accustomed to as it seemed to feed his vigour, straining his control. When our fervour calmed and we caught our breath amongst the mingling heat of our bodies I knew I was both sated and content.

I had not felt such contentment in such a long time, I felt replete and was soon lost in a deep peaceful sleep entwined as we were with each other. I was surprised at how deeply I slept, how soundly I drifted through the night and it was with a sense of the surreal that I woke to what promised to be a brilliant dawn just after the cusp of daybreak.

Even though as the morning arrived it still had a chill cast to it, with Andrews arm about me and Tango curled into my side I was far from cold. Moving though was another matter all together. My hair trapped me as Andrew slept on its length, I had not bound it and it was now binding me. While I couldn't have sat up, I could roll into his side and try to wake him. Positioning myself was easy, waking him was much more entertaining.

In sleep, his features were far softer than when he was awake and I wondered what his dreams were. Running my finger along his chin I waited for a reaction which never came. I thought the stubble along his chin line was nowhere near as heavy as that which I was accustomed to, even though it would be a day or so old now. I marvelled at how young he seemed, knowing he was older than I and the firm lines of his shoulders and chest fascinated me.

Carefully I ran my hand down over the texture of his chest, which was almost hairless and firm under my fingers and then deeper onto his belly beneath the camp blanket and watched as he stirred while my fingers drifted restlessly over his hip then leg, testing the heat around his wound very carefully, feeling the soundness of his body after our passion. His need for me stirred so easily and I smiled remembering the advice given to me about younger men. It seemed it was very true, even in sleep.

"Morning," he said softly into my hair, a rough note in his voice as he stirred to the day and I waited for him to wake properly, watching as he blinked the sleep from his eyes. He suddenly smiled down at me as I lay still looking at him in contentment, my own smile matching his as I considered him.

Capturing my fingers in his hand he swept them up to his chest resting them over his scars and held them there captive. "I have one more condom and I'm saving it," he warned, his eyes laughing as he kissed my fingers. "At least until we reach civilization anyway. I don't think there is much between here and there."

Amused I gave a chuckle and then shrugged. "I'm stuck here you know."

Andrew frowned. "What?"

"My hair, you're lying on it."

Lifting his head up suddenly he noticed the tangle of tresses beneath his shoulders and then suddenly sat up. "Oh sorry, never gave it a thought."

Easing myself up onto my elbows, I pulled at the length with a movement of my head checking it was free, and then sat up swinging the mass into my hand and ordering it in a roughly fashioned rope, then left it to hang down over my shoulder as he watched me patiently.

"Thank you," I said softly with a smile.

He reached for me, drawing me to him and claiming my lips with his then shifting me back onto the pillow easily as he playfully pinned me with his weight and moved to nuzzling my neck while I laughed.

"On second thoughts we could see if we can reach Camooweal by tonight," he whispered then running the tip of his tongue up my neck he toured my ear in a wet salute making me giggle and shiver at the cascade of sensation.

Immediately Tango growled, a sound low in his throat that froze us both as we both looked over at him surprised. He had made no complaints during the night, but now, for some reason he had decided to take exception.

"Tango?" I said softly, half scolding him, half questioning his reaction.

"No... no, it's OK." Andrew said softly, glancing at me. "Let me try something."

Easing himself up he watched Tango steadily, his expression intent as he drew deep breaths. Tango on the other hand watched me, though oddly enough he threw Andrew glances which I could have sworn were more argument than acceptance. Then suddenly he sat back with a whimper and sunk his nose to his paws, a silent protest.

Fascinated I sat up slowly wondering how it was that Andrew could worry him so much. "What are you doing?"

"I'm arguing," he answered, his eyes not leaving Tango's as he too leaned back supporting himself on his side. "And at last I think I am winning ground."

"You are?"

"Yes." Andrew broke eye contact with Tango to look at me and immediately Tango relaxed. Although he remained where he was I felt his confusion, his want to come to me and without thought I flicked my fingers and immediately he came, warily watching Andrew who was still propped on his elbow, once more with his eyes trained intently on Tango.

Tango's behaviour amazed me as he moved around putting me between Andrew and himself he then lay down, his head resting against me almost in a sulk.

Stretching, ducking his head around me and ignoring my look of incredulity, Andrew sort eye contact with him again. "Yeah you should be sorry," he said patiently.

"Andrew?" I questioned surprised more at his behaviour than Tango's.

"He's sulking now," he answered grinning. "Can't you see it?"

Swinging around to Tango I noticed the tortured look in his eyes and with threads of repentance I wrapped my hands about his neck.

"Is he picking on you? Ohh.. Baby don't you worry. I love you... Yes." Tangling my hands into his mottled coat I tried to comfort him as he responded immediately, his demeanour changing now from sulky to exuberantly playful. Stretching out on his back and settling into me as I knew he would. He lapped up the attention happily as I tried to sooth his uncertainties in a way I knew he would respond to.

"Will that work for me if I sulk?" Andrew tossed into the melee of tickles and cosseting I was lavishing on Tango and as I looked over I laughed at the expression on his face.

"What did you do to him?" I challenged. "He never behaves like that."

Andrew shrugged. "It's something I have always been able to do... but your mutt? I thought he was immune to it. It's good to see he isn't, believe me."

"He's not a mutt!" I chided, chastising him, but I softened my rebuke with a small smile. Then as I watched the look of irony cross Andrews face I was suddenly distracted again as he climbed out from the blanket to make his way over to the fire and I smiled quietly at the indignity I felt on behalf of my dog.

He made a fine figure as he moved about bringing the fire to life carefully and I remembered how the heat of him felt against my skin and the weight of him about me, then with a small pleasant shiver I climbed out of the tangle of blankets myself and picking a sarong carelessly from among those in my duffle bag, wrapped it about me and then grabbing another I took it over to him.

"Here you better put this on, you're way too distracting," I said laughing.

As he stood, he reached for the cloth and without his glance leaving me he tied it about his hips. "You couldn't have said anything nicer," he added softly. "So what would you like for breakie?"

"Mmm.. tea and scones I think. I'll rustle up the griddle scones and you can do the tea."

"Sounds right up my alley." Squatting back at the fire to continue where he had left off and I felt his eyes follow me around with some pleasure.

By the late morning we had the canoe ready for departure with both our bags and the camp packed up and cleared for the long hiatus between visits. Andrew had asked me about my vehicle and I had told him what I knew of the little green forester four wheel drive, which was scant information. For me vehicles were a means to an end but I fast realized this wasn't the case for him. I felt his frustration in my lack of knowledge and I teased him about his expectation that I would be actually informed about mechanical things.

My vehicle carried the necessary recovery gear and I had a UHF radio for emergencies but I had never bothered with mobile phones as I was never able to keep them charged, quite aside from the issue of reception. I found I could manage with communications when they were publicly available in any of the large centres I might pass through.

He on the other hand, relied on the mobile phone and hoped to be able to pick up reception as we neared either Lawn Hill or Riversleigh that afternoon though I doubted it myself, this land was too remote and there were no guarantees. So he didn't even bother breaking out the handset from its protective case, given the risk of it being on the water and the possibility of being dropped or damaged.

For me, I knew I would have reception on the UHF the minute I started up the car and if I had need, would be likely able to talk to someone by putting out a simple radio call. A device used by many travellers and most truckies, as well as those living in remote areas.

We debated the merits of the problems in communication while we paddled down the river in the canoe with Tango sitting happily between us. Andrew had taken the rear seat, insisting that he was the stronger rower and would better serve in the back position allowing me the front rider's seat. He wasn't entirely familiar with the management of the canoe but he would learn quickly I knew, even if his efforts occasionally placed the cargo and all of us at risk of a dunking. Something I made a point of mentioning every time it happened to his amused frustration.

It seemed our ride downriver was over as soon as it had begun and I had enjoyed the experience being shared. I showed Andrew where I had parked the car, concealed from the access tracks and we soon had our gear stowed. Manoeuvring the canoe onto the roof was much simpler with the added height and muscle Andrew was able to provide despite his tender leg and it wasn't long before we were out on the rough tracks and headed back south towards civilization.

It was always difficult leaving the arms of the bush, the beauty of the places I loved and the isolated serenity that drew me even though I had to also take on the bull dust and the dryness of the outback. Civilization arrived in stages though; first it would be the trucks and the occasional car along with the odd caravan rig. The dust would arrive with each encounter and then there would be scattered roadside buildings until once more they vanished into the bull dust. It was almost like a retreat that I would move onto the next isolated stretch and prepare myself for the upcoming arrival of outposts of civilization once again. Each time civilization would approach, one experience at a time until it overwhelmed me.

The late afternoon was a respite, a chance to revisit the quiet and serenity we were moving away from as we looked out for a likely camp-spot for the night. The choices were few, but along the rivers and streams of the channel country we could inevitably find something for a quiet night. That I travelled light and with a tent and swag for bedding helped. It was less conspicuous than a caravan or rig and with the small four wheel drive I could tuck into many spots that weren't able to accommodate other travellers as long as the conditions were dry and relatively flat, as well as being free of ants nests and the well worn tracks of wild life and those high enough not to be worried by the wild life, including croc's, not to forget the threat of any rising water.

That I had Tango with me often excluded me from many public and commercial campsites which were few and far between out here, but I considered without exception that I was safer with Tango than the company of strangers more often than not, and being a woman who usually travelled on her own now, or with a young child, this was a sound judgement. Though it wasn't uncommon for me to share a campsite with others, I had never had the experience of being threatened in any way though I knew it was always a risk and I largely kept to myself.

The camp beside the gully of a dry river where the trees grew thicker as they followed the path of the water, was cosy and we sat around and enjoyed the fire. Andrew had been quiet once dinner was over and we had settled into the camp. It was a lovely evening and because of that I had pulled out only the swag to enjoy the stars overhead and lounging on the canvas cover was as comfortable spot as any as we contemplated the following day.

Tango was settled and in no way appeared disturbed. He seemed to have accepted that Andrew would occasionally touch me and for the most part chose to ignore him, except when he made the effort to talk to him for some reason. He still wouldn't accept food from him though and staunchly ignored the small offering Andrew had made earlier. I didn't have the heart to tell him that Tango would not eat any offerings. He had tried so hard to convince him and still he left the food in his bowl. I also knew that while Tango would not let any other animal feed from his bowl, he also would disdain the food from Andrew's hand and it would likely be left to the ants until it was emptied out in the morning.

"I'll be surprised if we get into Mount Isa before lunch tomorrow, would you like to go straight to the agents and see if you can pick up a flight or a coach?" I asked quietly, wondering what he had planned.

He considered it for a while, the flames from the small fire flickering as he played with a stick. "Are you sure you wouldn't like me to come with you even as far as Katherine? I could get a ride into Darwin and fly out from there," he suggested with a smile. "I wouldn't have to go home with you;

you could leave me at the bus depot even. I don't like the idea of you travelling on your own."

Watching the concern in his eyes, I realized this wasn't just about travelling together. Stretched out behind him while he sat watching the flames I tried to reassure him. "I travel on my own all the time, I am used to it. Last year I was out the back of Bourke, literally for weeks!" I emphasized, aware that as popular a saying this was, that this time it was also a fact, but one that emphasised Bourke's isolation. "I enjoy travelling alone," I added. "Though admittedly I had Jem with me then, he wasn't much help but he was fun."

"You get to some strange places," he answered, shaking his head yet accepting my subtle refusal I was pleased to see.

"I was visiting friends and it was the quickest route from the Top End."

Stretching out beside me with something of a gruff invite to move into his warmth he gathered me into his side as we contemplated the stars.

"So, you gunna' kick me out at the travel agents in Isa? This is the plan? I might have a long wait?"

"You're a big boy, you can find your way to a hostel," I answered grinning. Then taking on a more serious tone I softened my grin. "Pals with perks, remember. I want to get home to Jem."

"Hmm. I know, OK." Sighing, he turned to me. "I like 'mates', it's a better term."

"No...Friends with benefits... Howz that?" I quipped happily.

Laughing at the mischief in my eyes he added. "Don't let me forget to give you my phone number will you?"

"I won't forget," I promised smiling. "I might even come down and visit you. You'll have to let me know where you are at."

"You really should get a mobile. How am I supposed to contact you?"

For a moment I thought about it and in doing so realized there was no way really. I wouldn't be staying in Katherine long, perhaps for a month and I hadn't yet decided on what I would do after that. I had a yen to move, perhaps further North into the Kimberley for a time.

"Mobiles are such useless things if you're not on the coast. You're never in range! I'll ring you by the New Year. I will know by then what I'm doing."

Andrew shifted me back gently as he moved to block out the night sky. "Mmm... promise?" he said, his look intent now on my mouth as he flicked his eyes to mine.

"I promise." I said softly and then he kissed me lingeringly as I had known he would. It was such a sweet salute which lingered in his eyes.

I loved the way he gently held me at first, his hand at my waist as he began a careful tour of my body shifting my clothes aside a little impatiently. He was impatient tonight and everything seemed to move so fast for me as he grew more impatient, almost a fear of losing me somewhere in the bedding before we could find the fulfilment we both wanted to hold.

By the time he reached for the condom, I knew I wasn't ready and I thought to slow him down but then I realized that perhaps this wasn't a time to do just that for a man, so I said nothing and he seemed to pick up on that I wasn't yet ready for him, in the way a woman reacts. His pace gentled as did his lips, his touch teased my body waiting for me to catch up and when he came to me, I welcomed the heat and strength of him as the sweet sensations began to sweep me along slowly.

In the tangle of bedding I shifted to gain a place where he would find it easier and as I moved over him, at first it seemed to be the best of both worlds. His touch fired along my nerves in a gentle onslaught while his skin glistened under the star light and then he moved too quickly. I know he tried to stop the path of his energy as he groaned tucking me beneath him easily, but he was lost to the demands of his passion and then I felt the waves of pleasure flow through him leaving me behind.

It took a moment for the tide to sweep over him, a moment in which he folded us back into the bedding and struggled to catch his breath, capture his strength, a moment when our heated bodies welded together and then he kissed the curve of my neck, tasting the fine film of moisture.

"I left you behind didn't I?" he asked softly with regret, when his body had slowed its pace, his eyes carefully trying to read mine in the star light.

"A little." I whispered still breathing deeply, feeling the fine edge of frustration.

"A little?" he chuckled. "A little is a lot." Easing his weight from me, he shifted after a long moment. The chill of the night touched me suddenly so that I tried to untangle the bedding and drag a light cover about us.

"Hang on, I don't want to leave you like this. Give me a minute, Beautiful."

"It's OK." I shrugged. "I know it's not always easy to control things, I don't expect you to," I said softly. "If I wanted to, I could do this myself you know".

For a long moment Andrew lay still, and then he carefully turned to me curious. "Yourself? You mean like I really missed the mark?"

I smiled and shrugged. "It's not target practice, but I didn't... I'm not..." shrugging I wondered what terms I could use that would convey my meaning gently. "I mean it was nice."

Easing himself up suddenly he looked down at me, with the bedding askew leaving me partially naked I felt a little exposed under the scrutiny of his eyes. I had never felt this way before and I found it odd, then wondered if it was just the chill.

"Nice?" he repeated softly, nodding almost in agreement yet in some way undecided about something. "Mmm.. That stinks!"

"Well I don't expect you to have the type of control... that well..." his frown stopped me as I chewed my lip. "Well you know what I mean."

He nodded. "That an older man has," he offered. "That's nice too," he added almost under his breath with a wry smile and I could feel his displeasure, which concerned me. I had not expected him to be offended by what was a simple truth. I wasn't sure what I could say or what I could do that would restore the fragile ego which seemed to be male.

Then looking around, his eye caught something and suddenly he was out of the bedding. I watched surprised as he started ratting through the tucker box and when he stood, holding the small plastic bag of bush honey that was left over. I then wondered if his leg was giving him trouble. I sat up expecting to help, to investigate what was the difficulty.

"No. You stay there," he said, coming back to join me. "I might not be as experienced as... some in your life but I have some good idea's." Grinning now, he settled down beside me and unclipping the bag I was fascinated to watch the way his eyes danced as he pushed the bedding further aside.

The colder night air bit at first but I was too distracted by the thin line of honey I felt hit the skin of my tummy and realizing what he was doing I laughed while he lent his tongue to the sticky line. It not only tickled but his warm tongue and gentle lips were as exciting as a mystery. I couldn't think of what he was going to do next as he moved over me and drizzled another thin line up around my breast.

"Lay still woman. This tastes great," he whispered softly chuckling, his tongue finding the darker skin of my nipples and then he moved back down to my belly in a heated sweep seeking every last sweet thread. Laughing I squirmed as I felt the warmth of his skin, the strength of his arms wrap around my hips.

It was a delightfully sensual feeling and I loved it. Then as his mouth ventured lower I gasped when I felt a fine tremor sweep through my belly. This I had not felt before and it was surprising as it was erotic.

It was the feel of the wet heat of his tongue along my inner thigh that surprised me next and the moan that escaped as he ventured further caught my breath, his touch touring my body left me breathless. My thoughts scattered and within seconds I was lost to everything other than a sensual flood of pleasure. It was familiar but so very different from anything I had felt before and as the passion built quickly it was like a sweet torture from which I didn't want to escape, it held me captive as the flood became a tidal wave of heat thrilling around my body.

I wanted him, wanted him so very much to stop the torture and come to me, stop what was so very enrapturing, but if he had stopped I would have begged him not to. I had not had such a pure experience of pleasure and I wanted to draw and hold him to me.

After forever, as the tide of heat finally burst and I shuddered under his touch. He moved up over me, himself trying to still the race of his heart and I could feel his need for me but he wouldn't move. His weight a welcome crush of passion and as my hands wound through his hair he shushed me, trying to quieten my small whimper telling him of my want. Trying to still my hands, my lips against his ear, his neck, he wrapped his arms about me and held me firmly. I felt like biting him hard, scratching him for not easing my want of him, but still his weight held me, even though my body felt sated, replete, I wanted him to be part of me once more.

"Shh.. I know... I know ... he whispered. Babe I can't. Honey I have nothing with me." And then he swore almost laughing at his own needs, and mine.

I quietened slowly, and after a time his heartbeat too slowed steadying against mine.

"I don't know if that was a good idea Babe, but I couldn't leave you like that." he whispered, once the throb of our blood had gentled. Shifting his weight, he drew a ragged breath and bent his lips back to mine.

He shifted again, trying to find comfort in his state and lent on his elbow, still partially over me grinning. "Don't ever compare me with your husband again please. It pisses me right off," he said softly, his eyes carefully searching mine as he said what was now foremost in his thoughts. "And don't... please don't take that the wrong way."

Biting my lip hard I tried to contain the small errant grin that sprang to life. "Sorry. I didn't mean... Well I mean is that how you get when you're pissed off?"

Andrew started chuckling softly and then he fell into a full laugh as he considered me. Drawing a deep breath he then said, "No.!" in such a firm tone that I had to giggle.

Snuggling into him again, as he began to relax at my side, I felt the deep contentment of a weariness bought on as only passion can do, passion which has brought the heights of its experience. For a moment I even considered how much I would miss him, miss his heat, his humour and his smile. These thoughts carried me into sleep as I lay cosseted in his arms. It was such a beautiful feeling.

It was late when we woke the next morning and it was Tango's wet nose and breath which disturbed my sleep. At first I just lay there, enjoying the feel of Andrew curled into my back, his arm stretched around me and his breath heating the back of my hair gently. Then as I moved, testing the tangle of my hair he woke, suddenly easing himself up, feeling the pull of the locks of my hair against his skin.

"Sorry, I'm on your hair again," he said sleepily and then smiled. "It must be a pain; But I will miss it when you lop it off."

"That's tuff," I answered carelessly, offering no condolences, it was my choice I knew. Turning to Tango I scratched his head absently as I waited for the morning to become the beginning of my day.

Propping himself up, Andrew considered me again. "I can't imagine it," he said quietly, curious. "You with no hair, well not long hair anyway."

I smiled and sat up slowly, now feeling the freedom to move. This wasn't something I would even discuss with him I knew. "We might have a quick breakfast I think we have slept in late," I said instead, wanting to do anything but this, but knowing the day had to begin.

"Hmm...I will get the fire started."

Climbing out from the bedding he stretched then climbed into his shorts and for a moment I took the time to watch him as I scratched Tango about the ears, not really wanting to move. The motion of his body as he set about building the fire, the strength of him, the gentleness in his eyes as he occasionally glanced my way. These are the things I would remember most I decided.

After we had washed and changed it was as though we were wearing the responsibilities of a different life. Seeing Andrew in his clean clothes, relatively unscathed from the time he had spent in the bush, it was like I was now with a man I didn't recognize

I was right of course; you couldn't know someone after such a short time.

What I knew of him was just one part of who he was. I would be fooling myself if I thought differently. It really was time to start a new day I realized as I moved towards a path which I knew would take me away from him, and towards everything which I also loved that was my life.

The drive to Mount Isa consumed our morning and we each kept our thoughts to ourselves as the car ate up the road beneath us. The distance seemed endless and yet the last thing I wanted was for it to end in many ways. But end it must for now I knew. It was time for me to say goodbye to my past and open the door to the future. I couldn't hide anymore from life, Andrew had shown me that, though I doubt he even realized it.

I owed him my freedom of mind and I realized that it was also time to set my past free also.

HOMEWARD BOUND

Andrew:

It had taken over two days, two long arduous days and two endless nights to get to Cairns and still I couldn't conceive of how it could possibly take that long but that was the vagaries of travelling though the outback in the Gulf Country of Far North Queensland.

It was two days of sitting on hard seats, waiting at stops, sleeping in strange beds and arranging pickups to get my backside into the seat of a vehicle. On my arrival into Cairns I contacted a car hire firm and made arrangements to take a car south to Brisbane. Often there would be vehicles to be returned south and if I had the time I could arrange to drive them at a nominal cost. Within a few short hours of reaching Cairns I was headed off towards Brisbane in what seemed an endless tour.

Two days of public transport with nothing to do but think of her and wonder where she was and what she was doing. At least now with a vehicle of my own under my hands I could take time to think in company with the sounds of the bush. Time to reflect and I wondered if that was a good thing.

She would be in Katherine by now I figured, I hoped. Unless she was waylaid with car trouble, or had cause to stop over and as I thought of her typically female attitude to cars my concern hit flash point. I feared most that she would be involved in an accident somewhere out on the tar with few people to help her, it was my worst nightmare. I hated not knowing how she was travelling, I hated that I couldn't contact her. I hated most that I didn't even know her name!

In my mind I had given her an identity that was other than words. Over the days she had become the sweet taste of honey in my mouth, the smell of acacia to my senses but mostly I felt the dark pool of calm in her eyes. This was my own private identity for her, one that was mine alone and which I couldn't share with anyone else even if I had wanted to. She was like a dream and she stayed with me in this way making my nights restless and my days lonely. It was the oddest experience I had ever had, knowing her in this way.

I had been a fool I realized, I didn't think I was in love, I don't think I even knew what that meant but I certainly felt in lust. I damned my pride for not knowing the most basic thing about her. I should have just asked her name and be done with it. At least she had my phone number, she could call... she might call? Not knowing if I would ever hear from her again was like torture, after all I owed her so much. Every day I thought of her and I hoped the phone would ring, even though I knew that there was likely no need for her to ring me yet. She had said maybe at Christmas and that was months away. I had to stop thinking about her, it was going to do me no good and get me nowhere but moody.

Trying to not think about her, not remember her eyes, the features of her face, the way she moved was simply impossible for me. To attempt not to think about her was to remind myself I had to forget about something I needed to recall to dismiss. It was so easy just to remember the smell of her skin, the light touch of her fingers. I didn't need visuals like I didn't need a name. I tried to convince myself of this and I found it in some way calmed me.

Three days to get to Cairns, another four on the road south over the inland roads at a steady pace and I was finally nearing Brisbane. Still I thought of her, she came to mind so easily and even when I managed to convince myself I hadn't thought much about her then my leg would remind me.

Maybe she had rung Aine's? I wondered. Maybe she had been unable to contact me, I may have been out of the service area, anything was possible. I had given her Aine and Jenna's land line number in case she was unable to reach me and needed to for whatever reason, it was a simple backup I had assured her. I knew they would take a message for me and make sure I received it in good time.

Yet even as I thought of this I knew she wouldn't have rung, there was no need for her to have done so. It wasn't even a week since I had left her side.

Impatiently I dismissed my thoughts and considered instead my return to the Community. First I would have to check in with the agency to find out what arrangements had been made and then hopefully I would have time for a trip down to Nimbin to catch up before I was based off shore.

Then my mind wandered, the last I had held her in my arms had been like trying to hold onto a bubble, so fragile and unknown. I did manage to annoy myself with the memory; it was a punishment for my idiocy. The time had been so short, as there had been nothing to delay us. A kiss as she had come to open the back hatch door to ensure I retrieved my bag OK. At least I had taken her in my arms and kissed her like there was no tomorrow. I knew, I feared, that this was the most that there would be for us. There were no guarantees; I would just have to accept that. We could be friends with benefits... those had been her words.

Even now I could so easily remember her over-bright eyes, she had had a fidgety manner about her as I had let her go. Her eyes had kept me standing at the curb after she had gone, even when there was nothing to do, no way that I could call her back to me. I had been such a fool and now I couldn't understand how I had simply let her go without even getting an address of someone she knew to contact her by.

She probably wouldn't have given me one I reasoned. She said she wasn't ready for me to meet her son. I could understand that, see the reason in it but it didn't help. Nothing seemed to help. What I needed was to get back into a busy life, wait for the time for her to contact me when she was ready, and make bloody sure I had the means to contact her next time. Even if it meant I had to buy a phone for her myself, attach it permanently to a car charger so that at least she would be accessible, she wouldn't even need to think about it. God! I wished I had thought of that in Mount Isa.

As I neared the busy Brisbane suburbs I felt my tensions ease. It had been nearly four months since I had been there, it had been that long since I had headed into Far North Queensland.

My trip so many months ago now had begun simply enough when I was headed north for initiation and my thoughts shifted momentarily back to the memories of the fight between Sean and Taipan's half brother. Then I wondered how Sean and Jenna were getting on now. Jenna had been so upset about Sean's stand but it had worked out in the end.

I was proud of my initiate scars and knew they would understand my pride. Sean had gained his in his first period of training and that was just as well, he had needed the skills then. He had needed those links to the Spirit Men.

For a moment I wondered if Sean would be in Brisbane, I hadn't thought to ask when I had rung and spoken to Aine, asking her if I could doss down at their place as I passed through, headed for home. You never knew if they had let someone use the spare room and it always seemed right to check before I lobbed up. Dianne, Sean's Mum had made a few trips to Brisbane to catch up with the girls and I knew she would make use of the spare room if I wasn't there.

Aine had been as welcoming as I knew she would be when I had rung, she had heard of my injury, likely from Taipan and her concern was for my health. I knew I would have to suffer their concern and I wondered how I was going to tell them about how my life had changed, the preoccupation I now felt. I wanted to draw my angel of mercy into my life but had left myself no way of doing so. Again I felt the frustrations of my stupidity, my pride.

Maybe if I simply said nothing, which was an option, they would learn about it later if they needed to, and then I remembered I had given out Aine's land line number, so she at the very least would need to be told. I would just have to deal with it. How could I explain that I didn't even know her name? It was alright to call her Honey, or Babe, to tease her as I had done in those last minutes, but I knew it wouldn't work with my friends who knew me so well.

I could also ring the Agency from Aine's, let them know of my decision, it would be at least two days before I could continue on my way south. Two days for the girls to figure things out and I knew they were pretty sharp in the way women were about relationships. Maybe I could fluff through it. They wouldn't ask much of my walk-about, knowing it was men's business but the injury on my leg would give them something else to focus on. I knew it was impossible to talk about that and not talk about her. It was a dilemma and I struggled with it as I neared the quiet street in anticipation of my arrival.

I remembered the sight of the house, more so than the address and finding it was a simple matter. The guys had bought it as an investment, a residence for Aine and Jenna and even now I knew there would be talk of who amongst the Community would join Jen as a joint tenant next year if they managed to gain a position in Brisbane to study, as Aine was completing her course this year. I knew even Sean would be toying with the thought, buying the house had been a sound investment, the kind of investment I should consider once I had settled into my job.

I had to admire the way Taipan and Sean had set up things, it was a lesson I was taking seriously and I planned to ask Ty about it when I got back to the Community.

Pulling the hire car into the open driveway I left room for Sean's ute to come and go, knowing the girls would be using it in his absence, I wasn't wanting to block anyone in. It was just after dusk, it was likely the girls would be home.

As I collected my rucksack from the back, I heard the front door open and the commotion of what sounded like a welcoming committee, I smiled. It was good to be back amongst friends.

"Andrew! I was worried about you coming through the peak hour traffic, you're late!"

Aine's smile was like a panacea, generous with the warmth of her welcome as she was, I gave her a quick hug, she was still as tiny and slight as I remembered as was little Jen. It was good to see the girls again and feel the warmth of friendship.

"Ty made me promise I would check your leg by the way, so you're not going to get out of that one, I have to give a full report. But maybe after dinner, Jen has a casserole on."

"That sounds great, though the leg is fine. It has healed really well," I reassured her as I moved through the house with them, dropping my pack in the lounge room.

Jen perched herself on the armrest of the long lounge while Aine headed for the kitchen, the open plan area across from what was the servery bar. Jen's hair had grown some, not much though and then I wondered if she had trimmed it again to a fluffier style. Somehow the cropped hair suited her, it sat on her neck neatly as though it had always done so.

"So tell us." Jen began happily. "What's she like?"

Surprised I looked up. I knew immediately who she meant. I couldn't believe I had barely got in the door and the girls were right on to what I didn't want to discuss.

"Who?"

"Your girlfriend!" Jenna said exasperated, chiding me gently. "Sean said you had met a girl. The one who saved your life you nut! Did you think he wouldn't tell us?"

"Oh her," I answered grinning, trying to hood the emotion in my eyes. Suddenly it was ridiculously hard.

When Aine came in with cool drinks, I thought to distract them with something, anything; but immediately I caught Aine's eyes I knew it wasn't going to work. She was studying me, studying my reaction and I knew I was doing this very badly.

"My... from the look in his eyes I do believe she's special," Aine said softly then looked across at Jenna. "I think he is quite interested in this girl," she whispered surprised as she put the drinks on the table and joined Jen on the sofa, her eyes pinning me.

"Oh come on!" I protested laughing. "That's not fair. I hardly know her!" Agitated I sat down in the armchair across from them trying to control my sense of irony along with its humour. I was going to bluff my way through this I told myself sternly.

Aine's eyes never left me. "Hmm... that's nothing," she said softly grinning. "You have to tell us all about her now. What's her name? Where does she live?"

"Will we meet her?" Jen added keenly.

"Look, you have it all wrong," I said opening my hands, avoiding it all adeptly I thought. "She's just a woman who found me in the bush, she was great, but she has her own life and even a kid. It's not like that at all really."

"Then why are you blushing?" Jenna asked in a tone that brooked no denial, or argument from me. "You wouldn't be blushing if she meant nothing."

Unable to argue, to deny what Jen said, I just shook my head with an accepting if somewhat annoyed smile. "She lives in the Territory, you will probably never meet her. I might never see her again. Who knows?"

I felt the weight of their keen eyes on me, and immediately I knew I had done it. I had managed to evade their questions. Relief flooded through me at the thought. Then Aine frowned.

"Didn't you get her phone number?"

I shook my head. "She doesn't have a phone, said she wouldn't use it she's rarely in range."

"So how do you contact her?"

"I don't. What does that tell you?" I said simply and shrugged hoping this was the end of it.

"You gave her your number though, right?" Jenna interjected. "Maybe she's rung, or messaged, have you checked?"

I shook my head. "She hasn't. I also gave her your land line, just in case. I know I should have asked but do you mind?"

Aine shook her head, smiling. "No. That's OK. The message bank will pick it up if she calls and we aren't here. What's her name?"

I felt the heat ride up through my skin. That was the one thing I couldn't tell them and I was annoyed again with myself as I growled in exasperation I swept my hands through my hair. I watched Jen's eyes widen, I knew I wasn't going to evade this.

Aine frowned. "You've forgotten her name?" she questioned confused.

"You don't know her name?" Jen said softly, incredulously.

How was it that they could get to the crux of this so damn quickly I thought as I shook my head, then I tried to explain. "She told me, seriously she did but I forgot. It was something strange and I have been trying to drag it out of my memory but... nothing. All I remember is that it isn't said with a G in it. Her dogs name I know, and her kids name is Jem but her name... I have literally racked my brain and nuthin!" I shrugged. "What was I supposed to do after two days... Excuse me, but what's your name again? I couldn't do it! OK. I thought I could figure it out, but there was nuthin' no letters, notes... it just got too ridiculous to ask."

"You spent weeks with her and you don't know her name?" Jen repeated softly grinning. "I don't believe it!"

"Come on... it wasn't weeks."

"Andrew! How could you be so stupid! Why didn't you just ask her?" Jen exclaimed.

"It wasn't like that. I couldn't ask... God she saved my life, Jen, she nursed me... she even slept beside me to keep me warm. I couldn't let her know I had forgotten her name, could I?"

Aine began to chuckle, softly at first and then more with irony. "Please don't tell me you slept with her and that you don't know her name."

I looked up, I had just told her that, but I knew it wasn't what she meant. The look in my eyes must have given me away, my look of exasperation answered the question Aine had asked I knew, when her mouth dropped.

"Andrew you didn't! Oh God! You idiot!"

"It happened OK. It was something we chose," I said clearly. "Neither of us regretted that. It was right, great... whatever it's you girls say when it's right." I wanted to emphasize the rightness of our relationship. Above every messy thing I wanted the girls to know that it was something that was as it should have been, would have been. It was to me the one thing we had that was so very right.

I had to stand, to stretch my leg and to ease my agitation. It had taken them what...! all of barely ten minutes to get to this and I still couldn't believe it.

"You know you girls are just incredible!" I said suddenly, facing them in my frustration. Then seeing the serious look in Aine's eyes I softened my voice. "I haven't been here ten minutes and you have what I wasn't even going to tell you. OK, I know it's bad but I'll work it out. She may never even contact me but I hope she does. I have to work this out somehow, and if I don't... then that is the way it will be. Just don't keep reminding me of how stupid I have been. Believe me I know!"

The two of them just watched me for a moment then Jen stood. "OK. Point taken, let's eat," she said suddenly, accepting my plea and I breathed again with relief. "You know we love you Andrew and if we can, we will help, but a last word," she warned and then smiled. "You got to admit it's bloody funny. You are going to have a hard time living this one down when Sean finds out."

I grinned. "Yeah I know that. Listen don't tell the guys, please. It's bad enough already and... well, she may never ring. I could live with that as long as they don't know... seriously!"

Jenna nodded, and I could see the empathy in her eyes despite the mischief. "That won't be easy but I'll try," she said, her impish grin springing to her lips, tormenting me despite her words.

While Aine nodded. "That's OK. It will be fun to have a secret."

I followed the girls over to the servery window which divided the kitchen from the lounge area, knowing we would be likely eating there and I watched Jen flashing the same mischief I had seen earlier in her eyes as she thought of Sean. Jen had grown stronger in her confidence and I wondered what was going through her mind as she pulled the casserole from the oven.

I thought again of the little handful Sean had, in trying to keep up with Jenna and the battle he had already fought in winning her away from Taipan. Jen would keep him on his toes if nothing else as she had developed a strong will of her own and you were never quite sure about what she was planning. Maybe I should just tell him about it all myself.

I knew she wouldn't tell him if I had asked her not to, but I felt as though I had aligned myself with the girls. I also knew how much both Ty and Sean concerned themselves about their women and the mischief they could get themselves into. Jenna had led both Sean and Ty off on more than one ill conceived adventure and Aine managed to tame Taipan in a way no other woman had ever come near to managing. Maybe I wasn't doing the right thing here... some how it felt wrong and I wasn't sure about this secrecy.

My training for the rigs kept me in Brisbane longer than I had first anticipated over the next weeks. As soon as I had contacted the agency they had organized for the training block, followed soon by an induction. I never even made it back to the Community. Safety was a major concern when life revolved around the particular isolation the large oil operations offered on the remote off shore rigs.

The men who worked the rigs were also of a particular breed. They worked long hard hours in the difficult conditions which come with deep drilling for oil out on the rigs. The isolation was a major factor and the hard long hours with heavy responsibilities took a toll. The teams you worked with were of necessity a tight group, and when you found your feet in this world it was a strong hold to be accepted amongst such men.

I found I loved it though, I loved the rough raw energy and I loved the open exposure of the rigs to the vast open oceans where I could hit a golf ball and watch it rise to the horizon. There was something untamed about the environment which spoke to me and in the quiet of the nights I could lose myself in my memories.

The subtle taste of her, the warmth of her skin would come to me, visit my dreams and disturb my sleep. Each time I returned to the mainland I wondered if I would return to find she had left a message, or had tried to contact me. Each time I was disappointed and after a time I refrained from asking, avoiding the careful scrutiny of Jenna and Aine. Avoiding the reality of my disappointment and I began to let go of the hope that she was going to return to me one day. It was time to move on I decided, it was something which simply hadn't worked out and I tried to convince myself that it was over before it had ever really begun. But I could still enjoy the memories that remained regardless of how much I tried to let them go.

In my work rotation I found that returning to the Community became the mainstay of my world. There was always something happening, always some way in which I was drawn into the lives of those around me and I enjoyed that so much.

Tom was busy learning about building, a project both Sean and Taipan were involved in and when I was home his build was something that I helped with. We were building a small cottage, a basic 'A' line structure that sat into the side of the escarpment on a levelled piece of land no larger it seemed than a pocket handkerchief.

The A frame for the external structure was simply erected and clad with corrugated iron, it sat on a metre of the more conventional wooden wall at ground level which also gave it some character. There was just one large room and this was relatively easy to get this to a lockup stage. The internals however were more demanding. Tom had designed a mezzanine which formed a second floor and this was eventually to be the only bedroom, high in the A shaped ceiling space. As we broke into the summer season proper it seemed the work ground to something of a halt when the younger men, Tom's friends, wanted to have more to do with the build and Tom slacked off somewhat having reached lockup.

Taipan and I then decided to leave the internal work for Tom to manage. That was when the build seemed to be going nowhere fast and until Tom could come to terms with controlling his circle of mates, there was little being achieved.

When the Christmas season approached Tom's mate Denis was visiting having travelled down from near Cooktown. I liked Denis, he was level headed and a good influence. He seemed to understand the things that concerned Tom. We had met briefly in the winter and that the two young men got on well together was obvious, also that the two of them had decided to take on the training of Shaman was also a good thing.

It was for Taipan to introduce them to the finer points of the men's Lore, which would in time carry them through to their initiations. This meant that Tom would be returning to Far North Queensland once he had finished his Senior year at school. He would be spending some time with Denis and his Dad to take on more skilling under his guidance.

It didn't take me long to realise this was a learning experience for Tom. He needed to manage what he wanted to achieve against the commitment he was prepared to undertake. We figured he would tire of getting no further in the build by winter. Tom, we were all glad, was showing more maturity in the matter of women though occasionally he would manage to get himself embroiled in strife, usually associated with some girl though he had learnt to not alienate the women in the community.

Ty on the other hand was spending more time in Brisbane as the building slowed down during the summer. I knew he was spending time with Aine, hoping to persuade her to come back with him to the Community and to use her skills with the kids. Sean was strictly practical; he was headed north into the city. I had my own theories about this and it had as much to do with spending time with Jenna, as it did with not spending time with his mother, Dianne.

As Aine had finished her course, there was the suggestion she would return to the Community with Taipan, so I offered to take over her tenancy with Jen. Sean spent most of his time there now and the three of us moved into an easy arrangement that suited us all. It was simpler to have the room available for me when I was on shore leave and I enjoyed the companionship.

It was a few months after Christmas, home from another rotation, that I arrived back into Brisbane to collect my car. I had grown into the habit of leaving the vehicle with Jen to use in my absence as Sean had need of his ute. It made sense to have it being used for the weeks I was away, rather than garaging it somewhere and wondering if the battery would be flat when I made it back into Brisbane.

I flew into Brisbane late on the Friday and was pleased to see Sean and Jen at the airport to meet my plane. It would save me the pain of public transport and I appreciated the gesture.

"Hi there, this is unexpected." I greeted Sean readily once I reached the terminal gates. My appreciation was more than evident as I shook his hand happily and gave Jen a kiss on her cheek.

"We were in town anyway, thought we would detour to pick you up after dinner." Jen offered.

"Well it's saved me some bother. Thanks."

"No worries mate." Sean said readily. "So you like this life then?"

"Yeah. I think I do."

It didn't take me long to collect my duffel bag from the luggage area and the trip back through the city was as congested as I could have imagined it to be on a Friday evening. It always took time to adjust after a rotation and I had found going to ground for a day or two, giving myself time to adjust, had a certain advantage to it.

Sean and Jen filled me in on a lot of what had been going on while I had been away. It seemed there was talk of Taipan and Aine heading to Sydney, returning to the cottage on the Woronora River on the old Shackles Estate for a time, though I undoubtedly would hear more about it when we got back to the house.

I was very much looking forward to the time on shore and wasn't due to return for a solid ten days, unless of course there was a problem, something which wasn't anticipated. While I loved the work, I knew there were others who would take the call if workers were needed.

When I arrived back at the house it didn't take long to settle in. I had taken over the third bedroom which still left Aine and Taipan's old room vacant. The arrangement suited me; it gave me a home base when I passed through Brisbane allowing me to share my time between the Community and the city.

It was the next morning, as we were discussing plans, I was considering returning to catch up with my family when Jen passed the phone table which sat just off the kitchen, and she pulled something from the paste board then handed it to me.

"You got a phone call last week. Some girl named Mary, or it might have been Marie. Said she was flying in Sunday and would give you a ring. I meant to tell you last night.

Frowning I took the small yellow post-it. I couldn't think who she was, but as my mind ran over the women I had met since basing myself out of Brisbane I could bring no one to mind. I knew it wasn't someone from Nimbin, I was sure Jen would have known her if it had been.

"Marie? Can't think who she is? Did she say anything else?"

"Not much. Just what is on the note, the flight gets in around 10:00am I think, she didn't leave any other details. I wrote what she said down. Maybe she wanted you to meet her?"

I shook my head, flicking the note between my fingers absently. I could think of no one off hand though perhaps it could be someone I had met while in Brisbane. I knew a few women, though they were mostly friends with the guys from the rigs. They were a group who I mixed with occasionally when we first hit the city after a rotation. Though by now I had learnt to either make arrangements to stay in town for the rotation, or head south to Nimbin to visit the family. Mixing the two groups didn't work very well so it was either one or the other.

"She did say something about going to the Gold Coast, a conference or something," Jen offered as she busied herself with breakfast for Sean.

Tucking the note into my pocket absently I headed out for the day to take care of business before I headed south tomorrow. I thought nothing more of it until later that evening and I considered what time I would leave to head home to the Community. I had planned to leave early, but again wondered who this woman was, who would ring me.

It occurred to me only then that most of the people from Brisbane knew my mobile number only. Few if any had been given the land line number, that had me sitting up suddenly and reconsidering the contact.

"That phone message..." I said to Jenna as we gathered in the lounge room after dinner and Jen had settled comfortably curled into Sean's side. "Her name was Marie you said?"

Jen looked up, "Yeah, something like that? Could have been Mary, they sound the same really sometimes."

It occurred to me that if I knew where she was flying in from it might give me a hint. The laptop which lived permanently set up in the corner was free and it was a simple matter to find these things out. So I went over to it. "Do you mind? I just want to check something."

"Sure, no worries," she said absently.

As I waited for the website to load, I considered the note. Moving through the flight schedule for arrivals I quickly realized I needed to know a city of departure, or at least a flight number. Impatiently I switched the computer off and wandered back to the lounge.

"No luck?" Sean added at my frustration.

"Nope. I have no idea who this is."

"You could try ringing the airport; they might be able to help out. You have an arrival time," Jen added.

I considered it, knowing that I would have to go through the rigmarole of airline security. I also realized that they wouldn't give names out of passengers. Besides, Marie or Mary wasn't a lot to go on. What stayed with me however was that there was only one person I had given the land line number to and the more I thought about it, the more I was convincing myself that this could be her, though the name... that rang absolutely no bells for me.

"I might take the coast road back home tomorrow, go via the airport. See if I can recognize her," I considered out loud. Then looked up, "I don't give out your landline to anyone. There is only...."

Jenna caught on quickly. "It could be her." She announced suddenly, her curiosity brimming.

I shrugged and tried to set it to the back of my mind. Sean looked puzzled but refrained from adding anything. He had planned to spend another week in Brisbane before he headed back, taking Jen with him when she finished her college term.

The more I dwelt on it, the more convinced I became that it was her. That she was headed to a conference on the Gold Coast added to the mystery. I couldn't imagine her doing that, but then I really knew so little about her.

The next morning the airport was busy as it usually was over the weekend and having parked the car early, I checked out the arrival schedule noting the arrivals for around 10am. That there was a flight from Darwin at 10:15 made me think and gave me hope, so I decided to wait and the best place to be was around the baggage carousels.

There was no guarantee that it was the Darwin flight. I could only hope that she wasn't travelling light and had luggage to collect. At least though, the carousels were near the main exit escalators down from the terminals and I could keep an eye on both.

Propping myself up against the wall I settled in for a wait watching as the human traffic moved steadily towards the baggage claim area. If I didn't recognize anyone, it would be of little account and I could be on my way by 11am having lost little time.

The river of people was hard to keep an eye on, so I went for small groups of one or two people, my eyes running over everyone, looking for any nudge of recognition but I particularly looked for honey coloured women with long hair, remembering the cascade of dark silk most readily.

It was however a sweetly figured woman who caught my eye. Her hair was cropped in a short pixie bob and it wasn't until I saw her then, that I remembered she had said she was going to lop it all off. It had to be her at a distance and I watched as she rode the elevator down though I didn't recognize her dress or style. She was trailing a small suitcase and turned towards the luggage carousel as she looked around and I suddenly smiled realizing that my guess had been right.

Her eyes ran over me absently and then past me without recognition and I debated if I could have been mistaken, though I found it hard to take my eyes off her. Perhaps she had simply not seen me as I stood motionless against the wall and I debated what to do about it. Then I remembered that I too had trimmed my hair and likely looked little like the bush man she had met in the Channel Country.

I watched her for maybe ten minutes as the crowd gathered at the baggage carousel. It was an interesting dilemma for me and my thoughts were going into overdrive trying to figure how I was going to do this. A plan was forming and I considered it closely as the first of the luggage off the flight began its circuit on the carousel. I waited impatiently now.

When she moved forward, obviously to collect a bag, I moved, coming up behind her quietly and while she struggled I reached ahead of her, greeting her with a smile I grabbed the cumbersome luggage.

"Hey you," I said softly, a greeting in my eyes.

"Andrew! Oh thank you," she said greeting me with the sweetest smile as I heaved the bag off the carousel and set it down back from the surging crowd clambering for their luggage.

Her smile was my reward and I returned it happily as she followed me the short distance out of the crowd around the carousel.

"Have you been waiting long? I asked, knowing the answer before I had even posed the question.

"No. I've just got in. I wasn't sure if you got my message, I was going to ring you again when I got to the Gold Coast."

"I was off shore when you rang. Jenna gave me the message when I got in a few days ago. Is this it?" I asked indicating the luggage.

"Yes. I have to organize a bus to the coast, I believe there is a terminal somewhere about here?"

"Yes, its outside. But I am headed that way, can I give you a lift?"

"That would be great, thank you again."

Getting out of the airport was a simple, uncomplicated affair and we were soon on the open highway to the Coast, filling our time with small talk. She asked me about my job which filled the conversation and I in turn quizzed her about her visit.

"I'm here for a nursing conference, it goes until Wednesday. I fly out on Friday which gives me a day off."

"Where are you staying?"

"An apartment just off the main centre I believe, I've been told it's quite nice. I think it overlooks the beach, I have the address here somewhere."

As she rummaged I considered putting my own plans aside for a few days. I could drive down from Jenna's and spend some time with her easily, but first I would need to resolve the other issues.

"Do you have plans for today? When does the conference start?"

"Tomorrow, I have the rest of the day to settle in. I was going to take a walk down the main strip and check out the shopping. There're a few things I need to get, the least of which will be swimmers for the beach."

Immediately my mind flicked to another beach, another part of the country and other memories. "Would you like some company?" and then glancing across at her I caught her eye. "I like your hair by the way, it suits you."

Subconsciously her fingers flew to the short neat crop of dark hair feathering her neck. "It has taken ages to get used to, but I am glad I did it. It was something I needed to do."

Her mood had sobered and I frowned searching for a reason for the mood change, then giving up, I wondered if she'd like company shopping.

Instead of persisting with my questions though, I decided that I would leave off and concentrate on taking the right exit instead. The trip took us only maybe thirty or forty minutes, we were fast coming up to the Labrador turn-off.

The apartment block was one of the older ones at the top of the Gold Coast strip. It was set back from the beach by a block or more, but it had magnificent views facing the south side out over the main drag which allowed the eye to travel down the length of the shore. The heavy ribbon of golden sand ran along to the horizon, swept constantly by the white cap of the ocean's rolling surf.

Like many of the apartments on the coast, it featured full length windows, floor to ceiling and while it was edging towards its use-by date, it was comfortable and well maintained. There were only three units on each floor, two looked to be larger, perhaps two bedroom, while one was a smaller one bedroom suite tucked into the corner. It was one of the smaller units which we travelled up to on the seventeenth floor. The unit also had a small balcony which offered alfresco dining which was only hampered by the view into the units above and below. Something I decided that it would pay to be aware of as I stepped back into the apartment and waited for her to join me while she settled her gear in the bedroom.

"This is nice." I offered as she wandered out to check on the kitchen facilities.

"Yes, it is isn't it? It was recommended to me, I think I love it. Just look at that view!"

"Hmmm...Would you like company with exploring, I could delay my plans.

Maybe we could head out for dinner somewhere? There are a couple of places on the coasts that offer some great dining?"

"I think I would love that, but somewhere close. Perhaps we can walk? I think I am over travelling for the day."

"Done then... when you're ready there is some good shopping along the main strip which isn't too far, maybe we could start there. I want to pick up something too while I am here." I suggested as she moved to collect her things eager for an excursion onto the central shopping strip.

Wandering down towards the main strip soon after, I couldn't get over the different feel of our friendship. It was amazing to me how things can change when moved from one environment to another and I wondered if she felt it too.

Geared for tourist trading, many of the shops were operating seven days a week so we found a few which catered for swim wear, mostly for women. While this was something I enjoyed immensely in that I was sharing this with her, as she scouted through the different styles of swimwear and I tried hard to be involved, it was difficult to concentrate to keep my thoughts on track. Shopping for women's attire wasn't my strong point even though it was easy on the eye. More than once I had to rein in my wandering thoughts and I was sure she knew it too. The whole experience was one we both enjoyed as we flirted through the shops.

It was later in the afternoon that I came across just what I was looking for and pulling her up I took her over to the counter.

"Could I have a rural phone, a pre-paid please, something simple with a sound antenna."

We discussed a number of options and when I made my choice the attendant handed me the necessary form and pen, I passed it onto her with a grin. "This is for you, fill that out and consider it a means to an end."

"What's this for? Really I don't need it, I don't know if I even like it," she protested surprised as she looked at the phone, like it was something alien.

"It's so I can contact you when I need to. You don't have to carry it all the time, when you get back to the Territory just connect it to the ciggie' lighter and leave it with the vehicle. But at least while you are in town, you can pick up messages and make calls. I am over not being able to contact you woman, now just do as you're told." I finished on a teasing note and grinned, hoping she wasn't going to argue, "I should have done this months ago."

"Andrew... really, it's unnecessary. I can't let you buy this."

Raising my brow I challenged her. "This isn't for you it's for me. Now just fill in the form and let me do this. I'll feel much better about it."

Breathing a sign she glared up at me, then thinking about it she flicked the form over and glanced at the sales man who was waiting expectantly. Taking up the pen silently, she began filling in the necessary user details as I relaxed, somewhat relieved at her side, and waited.

"I can register you at my address if you like, or you can use your own details," I offered pleased at her compliance, an offer which scored me a quick glance.

"Do they send stuff out?"

"No. A pre-paid means it can all be managed on-line. It's just an I.D. thing."

Taking the form as she finished it I ran my eyes over the details and grinned. I couldn't have been more pleased as I noted her name written clearly at the top. Ngaire; then I wondered how the hell you pronounced that. As I pondered the question I handed over my card to charge the phone for a twelve month term.

"Would you mind setting that up please," I asked the sales rep. "Could you register it on-line for us too, we don't have computer access at the moment."

As the man went through the process I turned to her. "You know Jenna thought your name was Marie, or Mary or something like that. I told her the G was silent."

"Yes, it sounds like Marie doesn't it. I get that a lot. Most people miss the N, you have no idea how many times I have to spell it and that doesn't help much. I think it was my Dads revenge on my Mum."

I grinned, I couldn't have been happier and it was hard to contain my relief. While we waited for the sales man I took out my own phone and set up the contact info for her, then sent off a quick text to Jenna, simply with Ngaire's name. She would know what it was I was sure, she would understand and appreciate my cryptic message.

It only took twenty minutes or so then we were done, impatiently I waited as the sales man ran through the basic features of the phone with Ngaire, I had trouble keeping my eyes off her as I married the name with her features and my memories. The rest of the afternoon was something of a blur as we picked up some basic foods for the kitchen and made our way back to the apartment.

More than anything I wanted to take her in my arms and celebrate, such was my relief. Something unfortunately which I couldn't explain and I wondered how long it would be before I could simply kiss her as much as I wanted to now.

WHAT WAS THAT?

Ngaire:

As I tried on my new swimmers in the bedroom while Andrew waited in the lounge I wondered if he would be up for a swim in the ground floor spa. Rarely did I have the opportunity to enjoy a heated spa and the thought was tempting.

I moved out into the short hallway and popped my head around the entrance invitingly. He was perched on the lounge and playing with the phone.

"How do you feel about swimming, we would have time for a spa before dinner I think?"

"Sounds good, I'll have to go down and get my togs though." Standing he smiled, putting the phone on the table readily as he moved around towards me. "Perhaps I could meet you at ground level? I can change in the change room down stairs."

"I'll just grab some towels then," I offered, ducking back in the room to throw on a loose button-through shirt and collect two towels from the bathroom cupboard.

The lift had a glass back wall, that offered views as we descended, something which while being fascinating was in many ways disconcerting, leaving us not knowing quite which way to face. Once we got to ground where the spa entrance, pool and BBQ area was between the main lobby and the lifts, I was looking forward to Andrew joining me in the spa with pleasure.

"You go ahead, I won't be long," Andrew said as he left me at the access door.

The water was beautifully warm and we had the whole area to ourselves though there was a small group out by the BBQ's enjoying the afternoon sun with a motley collection of kids, using the outdoor swimming pool. When Andrew got back he had his board shorts in hand and I watched as he slipped into the men's change room, making an entrance a few minutes later. He put his gear with the towels on the spa-side chairs as he bent to climb into the bubbling water. I had forgotten about the hatch scars deep across his chest which marked him a Shaman. I had forgotten how others not accustomed to these would now perhaps see them. While this wasn't my first trip to the city it was my first to the bustling holiday city of the Gold Coast but seeing his scars it reminded me of the bush and of the time we had spent together, I felt the thrill of recognition move through me.

My husband had never travelled with me. He had never wanted to experience the world of cities, civilization and commerce. It had been an alien world to him and that Andrew thought nothing of the same thing, nothing of mixing in the world with me, I found that I liked this side of him.

"Now this is worth the wait," He said in a low tone, grinning as he made his way over to where I was perched on the side ledge, adjusting my position in front of one of the turbulent spa jets.

"Go away, I'm not sharing. Find your own jet," I warned as he came close. He just smiled ignoring me and putting his hand either side of the spa edge, he trapped me with the mischief in his eyes.

I knew he was going to kiss me, his eyes flicked temptingly to my lips and as he raised a brow in question I smiled, then watched as he slowly bought his lips to mine. My lips met his willingly, a tempting touch before he pulled away slowly, moving to the ledge where another jet gurgled quietly.

His touch had been teasing, tormenting. A promise left off quickly and one left open. Andrew said nothing, yet he said a great deal in that gesture. His eyes watched me, smiling asking a question about what I would do.

"Your leg gives you no trouble?" I asked, curious about how it had healed.

"It's great, you did a brilliant job. I owe you big time for that." Pushing off from the edge he moved into the drift of water still bubbling contentedly and invited by his eyes I followed him.

"You're welcome."

He caught my hand as I went to pass, and pulled me gently into his arms. "I'm glad you rang, I've thought of you often over the last months. I had almost given up on hearing from you."

"I was going to ring, but I never seemed to be near a phone when I thought of it. When this trip came up I jumped at the opportunity. It's not only something I will learn a great deal from, but it meant I might catch up, plus I enjoy the coast and it seems I rarely enough get a chance to visit."

His hands on my waist were warm and firm, and I enjoyed the possessiveness of their strength as I slipped my arms loosely about his shoulders to support myself. He grinned and pulled my body up against his, slipping his arms about me as his head dipped to the curve of my neck. I could feel the response of his body against mine and knew why he moved suddenly away putting a slight distance between us, but not releasing me.

"So you didn't come just to chase me?" His chuckle danced along my shoulder as he finished on a sigh. "This was maybe not such a good idea," he said softly, a rueful smile playing about his lips.

Instead of answering him, I pulled from his arms and moved to the steps climbing from the spa, gathering my things absently. "Maybe we should go upstairs?"

Andrew wasted no time in joining me, his look never leaving me as he bent to gather his things and silently we moved out of the swimming area back to the apartment. He took the swipe key from my fingers as I went to use it on the door and opening it ahead of me waited as I moved into the apartment. The moment the door closed though, I felt his warmth about me and laughing I turned to face him, my hands tangling in his damp hair, inviting him.

He growled a sound rumbling mixed with the breath he could no longer hold as he allowed the tension between us free reign. The heat of his hands touring my skin and the breathless pace of our heart beats drove the demands of our lips against each other. He lifted me suddenly, I surrendered to his strength as he carried me through to the bedroom, his mouth moist against my neck, my body thrilled to the demands of his, his arms like bands about me. It seemed like it had been so very long ago that I had been touched and I thrilled to his fingers exploring my skin, his weight moving over me, his hands almost impatient as he dealt with the skimpy fabric of my swimming costume. I had no thought for our dampness as we became lost in our need for each other.

When his body fitted so neatly against mine demanding accommodation, I welcomed him. My need was as urgent as his and as our bodies became one, our minds seemed to meld, meet the demands we both understood. It felt right, our need for each other, tasting a certain urgency so complete as I felt the power of him move within me as part of my own journey and the welcome tide came quickly scorching through me in a vibrant flow of its own making. Releasing me to the tempestuous heights to where he drew me. It was such an impatient passion though none the less it was precious. My body thrilled to his and I became lost to the sweet demanding dance that left us breathless and flooded with heat, revelling in a fine exhaustion.

It was a time before we were calm, before the sweetness of the heat calmed and we lay still, our skin was damp as we gathered our scattered thoughts. In some part surprised at the demands of our own bodies and our need for each other, we lay entwined the bedding twisted about us, it was such a delicious confusion.

Andrew eased his weight onto his arms, his hand sweeping my face gently as he carefully shifted his body allowing the cooler air between us.

"You OK," he whispered still threads of a breathless passion between us. As I nodded in response and smiled at his hesitant expression, his smile opened and spoke easily of his pleasure.

I stretched as his weight released me and I felt the languid heat of deep satisfaction shift along my body, then I moved snuggling into his side, spreading my arm about his middle not wanting the heat of him to go, as he gathered me back into the circle of his arms and we took the moment to wonder at the unexpected urgency of our passion.

"I didn't plan that... we took a risk..." Andrew whispered, suddenly tense with the unexpected impatience of our passion. "I'm sorry Baby..."

"It's OK. I've not long finished my period, I'm not fertile now," I answered also in a soft almost breathless whisper. "I know my cycle, it will be alright."

His tension relaxed as he ran his hand soothingly over my arm. "God that was thoughtless of me Babe, I'm really sorry. I had a medical a few months ago, there's been no one since," he added with a gentle reassurance.

"A medical?"

"Hmm... with my job."

I considered his words. "I never gave that a thought."

Andrew turned towards me, his eyes capturing mine as he smiled and kissed me gently. His hand running softly down over my body, following the curve of my waist and hip in a manner that made me shiver, despite the recent heat of my body remaining.

"You're gorgeous you know. You're hard to get out of my mind Ngaire. You wouldn't believe how much I have thought of you."

"That's gratifying." I whispered with a small giggle.

Looking up, I studied the firm cast of his jaw, running my finger over the light stubble on his chin. In turn I couldn't bring myself to tell him how many times I had also thought of him over the past months. I often felt like I was missing part of myself, but I didn't think that this would be what he wanted to hear. It sounded so possessive so I kept this knowledge to myself.

We had discussed this, we had been down this road and I knew while hopefully monogamous this wasn't a committed relationship. Friends with benefits, we had agreed but knowing there had been no other women while we had been apart gave me a certain satisfaction.

"How is that dog of yours by the way?"

"Are you missing him?" I quipped with humour.

He laughed his eyes teasing me. "Hardly! He always made me feel he didn't like me much."

"Well he's fine. Tango is with Jem, they are probably enjoying my absence."

"You still near Katherine?"

"Yes. Jem has school there at the moment so I have a place nearby. I thought it was important that we have somewhere settled for a time."

"School? I didn't think he was old enough."

"He started this year. It's only preschool but he loves it, well sort of. He wasn't so keen when he discovered that the school work was more important than the play ground but he is getting used to it."

Andrew chuckled, a sound born deep in his chest as he lay back and stretched out relaxing. "Maybe I'll meet him one day," he teased.

"Maybe." Absently my fingers followed the line of the hatch scars across his chest, following them as they dipped over his ribs, then I softly let the weight of my touch drift down onto the planes of his belly then deeper, running over him in a gentle torment.

His laugh was rich as he growled and shifted back over me, pinning me again with his weight.

"If you're not tired, we can do this over again only a damn sight slower this time." He suggested hopefully, his smile teasing me.

"We can? Are you sure?"

He laughed, his lips moving to gather mine. "Oh I am sure," he said as his own fingers began to explore a gentle path over my body which was still sensitive from our lovemaking. It was thrilling once more to feel the promise of his now gentle touch.

"But I'm hungry," I teased laughing at his invitation.

His look spoke of his impatience, but with a sigh he shifted his weight. "OK. Food it is then. Up you get woman and get dressed."

Slapping me on my rear in a teasing way he climbed off the bed. "You hungry for Italian, Japanese, good old steak?"

"Mmm... Japanese I think."

"I know just the place. I'll have to change though, do you mind if I bring my duffel bag up?"

For a moment I thought, then smiled. "Would you like to stay with me tonight?" Deliberately I stretched, I knew his eyes followed my movement as I climbed off the bed and moved towards the shower. I giggled at the physical response of his body that was so apparent as he stood there naked.

Again he laughed readily, "What a stupid bloody question." Growling as I scooted ahead of him, he moved quickly to follow me.

Dinner at the restaurant Andrew chose was enjoyable. I loved to hear him talk about his work and what had kept him busy over the last months. In turn I told him about the Health Centre where I was working part time and about what Jem had been up to at school with his difficult transition into education.

The evening was full of light and pleasant chatter. I loved sharing it with Andrew, knowing that we would also be sharing the night, sharing the warmth between us that offered so much promise. I knew I had missed him though I didn't feel I could tell him just how much.

Seeing him in his world here was like learning another side to him about which I knew little, it fascinated me and I encouraged him to talk about the Community where he lived.

"You mentioned that the coast was on your way at the airport. But you didn't say where you were going?" I asked after dinner, as we enjoyed coffee and light conversation.

"Yeah... I am on my way to Nimbin for a few days. I have a couple of weeks off between rotations on the rigs."

"Will you be back in town at the end of the week then?"

"For you...? Yes," he said softly, his eyes dancing with mischief. "I was wondering if you would like to come up to Brisbane with me Thursday. I have a share house with some friends who I would like you to meet. When is it you need to fly out, you said something about Friday?"

"Yes, Friday afternoon."

"You can stop over at the house with me if you like? I have a room I rent in a house with my friends. I can get you to the airport Friday."

"Thanks, I would like that I think."

His smile spoke of his pleasure in the arrangements, reflecting my own, and later that night as I lay in his arms I was torn between my need for sleep and my need of him. It was as though my body recognized his and knew of our imminent parting, something I didn't want to think about. I loved to touch him, feel his skin under my fingers. A feast for my eyes, he was so different from what I was accustomed to. The power of his shoulders and the tightness of his chest and belly were a field for my hands and it fascinated me.

"Tell me about your friends," I asked softly into the evening quiet, propping myself up to better watch his expressions as he spoke of the people who shared his life.

"You'll like them. Sean is my oldest friend, we ranged around the forest on the caldera rim as children together and Jen, well Jen is his woman and his life. They sort of grew up together though Jen didn't come into the community until she was a very young tweeny. Sean stole her from his elder brother. It caused quite a stir at the time."

"Really?"

"Yes. It's a long story but you should get Jen to tell you about it."

"Mmm... I might. It must have been messy, how did his brother take it?"

"His brother is a Karadji. He fortunately didn't mind so much, he had someone he was devoted to. You spoke to Jen on the phone; she and Aine shared the house in Brissy originally. Aine is Sean's brother's woman... it all sounds a bit messy hey?" Andrew finished chuckling.

"Well, yes."

"It was for a while, but not in their feelings for each other, only in what everyone's expectations were. Sean ended up fighting for Jen against two of his brothers, though I guess the other guy wasn't strictly speaking a brother really, only Taipan's half brother."

"Taipan? He is the Karadji?"

"Yes. A really nice bloke, though he is torn between Aine's need of her family in Sydney and his need to be in the Community. It's a bit of a battle I believe."

"Family over friends? That must be difficult."

"No. Not because of Sean and Jen. Aine wants to live in Sydney, her sister is there and they're close, I think she misses her family. They are still talking about it but I think he will follow her. If ever there were two people who belong together it's those two."

"Well I think that is nice, that he would do that for her," I added softly, wondering if one day I might meet them. "Anyway, it would be nice to meet Sean and Jenna. I would like that."

"It's settled then, I will pick you up on Thursday morning .How does that suit?"

"Great," I said happily as I settled back into his side, his fingers trailing along my back in such a pleasant way I could have lain there for an eternity.

The next few days moved along quickly and as much as I enjoyed the conference and the companionship of other nurses, I looked forward to Andrew's arrival. On Thursday morning I was up early wondering what time he would get back from the Community.

It was then that I thought of the phone, I had set it aside and thought little of it but now I picked it up and tried to remember what it was that the salesman had said. It was a pretty basic model I was pleased to see and it wasn't long until I found Andrews number at the top of the few phone numbers listed. Pressing the call button I waited, but the phone rang out offering me a message option which I wasn't too sure about so somewhat disappointed I set the phone aside again. My opinion about the necessity of a phone was shored up by the lack of being able to use it. I couldn't help thinking Andrew had wasted his money.

Restlessly I paced around the unit, aware of the time passing. I knew I had to vacate the unit before lunch and wondered if I would need to wait for Andrew in the lobby. Sitting on the small pocket sized balcony some time later, with a cup of coffee, watching the buildings and business of the world around me I heard the soft tones of a phone and wondered what the people were doing.

As the ringing persisted I looked around, wondering just where it was then I jumped. It was coming from my apartment, it had to be my phone and I nearly tipped the chair up in my sudden rush to find where I had tossed it.

It was a scramble, but I found it and nervous at the sound it made I pressed the little green button still agitated and held it to my ear with trepidation.

"Hello," I whispered, only to hear the deep chuckle on the other end. "Hello Andrew? Is that you."

"Yes." He answered still laughing. "It took you long enough to find the phone, this is my third time around the message bank."

"Well no one calls me but you!" I protested seriously. "It had to be you."

"You mean you haven't even used the phone, you didn't try to call Jem?"

"Well no. It has to be too expensive," I answered somewhat confused.

"No it's not. You are on prepaid plan, and I know you hardly use the thing. You should have tried to call him at least."

"Well I never thought of it. Where are you anyway?"

"Down in the lobby, you will have to ring me in. Press the button that opens the door."

"Oh hang on... I know where that is." Tossing the phone aside I moved over to the wall to release the door... "There, did that work?" I yelled at the phone and heard nothing. I realized then that I wouldn't have heard an answer and moving back I picked up the phone and listened. It was quiet, so I shook it and listened again. He must have hung up I realized so setting it aside again I headed out to the lift.

Andrew stepped out about the same time I arrived. He looked taller somehow but as he moved to kiss me I thought that perhaps it was just the illusion of space around us.

"Hi... How was your seminar?" he asked as soon as he released me and surprised I smiled.

"Great, I had a great time."

It had been so long since anyone had thought to ask how my days went, that I found it odd, but I guess it wasn't really. As I keyed us back into the room

I was conscious of his hand, gently placed on my back ushering me ahead of him. "I'm all packed."

"Good, then we can get underway. I've been driving since early this morning and if I stop I will stay stopped, so we might as well get going. It's only an hour or so from here though I could go a drink if there is any left in the fridge?"

"A drink, of course...I should have thought." I apologised, moving to find anything available..

Having Andrew leaning against the servery between the two rooms watching me was nerve racking. I was nervous enough now about meeting his friends but Andrew seemed calm, his expression alight with expectation and the enjoyment of the day. It wasn't long before he had me calmed however and soon we were on our way along the highway.

I was glad that he knew where he was going, I had difficulty understanding the metropolis that was Brisbane, where the suburbs seemed to go on forever but when we pulled into the neat low-set house I was very much looking forward to meeting Sean and Jenna. Andrew had told me some of his teenage stories, mostly involving Sean but occasionally with reference to something Jenna had done which had confounded them. The least of which was her decision to run away a year or so ago. I must admit that he had turned it to a humorous twist but I could imagine the shock she must have felt to find Sean had been waiting for her, when Andrew had dropped her at the transit centre.

Andrew let us in with his key and announced our arrival to anyone who may have been home and it was obviously Jenna who came around the corner from the lounge, her hair still cropped short though it had been some months now Andrew had said, since she had hacked at it at the corroboree. It wasn't this though that surprised me and held me still. It was the candid clarity of her eyes as they caught sight of me, the look of her expression which spoke of an impossible recognition and as Jenna moved towards us her words stilled with her step as her candid glance swept between Andrew and I.

"Andrew, Ngaire... Hi... it's a pleasure to... well to finally meet..." Jenna greeted us hesitantly.

"Jenna?"

"Yes. You're Ngaire, Andrew's friend. But I'm sure he said you had long hair?"

"I did, I mean it was, but I have cut it now and it's still growing, it has only been a few months really?" I reassured her and then I had to say something. "I'm sorry, but I am sure we have met?"

I watched, hesitant as Jenna scraped her fingers through the short elfin wisps of her own hair which lay against her neck and it must have been Sean who came up behind her, a frown growing across his forehead. Then Jenna spoke softly.

"Mindindi, that's my name... I mean that is my spirit name."

"Mindindi?" I repeated softly and then I felt the surge of pleasure run through me. "I can't believe..."

"I know... It's you isn't it?"

"Yes... I mean yes!" shocked I looked across at Andrew. "You never said..." and then I couldn't help but return my attention back to Mindindi. She had been so much part of my life for so long, so much a friend that I couldn't believe that I had finally found her.

"Hang on... you know Jenna?" Andrew asked clearly shocked.

"Yes, well yes. But no... not really... I mean?"

Confused I wasn't sure how to explain this. I had known Mindindi but I knew I didn't know Jenna. Well not in the way Andrew would see this. Andrew would surely understand it however.

"No... no, we haven't met." Jenna said firmly and then turning to Sean she tried to explain somewhat hesitantly. "But I do know Ngaire, only I don't know her. I mean we have journeyed together Sean... many times."

Jenna grinned suddenly at the men and then with a careless flick of her hair she turned back to me. "Hi, Ngaire. I'm glad you're here please come in. Let's go into the kitchen where we can talk, you guys don't mind do you?

This is really weird... " Then without any more preamble she held out her hand by way of invite.

I couldn't resist, the look on Andrew's face which I caught in a glance as I joined Jenna made me grin and we both escaped to the kitchen leaving the men in the hall confounded. They were likely as surprised as we were.

I couldn't believe that Jenna had recognized me but I could feel her spirit, it was truely as though we were sisters, as though we had always known each other and it was a warm familiar friendship which enveloped us.

"I'm sorry Ngaire, I hope I didn't shock you or anything." Jenna added as she turned back to me excited, the light of a rare pleasure shining in her eyes. "It's really odd, but I do know you. Well I feel I do."

"I know," I laughed. "Yoonda told me all about you... Ohhh a year ago or more now, we spoke about you often. I can feel it too... the Skystone I mean. Yoonda said I would know you. That I would feel its presence about you."

Jenna's hand went immediately to the locket around her neck. "Yes, I still wear it. Sean would rather I am never without it, though I don't think there is a threat now. I can't believe she told you about it, so few people know."

"Sean is right, you should always wear it Jenna. It was my husband who fashioned it for you and when it's time for you to pass it on you will know it. But until then, it's yours to protect you."

"Your husband?"

"Yes. Your father came to him and asked for a talisman, one that could protect you. This was many years ago." I added as I saw the sad wonder in her eyes. "My husband was a man of power, a Shaman for his people and he was well regarded. Your father sought him out, he felt there were things that he didn't want you to deal with, so they fashioned the Skystone for you. It will protect you all your life or for as long as you need it."

I could see the moisture build in Jenna's eyes, she was so young I realised. Even though she was only a few years younger than me, it seemed there was a world of experience between us, something which I had not known before now. The sadness in her face drew me and as I moved towards her I gathered her to me, comforting her in some way.

"Could you tell me of my father?"

"Oh Jenna, I would love to but I can't. I didn't know him for very long and it was four or five years ago now. You must have been barely a woman when I met him and I was only young myself. My husband knew him well I believe. It was he who brought the stone to the old Shaman of the opal fields, Old George, and asked him to keep it for you. Yoonda also knew of the stone, she is one who guards their stories."

"Call me Jen. Jenna sounds so strange coming from you. Mindindi sounds much better but I don't think it's fitting here, it belongs to my Dreaming."

I smiled. She was right, it belonged to the Dreaming, it was a gift of the Spirit from her father and that was as it should be. I nodded. "I would like that. But tell me about yourself, Andrew has told me some things but I didn't realize it was you."

"I can't believe you're here," she exclaimed softly. Then glancing out at the men who we could see through the hutch which adjoined the kitchen, she smiled. "We can talk in my room, the guys won't mind I am sure and if they do... well tough." With that she laughed, it was a quiet conspiratorial sound which danced around us mischievously. "There is so much I want to hear, please."

"Of course."

For hours we talked, there was so much to say and to be with such a friend as Jen was something that I had never known. I had childhood friends, many who in time had moved on in their lives as had I, but Jenna, she and I had a bond which I doubted would ever be broken.

We spoke of our lives and I told her of my own early marriage, how content I had been and the loss I had experienced. We marvelled at how close we had come to meeting on the opal fields. Only a few short weeks had separated our visits to Yoonda, though it had been a life changing experience for both of us.

I shared with Jen the comfort she had bought me then.

"Yoonda told me so much about you, it took me from my grief, drew me out of my misery. I heard how you had chosen Sean over his brother but I never realized when Andrew said the same that it was you. I should have done I guess, when I think of it now."

"I don't know if I chose him," Jenna said softly, smiling. "I think we were perhaps just meant to be together. It wasn't really a choice, he is just so much part of me, of who I am. I love him heaps but well... we don't always see things the same way. You have Andrew now too, You do like him don't you?"

"Andrew... yes." The question from Mindindi threw me into confusion. It wasn't so much the question, but that it was Jenna who asked it. It was as though I couldn't answer it, in all the nuances of what the relationship was between Andrew and I. Our feelings about each other felt so new and yet it felt as old as time itself, not unlike how I felt about Jenna and I didn't know how to put it into words.

Part of me wanted to say Andrew and I had found something which was growing between us and was strong and would last the test of time. Then, I knew that what was between us was so young, so new and so very much unexplored, that I couldn't give the commitment that I was so tempted to give. So instead I attempted to explain so that Jen would understand.

"We haven't really known each other for very long," I said softly, answering the curiosity in her eyes. "And there is so much that we don't know about each other. I mean there is Jem, my son. Did Andrew tell you I had a son?"

"Yes, he did. You will have to bring him down to meet us, perhaps a holiday. I would love to meet him."

"He would love you Jen, though he is such a terror at times. Perhaps that is something we can work out before he starts big school, maybe I could return with Jem or you could maybe visit?"

"That would be great... we should organize something. Sean has a sister, she is only little, she started school last year, she lives in the Community at Nimbin. Oh there are a number of kids that age and I am sure Jem would fit right in. We should organize something, you can't just go away now I have found you."

"No. We must stay in touch. I can't imagine not doing so... Oh I have a phone! Andrew got it for me, you can be someone else I can ring," I said laughing.

We talked well into the afternoon, not even thinking of something to eat until Sean tapped softly on the door and Jen, surprised opened it, we had not realized that so many hours had passed.

"Are you two ever going to surface from here?" he asked in a comic tone, his expression voicing his doubts that we were even going to emerge for dinner, having missed lunch and not even felt it.

Jen laughed, "No. What are you doing disturbing us?"

"Well I wondered if you wanted something to eat? It's hours past lunch."

"Oh good... I'm starving," she answered giving him a cheeky look. "Can you call us when lunch is on? A BBQ would be nice, we can turn it into dinner," then to the surprise of us both she closed the door.

I could only laugh at her mischievous expression as she stood with her back pressed to the door trying not to giggle herself as she whispered, "We'll go do some salads as soon as he gets over the shock and moves. I like to shake him up a bit every now and then."

Jen in her life, I could see was less involved with the more serious business which always married with the Dreaming. I was most familiar with, and more accustomed to the spirit of my Dreaming friend who shared our adventures as we moved through discovering the meanings of our world and finding our way along the paths of our lives. It was a knowledge we drew from the Dreaming which helped us in our daily lives and Mindindi wasn't half as mischievous as Jenna it seemed.

Now, though I enjoyed the open laughter in her eyes which I wasn't familiar with and I realized that I was going to enjoy her friendship even more. For the first time in many years I felt the warmth of a sister surround me. It was a feeling I welcomed and embraced as I realized that this was something gifted from the Dreaming Spirits. Subtly I felt the breath of my husband and his care of me reach out from the world of the Dreamtime. I felt his shadow touch me. It seemed my world was taking a path which led me away from the loneliness and the isolation which for so long had been so much my life and I welcomed it with delight. I had found a true friend from my Dreaming and she was to also be part of my life experience.

In some way, for some reason I felt a completeness envelope me. It was a delicious sensation and it had a lot to do with my friend Jen, and much to do with my feelings for Andrew. It was as though I had finally found what I had been missing, what I had been seeking for so very long and yet it frightened me as much as it thrilled me.

A DANGEROUS KNOWLEDGE

Jenna:

The evening was one of the most memorable evenings Sean and I had both truly enjoyed in the company of others for many months. It had been hard with my college work, the performances I shared with my college mates and the involvement of the studio, to find time to share with friends we both enjoyed.

When my college studies became too demanding, Sean usually would simply head back to Nimbin for a while giving me the space I needed to devote myself to dance and performance. He would return, when my focus was less on my studies and the friends I had made. It was more about enjoying our time together then.

Since his return from his time with the Shaman up North last year, Sean often needed time in the forests and among the men. He seemed to crave the community he found there and I knew it strengthened him, fed his hunger, it nourished his Dreaming Spirits too. In the same way exploring movement in dance plus the total involvement of my mind and body in the story of the dance, nourished mine. This was a time in our lives for exploring and learning all that was what we were.

I missed his presence when we were apart, his smile and the warmth of his eyes on me but I also enjoyed my own space and the friends I had made at college. What I really missed in his absence though was the sound of his voice, the gentle companionship we shared as much as the touch of his body against mine. I had come to love the heat and the strength of him and how he could fire my own body so easily. He could make me flame in a way that was purely his doing, and I loved when we had time to share these things. I craved him often when he was away but it wasn't yet the time to be with him always. There was so much in life to enjoy and learn about.

Having Andrew and Ngaire share our evening was a particular delight. Andrew was such a wonderful friend and we had enjoyed each other's company in the time we had been sharing the house. He and Sean, mates since they were children, shared a bond which wasn't unlike brothers. But that I could now share my friendship with Ngaire was equally rewarding for all of us. It was as though the four of us had always been friends, as though we had always been linked in spirit and the fun in knowing each other well, beyond what was a simple friendship was something apart from any other of our friendships. It was a wonderful evening, one of those truly rare occasions where everything in your world is right.

Ngaire and I enjoyed our simple BBQ and later fooled around as I tried to teach her some of my dance steps; it was easier when Sean bought out his guitar though the boys struggled to find music for us to dance too. After a great deal of laughter, we settled to half listening to the boys take turns in strumming tunes while we talked. To see Andrew so happy, so involved in Ngaire was the best part of the evening. I had never seen him so engaged with a woman, nor so content in simply enjoying her company.

Ngaire and I talked about our experiences. I heard how she had grown up around the Kimberley's living mostly with her Mothers and Aunts until her marriage. I knew now how she had loved her man despite the huge age difference between them. It was a much greater age disparity than that between Taipan and I. Yet we sat here now, enjoying the evening with men we had chosen for ourselves and this was a special joy. It was as though we had both been set on the same path, yet each of us had found our own way, only to once more find where our paths again joined.

"I would love to meet your son Jem." I said hopefully to Ngaire, after once more listening to something of his antics with so much delight. Thinking of her young son, it was as though he was also a part of my life and yet I had never met him. I wondered about his world and if such a young child would miss his mother in her absences and how he would cope. I felt such a need to know him, draw him into my world, it was as though he was already such a big part of those who were gathered around me, a part that was now absent and it was an absence I felt deeply.

"Yes, I would like that too."

I could see the wistful expression in her eyes, I could see how much she missed her son and I felt I understood the need drifting across her face.

"How come I didn't get that reception? This is not fair!" Andrew protested half laughing, but I could see the hurt in his eyes and wondered at it too.He enjoyed kids, but had never wanted to be so involved as he looked to want now and that more than anything spoke of his feelings for Ngaire.

Ngaire's face flushed uncomfortably with guilt.. She hesitated, "It's not the same Andrew. I have known Jen for ages and I know she will always be part of my life. You and I really haven't known each other for very long," she attempted to explain. "There is so much we don't know about each other."

Dumbfounded Andrew frowned. "But... no..."

Ngaire quickly answered wanting to spare ill feeling. "Andrew, really it's a girl thing, it isn't that I don't want you to meet Jem." She struggled to explain. "It's just that Jem's experience of women is encompassing. At first Jenna is another Aunty or Mother, one of many in his life and in time this may grow and change. It really doesn't affect him. Jem has grown with women always around him. If a man is introduced into his life, the equation changes, his life changes, his experience changes. I have to be very careful of that, especially with someone who is as close to me as you are. So in a way it's a compliment."

Frowning, Andrew was silent and I could see that Sean also would have liked to say something but it was Andrew who spoke first. "It seems to me that Jem needs a man around him. He needs to experience the world of men, of boys and mates. It's important"

My friend flushed and considered his words. "He did, when his father was here but for the last few years it has been different. I don't have much contact with his family."

"Maybe that's something. I can see what Andrew means..." I offered.

"No. You don't understand," she said interrupting me. "They are of the Mimi. I cannot let him go there, and I cannot go there without cause or reason. I am not ready for Jem to meet his father's people."

"The Mimi? But how can that be?" I asked surprised. I had heard of the Mimi People and what Ngaire was saying seemed impossible. I had never met anyone who knew of the places of the Mimi and I had even considered as did many, that they no longer existed. Now I wondered perhaps if they might still be part of this world.

Sean spoke up. "The last few years... that is half his life Ngaire but I can see what a dilemma this is. Look maybe this is something that we don't have to work out now, but it's the experience of men around him that a young boy needs. Maybe we can help with that, I know Andrew would like to and so would I. Would you perhaps consider that? I have known Andrew nearly all my life, he is a good bloke and I know he wouldn't hurt Jem. He is great with kids."

Watching the play of glances between Andrew and Ngaire I understood her doubts and yet I could see that Andrew was committed in his regard for her, it was something she could not perhaps recognize and my heart went out to him.

Ngaire's words were apologetic as she answered Sean. "I know. It isn't that simple though. Look, I'm really not ready to talk about this. It all sort of scares me a bit and I'm not even sure what I want to do about it. I know you mean well, but... I'm not ready."

"OK..." Andrew said suddenly, "Look guys, we don't have to talk about this. Ngaire is right, it's too early. So let's just talk about something else. I can accept her decision. I will meet Jem when she's ready. Let's just give it a break hey?" For a moment we all drew breath, struggled to do what was best and then Andrew looked up, wanting to divert the subject. "What is Jem short for anyway...? It's an unusual name. Is it one his Dad gave him?"

Ngaire smiled at Andrew, she was glad for this turn in the conversation. "Yes. His full name is Jiemba. His father said he was a gift of the skies, we never thought to have children but he arrived none the less and he is my special treasure, from a world that seems so far away now."

Andrews effort to distract us could easily be seen and I knew then that he really wanted to get to know Ngaire's son and in doing so learn more of Ngaire. Yet for some reason she was shutting him out. He in his own way was fighting for his right to be in her life and as I watched the glances between them I knew he was slowly winning.

Much later in the evening, when Sean and I were tidying up the BBQ area and the others had retired for the night, Ngaire's words came back to me and I wondered about the constraints which held Ngaire from reaching out to the

Mimi people. It was something I had not considered, something about which I knew little and yet I knew that it was part of my own heritage, part of the legend of the Wandjina.

The Mimi were part of the stories of my father's people and Granny had spoken of them rarely because so little was known of them, they were thought to now be wholly part of the Dreaming, wholly one with the Spirit creatures. A place they had chosen for themselves in the existence of their world. I had heard that they were not able to exist well in our world they no longer held the ability to live as we do, their bodies no longer able to sustain the demands of our world and so they had moved towards the Spirit world of the Dreaming. They were thought to have become creatures of the Spirit and it was a choice they had made to survive. This was all we really knew about them from the old stories.

That their legend had ventured into our world was testament to those who held ancient blood links with the Mimi. I had thought the stories were more legend, which spoke of links to a world like my Father was said to have had, and like the links which Ngaire's husband had also held. These were the Mimi people we now understood and it was believed they were lost to our world. I was left wondering if there was something, perhaps which might be a quiet secret, one which Ngaire went in fear of?

As Sean took the last of the dishes into the kitchen I took a moment, settling myself up on the BBQ table under the evening sky, using the stool as a foot rest, I considered the brilliance of the stars which peeped occasionally through the light cloud cover of the night.

The ancient peoples of the Mimi were almost unknown, yet they must still live in the rocks and mountains of the Outback and I wondered how extensive, their communities might be, if they existed at all. They were a part of this world and yet they were not and I tried to recall what I had been told of them. They were a mystic people who it was said could move in and out of our reality. They were a peaceful mob, taller than most and rarely ever were they caught in our world, moving as easily as they did between worlds.

I knew that when the Wandjina brought the knowledge of living to our people, they left a great legacy, when they returned to the sky it was the Mimi who remained. True children of the Wandjina, they moved between the sky and the earth, they vanished easily in the wind. They were a peaceable people though mischievous it was said. Few had passed into their world and even fewer returned. It was said that only the Featherfoot, those who understood the lore of life and death, could move as easily as the Mimi between the worlds, and then only a few of those sorcerers would be accepted by the Mimi.

It made me think of our visit into the rainforest of Far North Queensland, that time where Sean and I had been so much at odds, when we had stayed with John and his family. I had learnt then that John was a Featherfoot. Even when I had first met him I knew there was something about him but it was when I had recognized the distinctive marking of his initiate at the Bora ground that I had truly known that this was a Shaman not to be crossed. He was a powerful man, a sorcerer of note; the women had then told us much of his deeds as a young man.

"What trouble are you dreaming up Baby?" Startled, I turned to Sean and wondered how long he had been watching me as my smile welcomed him.

"No trouble," I protested happily. "I was thinking about what Ngaire said tonight is all."

"Hmm... Yep. It was a surprise, to hear she had links with the Mimi. That is something Taipan will like to hear I think."

"Taipan? How come? Because of his friendship with John?"

"Yes, that too. But mostly because of Tom."

Surprised I realized that it would be very relevant to Taipan, of course. I was a little surprised that I had not seen it. "Tom has started on his initiation into the Lore hasn't he? I had forgotten that. So he wants to be a Featherfoot?."

Sean chuckled as he moved to gather me closer to his warmth. He perched on the edge of the table close beside me, leaning over he stretched to kiss the curve of my neck and waited to see what type of mood I was in.

I smiled, leaning into his caress initially, then suddenly I sat back. "How is that going? Tom's initiation I mean?"

Reluctantly he left off, laughter in his eyes as he watched me. "Well." He answered with a sigh. "You want to talk about it don't you?"

"Well of course," I protested. "Toms like... well he is a brother to me. You know that, and Ngaire is like my sister. Sean I know her, I have travelled with her since... well since we visited old George. He and Yoonda introduced us in a way. She is a spirit sister and if it wasn't for her, it would have been so much harder... things would have been so difficult for me. These are my people Sean, they are people of the Wandjina."

I needed to explain this to Sean so that he understood. I needed him to know how much this meant to me. Yet I wasn't sure if I could get him to understand. I wanted him to talk about the secrets of the Shaman, help me to understand what he knew of my fathers people, even the secret things.

"Sean, the Skystone..." I suddenly said, realizing that this was a way. "That is the magic of the Mimi. It was Ngaire's husband, a Mimi Shaman, who fashioned it for my father. Ngaire knows all about it, she can even feel it, she understands it." Fingering the locket I wore about my neck, I could feel its warmth drawn from my body. I never took the locket off, knowing as I did that it held the weight of the Skystone and the promise between Sean and I. It was the most precious thing I owned.

Surprised as he was, I knew instantly that I now had his attention. "Where did you hear that? Did Ngaire tell you? Or did you tell her Jen? Very few know of the Skystone Baby, it's not something you should share."

"No, I said nothing. Ngaire was first to mention it when she arrived today, she said she could feel it about me, though I didn't say that I was wearing it. She told me that her husband, Jem's father, Sean..., fashioned it for my father, giving it the power to protect me. Ngaire knew that and she shared it with me."

For a long moment he was silent and I knew he was placing the pieces of a puzzle into place, he had pieces I knew nothing about, I suddenly realized and I needed him to tell me.

"Sean if I am going to tell you these things, then you need to confide in me. You know something, I can feel it. Why don't you tell me? I can just as easily stop telling you these things also you know."

I heard his sigh and I knew I was right. There were things he wasn't telling me and as I watched him, I at first I became anxious, then I felt my frustration with his reticence steel my nerves. "Sean...?"

"OK... Look don't get annoyed Baby," he said suddenly. "This is serious stuff, I shouldn't be telling you this. I don't know if I can..."

"We have been over this." I said impatiently as I moved to climb off the table. I would make this a fight if I had to and I was getting better at arguing with him even though I knew he wasn't too happy when I did challenge him. "If you don't understand that I can know these things, then Sean... I am going to stop talking to you!" I said testily.

"Jen, Baby... come on. You know why... "

"No Sean. I don't know why... all I know is you expect me to tell you and yet you won't show me the same trust," I said, now growing angry.

Reaching for me, he effectively stopped me from storming off as I wanted to do. But also, I knew he was wavering in his position of keeping safe this small business of the Shaman. "Baby... look... OK..." he reasoned suddenly, frustrated resignation showing through his expression. "But I am going to have to tell Ty of your knowledge, he will need to know. This is no light matter."

I knew what that meant. I knew if Ty didn't agree then I would come under his scrutiny and that was never a pleasant thing. I risked his anger but I knew I was right. I doubted he would be angry with me because this also was the business of women and the Elders amongst the women would protect me. Taipan was aware I was told much of the business of men, or how else could I be a story teller to my people, to the community and most importantly to the young boys.

Taipan risked having to deal with Granny if I was dealt with in a manner less than strictly fair. I considered this as I looked at the doubt in his eyes and then I reached up, winding my hands into the hair at the nape of his neck and while I recognized the sudden laughter in his eyes, I pulled his lips to mine. He might know what I was doing, but that wasn't to say that this wasn't a ploy I could use if I chose.

When he groaned softly, I knew he had conceded and I felt the firm frustration of his position against my lips as he faced the last of his reservations. I couldn't help the small giggle which escaped speaking of my mood.

Matching the light punishment of his lips with my own, I knew he would acknowledge my trust in him. If I told him things which were strictly the business of my Dreaming, things I felt he had a right to know, then he too should do the same.

We dealt with our small reservations in a way that I so much enjoyed as I felt the response of him against me, and my own body answering his. I knew that I had won a small battle in the delightful war of our growing trust and love for each other. It was a love that warred with an ancient Lore that was settling to a sleep, in a time no longer patient with age-old fears.

He braced himself, leaning back against the table again, supporting us both and then when our lips broke apart I felt his grin in the curve of my neck. "You do not play fair Jen," he whispered.

"I do." I challenged him softly, smiling myself. "You needed to be kissed to remind you why you are here with me. Why we can have this conversation. Conversation, in some ways it's a different world Sean." Then I giggled, my eyes dancing for his, "So what is it you are going to tell me."

His sigh was fun to hear. "OK... Tom, it's about Tom."

"Tom? Well I wasn't expecting that." I said lightly, encouraging him. "I thought it would be about John up North."

"Yeah well... you know Tom is undergoing an initiation with the Featherfoot, so it does have to do with John. It's not easy, this isn't a skill we know much about but John is a strong Elder, as are the Shaman from up near Cooktown. So they are helping."

"Oh I know that, that was easy to work out." I said softly. "That isn't even a secret."

"Yeah... well what you don't know is the extent of Tom's skill."

I frowned. "He has a skill that is definable already? Isn't that a bit early, he is barely out of his initiation, Sean."

"Yeah well, that is about when it came to the fore. We aren't quite sure when, it's hard to define."

"Well what is it? I thought it was perhaps just an instinctive awareness. I mean I watched him, he is very good at observation, you can see he pays a great deal of attention to what is about him. I thought that was a good thing, he seems to interpret it strangely sometimes but that is OK."

"Yeah... well you're right. He does pay a great deal of attention." Then Sean sighed, as though about to surrender something important reluctantly. "He sees the spirit world Jen, he has to pay attention or he gets the two confused."

Surprised I knew my mouth fell open. "But how do you mean?"

"We are still working it out. It's sort of like what Debbie sees we think, only he well... he participates, the spirit people participate in his vision."

"You mean like people?"

"Well yes, sort of, it seems though it's only the women who participate, the Spirit women. We don't think the warriors; or the Shadows of the men in the Spirit can see him as part of their world. At least most of them don't, there are one or two who do."

"Do the women Elders know this?" I asked shocked that they may not.

Sean shook his head. "John asked us not to tell the women yet. They..., we need to work out who they are and that is the business of Men. The Spirit, what mob they belong to or we could do a great deal of harm. We need to understand what this is and what is its proper place."

"Oh, I see. Trying to make sense of it I could see what he meant. This was a dangerous skill which needed care to control. "Do you have any idea what mob the Spirit women are?" I asked suddenly.

Sean watched me carefully and I felt the thrill of adrenalin hit my nerves as he spoke softly. "We think they are of the Wandjin or the Mimi though we aren't sure. It's only some who choose to interact with Tom."

"The Mimi?" I repeated softly. "But Ngaire...? She should know..."

"No. Jenna. I forbid you to tell her." Sean said in a tone I wasn't accustomed to hear from him and it shocked me again. "What if they are not the Mimi, what if they are the warriors of the Dreaming? If they are our people..., some are and we know this, then it's no business of the Mimi. But we don't yet know the whole of it. We aren't sure what it's that Tom sees, or why he even has this sight."

I shook my head, more to clear my fright but Sean took it other than that.

"Jenna! I can't allow you to tell her. This is the Featherfoot you are crossing, an' this could be dangerous for you. Don't even go there Baby."

"No... no... of course, that is not what I meant. Of course I won't tell her though... though how can I not?" I said softly again, realizing that while I may say nothing in this world, could I keep it from her in the Dreaming. I didn't yet know how strong our links were now in the Dreaming, particularly now that we shared a friendship in our real world.

Sean drew a breath, to steady his own thoughts. "It's not the time for this, it's way too early. It may not even be the truth Jen. This is why I must tell Ty and leave it to him to tell Tom. See if he feels he needs to know more about your knowledge. The world of the Featherfoot Jen... you must think of the consequences. Tom will need to take this knowledge there, let their Shaman deal with it. They will protect the knowledge if they need to, they will understand how to protect the Lore, and you from knowing things which are not meant to be the business of women."

"I can see why now, you didn't want to tell me." I said, almost repentant.

"Yeah well... bit late for that. Look, I need to contact Ty... I don't know where he is, he likely isn't in range. You go on in, and I will be just a tic."

"OK." I said softly and then reaching up on my toes, I kissed him. Something he returned in a short distracted way.

"Oh... an' another thing young lady. I want you to understand that you are not to remove the Skystone. It hides you from the Spirit men and there must be a reason why your father felt you needed this. Promise me."

I nodded silently, aware of the serious note in his voice and the steady look we shared.

I felt guilty as I moved indoors, I found myself wondering whether I had done the right thing in forcing this confidence. Well it was too late now... and then I thought of Tom. What did it all mean and how was it that he could see the spirits of the Wandjin?. Or perhaps this wasn't who they were? Sean was right, they needed to understand who it was who intruded into Tom's life and for what reason?

As I readied for bed, questions filled my mind. I would need to shift my thoughts I knew, move them away from my conscious. I decided then that I I didn't want to carry them into the Dreaming with me, it was too dangerous.

The penalty of knowledge, even that ill advisedly discovered, I knew was often death. It was an ancient penalty and a price many had paid in past times when they had learnt about things which were not theirs to know. Such a penalty was judged by both men and spirit for such a crime as breaking with the Lore about that which should be secret. The men of the Spirit world would act upon their right of silence, about what was their business alone and I hoped I hadn't angered them now in my want to know these things. As I touched the Skystone around my neck I once more felt comforted that they could not find me.

Sean was waiting for me when I got back to our room from the bathroom. I loved that he was there and I knew that he could help me, distract me in ways no one else could. We might fight more these days but we also had learnt to make up in ways that were all our own. Climbing onto the bed I settled at the end, cross legged just watching him as he finished texting.

"Did you reach Taipan?" I said quietly with what was an apologetic smile.

"Nope. I left a few messages though." Setting the phone aside he considered me for a moment, perched as I was at the end of the bed. "What are you up to now?"

"Nothing. I don't want to disturb you when you're busy texting."

Sean smiled, "You're feeling guilty?"

"Well, maybe just a little."

"Come here," he said softly, the light of laughter in his eyes. "I would not have told you anything if I had thought it would place you at risk. This is business that you would have learnt about eventually, as we all accept the skills of little Debbie. Don't worry too much over it Baby. You know little enough and the knowledge itself cannot harm you. It's what you do with it that is dangerous to you now."

I climbed over towards him. I wanted to make it up to him, reassure him of my faith in him and how much I would try not to reveal the Shamans secrets. I wanted him to have confidence in me.

"Don't feel guilty... OK," he added. "Do you know how hard it has been for me to keep that from you, knowing your interest in your father's mob. I am glad you now know but you can't tell anyone. Definitely not Tom, you are not to mention it to him. It's not to become a point of conversation between you, or anyone else. He is too young to deal with you Jen and I don't want him to even have to try. OK?"

"I know that is very chauvinist of me," he continued chuckling. "But you have a whole arsenal that he has no idea about and it will not be you who introduces him to that side of woman."

As he nuzzled my neck, I couldn't help but smile. "I wouldn't do that." I knew I had no interest in revealing to Tom the joy between men and women, and Sean knew enough already I thought."

"Hmm... I don't think you know half of what you can do," Sean added. Chuckling as his hands found the warmth of my skin at my waist as he began soothing me, then teasing my breast gently, distracting me completely.

"I don't?"

Sean laughed. "No Baby, you don't. Now shhhh..., come with me while we find something else for you to think about.

I giggled as his lips dipped to my skin, trailing a moist path along my body. "You're distracting me, this is good," I whispered in response, encouraging him.

"Yeah well, I can do that," he said confidently, laughing. "Now shoosh... and stay with me."

THE MIMI

Ngaire:

The morning was still quiet as I walked around the kitchen looking for something to eat. I didn't think Jenna would mind but I was ravenous for some reason and I knew there were left over lamb chops and salad in the fridge. As I gathered myself a plate of left-over's I wondered if Andrew would be awake... perhaps not. He had been sleeping deeply when I had stirred and I had been careful not to disturb him when I had slipped out of his bed. Knowing that I was leaving today had bought a particular edge to our time together, neither of us had wanted to lose much time to sleep and we had talked well into the small hours, talked and played.

It had been a great evening and while I knew I had to go today, part of me wanted to stay on. I wanted to continue to enjoy the carefree company and I wondered how long it would be before I could indulge in the fun of being with such good friends again. I had loved the time Andrew and I had been able to share and I felt a wonderful sense of security in our relationship, while I was wrapped in his warmth, in his arms.

At home, I knew I would be again immersed in responsibility and while I didn't mind this, there were times when I wished I could share my life with someone. A man who could help distract me from all the small troubles life brings, share with me the small joys.

Jenna was fortunate in this and I wondered if she realized it. Yet the thought of taking on the responsibilities of another person in my world checked the wanderings of my mind, I wasn't at all sure that was what I wanted. How could I be at such odds? Wanting Andrew and yet so uncertain about his presence in my life left me conflicted.

As I mused over the responsibilities waiting me at home I enjoyed the chops, making my way happily through them, picking at the salad and listening to the noises of the morning about me as city life woke to the dawn.

It was only a short time later that Jenna walked quietly in from the hall and smiled.

"Morning."

"G'morning Jen. I hope I didn't wake you? You don't mind do you?" I added quietly, conscious of the early morning as I pointed to the plate now mostly cleared of the good food that had been in front of me.

"No. Of course not," she said as she too opened the fridge and helped herself to the last of the lamb chops, pulling a stool up across from me at the small mobile chopping table, not bothering with salad.

After a moment she looked up, a conspiratorial smile turning up her mouth. "You and Andrew seem great together. Do you like him much?"

Answering her smile with one of my own, I felt the flush of the pleasure I felt around Andrew, especially when he looked at me in that way that made me feel weak in a womanly sort of way. "Yes... yes I do. Though don't tell him, he's possessive enough already."

Jenna grinned, "I'm glad. We are good mates and I would hate to see him hurt."

I dropped my glance from Jenna's. I knew what she meant and I really wanted to explain but it was difficult. It was going to be even more difficult the longer I left it.

"I don't mean to exclude him in regards to Jiemba, but it's difficult Jen..., very difficult."

"Can't you tell me? Maybe I can help him to understand. I had the feeling there was more to it than we spoke about yesterday, yet you're sort of... well, reserved in talking about it."

Drawing a deep breath I considered how I felt. I knew Jenna would be interested; it was about her people too. I had always known that and with the strength of the Skystone protecting her it was fitting. My husband had judged it so that the business of the Mimi was Jenna's, as had her father or he would not have named her Mindindi. Even Sean would see it so; both he and Andrew were Shaman and they would have the wisdom of the Shaman to lean on. They would understand the need for secrecy in regards to the Mimi even if it wasn't a knowledge they kept as their own.

"It is the Mimi people Jenna, my husband's people and Jem's people, though my family don't want to lose Jem to the people of the rock. It's why I will not take him into their lands."

"Who..? Jem? He is so young, too young to be drawn into the world of men. I am sure the guys realize this. I don't think they meant for you to lose him just yet."

I knew this was going to be difficult for Jenna to understand but I also knew I had to try. "It isn't just his initiation, it's his whole life. He has mothers in the land of the Mimi people who would care for him, perhaps better than I. I can't bear for him to be separated from me for so much of his life. I already feel I have him for such a short time, it goes so quickly."

"But surely, that isn't a problem. It isn't as though he will be gone forever Ngaire."

Again I hesitated. Would Jenna understand? Perhaps it was her strength that Jem needed, perhaps this is why we had been bought into each other's lives, bound together in the ways I knew we were.

"Did Yoonda tell you that the Skystone has a twin?"

I could see Jenna was surprised, shocked even, then she shook her head in wonder. I realized in that moment that it was something she should have been told.

"It does. Its twin is a dark as yours is white. The lightning in the stone is a blue while yours is red. It's the blue of the sky as yours is the red of the earth, they are opposites but one. Together they make the whole and they are powerful. Jem wears the other stone about his neck on a short string amongst other small stones. His father gave him his stone when he was born and it protects him. It was given to him until such time as when he goes to live in the world of the Mimi people. That world is too close to the world of the Spirit Men. His stone protects him, hides him from the Spirit Men in our world and it was meant to hide him until such time that he enters the world of the Mimi. In their world he does not need the Skystone because the world of the Mimi is also close to the Dreamtime and the Spirit men have no strength there."

"Like mine hides me," she said softly, fingering her necklet. "I didn't know that there was such a difference in the world of the Mimi or even that such a place existed."

"Yes, there is and it's a secret world. But you must never leave your stone aside Jenna, this is important, as important as it is that Jem never leaves his aside. The Spirit men of the Dreaming would interfere too greatly in your life if they knew where to find you. If they knew you even existed and about what you were doing, how you were influencing people around you. Your very existence changes the world around you and others."

"Am I such a threat to them? I never understood their interest. I do nothing but live my life."

"Like Jem will one day, you may reach many. Your way crosses many paths, bridges many lives and this places controls on the Spirit Men, perhaps this is what they fear the most. The Mimi world is close to them, it's a world that fringes on their reality but they have no strength there." For a minute I paused, gathered my thoughts and giving an order to the things which I understood and I ordered them again. "I really don't know the answers. I only know what I have learnt at the side of my husband. I know he feared their influence on Jiemba, as your father feared their influence on you. They feared those influences enough that they found a way to hide you both from the sight of the Spirit men. In your life you have a place or a purpose that is important to the Mimi, so much so that the Skystones were created."

"Is the world of the Mimi people so different, so close to the Spirit Men? I had thought they no longer existed, that they had shifted into the Dreamtime."

"In a way they have. Many no longer can move into our world, their lands bind them to their world. Some do return; their Shaman often leave their world to join ours and some of the women also can move between the rocks. There are things in our world which make theirs easier to live in. To some it's like a play ground where they can make mischief then return to their comfortable world."

I watched the frown gather on Jenna's brow and knew she did not understand. She had not been told many of the stories and I knew that she should also have been. She was a storyteller, well respected I knew from what she and Andrew had said and I felt the need to introduce her into their knowledge and the Lore of the Mimi, a Lore all children of the Wandjina should understand and I wondered how I could do that.

"I don't think I understand," she said softly after a moment.

"They are the children of the Wandjina, Jenna. They are a little different to us, though we also are of the Wandjina, we can live easily in our world. It is after all our world. They cannot, they are more like their Dreamtime ancestors. They waver between the worlds, they waver in our reality."

"Waver?"

"Yes, their reality, their very presence in our world wavers before our eyes. They cannot sustain a presence in our world. I was once told that it's akin to being part of the Spirit world, though it's not like that for them, it's simply their world. I don't fully understand but it has something to do with where they live, in the rocks that protect them. It's the same red rocks and mountains that bind them to their reality. I think it's something in their mountains that sustains them."

Jenna shook her head so I searched for a way to explain it.

"I have often thought it was a magnetic thing or perhaps some quality in the land where they live. When I have travelled into their world I wear bracelets which hold me to their world. If I don't wear these, I get sick. It's something about their lands. The bracelets help to quicken the body, in some way they change something in us like a vibration and this allows us to move through their world, to see them. Otherwise I could walk through their lands and likely not see them at all, unless they were strong enough to choose to show themselves."

"Where is their world?"

"In the mountains, the red mountains, it is in these mountains that they don't sicken. It's something in the ground that tempers their world and allows them their existence in our world. You have to understand that there is another world that is theirs, a world into which we can't move but it's their reality. Worlds living along side of each other, not unlike the Dreaming which is a special place as you know but the Mimi can cross between these two worlds, ours and theirs. We can only cross into the world of the rocks; we can't go into their other world where they live. It's only these sacred Communities that can move between the worlds, their rocks are like the gates to other worlds."

"And if they leave their lands? They get sick? How can that happen? What is this other world where we can't go?"

I shrugged, "I don't know that. What I do know is that they waver before your eyes as they shiver between both the worlds. They sicken sometimes also when they are in our world. Their very bodies waver as though tormented by the wind. Many can't exist away from their rocks or their mountains. They don't even want to, they are happy in their world amongst the rocks which is very beautiful from what I have seen. My man has told me that it's the best of both worlds, there is no war, no hate... just people who are happy with their lives."

"But how can these be my people?"

I smiled. I could answer this because it was also the Lore of my husband. "They are the children of the Wandjina and their people were born in the Dreamtime. Their Shaman are the Banman, they also move into our world with ease. I guess they are strong and they often take wives in our world. Jem is child of such a union, as are you."

"My father was a Mimi Shaman?"

"I have told you this and I am sure others have also."

"No. Well yes;" she corrected. "I was told he was of the Wandjina, but I didn't... didn't understand what that meant."

"Not many understand their world."

"But you do?" she added softly, somewhat in wonder.

"I have been there, yes... to one of their places. As a healer, I have travelled into their lands accompanied by my husband and other Shaman who have the strength to bring others into their world."

"One of their places?"

"Yes," I smiled. "There are a number of communities, mostly in the north. They choose their friends carefully. Many are among the Featherfoot and 'Men of high degree' who know these things."

"Could I go there?"

Surprised I frowned. This was something I had not expected. "I... I don't know. I... I guess you could, you are after all of the clan... partly," answering hesitantly I considered the question. If I could travel there, then so should Jenna be able to. Perhaps she would have less trouble than I, though this wasn't Jenna's father's community I knew, but they are his people. Would it be allowed none the less?

Then I realized that as their Shaman travel into our world with ease, Jenna should also be able to travel into theirs with my help and the help of others. I knew the people of the Community I visit would allow me a helper and Jenna could fill such a role. "I guess you could."

"I would like to go there if I could. I want so much to hear of my father's people Ngaire, could you do this for me. Please Ngaire..."

I knew the risks, but we were women. The risk would not be ours, as we were not men. It wasn't the women that the Mimi needed in their world. It had been the only reason my husband had taken me into his mother lands, he had known I would be allowed to return to my own world.

"We would have to go alone. We cannot take Andrew or Sean there." I said with reservations, not really knowing if the men would truly be at risk but not willing to test it. The Mimi women were often beautiful, tall and finely built they had an instinctive grace and they understand the power of women, it is their culture.

"Why?"

I drew a breath, steadying my thoughts. "The Mimi are a people who are slowly moving away from our world and closer to the Spirit world. It's the Shaman who bind us now. The Mimi above everything prize their Shaman, their Banman. This is why I won't take Jem into their world."

Trying to explain this to Jenna I hesitated, and then continued. "He is the son of a man of high order and the Mimi people would want to keep him amongst them. This is something Jem must choose for himself when it's time. He must choose his world, it must be his choice as it must be Andrew and Sean's if they were to visit the Lands. I would not take them into the Mimi world unless there were things to draw them back to their own world. Their right to choose is greater here in this world, than it's in the world of the Mimi people. For Jem, I want the choice of how he lives his life to be his and his alone and he is way too young for such a choice now."

For a moment I struggled with the look of confusion in Mindindi's eyes, knowing she was having trouble grasping what to the Mimi of the rocks, was a simple truth. "You have to understand that it's about choice, where the choice is known. If you do not understand this then you accept the world into which you are born as being yours and the only world there is. It's the children of the Shaman, born to this world, who do not understand that there is a choice to make. If they are not trained, do not learn these things, then these secret places are lost to them and the sacred knowledge that should be theirs is also lost. They will never learn their own strengths, strengths of their own blood. This is something which only their fathers may teach them. This is the business of men; women can only teach the boys so much before they become men and are lost to us."

"But how could that keep Andrew and Sean from going there?"

"It wouldn't stop them from going, but from returning from the lands. The Mimi people would do much to keep the Shaman with them. It strengthens their people and even I can see how strong Andrew and Sean are, who understands the limits of their strengths? They are already well disciplined and the Mimi can offer them a great deal. I can see that and when I met Sean, I realized it would have to be from the same place where Andrew drew his strengths. I thought men like them were only to be found in Arnhem Land. To see that they move with such ease in the cities is amazing to me. How has your community managed to have such men?"

Jenna smiled. "You are right I think. I forget sometimes but Taipan, Sean's elder brother is a strong Shaman, he is a Karadji who is greatly respected for all that he is still younger than many of the Karadji. He is like a brother to me and he watches over the young Shaman carefully. Also the council of Elders are strong and wise and they guide him where his wisdom and experience may not. The Elders take care with their Lore."

"He was the man you were promised to?"

Jenna nodded her head and smiled. "I tossed him over for Sean," she added candidly and I laughed at the light dancing in her eyes.

"Andrew told me some of the story. I would love to hear it all one day."

"I will tell it to you one day. I think you will enjoy it, after all I think you are so much a part of it in many ways. But could you take me to the mountain of the Mimi sometime?"

"I don't go often, but I know I am to go soon. I had expected to go before I came south but the Shaman haven't called for me."

"They come to take you?"

"Well yes. I go to do a clinic with their children. Usually their own healers tend to them but I am called sometimes. I think they like to keep the links between the worlds open, it teaches them a lot and it helps them. The worlds are very different and each has its promise."

Jenna shook her head again. "It's really hard to understand you know... You make it sound like they live so remotely and yet, they don't sound as though they do."

I understood the difficulty Jenna was having, but there was no way to explain to her what was the world or existence of the Mimi people and it was that more than anything which helped me to make my decision.

"They don't live so remotely in many ways... and yet in others they do. Their physical world is ours, they see the same mountains, feel the same rain and fish the same rivers but we don't see them if we move through their land unless they choose for us to, and then we need to have the strength. I was once told that the Mimi people are like the substance of a cloud. Some clouds are thick and easy to see, others are thin and wispy. The closer you come to a cloud the less substance it has. The more water in the air, the easier they are to see at a distance; but up close they are without substance. It is the light that reveals them and each person is unique."

It had taken me some time to understand the explanation as I tried to explain it to Jen. It had only been after my first visit to their lands that I had really begun to understand it. Realizing this I added, "I think I would like to take you there, would you be able to come? It will be soon, perhaps the Shaman have already tried to contact me even now." Then a thought occurred to me that I should have considered, "I should ring and find out. I will never get used to this phone Andrew got me!"

"How do they contact you?"

"Oh, they will leave a message with my family. As I said, I was due to go, they prefer the wet season to shift others between the worlds and it's the ideal time now, so it's something I am expecting. The Shaman once told me, it has something to do with the water which makes moving into their lands easier."

Glancing up at the clock I realised it was far too early for me to ring across the time zone between Central Desert time and Eastern Standard, they would still be asleep "I can ring later this morning but perhaps you can come up to Katherine with me anyway. I would like you to meet Jem."

Jenna bit her lip, her eyes alight. "I would love to go... do you think...?"

"Would Sean mind?"

"It's not for Sean to say, and anyway I wouldn't be away long, maybe a week or two, we are in a break now so now would simply be ideal."

"That would be plenty of time, I might even be able to arrange that we go on our way into Katherine, the clinic visit in to their land will only take a few days. I just need to contact the Shaman and arrange for them to meet us... Oh I love the idea, we can even try to get you on the same flight this arvo... oh Andrew would be a bit... well put out, but I think it's a great idea."

Andrew was a little put out, but he said little. I think on the whole he thought that it was a good idea that Jenna would meet my family. It seemed a step closer to linking our lives. I know it seemed that way to me and somehow I liked that.

Sean though had been less enamoured of the idea I could see as Jenna put the proposal to him. It was for this reason I am sure, that she didn't mention our proposed visit to the land of the Mimi. Both Jenna and I knew without being told, that he would be even less happy with the trip if he knew our intent.

I didn't know how much Sean and Andrew knew of the Mimi people and their world, though I knew they would not know of the community I was familiar with. If they did, then I would have been aware of it, it was a relatively small community.

Having the opportunity to talk to my son on the phone later that morning was wonderful, it was so good to hear his voice and it was then I decided that this phone business was perhaps a really good idea. I could hear the excitement in his voice, as hesitant as I knew he would be and I could imagine him gripping the landline hand-piece when he held the phone to his ear. I tried to coax responses from him but his obvious confusion at hearing my voice and not seeing me made me smile and I missed him all the more.

 The call too had been opportune when I was told that Billy Black had been into town looking for me. Billy worked as a roustabout and musterer on one of the homesteads out from Katherine but he was on walkabout now. He had called into Katherine looking for me as it was time for me to visit his mother lands. He had come hoping to make arrangements for my visit which was much overdue. He was waiting word of my return I had been told. It would only take a call from one of my Aunts to the Outback Station and I knew Billy would meet us, collecting us in the small Station chopper he used to muster cattle. This would lift us onto the plateau and from there he could escort us into the lands.

I rang my Aunt in Katherine and she had bought Jem to the house an hour later to take the second call from me. I was beyond delighted about talking to him, reassuring him I was on my way home and that I had a special Aunty who I wanted him to meet and it would be a scarce few days until we were there. He would be disappointed that we first planned to make the detour into Kakadu but he understood and I knew he was happy regardless of the delay.

Helping Jenna pack was a lot of fun, Sean sat and watched the proceedings from the lounge-room. I could still see his reservations but Jenna was all keyed up and it was hard not to become swept along by her buoyant mood.

Eventually we settled on a small selection of cotton clothes, to go in her back pack and as I explained we would be spending a great deal of time in the water as I knew the humidity was high in the wet season so water was often the best place to keep cool.

When Andrew managed to secure Jenna's seat on the same plane that I was travelling on, our plans were complete and as we headed out to the airport it was with a sense of adventure and anticipation. Even Sean had softened in his reservations and wished her an enjoyable trip. I think though, once he had booked her return flight for just over a week later his confidence grew several fold.

The flight between Brisbane and Darwin was just long enough for me to overcome my sense of loss at leaving Andrew, knowing as I did that he had only a week before he returned to the rigs. Our time in Darwin was good as it allowed me to collect the necessary supplies for our journey onto the plateau where we could reach the Mimi lands. It was a delight to have Jenna with me as we shopped in Darwin There were things which I knew would be welcome on our visit, not least was a big bag of sugary lollipops for the children, though I always took enough for the adults as well. They were much prized and enjoyed by all. Having Jenna to help me stock up on such things made our shopping so much smoother.

The difference in climate between Brisbane and Darwin was great. Darwin was hot and extremely humid now unlike the east coast. The moisture in the air built slowly to peak with the afternoon rain storms in the tropics. At this time the storms shifted across the land in torrents and a raw and savage, but spectacular storm was a daily occurrence. Darwin's climate was tempered by coastal influences but it would not be so on the Kakadu plateau where the humid weight of the air could become oppressive. It was only the beautiful gorges which offered a more temperate shelter from the full flush of the tropical summer.

Due to the difficult assent onto the plateau most people only ever stayed down below the escarpment in the wetlands. Access to the plateau was controlled by permits, this of necessity for more reason than apparent as well as safety. These were Aboriginal Lands with many sacred places and others where the Spirits of the land dwelt.

We really only had a few hours in Darwin to collect the things we needed before we were headed out towards the base of the Kakadu escarpment where we would meet up with Billy Black. Arrangements had gone smoothly and Billy knew where we would meet him which was near a now abandoned mining interest. A place that allowed my little forester to reach into the low lands of Kakadu without any difficulty as the roads were prepared for a much heavier vehicle than my little car. I had collected the forester at Darwin airport and now trundled happily into the mining camp, which was now cared for by a sole caretaker.

I knew that Billy would be there waiting for us along with another helicopter pilot who would take the small craft back home having bought it in for Billy to use.

We had only a few hours to climb up onto the plateau but I had every confidence in the flying skills of Billy Black. He was an extraordinary stockman, familiar with manoeuvring the small chopper around trees, negotiating the often erratic movement and control of cattle from the air and moving competently over the land. He was also a Shaman of high order, a wise man whose knowledge shone in his eyes and I would trust him with my life. Which was just as well because flying in the wet and up over the Kakadu escarpment wasn't a simple matter. He held our lives in his hands though he handled the little craft with such skill that I wasn't sure if Jenna realized it.

In the small air craft it was hard to appreciate everything that Billy Black was. Tall and solidly built he spoke little, and at first I wasn't sure if Jenna understood the meter of the man who piloted the craft. But his broad smile welcomed her, making nonsense of my reservations. Then again perhaps it was the promise of his time in the lands of the Mimi as he escorted us, which bought the light to his eyes. I knew he had family there and the opportunity to visit with them was something he would not take lightly after the long months working on the land.

As Billy manoeuvred the little craft safely onto the natural rock platform, leaving it then to the mastery of the other pilot accompanying us to return. The sun was just making its descent beyond the horizon and I knew it would leave us little time to get down into the gorge. There was little for it but to set up camp overnight and make the descent into the gorge at the first light of day. It wasn't the first time we had needed to do this and there was a small campsite nearby which had served us well before.

Billy worked quietly. He began to bring the campfire to life. Our meal was a simple one shared in view of the endless expanse of the plateau under a now beautifully clear night sky. It was good to feel a sense of being home in land I knew well.

As we sat around the camp fire and talked of our day, I knew that Billy was making his own assessment of Jenna and as his eyes occasionally met mine I smiled in acknowledgment of this. It was after our light meal as the evening settled into the night that I decided to ask Billy if he thought there would be any difficulties ahead.

Jenna looked up surprised at my simple question, wondering at its meaning. Billy however just shook his head as was his quiet manner, the expression in his eyes confident.

"Is there some risk I should know?" Jenna asked suddenly aware of the language between us.

"No. It's fine," I reassured her. "Billy has the sight to see if our passage will be smooth tomorrow and he is confident it will be fine"

She looked to the man seated with us around the fire, curious as to the choice of my words. "The sight? You can tell ahead?"

He nodded, "You have about you the light of the dawn, it strengthens even now as you are in the mother land which gives this aura its strength. The cast of the light about you moves to the richness of the red dusk light. You will move with ease into the Mimi world," he reassured her softly. "You must have blood links with the Mimi for the light about you to be so."

"Jenna's father is of the Mimi," I explained and watched as Billy nodded. Knowing the questions which would be plaguing Jenna I tried to answer some of them for her as I then turned to her. "Billy is gifted with the sight to see the aura around you. He sees the quickening of your body to the mother land of the Mimi. This is why he is so valuable a guide for us."

Billy chuckled at my words and then added, "Jenna does not need the stones as much as you do Ngaire. It has been too long since you visited our lands, perhaps you should begin to wear them now so that they may work their magic."

I flushed, recognizing the gentle rebuke as I watched Billy reach for his own pack and taking the small pouch from its depths he began to untangle the strings of brilliant black beads, handing us each strings he selected.

Taking the strings I helped Jenna with hers, which I realized where not as long as my own as we wrapped one long string about a wrist, securing the ends with knots and another about an ankle on the opposite side of our body, creating a polarity as I explained to Jenna.

"How is the community Billy?" I asked as we managed to secure the heavy strings of small round stones.

"It's well. The children need your attention though, there has been a little one born who the healers can't help."

"Oh?"

"Yes. You will see, I do not know much but I do know that the women wish you to advise them. There is something wrong with the way the baby feeds and it concerns them a great deal."

As I considered his words, Jenna distracted me.

"What are these beads and what do they do?"

Billy answered, he was used to such questions I guessed. "They will help quicken the body and allow you to move amongst the people."

"Quicken the body?"

His look spoke of his tolerance to her questions, he must have heard such questions many times and I remembered how I had plagued my husband with such questions as this, and it made me smile at the memory.

"Yes." Billy answered simply and then I realized that he was gathering his strength.

Jenna picked up on my own sudden stillness, perhaps also at the sudden heightened energy in the air as Billy became deathly still, almost trance like and then his body, his form wavered in the very light wind as a shiver seemed to overtake him. He seemed to vanish slowly, the reality of his presence was thrown into doubt, his form quivering and shimmering in the light of the camp fire. He seemed to vanish in part and then once more he took on a solid form, returning to us, drawing on everything within his aura.

I heard Jenna draw a surprised breath as Billy's form shuddered again and moved back to our reality becoming as solid as it had been before, then as he became slowly more animated he smiled, a broad and almost cheeky grin.

"It's easy for me to quicken my body," he explained. "I no longer need the power of the stones, but you do, as does Ngaire. Perhaps if you too, spent more time in our lands you would not need the stones."

Jenna's answering grin was delightful. "You shifted," she challenged suddenly surprising both myself and Billy. "That was a shift to another reality; it's so like a shape-shift."

Suddenly Billy's stance became alert, his eyes sheltered. "You have seen this before?"

"Well yes... Not quite like that but something like it. My man does such a thing, he is a Shaman also but it's not as your own skill, he draws a form, a spirit animal to him." Then she paused, as though realizing something and I wondered what was going through her thoughts. I had wondered at the strengths of Sean and of Andrew and Jenna's simple explanation told me a great deal I realized as she continued, fingering the beads about her wrist while she spoke. "These beads..? They will help me transition like that, like what you just did... into the world of the Mimi?"

It was some time before Billy answered. He too weighed the value of his words as we quietly waited expectantly. "In these lands, yes the beads will help but they need the land. It's not so much that you transition, but that they hold you in a quickening. They talk to the Spirit of this land of the Mimi and then allow such a thing. Away from the land they are perhaps just small stones. On some people, most people, they are just stones. It is only the children of the Wandjina they talk to. It is only they who can be drawn into the lands. Perhaps this man of yours has such links and doesn't realize it?"

"No... I don't think so... but perhaps it's the power of 'Clever Men' such as Sean who can shift with the strengths of the Spirit Men, it seems very alike to me. But where do they come from, the beads?" Jenna added suddenly, still fingering the small beads wound about her wrist.

"You ask many questions," Billy challenged not without candour.

"I have many questions," Jenna answered equally candid. "My questions are for the children. I am a story teller, a dancer around the fire at night."

Billy nodded as he considered her and I watched, knowing he explored her place in this world and then he nodded again having reached some decision.

"The whitefella's call these stones 'australites', no one knows where they come from but the Wandjin people know they are from the sky, a gift of the Creator Spirits of the Dreamtime which are to help us. They help us mostly in places of the Spirit, help us to move between our worlds," and then after a moment Billy once more grew still. "Help us as you also help us. You Jenna can also move between the worlds, you have a great value to our people."

The stillness about us was heavy and for reasons I didn't understand I held my breath. I felt a fear I had felt only in regards to Jem and suddenly I was frightened. I felt I had to do something and do it quickly, I didn't understand this feeling at all.

"Billy?" Desperately I tried to distract his sight from Jenna. "I should perhaps tell you of Jenna so that you can understand. Jenna's man is a Shaman of considerable skill, she is under the guardianship of a Karadji of high esteem and I have bought her here to learn of her father's people. She travels with the blessing of her men and is under their protection. She also has the protection of the Mimi Spirit Men, guarding her."

My words shifted restlessly about the camp but I felt it, I felt the slow lifting of tension. In some way I had touched him and my fear began to ease even though I knew I had perhaps stretched the truth a little in regards to Jenna's protection. I knew Billy would feel the power of the Skystone Jenna wore even now, and wonder at it. The fear I felt, I didn't fully understand as I watched the wise Shaman's glance go towards the flicker of the flame. Once more he nodded silently.

Jenna was confused at my apparent need to explain. A confusion I too felt and I wondered if I had been right to bring Jenna to this land, but it was too late now. I would have to be careful, very careful or I would be answering to Sean and perhaps even his brother, and I wasn't too keen to meet Taipan, something about him frightened me. He reminded me too much of the powerful Karadji my husband had kept company with in Arnhem Land.

"I am very much looking forward to weaving the stories of the Mimi into the world of the children." Jenna offered suddenly, almost quietly presenting her position to Billy. "So little is known of your people and they hold so many secrets of our people and our land."

I watched as Billy nodded. "Would you also bring stories to our children?" he asked suddenly. "I too would like to hear the stories of your people, of your man and of other mobs."

Suddenly Jenna's ready smile lit the place around the camp. "It would be a privilege and I also have promised Ngaire a story, the story of my own and it's one of the Karadji Council. Perhaps I can bring this to your campfire tomorrow night."

Once more I watched as Billy nodded and I knew a danger had passed. For some reason the threat had lifted and again I wondered at it.

The next morning, the tension around the camp fire the night before seemed to be a distant dream. Billy was as cordial as usual and Jenna it seemed had become a good friend. He watched her with care, conscious of her mood and comfort.

I on the other hand tortured myself with doubts. I knew now we should have told Sean and Andrew about our plans to visit the Mimi lands and I knew without a doubt that the men would be angry about our deception if they discovered it. I knew I should have known better and I worried myself into a world of doubts about taking Jenna into a land, so much closer to the world of the Spirit men. More than anything though, I knew I would not bring Jiemba here. Not until he was much older and I would have to find some other way of finding his path into the world of men. I would not wait for his kin amongst the men of the Mimi to claim him for his initiation into manhood; I would find another path for him.

Dawn was still breaking when we began the drop down into the freezing gorge. It wasn't far from the night camp and Billy Black was keen for us to be underway before the flush of the afternoon rains might fill the caverns dangerously. I understood the risks, but Jenna I knew was better off not knowing the inherent dangers. Billy would guard our safety well and know the best times to cross into the lands, those the australite bracelets were preparing us for as we wore them idly about our wrists and ankles.

There were only two options to gain access to the beautiful gorge where the Mimi lived. One was through the caverns, which was scary enough, the other was by dropping down over the escarpment cliffs of the gorge and that was terrifying. The gorge walls of the Mimi were sheer and slippery, breathtaking in their soaring height. The escarpment cliffs were much more than they seemed to the uninitiated, not only did we risk our life against the slippery stones but also against the ire of the earth spirits. It was a greater risk than the Mimi people were willing to undertake so they kept to the ancient ways into their land.

We descended slowly into the freezing gorge via an amphitheatre of scree, one which spilled into the gorge. Here beneath the water flooding the floor of the narrow gorge there was a hidden maze of tunnels mostly flooded and submerged beneath the icy waters. This place was known to some but its secret caverns where only known to a few. The sheer cliff walls carved by the water were so close together that they sheltered the icy stream from the sun for much of the day. They were also slippery with moisture oozing through them, seeping down the walls and feeding the permanent flow. The gorge was one of many scars across the plateau, before it dropped down the escarpment walls and onto the vast wetland below.

The descent into the gorge was difficult, the top layer of the track slippery, the scree loose underfoot and tiresome but eventually we made the gorge floor where we could use the icy water of the streams flow to move down to the cavern entrance. Jenna was wary of entering the water at first. The stream here wasn't deep, but I knew further along it dipped to deeper permanent pools and as Billy Black coaxed her along, crossing from rock platform to another often submerged rock, I followed confidently. I enjoyed the icy touch of the water. After our suffering and the humidity building on the plateau this was heaven and I intended to appreciate it.

Our light backpacks were floated in large water tight plastic bags, Billy took responsibility for these, taking particular care with the medical kit and supplies. Dealing with water in the top end tropics was a fact of life, it was something we often gave little thought to and something we took the opportunity to enjoy though I knew Jenna would find this unusual.

Jenna took it well though and it was then that I remembered that she had been raised as a child in the rainforest; I should not have concerned myself.

When we reached the sheer rock face with its deep pool, we took a rest on a relatively dry ledge. I took the time to explain what was required of us as I watched Billy prepare to pass into the caverns on the other side of the deep pool.

"Beneath the cliff-face is a cavern entrance, directly below in the water where Billy is now." I explained carefully. "We will need to dive to gain entrance but it opens into a cavern. Jen, don't be afraid. I will help you and so will Billy. He is now tucking the gear into the current that moves beneath the water, our gear will go ahead. It only is about three feet under the water level now and once we enter the caverns we will be in the flow of the waters current, you will feel it draw you into the cavern opening. I guess it's like a drain, you can't go wrong."

"Do you mean it drains out... the water from this stream?"

"Yes. Once you go beneath the surface at the cliff-face you will feel its pull. You only need to be underwater for a short time, there is a cavern pocket on the other side and we can move down through that. The current will take us."

"What about our gear? Will it be OK on its own?"

"Billy will take care of that, it will be on the other side waiting for us. You ready?"

"Isn't there an easier way?"

"No. This is the easiest way", I reassured her. "You can do it. It really is simple. Billy will be on the other side and we can go together."

I had watched Billy Black signal that he was again submerging into the current which swept into the cavern, while I spoke quietly to Jenna I knew after he had ducked beneath the surface for the third time, taking our packs with him, that he would be expecting us to follow him on the next run. Billy was just releasing the last pack to travel with the current to its destination and it was time for us to go.

When he surfaced again, he looked over expectantly and waited. "Come on Jen, you can go down with Billy if you prefer, he has done this a million times and I can follow."

"God this is scary. Are you sure..?"

"It's fine. I have done this half a dozen times, it's quite safe. Billy will make sure no harm comes to you. Just hold your breath and do as he does."

We made it over to where he patiently waited. I knew his foot would be balanced against a tiny ledge and I sought the same small foothold, allowing me to rest while Billy took Jenna's hands and braced her.

"OK... draw a breath and follow Jenna girl," he said confidently, not releasing her hands but squeezing them to reassure her. "We will just duck below the surface and you will feel the draw of the current, it will take us. We will be underwater for barely a minute and there is nothing to be afraid off." Glancing across to me, he nodded. "You ready?"

I nodded happily, I had done this and I was confident of the passage we took. Jenna looked frightened though.

"Let me go first, if you open your eyes under the surface Jen, you can follow. It's very clear."

"It's getting bloody freezing," she said with a nervous laugh. Billy smiled also, still holding her hands supporting her carefully.

"OK meet you on the other side." I said in a challenge and with a bop and a breath... slid confidently beneath the surface.

I felt the gentle current catch me and with an encouraging sweep of my hands continued my short descent before it gathered me quickly and swept me through the cavern entrance. It was a short distance, almost a pleasure ride. I was learning to enjoy the sensation of swift passage through the cave entrance, then in a moment I was on the other side. The sudden burst of light above welcomed me and I kicked towards the surface on the other side barely a few seconds later. Billy and Jenna were hard on my heels and it was as I gathered another breath I watched them surface nearby, Jenna laughing delighted as the current kept us in its gentle tow.

"That was great," she squealed, relieved to be drawing air, relieved to have surfaced and I watched her delighted expression, as she grew enthralled at the wet cavern walls around us, the dull light vanishing slowly as we were swept into the back of the cavern, towards the dark patch. The water moved swiftly around the corner of the streams path before it swept us towards the light of day. It was always a relief to see that light. At first it was merely a spill of light on the water from where the cavern opened into a deep pool of the gorge. We were soon swept through leaving the dark, the late morning light greeted us gradually as it grew in strength.

The current slowed as it reached the pool and it was only a moment before we found ourselves swimming in calmer water. The packs had also made it and were edging up against the shallower bank where a few youngsters were hauling them from the water delighted to be at hand for the arrival of guests into their world.

"We have a welcoming committee." Billy said as he struck out towards the shore and we followed more slowly.

I knew that Jenna would be enthralled, and it was difficult not to become lost in her wonder as we climbed, chilled despite the humid heat, our clothes sodden from the water would be quick to dry though the dampness of the fabric would keep us comfortable for a time.

"Welcome to the Mimi's gorge Jenna," I said laughing at her expression as she looked around the closed sheer cliffs of the gorge, taking in the tumble of rocks and sweep of the tropical plants sheltered in beneath the shadow of the cliffs.

"The children... they are the Mimi children?"

"Yes. In the shadow of the gorge cliffs it's easy for our worlds to be one. Your body has quickened and the bracelets hold you steady in their world. These are the children of the community and they live along the gorge. Come and I will introduce you to the families, they are a lovely people. We will head up to the main camp area, it isn't far."

Billy Black grinned across at us as he dealt with the eager hands of the youngsters. "I will have the kids take your gear up. Take your time and it will give the women a chance to gather, and to celebrate tonight after the clinic and they will want notice of your arrival so that they can begin to prepare for a celebration tonight."

"We will be following behind; I know we will be delayed just a bit. I would like to speak to one or two of the families on the way up."

Waiting for Jen, I watched as her glance took in what she could see of the gorge and I knew she found it as breathtaking as I did. It was going to be fun introducing her to the Community, she had such a lively curious mind and it would be interesting to see how she would cope with the interest her visit was going to engender.

Our first stop would be at Derain's camp which was a little way down the track, I smiled at the thought. Derain and his youngest wife Arika lived not far along and their baby would be now over two years old. The baby was a little boy and I knew he would be much loved and spoilt. It would be good to see how he had grown, though what Jenna would make of Derain I wondered, he had a great deal of pride and a marked presence. His wives usually got on well and Derain was a good man but he had a wandering eye common to younger men, an appreciation of women. I thought about whether I should warn Jen then I decided not to, after all she might enjoy the attention. He certainly had a charm that was all his own and without my own husband at my side I knew I was also going to be attracting a degree of attention myself even though there were many more women than men in this community. Jenna may present an alternative focus.

With these thoughts I moved up towards the track which wound its way along the small creek bed which then rejoined the main stream again. It was good to be here, I intended to enjoy the visit and the opportunity to catch up once more with friends. A few of the children followed us along, having lagged back from Billy Black's progress and as the chatter built around us I relaxed and slipped easily into the light hearted mood that always accompanied my time with the Mimi. It was good to be here again.

THE DREAMING SONG OF THE MIMI

Jenna:

The country about me was stunningly beautiful, a feast for my eyes which couldn't resist climbing the sheer high cliffs of red water-washed and wind carved stone, which in places bled a clear crystal water that dripped from ferns and fronds captured in undercuts the rock nursing the delicate moss gardens clinging to sheltered spots in the vertical walls of the gorge.

The path of the gorge narrowed in places and widened in others. It wound like the passage of the serpent across the land gouging the stone to create what I knew was a hidden world. Even the water of the creek, which the path followed, was a brilliant crystal. It was so clear that the level of the water was difficult to see as it tumbled over the rock beds and when the flow dipped to feed deep pools, the water took on an almost ice blue tone in its depths, growing in hue as the pools deepened.

As I followed Ngaire along the path, coaxed along by the few children who were as fascinated with us as I was with their world, I wondered how such a place of such beauty, with such clarity of light could exist. Although it courted the feel of the rainforest, it had a drier feel about it and the clear ribbon of blue sky above which crowned the gorge was bright and warm through the foliage of the gorge floor, it kept the air cooler than we had experienced on the plateau lands.

It was a world of birds, a world with such particular clarity. Tame animals which foraged in the under growth startled me much more than I startled them. There were small wallabies with a sweet faces and others that were a fawn colour not often found anymore. The trees were alive with animals and in the deeper shade evidence of possums and gliders could be seen and the sweet song of birds filled the air. I made a promise to myself that I would venture out in the night to discover the night world of the gorge creatures if the opportunity presented itself.

"How can the men hunt and yet the animals not be afraid?" I questioned Ngaire as we made our way along the path.

"The Mimi rarely eat red meat, so most of the game has little experience of the hunt. Their diet is mostly fish and birds and food from the forests and palms. Though they do hunt crocodiles, mostly the freshies but occasionally they will venture out into the wetland for the salties which are considered something of a ceremonial food. Salt water croc's rarely make their way up onto the plateau, let alone into the high gorges."

"It's amazingly beautiful I can see why they prefer not to leave their land. Everything is here for them."

"I think so too, they have a huge respect for their lands and they manage them well, after all, this is the only land where they can live in health."

Her comment made me think and I wondered about their network of communities. "Do the communities stay in contact with each other?"

Ngaire tossed a curious look back at me which made me wonder, but she answered none the less. "Yes, their Shaman often talk but they have no need to meet unless there is something or great importance. It is a ceremonial communiqué almost unique to the Mimi now, I have only heard of it and wondered too, the Shaman won't say."

This was something which I knew some Shaman were capable of, the knowledge of others, their welfare and movements without the need to talk or undertake a physical trek. I had heard it said that long ago they could travel great distances following the subterranean path of water in no time at all. Like a ribbon which connected them to each other, a flowing path upon which only the Men of High Degree could walk.

I could catch glimpses of the different small home settlements scattered along the track, each marked by a lightly trodden path to its location and occasionally I could glimpse the people in the dwellings. They had simple though comfortable structures, often built up against the dry stone of the gorge walls. We were gathering a small following of tall and graceful women who spoke mostly to Ngaire in a dialect I was unfamiliar with, along with the building troop of children of all ages. She seemed to understand them well and their conversations were animated as she apparently explained my presence to each who enquired. I felt welcome, even though I couldn't understand what was being said.

After a time we went up along one of the paths and a little surprised I watched as the women went on ahead along the main track, leaving us.

"There is someone I want to see first. Once we get to the main camp we will be flat out with the clinic, that is what the women are now going to prepare," Ngaire explained at my questioning look. "This is where Arika lives, she is quite young and has a little boy who would be about two now. The baby was the first to be born under my care and I feel a certain attachment to him. I want to make sure she brings him to the clinic, more so that I can talk to her than check the health of the child. Her husband has an elder wife also and I don't think they get on, though he is able to control his wives, often men will overlook things."

I nodded my understanding but I too wanted to visit one of the home campsites. This could have been my life I realized and I wanted to understand the ways of the people.

Arika was obviously the first to greet us from the small campfire where she was working as we stepped into the campsite, it was a greeting of surprised delight. She was a tall, slim and graceful girl, very attractive with the firm roundness of her breast which spoke of child bearing. Ngaire greeted her and introduced me also, it was clear that Arika's attention was on Ngaire though, then another woman appeared from behind a woven screen which was used to create a shelter under the undercut of the cliff, obviously their home. I could see that it was a home which was made comfortable and welcoming by the women.

Over to the side of the camp there was a shallow pool and a small stream fed from the cliff face. A small child was playing with an older girl, both obviously happy and healthy children and I realized from the conversation and gesturing of Arika that this was her son. Making my way towards him, the older child reached for the two year old and hoisted him onto her hip, waiting for me to reach them. She wasn't willing to let me touch the younger child, but quite happy for me to delight over him at a distance.

"Hello, is this your brother?"

The girl frowned, and I remembered she likely didn't know what I had said. "Oh well never mind, he is a gorgeous little boy isn't he." I cooed happily, hoping the tone of my words would reach her.

The young girl tolerated my babbling and allowed me to touch the child but wasn't willing to give him up, so I contented with trying to coax a smile from the youngster. After a short time Ngaire moved up behind me.

"He is a strong little guy isn't he?" She said running her fingers down his face as he fidgeted, tucking his nose into his sisters shoulder. "And quite a healthy little bloke I think," she agreed, her glance ducking across to Arika's as she said something in dialect.

Arika nodded, but her eyes flicked to the older woman before returning to Ngaire and I thought I saw in it the glimpse of a challenge, it seemed Ngaire had been right in her judgement concerning some animosity between the two.

However she didn't acknowledge the challenge between the women, but instead spoke, once again in dialect to the older woman. I didn't understand what it was about but the elder of the women spoke back, tersely, though not unkindly and Ngaire agreed to whatever it was that was said.

"We'll get going I think," she added softly to me. "Both the women will be at the camp tonight and I can catch up then. You ready?"

"Yes."

Together we moved off retracing our steps down the narrow sand track until we reached the main track and Ngaire turned towards the path the others had taken.

"Did it go well? I didn't have a clue what was said you know."

"Yep, it's well. Arika gets a hard time from the older woman, but that her child is a boy and that he is adored by her husband is a good thing."

"Is it so important that there is a son?"

Ngaire's glance was humoured as she answered me. "Yes. Men are often too quick to leave the community, particularly the Shaman, which is why I would never, ever bring Andrew here," Ngaire added with a laugh. "You can see how beautiful the women are, it seems to me that they are all like that. Most men would be absolutely delighted at the attention they would get in this community I am sure."

"Then why do they leave?"

"Well, take Billy Black. He moves between the community and the outside world if you like. He has the best of both worlds, he also has a family here and the women idolise him not only because he is strong and can provide well for them, but also because he brings much to their lives when he returns. I dare say his wives go out of their way to ensure he wants to return to them. In the meantime his sons have grown old enough to take on much of the work he would do for his women. It's a pretty good setup. Billy would no sooner give up his life on the outside than he would give up his life here."

"Doesn't he miss his family though?"

"Probably, it's likely that he also has a family in the camp at the homestead station where he works. The young men are accustomed to this way of moving between the two worlds, while the women tend to stay in their communities, particularly the Mimi women who find a secure and contented life here. In this particular community the women have a large say and it seems to work for them."

"I see," I added, wondering how Sean would react to the community. That thought kept me busy until we reached the main camp.

The cleared area running alongside the bank of the main stream was alive with activity and as Ngaire and I entered the clearing out from beneath the canopy we were immediately greeted by the children and some of the women, though the men there were few and they tended to hang back.

Ngaire made her way over towards a large shelter of woven palm fronds where an Elder sat with a cluster of others. He was a big, solid man and he watched intently as we approached. Ngaire slipped to her knees on the woven mat before him and surprised I joined her.

"Adoni..." She greeted him, then spoke a dialect that was so foreign to me.

Looking towards me, the Elder acknowledged my presence with muted pleasure and immediately I relaxed as he returned Ngaires greeting with obvious ease. I was surprised though when Ngaire mentioned my name and then when she had finished her dialogue the proud old man turned to me noting I had dropped behind Ngaires kneeling figure respectfully.

"You are welcome Jenna. Word of your talents comes before you. I hope that you will tell us some of your stories tonight. The children would love to hear any of your telling."

"Thank you... I would love that."

"I also will look forward to hearing your stories," he added and I almost became lost in the dark depth of his eyes which held me in a way that was respectful. As Ngaire climbed to her feet, so did I and taking our leave I followed her up through the campsite, accompanied by a growing number of women and children. I guessed we were headed towards the area set up ahead, obviously the clinic space as I could see Billy laying out the stores we had bought along with Ngaire's kit.

"Adoni is very taken with you Jen," Ngaire said softly as we approached the small clinic space. "I think he, as well as the Elders would have you stay if you could be persuaded. I think Billy has sung your praises though I am sure Sean would not be so happy about that," she finished chuckling softly.

"Oh I am sure too," I said, considering the very idea of me staying here without him as quite remote.

Through the remainder of the morning and well into the afternoon I met many of the community children. They were lively, happy kids, often with over anxious mums which I tried to calm, not always successfully. Particularly when Ngaire, made reference to a large clinic book which Billy had produced, and began the process of administering inoculation doses and vaccinations along with the other medications and advice. We were helped by a very competent woman, who I guessed was also a Healer if the deference she was treated with was anything to go by. However it was towards the late afternoon when things finally slowed down and we were enjoying a lull and some light foods that I saw a younger woman approach carrying with her a small bundled child. Ngaire seen her coming well before I and had risen to greet her.

The little boy was a chubby happy little thing, despite the obvious concern his mother showed I stood back, and refrained from interfering although I was wanting to understand what the problem was.

Ngaire however dealt with the examination competently, listening to the advice of the Elder woman and I could see that this was something that was raising a great deal of discussion. It was a good hour before Ngaire rejoined me and by this time the baby had become fractious. It was when the mum settled in a quite spot to feed the baby that Ngaire wandered over to where I was waiting

I had finished clearing the small service table with the help of Billy who carefully took charge of the community's medical kit, refreshing it from Ngaire's own kit, something I realized that was his carefully considered responsibility.

"Is it serious?" I asked conscious of the frown Ngaire wore.

"Not life threatening, the baby has a cleft palate. It's something that the community has not had to deal with before. Fortunately it hasn't carried through to the lip, there is a bridge of skin but it affects his feeding and I am very concerned about his hearing."

"Can't they get someone to take them to the hospital to see about it?"

The look on Ngaires face at first puzzled me, and then I remembered where I was. I couldn't believe I had forgotten and as the realization registered, Ngaire nodded.

"Yes, presents a problem doesn't it. The baby needs to be seen fairly soon before any damage can be done to his hearing. He will need surgery eventually, a few surgeries perhaps and ongoing care."

"Isn't there something that can be arranged?"

"Well fortunately the mother is managing well with feeding and the baby certainly isn't suffering there. He's able to suckle, the Elder Healer has managed to help the mother with that, but we need to get his hearing tested and show the women how to keep an eye on it. Then there is the problem of plastic surgery, I don't know how we are going to address that, let alone ongoing remedial surgeries that may be needed."

"Can we take the child out of the community?"

"We don't know yet. It could be possible but we would need the help of the Shaman. Fortunately we have time, but the issue of possible damage to his hearing can't wait and I would like a specialist to examine him to advise on treatment. It's a real problem."

I could see the difficulty and as I thought about it the more I realized just how complex the problem would be. I couldn't think of any solutions. Medical attention was a huge problem in many country communities, let alone one which wasn't only remote, but hidden such as this one was.

The women of the community had prepared a small shaded area where we could rest before the night's corroboree and I was glad of the cool moist shade of the cliff overhang. The camp activities buzzed happily around us and playing with the children down at the stream was also a lot of fun. I listened to their delighted babble and things they told me about their daily lives with very little need for me to coax them along.

In the stories I would later tell, I needed to be able to give them a something they could relate to their lives making the stories relevant to them. This was the ideal time to gather threads. Storytelling to the children was something which they would carry throughout their lives, a memory and a subtle lesson which would return to them when they needed it.

The feast around the campfire that night was a delightful surprise. It was organized with the arrival of Billy Black and it had been decided that in honour of our visit some of the men of the community had taken themselves off to the hunt for a feast.

I realized then that there was obviously another way down through the gorge though I little knew the details. Ngaire had told me that there were no saltwater crocodiles up on the plateau and yet the men had returned with a large saltie for the campfire. I watched as the community prepared to bake the large reptile on the heated bed of rocks and sand tempered with bark and leaves in the earthen pit. The croc had taken two big men to carry it into the camp, strung as it was from a pole allowing them to manage it and it was more than entertaining to watch the community prepare for the celebration.

I considered asking Billy where the men had been to find the animal and as I thought about it I realized that we had yet to get out of the gorge and I didn't think we could leave the way we had arrived. Perhaps I would learn more when it became time to go, so rather than attempt to coax information from my hosts in a manner that may be unwelcome I decided to wait.

As we waited for the food to cook the men honoured us with a dance and it was really something spectacular. Their heavily decorated bodies weaving about the camp in movement that was carefully studied with powerful steps to the beat of the sticks, movements expertly measured in the sand, I was absolutely enchanted, watching the life of the dance.

I loved the way the children were drawn into the dance and the humour the dances entertained their mob with. Their slim bodies coloured in white clay, markings they bore with pride and delight as they danced to the steady beat of the bush. As the dusk slipped into evening the gathering became more animated, then when the feast was produced from the ashes and sand it became a wonderfully unforgettable night.

Later, when our bellies were full the community settled and the storytelling began. The first tales were in a dialect which I didn't understand but as the Elders took up the telling they switched to a corrupted Australian, mixed with words which Ngaire would translate softly in my ear, often causing much amusement. I guessed the Story Keepers realized that I was unable to understand much of what had been initially said so in general they switched to a mix of a language I could mostly understand.

When I was invited to join in I knew that I would need to animate my tales for the children to understand and follow me. So I began my tale told with a marriage of dance and expression, one I had told before of the battle between the brothers for the protection of a young woman of the mob. After a time I invited Ngaire to play the part of the Spirit Men and creatures who were the essence of the tale. She made tactic comments in their own dialect on how the spirits played with the fates of the characters. Her humour enhanced the story and while she may have deviated from the tale, she allowed the children to be a part of the telling, drawing them in with her mimicry of the Spirit creatures and the mischief they could create.

Ngaires inventiveness often wove a new thread into the telling, but it was an entertaining thing and I couldn't contain the look of delighted surprise when she occasionally hit a note of truth in the mischievous characterisations of the Spirits, even if it made me laugh. Though as I danced and told the story of Sean, Andrew and Taipan's confrontation with Warren in the Bora Rings of the Daintree forests it lost much of its seriousness when Ngaire enhanced the telling, leaving me wondering if she understood the dance and my interpretation. Warren was portrayed as a Spirit man, one bent on strife and if left me wondering just whose interpretation was the more accurate in the end, hers or mine.

Interpreting her words by deed as well as movement was often somewhat comic. I found the telling and her input to be as entertaining for me, lending depth in part to my tale and it was as fun for me as it seemed to be for the laughing children, as well as their parents who perhaps understood better the underlying story being told.

The tale changed often, and some of it became lost but important was the understanding of the audience and the subtle lessons learnt.

Ngaire sat quiet though relaxed after the tale, happy to have been able to participate as I wound up the story for the children, finishing with a small dance. I could see the community understood much of the tale though and as I returned to my place on the mat by the fire the gathering broke into animated chatter, some were asking questions where they could and others were wanting more to be added to the tale. It was the most rewarding of experiences, then when some of the youngsters began to imitate the dance with their childish movements, it was truly for me the most rewarding part of it all.

It was as the children began to settle against each other and their parents that Billy Black began his tale. He had a low melodic voice, one that wove its own spell about our thoughts and it was clear to see that the kids often hung off the words he wove into his ancient story. I was as enchanted as they were so I settled to listen carefully.

"It was long ago, at the time of the Dreamtime..." began Billy, easily drawing the attention of all. "When the Wandjina, the Great Creator Spirit had retired to his mountain, he was so old and he had seen so much and he knew that often telling the children of the Dreamtime less, was more than enough. He knew that they didn't need to know all the secrets in the world which Baiame had created for them."

"The creatures of the Dreamtime still roamed the land and they all knew that one day they would gather together again. One day their time on the land would be done and they wanted this. The time for the Spirit Children to be left to their land and to become part of this land was approaching, but it wasn't yet."

"The fiery Rainbow Serpent still wandered across the country, he was a good friend of the Wandjina but when the Rainbow Serpent climbed up the mountain of the Wandjina he boasted to his followers that he could bring about the great gathering of the Spirit creatures. He said that he could be the Wandjina and that he could bring the people together and he angered the Wandjina with his claim as it wasn't the time for the gathering."

"The Wandjina knew that the Rainbow Serpent wanted to be like the great Baiame, the Father and do what the Wandjina had always planned to do for Baiame when the time was right, but that time wasn't now."

"The Wandjina also knew that the Rainbow Serpent could gather the people, he had many friends and many followers in different tribes and it worried him that the Serpent had this false idea that he was all powerful."

"The Wandjina thought about it for a long, long time and Dreamed about it. He worried the false reasoning would destroy the people of the tribes, because they were not ready. It troubled him deeply but he would not talk about it and he had decided to remain quiet. He is often painted with no mouth because he decided to let his friends and followers talk for him. He knew that in not speaking that this too would slow the Serpent down for his old friend would now need to talk about his plans amongst his friends and followers, and couldn't mimic what the Wandjina said."

"He decided also to remove the wings from the fiery Rainbow Serpent and throw him down the mountain. Because this would also slow him down, he would have to climb all the way back up the mountain and would not be able to move as quickly across the skies."

"The Wandjina didn't want to hurt him, because he was good at bringing his friends and followers together for celebrations and ceremonies. So removing his wings and cooling his fire was the only way to slow him down from reaching the mountain top."

"He decided that he would wait for his old friend to climb back up the mountain, as this would allow for much Dreaming to take place, both good and bad. There would be more for the Rainbow Serpent and his friends and followers to think about, to reason with and to learn from."

"The Wandjina knew that given time he would not have to force his own Dreaming and reason upon the people and that they would learn much if they had time to think about it and learn from their Dreaming."

"He was wise in this, but the Rainbow Serpent had to remain amongst the people of the Land when the other creatures of the Dreamtime gathered and left the world of Men. Our mob, the Mimi also followed the Spirit creatures towards the Dreamtime because we also were not of the land as were the followers of the Rainbow Serpent, we belonged to the Sky people. We belonged to the Wandjina."

"Because the Serpent had no wings or no fire he needed to teach his followers how to make fire and he had the brothers of lightening show them these things. The Rainbow Serpent found his way through the sacred caverns and it was a way for him to return to the Dreamtime, the place of the Dreamtime creatures. This he also taught to the strongest of his followers and they guard these secrets carefully even now."

"These are the stories of the Shaman who are our friends and yet are followers of the Rainbow Serpent and we must remember these things. We are the followers of the Wandjina, we are the sky people and we should remember that the Rainbow Serpent and her followers are our friends, they protect our secrets also."

"We don't know all that is in our world, but you should listen to the Dreaming as this is how you find your way towards truth. We are different, but we are all the children of Baiame like all the creatures in our lands."

The quiet around the campfire seeped into our awareness as we all thought about the story Billy had woven for us. Its truth's and its lessons stained our thoughts and as Billy cast his glance around the gathering I became once more aware of the soft song of the Songman who sang in the background, beyond our conscious awareness. We knew because of this that he wasn't finished with his tale and expectantly we waited.

"We here are the Mimi, we are the followers and children of the Wandjina.

The followers and children of the Rainbow Serpent are our friends also, but they have not yet climbed our mountain, it's not the time for this yet. It may never be time. The people of this land are now losing their Dreaming, it's a sad thing if they become lost."

As the Song-man suddenly stopped, I knew the tale had finished and the note of sadness that filled the audience was edged sharply with the knowledge that our Dreaming was the most important of things.

For the first time I truly understood its importance in my life and I realized in the telling of this story, Billy had told his mob their own histories and it was clear to them within the telling of the tale, what was their place in the world. He had explained their whole existence and their world apart from ours in what was really such a simple tale.

As the gathering began to stir once more I was still lost to the old tale as someone else began to tell another tale. It recounted some amusing event of the day, lifting the sadness from about the camp, making the children laugh as they left the serious note of the lesson behind them.

The evening moved into a quietening pace and the circle about the camp fire pit grew smaller it was then that I most noticed the attention of the men. Most of the children had departed with their mothers, though some remained curled in their laps, many of the Elders had moved off leaving the group of young men and women to the comfort of the fire.

Ngaire and I still sat together and at first I had thought the interest was about the dance woven into the tales. It was a natural interest for the men, and I too became involved in the science of the steps other dancers had used.

What surprised me most was that the people had no difficulty in understanding the Spirit Animals from the Kadimakara which had been part of my story, the ancient animals who no longer roamed the earth, and I thought that perhaps they had preserved much of their understanding from the Dreamtime. That was something many lost, but then they perhaps hadn't suffered as a people in the tribes outside the gorge had suffered in the last centuries.

One of the male dancers, Derain, had introduced himself. His grip on the Australian language wasn't as firm as the Elders but I was still able to talk to him with the use of gesture and laughter. Derain was more persistent in wanting to talk more than the others and the expressions in his lively face were easy to follow. Ngaire joined in on our conversation, enjoying the exchange also and as the chatter turned to the story we had woven she didn't hesitate to identify the characters, something which I wasn't accustomed to.

"Was it Sean and Taipan who found you in the mountain?" she asked easily, having obviously followed the gist of the storytelling. Her simple question caught me off guard though I realized she would recognize the flow of the story.

"No…, no, it was only Sean," I answered.

"But so many spirit animals? Jenna, such a tale speaks of a powerful man. Is Sean really so strong?"

I glanced about the company wondering what they understood of Ngaire's question, deciding that in this company, a people so close to the Dreaming that it would likely be of little account, so I relaxed somewhat and eased into the answer I knew Ngaire would understand.

"He is strong. As is Andrew, though Andrew's strengths are more subtle and it's harder to get anything out of him than it is Sean," I finished chuckling a little. "We should swap notes some time," I added, knowing that my words held a sisterly challenge as well as camaraderie within the meaning.

"Andrew has said little you know, you likely know more than I. I can just sense the strengths he has, though his influence over animals is clear. It's something I have yet to experience and well... I may never do that. You have known Sean for so very long that you know each other well."

Derain interrupted our quiet exchange, unsure of his understanding. "This is your man?" he said to me, his expression a little surprised as he tried to portray his meaning also with his hands.

I nodded.

"Ohh…"

The disappointment on his charming face had me grinning, and Ngaire began to chuckle softly as she spoke.

"You have a good wife, two good wives," she corrected with amusement "Derain, you could not handle Jenna. Even Sean, and he is a man of strength, he chastises her often."

"He does not," I protested smiling. "Well... mostly not," I added, but this only made them laugh and Derain shook his head.

"I see... it would not be easy. But ... good," he argued, his glance quickly running over me, his smile clearly an invitation.

Immediately Ngaire broke into dialect, a stream of quick and humoured words which had Derain drop his attention to his hands, though the smile did not leave his face as he again met her challenge and on finishing, she turned back to me.

"You are not serious in this?" she asked softly surprised, I shook my head and tried not to giggle. "I didn't think so. Derain is hopeful, but I think I will call over Arika," she said the emphasis clearly on his wife's name... conveying a clear message to the man who had made his way to my side earlier.

He laughed and said something rapid in his language which also bought a smile to Ngaire's lips.

"He says she will be happy to have you to help her. His first wife would be more circumspect with you and it would bring harmony to his world."

"Oh I'm sure," I also added with amused conviction. "But Sean would not be happy."

Derain nodded regretfully, "Perhaps you will bring Sean?"

That had me smiling. I don't know what Derain imagined he could say that would change Sean's mind but it would be interesting to hear I thought.

"Sean is a long way away, he is very busy," I suggested carefully. "But he knows when I have done something that upsets him." I added for good measure, at the same time realizing ruefully that this was often the case.

Once again Derain nodded and then sighed.

That night we slept comfortably around the camp fire as did some of the others. It was a peaceful night and as I lay under the ribbon of stars framed by the tall escarpment of the gorge I thought about Sean, and missed him. I wondered what he was doing, likely he was on his way to the community, or he would be spending the few days with Andrew in Brisbane.

Tomorrow we would leave and make our way out from the world of the Mimi. They were a wonderful people and in part I envied them their world but I missed my own and as much as I treasured the time here with my father's people. This would not be a world I would choose no matter how much I wished I could. There was too much in my own world to hold me near the people I loved. I could never abandon Sean, it was unthinkable.

The trek out from the gorge began in the early dawn. Billy had assembled most of Ngaire's medical pack which he took charge of when we began to gather our things together and we said a respectful goodbye to the Elders and a more comforting farewell to new friends.

Billy led the way down the gorge following the stream in the opposite direction in the way we had arrived. I understood then that this meant that there was a different exit. The going wasn't uncomfortable, though we crossed a lot of ground. We followed the stream until we were unable to continue ahead. The gorge walls had pulled together slowly until some hours later the cliff-faces joined and I wondered if we would need to climb up the sheer wall ahead.

Billy however called a break and began to assemble a light meal as we rested our legs from what had become a demanding trek.

Ngaire was tired and even Billy noticed her tired movement and expression. After only a few moments he approached her, squatting in front of her to closely observe her colour and breathing.

"You are not well?" he questioned intently, his eyes not leaving hers.

"It's OK Billy, I'm just very tired for some reason and dizzy at times."

Silently he studied her before he continued, "The caverns of the Unggur Spirit will tax your strength, but if we stay here you will weaken, your colour... is not good." Carefully he began to untie the string of beads about her ankle as Ngaire, realizing what he was doing began also to undo the knot that bound the beads to her wrist so I moved over to help her.

"What is wrong?" I asked, noting the sticky pallor of her skin.

"It's nothing, I just feel a little off colour. I should be fine once we get down off the plateau. It's just this headache, it comes and goes."

"Is the way very hard?"

Billy Black answered as he tucked the beads into his pack and moved to also remove mine. "We need to pass through the caverns ahead. It's a place of the Unggur Serpent, I will need to go ahead to prepare the way for you. It will be good if she takes the time to rest."

Ngaire took up the explanation, though I had heard of the serpent before. I knew the Unggur was a powerful creature of the Dreaming who had ways similar to the Rainbow Serpent of the Channel Country to the East, and a serpent of the Bama people.

"The Unggur Serpent is a creature of the Mimi Shaman, Billy will be able to escort us through the caverns without coming to harm though it's in part a difficult passage. Billy is a Banman of a high order we will be safe with him. He is a man of the Unggur Serpent Lore."

It wasn't long before he left us to prepare our way through the caverns of the Serpent. Passing through such a place wasn't a passage to be taken lightly and if respect wasn't paid and permissions not granted then the penalty in disregarding these things was often serious. This was a place through which only the Shaman or Banman, as known by their own Lore, could pass. I realized that this was where the Unggur Serpent guarded the gorge and the lands of the Mimi. It was a way which only those who knew the Lore, and those who respected and understood the Unggur Serpent could enter by, venturing into these subterranean caverns safely.

Taking the time to rest while Billy Black undertook to seek permission of the Spirit for us was a welcome reprieve. The trek along the stream had been tiring and I was concerned for Ngaire, though she looked better now that she had rested.

The chance to say goodbye to the beauty of the Gorge though was something I was glad of. The place had its own scent, a subtle almost sweet moisture in the air which helped cool the floor of the gorge and even here in these far reaches, the animals browsed contentedly as we moved into the heat of the day they could more often be seen sleeping under palms and bushes.

The smallest of the birds could be heard in the trees and brush while the water birds seemingly lazed beside the stream in their favourite places. Overhead the sea eagles soared with their striking white plumage, catching the updrafts of the gorge winds and it reminded me of being at home. It was beautiful and as I committed it to memory, I hoped that one day I would have the opportunity to return.

It wasn't long before Billy returned with news of our welcome so we gathered our things and set out trailing in his shadow. It was important to gain permissions I knew and as we approached an aged darkened wooden canoe, settled in what seemed an impossibly small pool I considered the Spirit of the caverns we were about to enter.

Billy held the craft steady for us as quietly and respectfully, we settled on our seats. With some curiosity I waited patiently for him to manoeuvre the long rough hewn craft around the rocks and sands then into the flow of the stream which wound its way towards the towering cliff face.

The waters moved steadily and as we approached the broad undercut of the rock into which the water flowed, with little direction from Billy we found we had need to duck down, holding ourselves to the floor of the small wooden craft while the low roof of the rock swept above us. It wasn't a comfortable position but it was soon passed then we found ourselves drifting across a wide dark pool which curled about the caverns. It was as though the strength of the Unggur Spirit serpent drew us along in a path over which we had been granted permission to pass.

The pool of the Unggur Spirit was a quiet place, lit only by the seepage of light in a few places, and as we drifted out of one muted pool of light and into another, crossing the blackened depths beneath us, we could feel the Spirit. I felt the power of the serpent move along the waters until it seemed we were drifting into the very rock itself, onto a strange ledge of light.

With a bump of light wood against stone the canoe came to a halt, steadying it Billy climbed onto what I realized was a shallow shelf barely beneath the water. The water spilled quietly over the rim ahead, seemingly slipping into another world at the bottom of the steep drop though I could only see the top of this spill; I heard its splash into the pool below as a muted sound. It was like a curtain spread over the rock as it slipped away and I listened carefully to what Billy then said when he broke the silence.

"Follow the edge of the rock shelf as far as you can go but be careful it's slippery. There is a turned vine to help you down the edge of the spill by the wall of the cavern, I will follow behind. Do not let go of the vine or you may drop down the rock. It's an easy path to slide along but it spills into a pool below and old man crocodile lives there waiting for you."

I could see his grin in the muted light but it was no joking matter. Carefully I took hold of the hand Ngaire offered me and together we moved across to the rim of rock wall to where Billy had indicated, we found and held onto the thick and slippery vine which was covered with moist lichen or moss, it was our lifeline.

It was a difficult and slippery descent down over the sloping face of the rock but I was very conscious of the pool at the bottom and particularly of the promise of old man croc'. Glimpses of the water which allowed us to see the hazardous descent did look threatening and as we neared the end of our hold, a breeze rippled across the surface of the pool below as Ngaire stepped carefully around onto the soil lip not far from the bank and then safely onto more solid and dry land, stepping into the filtered light.

Never in my life have I been more conscious of the slippery wet rocks joined by occasional patches of dirt and lichen where we could also see where others had left a foot print. There were small slides of mud where feet had slipped and these frightened me all the more.

We didn't hang around to greet the old croc' at all, in fact I didn't even care for the thought of him. Ngaire moved off quickly and I didn't hesitate to follow, I was only glad that I could. I wondered if the canoe left back in the rock pool now high above us was left it for another time, perhaps someone would collect it later or would others return it. By the time I had formed the question to ask of Billy, he had taken the lead along the track and I was soon too engrossed in our path to remember to ask the question.

The hike after that seemed long and dry though Billy found water easily enough to keep us from being thirsty. Ngaire seemed to recover also and even teased me as I lagged behind. I wondered what had become of the chopper we had used the day before, when I asked, Billy explained that it belonged to the homestead and we would need to hike out along to the plateau escarpment then drop down at a pass near the falls, to make our way back to the old mining camp.

It was a long, hot, tiresome trek but by the late afternoon we had reached the escarpment and I wondered at the descent we now had to undertake. The view from the escarpment edge out across the wetlands was magnificent. We had returned to a rivers flow, over loose rocks which presented some hazard to our balance, but when we reached the fall of the water to the first level of the drop down off the plateau, it was as though we had reached the edge of the world.

Here a tropical thundering storm swept in to drench us and as Ngaire and I scrambled for shelter, Billy just smiled and seemed to enjoy the cold wash of rain. It wasn't long before Ngaire and I followed his lead and stepped out into the cold pour of the storm from the heavens too, enjoying the welcome relief from the humidity and heat.

Billy wanted to move onto a camp at the base of the escarpment before dark and he soon had us following him down a scree bank, which was scattered with struggling trees which clung to the rocks. It was a hazardous descent made all the more slippery by the rain. At times we had to throw our light packs ahead of us and I was so tempted to simply toss the thing to the winds and find it, where ever it might fall and land at the base of the climb once we had made the low wetland. But uninvited I guessed that neither Ngaire nor Billy would allow me such a fit of temper so I held my peace and followed behind, all the time wishing simply for a sturdy rope and long drop to facilitate a quick descent.

It was just as dusk was making its swift descent that we reached the low wetlands beneath the escarpment, I was exhausted. My legs ached mercilessly and I was hot, muddy and wet. Ngaire didn't look much better but at least she was smiling so I guess she had known the camp from before.

Though when Billy laid down his pack and walked over to the fire pit to check and replenish the shallow hole I knew the day had not finished.

There were a few things to do, not least of which was collect some sticks for the fire though there seemed to be a reliable supply.

"There is a dry supply of sticks up against the rocks over there we just need to replenish what we use. We can take a swim safely in the shallow of the stream, I vote we rest first... is that OK Billy?" Ngaire asked.

"Yep, I can manage here. Take young Jenna with you, I can get the fire going and something for dinner, will noodles do?"

"Oh yes please," I answered gratefully. Eagerly I ditched my pack and began to strip on the way to the stream. The thought of being able to soak away the mud and sweat in a cold stream was divine so it was only a few moments later that Ngaire and I were both flopping about naked in the shallow waters which ran over the rocks, soaking up the cool in the last of the light of our day. It was simply the very best way to end the day.

A ROUTE UNKNOWN

Sean:

The wet tropical summer heat of the Territory was oppressive, but at least up here in the sky it was cooler and I felt the air whip along my body. Cutting up over the escarpment was simple but it was the spiralling rising heat of the rocky plateau that I could feel. It was like a sea of hot air rising slowly, flowing like a tide and taking me with it.

I didn't know what Jen was doing here and I felt the drive to find her, it was a single minded determination that was all absorbing and I knew the savage twitch of clawed feet in my impatience. Missing her and her absence from my side was as though I had been robbed of part of myself and there was no room left for reason as I was driven to find her.

What I was looking for was the evidence of a camp fire, I had seen a few, a very few but still I searched for the telling markers on the land in the direction my senses were being pulled as I searched for Jen. Camps in the wet season were few enough. Many people avoided the annual wet of the north, travelling elsewhere rather than spending these few humid and wet months in the tropics while the land renewed itself and this made my search much simpler.

Kakadu was generally cut off even from the thick flow of tourists in this season of the Wet. A season when the wetlands flooded and the roads and tracks became impassable to all but the strongest of vehicles. But there were still a few locals about and those who understood the beauty of the Big Wet and who knew how to cope with it.

My mood affected my spirit animals, but the eagle part of me if anything sharpened my instincts. I didn't know what I would do when I found her, but not finding her was an option I would not accept. She was somewhere here, she had not made it to the township of Katherine. I could feel her presence and for some reason this afternoon, the sense of her had grown stronger. I didn't know what had changed, but I could feel her closer, I was sure of it.

I had arranged my ticket into Darwin for the following day when Jen had been flying out with Ngaire. This at the same time I had arranged our return, Jenna's and mine together, though she hadn't known of my plans to join her.

I had planned to surprise her by meeting up with her in Katherine. There was after all no reason why she had to return on her own. It had suited me and it had been the only thing which had calmed Andrew. I recognized his sense of attachment to Ngaire, it was something we had discussed and I empathised with his want to follow his woman and keep her safe. I also knew that at the moment it was something he could not do.

It was only a week out of my plans but it could be one that Jen and I could enjoy together in a place that was new, somewhere with a promise of adventure. It was such a beautiful region. I had even decided to give Jen and Ngaire a day or two on their own to travel together then I intended to surprise them, when I caught up with them today. They should have been in Katherine and that they weren't had heightened my sense that there was something terribly wrong.

I had first felt it the evening after they had left, it was like a thread of fire along my nerves which had lasted for a frantic half hour, and then it had settled... settled to nothing and that had been worse. The sense of nothing had grown until I couldn't feel her at all, couldn't answer my need to feel her Spirit about mine and that had sent my fears into overdrive.

Andrew had tried to calm me and moving my flight ticket for the next day forward by hours had been fairly simple. My first instinct had been to get into my car and drive, but it was a drive of some 3,000 klm so it was that to take the flight was the best choice.

I had wasted no time passing through Darwin, there was no need to stay. I knew they weren't there but when I had rolled into Katherine around midday and found no evidence of either of them I had begun to feel once again that sense of dread.

The Healthcare Clinic where I had hoped to find news of Ngaire had been closed for the weekend so I had abandoned Katherine very quickly, as quickly as it had taken for me to realise that Jen's phone wasn't in a service area, she wasn't in Katherine. That is when I had needed to rely on my instincts to find her, so I had found my way in the hire car into Kakadu and the closer I had travelled towards the escarpment, the greater my sense of her had grown. That at the very least was satisfying.

Travelling along the Kakadu Highway I had stopped when my sense of her presence no longer led me forward, it was a simple matter to park the old four-wheel drive and take to the skies, my path now was more direct.

There were few enough camp fires to distract me, they were more easily seen in the growing dusk and it was simple to take to the skies, to take a moment to rest on the high wind as I surveyed the land looking for the camp and explore my intuitive sense.

I had done this before to find her, back in the rainforests of Far North Queensland and it was a sense I had heightened and trained over the months since then. That was something I was now inordinately pleased about. I could feel her, and I knew that feeling well. This particular skill in regards to Jen, I considered my greatest skill of all.

It was just on dark when I found what I had been seeking for two days. It was the feeling of peace, a quiet ease of my muscles when I at last recognized the naked figure playing carelessly in the stream below. For a few moments I just sat high and watched her, enjoying the ease of the tight stress which had tied my body and driven me on relentless. Then as the same ease bought a driven need, I knew that this was dangerous in this form so I dropped to the ground, my body shifting back during the descent to the shape that could deal with the desire which was my need to have her nearby.

Quietly I stayed in a comfortable squat and simply watched from my vantage point. I didn't know what she was doing here, nor why she hadn't told me of her excursion into Kakadu but what worried me most was when I had lost sense of her. That had never happened before and it was a puzzle I needed to solve. I had to understand how this could have come about. It was like losing control of part of me and I detested the feeling. It made me realise how much Jen and I were bound together and how strong these binds had become.

Resting on a gentle sloped ridge that was leaning up against the sheer escarpment wall, I was in a good position to watch the camp below. I could see the tendrils of smoke from the small cooking fire nearby, also I could see the girls were relaxing in the shallow flow, though I could see no vehicle parked near the access track. In the wet, as it was now, it wasn't uncommon for the tracks to be closed and impassable, however it seemed unlikely that the girls had trekked in on their own, but it wasn't impossible. Perhaps Ngaire had decided to show Jen some of her lands, the beauty of the country and the history in the many ancient sites which abound in this remote area. Maybe this was what had bought them off on this trek and if it was a women's camp then I knew I had no right here, though that didn't answer the question upmost in my thoughts. Why had I felt the loss of Jen's presence?"

For an age I watched the girls, assessing the situation as darkness began to fall more deeply and move towards the ink black of night. I debated whether to join the girls or leave them to their journey for the time being. If I decided to join them it would be best to make my move soon and not wait until the dark of night.

"Move and you will pay for it!" The sudden coarse whisper slapped the air against my ear and I went rigid in surprise.

In an unexpectedly swift move I felt the cold blade of steel press against my throat at the same time a dusty hand gripped my shoulder from behind, my body went rigid in shock.

"What is your business here?" The voice was heavy with authority, and behind me, I could now feel the weight of his presence, the heat of his skin and smell the sweat of his body. I knew that my preoccupation with watching Jen had blinded my other senses. The knowledge marked me a fool and mocked me.

"I have business here." I answered tersely despite the scream of my body to shift in reaction to the threat. I fought to hold the response still; it would not help until I knew what this was."

"And your business is...?" The man demanded with steel in his voice. He was in no way disconcerted by my naked presence, in no way confused by my interest in the girls, he simply sought an explanation. He was a man of the tribes I knew; his scent wasn't that of a city man.

I recognized immediately when my body shuddered and felt the heat of the shift I had struggled to hold. I felt his shock as much as I heard it, sensed it, aware of him as I now was. My shift spurred on by the drive to survive was like the whip snap of oiled leather and as I realized I found myself slithering rapidly across the ground, then I instinctively swung about and coiled to strike at him.

I stilled and struggled to take my form again into a shift back from the serpent. Fighting with the instinct to do so, in the knowledge that I didn't want to kill this man and in my normal form this was less likely.

My reaction to him was swift, like the flow of heated metal, which had burnt his hold. To shift from the threat into the form of the serpent and again to find myself in seconds spread along the ground devoid of the weight of his hold, or the mark of the knife against my throat. Then to shift again, swiftly taking the natural defence on all fours as a man, hands to the ground, feet braced to spring as I faced him. But I held fast to the ground as I held fast to the shocked look of him as he too struggled to find footing in the loose ground which he had flung himself back against.

"Who are you?" I demanded angry now. I was angry at his threat, at his intrusion into my business and my thoughts, angered at his imposition in my world so I ignored the shock and confusion in his eyes.

I could see now that he was a solidly built man of the tribes, a serpent man. He broke into a fast flow of words, words spoken in a dialect I little understood though there were edges of words I could hear and understand.

I too then broke into dialect, that of my mob which I doubt he understood but it was enough to declare myself. My words were short and sharp still braced with my anger and they silenced him.

For a moment we watched each other, measuring our strengths and then we both heard the faint chorus of the women below, unconsciously we turned toward the sound.

"Billy...?" and then more softly. "I wonder where he's gone...?" Ngaire's voice floated up from about the camp.

I watched, understanding more as the man put his fingers to his lips and whistled as he gained his footing more surely, gaining also their attention.

"Billy...?" I asked. "You're with Ngaire and Jenna?"

"Yes. I'm with the women," he said then I could feel my body relax, my breathing became more settled.

"I'm Sean, Jenna's man. Do you know what they're doing here? It isn't at all where they said they would be," I asked as he too relaxed from the sense of threat we had both shared, which now was slowly slipping away.

"I've been escorting the women into a clinic on the plateau."

"A clinic? There are tribal people still in Kakadu? I thought they had moved across into Arnhem Land or into the Kimberley's?"

"No. Not all."

"OK... that's news," I commented, slowly adjusting my nerves to new knowledge as my body tension wound down.

The man climbed to his feet, as did I and steadily, very carefully, he offered his hand. "Billy Black," he said introducing himself. "Jenna had mentioned you but she said you were back on the East Coast, I'm sorry about... before. If I had known..."

Taking his hand I measured his strength, noting the lack of surprise in his glance. He too was a man of skill, a Shaman and his ways were not unlike my own I thought.

"Pleased," I added in a fitting tone. "I had reason to find Jenna, something about her situation alarmed me. But it seems she is fine now, I can feel the problem has passed."

Billy considered my words and nodded, "She has been into the Lands."

I frowned. "The lands?"

"Yes," he said slowly, measuring the weight of my own knowledge carefully. "The Lands of the Mimi?"

Surprised, I wondered what on earth could have drawn her into those Lands. Then I remembered Ngaire's association and realized what I should have realized before. Jen would be unable to resist such knowledge, the promise of such access. "No wonder..."

"Yes. The Mimi Lands, they're nearby," Billy confirmed softly and then taking a step back he considered me. "Your bond with her is strong?" he added somewhat surprised.

"It is. Though I doubt she realizes how strong and perhaps it's not time for her to understand this. She is still very young."

Quietly I too took a few steps back from the man, more to observe once again the camp where the women were now moving about the small fire, there was quiet laughter and chatter in the air. To better see between the low trees I squatted once more and watched steadily. This clearly was a comfortable camp and I smiled pleased to see it so, then looking across as Billy too joined me observing the women, I considered the circumstances.

"Are you bringing the women out from the Lands? Your done?"

"Yes, for the time being. Will you come down to the camp? Jenna will be pleased of your company I think."

"No... Jen needs her space. Perhaps in the morning, I might see if I can bring my vehicle into the camp along the tracks. Did you plan on walking much further?"

"We are headed to the old uranium camp to the East, where the women have their own vehicle waiting. I will leave them there and return to my Country, it's a day's walk away."

I considered the walk and smiled. I knew Jen could think of other things she would rather do than to trek for a solid day across the crocodile infested wetlands in breeding season.

"If you would like to wait until tomorrow, hopefully before noon, I could get the forbie in and meet you in camp. It would save you the day and you could return sooner. Then I could take the girls back to their car? It would give me a chance to help Jen see that she should tell me about her plans, she obviously doesn't realise how crazy she is sending me."

Billy laughed, his grin splitting the growing darkness. "It's a good plan," he eventually answered as his laughter subsided, "She's a good woman, a woman such as Ngaire."

"She is," I added grinning myself.

"Then we will stay in camp tomorrow and wait for your arrival. I am thinking though that it would be best to take the day and perhaps we can leave our departure until the day after. I would like to share the campfire with a man such as you."

My glance measured his and I smiled, "As would I," I added confidently.

Standing, I once more held out my hand and felt the strength of his grip. "Tomorrow..." I added.

"Will you be camping up here tonight? You are very much welcome to join us regardless."

"No. I'll join you tomorrow. I think it's best if my woman doesn't know about this just yet." Smiling I stepped back, knowing I would not need to explain to this man and drawing the heat to me I felt the tremor of the shift as I spread the blades of my shoulders into the motion of the flight and took to the skies in a swift sweeping movement.

I knew Billy watched me as I swept lower over the camp to once more check on little Jen and I wondered if she even noticed the silent path of the sea eagle overhead. Sweeping towards the escarpment I caught the warm updraft and soared higher into the skies to plot my path back to the vehicle and check the access tracks. Instinct took hold and my mind once more sharpened to the path ahead, now lit by the growing star light of the night sky. I hadn't felt this peaceful in days and it heightened my senses, sharpened my mind. It was good to be so clear in my path and I was inordinately glad of my meeting with Billy Black. It had been a good thing. As I slid into the darkening night, the last rays of the sun dropped beyond the horizon behind me, tipping the day into darkness.

It was late into the morning when I next approached the camp; I'd been bringing the little forbie up the access track as far as I had been able. I had need to find a safe rapid water flow along the river to cross. Knowing that while I could easily cross, the girls would be unable to do so, their safety was a very important consideration.

The crocs 'which inhabited the waterways here could move like lightening regardless of their size. There was one chance with the croc's I knew and it wasn't possible to know where they would be settled. Crocodiles..., salties, would watch first, observe and then attack. The first person to cross in the warm still water was likely to make it, the second wouldn't be so lucky. Being able to get high above the water undertaking my shape-shift as an eagle had allowed me to at least assess the water crossings. It hadn't taken too long to find a safe enough crossing near where I could leave the four wheel drive vehicle.

The noise of the camp reached me well before I reached the edge of the clearing, the girls were chattering and I noticed that Billy was away from the camp. Jen and Ngaire had obviously taken the lay day to tend to some washing which was strewn over branches nearby and both the girls were wearing sarongs, draped and tied around their bodies. It was an enjoyable sight and for a moment I stood at the edge of the clearing watching Jen.

Her cropped hair was wild, but somehow it added to the vision of her. Slim and small the fabric of the sarong draped and flowed around her enhancing the slight curve of her hip, clinging to the roundness of her breast and for a while I stood there enchanted. I was also conscious of Ngaire, but nowhere near as observant or aware of her as I was of Little Jen.

"Sean!" Ngaire was the first to greet me, surprise in her voice, though a pleasant surprise I thought as she froze in her movements.

"What?" Jen echoed seeing the direction of her friend's eyes; she swung my way in shocked surprise while I stepped into the camp clearing.

"Sean! What on earth…?"

"Hi Baby. You've given me a royal run around do you have any idea what mischief you've caused?"

Jen shook her head, still shocked, while I moved over towards her.

"Baby, I lost sight of you. I couldn't feel your presence or find you," I explained while my glance checked that the locket still lay against her skin, reassuring me as I took and held her steadily between my hands, feeling the warmth of her within my touch again. "You know what that would mean to me, I had to find you."

"I... I... I mean, I had no idea." Glancing towards Ngaire, she then looked back at me, "I'm fine. We have just been up on the plateau, to a clinic. There was no need for you to follow me."

Ngaire stepped forward and interrupted. "We have been with the Mimi, Sean. I'm sorry, I didn't realize, I mean I well... forgot that you would have lost sight of Jen. It's my fault really... I should have known... realized."

Sighing I nodded. "Well no harm is done, it's all good." Releasing Jen I smiled, "I met Billy earlier, he told me where you had been. Though I had no idea it would hide Jen from me, I haven't come up against that before."

"It does," Ngaire confirmed. "I should have realized. I really am sorry."

Frowning I tried to follow the way of Ngaire's words. "Jen has told you of the Skystone I gather?" I spoke knowing Ngaire's links with the Skystone, however I wanted to hear the story from her perspective. The knowledge was valuable.

"Yes. My son has one also, I can feel the power of the stone around Jen and I understand she must be carrying it with her. It was my husband who fashioned them, both for the same reason." Ngaire said firmly, wondering perhaps if I would understand her meaning.

"There is another?" I asked surprised. I didn't know the extent of the confidences the girls shared and I trod carefully not sure what I could be told. I could afford Jen her secrets but this was something different again.

"Yes."

"There is," Jen agreed with a small conspiratorial smile, breaking into my pursuit of the truths of the stones. "It's not the same as mine, but the opposite I believe." She looked at Ngaire for confirmation, Jen waited.

Ngaire nodded and smiled. "I think it's time to talk about this. It's time perhaps that these things are spoken about between us. You need to understand why the Skystones are so important to those who have been given them." Ngaire glanced about, seeking Billy Black I realized and unable to see him she signalled towards the fire then we moved closer to it, it was a natural place of meeting and talk.

"Sean, I know you understand the strengths of the Skystone, but perhaps you don't fully understand their purpose. We need to talk about that and you need to understand. I realized this when I took Jen into the Lands, I took a risk but didn't realize it until we were well along the path. I'm sorry for that."

Frowning I followed the girls as Ngaire spoke. I had thought I had known all that was required of me, though I knew there were things I could learn more about. Ngaire looked up gathering my attention with her smile, then she continued speaking softly.

"Both Jem and Jenna are children of the Mimi people. Though unlike many they live comfortably in our world, they are also able to live in the world of the Mimi. You need to understand that the Mimi people move ever closer to the world of their ancestors and as time goes by, they are losing the links with our world. I was telling Jen about this earlier," she added smiling across at her. "There are many things valuable in our world that the Mimi do not wish to lose and the ability to move easily between the worlds is one of the most valued."

Ngaire took a moment to stir the embers of the fire before she continued. "Jenna will one day have children and the children will also have some gifts, the Mimi would choose that they be the gifts of the Mimi people. They would choose that the father of her children would be of the Mimi, able to strengthen the ability of their people to move between the worlds. With Jiemba my son, it's the same. Can you see where the risks lie?"

The question took me off guard, I was still struggling with the thought of Jenna and another man of the Mimi people but I tried now to leave that aside to think hard about what Ngaire was suggesting.

"The only risk I can see is that I would lose Jenna," I said still blinkered by my love for her. I couldn't get past that and I looked over at Jen almost apologetically. "I would not allow that to happen," I added with conviction.

"Nor will I allow that to happen to Jiemba. I will not lose him to the world of the Mimi people and I understand what you say and how you feel. I am welcomed into the Lands of the Mimi often, but there are a number of communities and they are closely linked and well guarded against intruders. I would have great difficulty entering their lands should they so choose it, as would you. The Mimi guard many secrets."

"For this reason your man empowered the Skystones?" I asked tentatively.

"Yes. Those who can move easily between the worlds grow fewer in number. Billy Black is one who can. He recognized this in Jenna when he first met her and it was then I realized the risk I had placed her in without thinking. You need to watch over her carefully Sean. The Skystone will hide Jenna from the Spirits but not from the Mimi, the stones have no power in the Mimi lands. The Skystones were made so that it's only in our world they can protect the children of the Mimi from the Spirit men and creatures. In this way the Mimi may still find their people and bring them back to their Country."

I grinned, locking my eyes with Jenna in reprimand, "And you need to tell me what you are doing woman!" I added ruefully. Finding it easy to understand what value Jen could be to the Mimi

Ngaire laughed suddenly at the ease of our banter, grinning when Jen playfully poked her tongue at me, scolding me in her own way, her eyes laughing. "I am sorry, that was my fault really," Ngaire said trying to mollify me. "I am unused to having to deal with others, I think of only Jem in regard to this. I will not put Jenna in harm's way again. I promise. The Mimi would welcome Jenna's strengths amongst them and they would try to influence her to remain with them. The Skystone will not protect her from the Mimi, but the Mimi lands alone would be her greatest protection from the Spirit men."

"But these are my father's people and I don't wish to be afraid of them," Jen suddenly protested. "I would like to return to the lands again one day. Surely I can make up my own mind about this."

Ngaire frowned, then looked up as we all heard the tread of another foot. Billy Black was returning with a good catch of fish and immediately I saw him, I stood to greet him as did the girls.

"Sean, you've found your way here I see."

"Yes, Billy... I was telling the women we met earlier."

Nodding, understanding more now, I turned to Jen but my words were for Billy and Ngaire. "And I was explaining to this woman of mine that she needs to let me know what she is up to. Sometimes I think she feels I am being obsessive." My grin softened my words, but I knew how much Jen was beginning to value her sense of independence lately and to see a gentle flush move along her skin merely confirmed my thoughts.

Jen and I had battled a number of times over just this issue and later as they told me of their experience I realized just how much Jen would have enjoyed her adventure. I was pleased she had the opportunity to visit her father's people, even though I had not shared it.

As we settled around the camp, I helped Billy with the preparation of the fish the girls tended the fire, I listened as they continued to talk about the Mimi people, drawing Billy now into the conversation.

I had known of the people and met some of the Shaman in my time in the North but had never been invited into their world. Invites were not common nor were they received well as many knew the Mimi were a powerful people and they were afraid of them.

Tales of them were scattered and were often told with threads of fear, the greatest being that it might be difficult to escape their world if they should enter it, but as I listened to Ngaire and Jen, I didn't voice my knowledge.

Around the campfire that night Billy joined in the conversation with a companionable eagerness, glad to be talking of the tribal experience with the Mimi and drawing the odd comparison between his life in the gorge with his people and living at the homestead station where he worked for months on end.

Both Ngaire and Jenna found his stories entertaining, as I did. I listened, as they spoke of some of the people the girls had also obviously met but I couldn't help but feel a slight sense of exclusion as I wondered about the characters they mentioned.

"Sean... there's this baby so tiny still, which lives in the Lands. He is gorgeous but he has this mouth problem and we are really quite concerned about it." Jenna added into the conversation suddenly quite serious, a seriousness which spread instantly to the others, also enveloping me. Jenna's tone set aside the laughter of moments before, as she tried to tell me about what was now obviously a concern to her and to the others.

Ngaire took up the explanation. "It's a cleft palette, not too serious fortunately, but it really needs to be seen to but I don't know quite how we are going to manage it. We don't even know if the child can be bought out from the lands, but if it's to be fixed then that certainly needs to happen."

"Can the healers do anything?"

"Well yes. But that's very limited, I am most worried about his hearing and how the condition will affect that, but the condition is such that it may need plastic surgery or a repair of the palette which will mean he will need to go to a hospital."

I could see the problem. "They can't bring him out from the lands? Are you sure?"

"No, not at all, a child has little control over such a transition. It could be quite dangerous, though we can find that out, then any surgery needed can be done, that is why a doctor would be best to assess the condition."

Jenna added, "Taipan may be able to help do you think? Perhaps he knows someone?"

"He might," I agreed. "Is there maybe anyone in Darwin?"

Ngaire shook her head, "Not in this field."

"Well I guess then our best bet would be to ask Ty. See what he can suggest." I turned to Billy, knowing he would best be able to answer me. "Is there anything the Shaman can do?"

"Well, yes. We could try to bring the baby out but he is so young. It would be best to wait as long as we can but I don't know if the baby can wait? I would need to stay with the child, we don't want him vanishing... might upset a few I am thinking, if he drifts back away from his Land."

His grin made light of the problem but it made me realize the seriousness of it. I nodded in agreement and sought to confirm my understanding. "The child cannot be seen by everyone?"

"He is of the Mimi people. He fades into the rocks and he may well sicken away from his lands, we can't know the strength in one so young. There is not much of this world that runs through his blood. I am thinking he will not transition well into your world. If we could bring a doctor of skill into his World it would be best."

"You can do this?"

Billy nodded, "There is little I can do to help the child in moving into this world. The stones I use will not work well they need the land around them to work best. It's these lands which make them work as they do, away from these lands they are just pretty stones so we can't take him far. But drawing someone into the Lands of the Mimi who does not have links with the land can also be risky. It depends entirely on the person, though I could judge perhaps if we were able to do so."

"It will be a difficult life for him if something isn't done," Ngaire added. "It's a problem I would like to solve for the child, if you can think of anything... perhaps if Taipan could even think of something I would do anything to help the child. I can test his hearing and give advice but that is about the limit of the help I can give and it's very frustrating."

I nodded. It was something I decided that I would take away with me and I hoped we could find a way. "Sure, I will ask and see if there is anything. I can let you know."

"Thank you. I hadn't thought of your brother, but it would be ideal if he could help, even if he could visit the child and give a medical opinion that would be a great help. It would reassure me, though the Mimi people are very wary but I think perhaps if Taipan..?"

"Ty is familiar with such situations. He has worked with other tribal groups before and knows how to move amongst other tribes."

"Then please let me know if he can help," Ngaire said eagerly. "We can perhaps bring him north for a visit..."

Billy suddenly looked up. "Your brother...?"

"He is a Shaman, a Karadji of our mob and he has some medical training."

I explained, "He is better known in North Queensland where he has family links."

Billy nodded but I knew there was something he wasn't saying, perhaps because of the presence of the women and I wondered at it.

Later around the fire that night, after the girls had settled on their blankets Billy and I still talked, it was when he felt that the women were well settled that he broached the subject again.

"Your brother, Taipan, he is a strong man?" he asked softly.

I nodded my expression serious, knowing that he was seeking information.

"I have heard much of the Shaman of the Far Northern country. The Communities there speak much of the Featherfoot, they are highly regarded amongst the Mimi people there. Our meeting Sean, has perhaps a reason for it."

Again I nodded, "Ty also has close friends amongst the Featherfoot. I will tell him of the baby and perhaps he can do something."

"Your brother is of the Featherfoot?"

For a moment I paused, not because I did not wish to say but because I have more than one brother and Billy had no reason to know this. "Taipan is not of the Featherfoot Lore, but he is learning much of their ways."

"I would like to meet such a man. Hopefully you can bring him to us and we can share our knowledge, share the ways of the Mimi people with him. I can draw him into the Lands without risk while the wet season is with us, but during the dry I will have trouble and I may not be able to do it."

"I understand," Agreeing I considered the possibilities. "Leave it with me and I will see what can be arranged, something timely with the seasons perhaps."

I knew Billy was content with our understanding and I also knew that Ty would find the knowledge I bought back with me to be of great value. I would be surprised if he didn't wish to be a help to the community, but more so help the child which Jen was so concerned about.

The whole thing played over constantly in my mind as we travelled through the next day, having said goodbye to Billy Black when he headed off early, back up the escarpment at the break of the day. Finally we reached the abandoned mining settlement by the late afternoon and picking up the girls car, we found ourselves headed into Katherine by the end of the day.

It had been a long and demanding trip and I knew I for one was looking forward to a few of the comforts the town of Katherine could offer us. But mostly I was looking forward to meeting Jiemba, Ngaire's son. I knew that Andrew would be interested to hear all about the lad, not to mention the reassurance he would feel at this gradual move into what was Ngaire's life.

The girls travelled ahead of me in the more powerful car and although I often fell behind, Ngaire would wait for me, which afforded them a few breaks in the long drive. By dusk we rolled into Katherine and as I followed her car through the streets of the town I wondered just what we would find when we arrived.

THE BREATH OF CHANGE

Ngaire:

As I watched them play, I couldn't help but enjoy the experience, it was such a special delight. Tango bounced around confused, but delighting in the insane game while Jem laughed riotously. Sean couldn't have been any less serious about this game of backyard cricket if he had tried and Jenna was so bad at hitting even the slowest of balls that Sean had made a riotous mockery of her spectacular lack of talent.

Watching Jem with the two of them warmed my heart. I would have loved to join in with them, but my annoying headache had not gone and despite taking some tablets I felt little the better for it. I would need to see the clinic doctor tomorrow I decided. It seemed my head aches were becoming more severe and I hoped that it wouldn't mean that I would have to return to the blood pressure medications, something I hated.

It was enjoyable watching Jem being taught how to hit the ball with the small bat Sean had fashioned for him from a light plank of wood with some bandages around the handle for a better grip. I wondered how long the bat would last... it didn't seem as though it would be much longer as it kept connecting with the ground as Jenna stumbled with it yet again, making me laugh.

Watching Sean with Jem made me think of Andrew. I had enjoyed the short entertaining messages he had sent me via the phone, though it was an arduous task replying to these as unused to thumbing replies as I was, but I was getting better at it under Jenna's coaching. It had been a delight to talk to him before he had gone off shore again. Perhaps I could invite him to join us in Katherine when he returned after his rotation, though it was a good few weeks away yet. I had plenty of time to consider it. It was time to introduce Andrew to Jiemba I had decided, and I wondered how Jem would adapt to another man in my life.

As Tango lunged for the ball yet again, I could hear Sean's moan of protest and as the three of them began to chase the dog around the yard once more, I couldn't help but laugh again at their antics.

It was a breathless and hot trio who joined me in the kitchen some time later as the sun began its fall behind the horizon and I knew they would be a hungry crew. So ignoring my aching head, I slipped some frozen pies into the oven, along with a tray of chips and headed for the bathroom to run a cool bath for Jem, leaving Jenna to organise a simple tossed salad.

The evenings spent with Jenna and Sean were both enjoyable and taxing. Difficult because it was so obvious that they were very much in love and enjoyed each other's company in a way that people who know and understand each other well can. It was almost as though they were each one half of a whole, such was their confidence in each other and I envied them the apparently simple honesty of their relationship even though I could only guess at its depth and complexity. I found that my thoughts would drift to Andrew, and as eagerly as I looked for those small text messages, I knew he would be unable to send them from the off shore rig where he now was.

I had never felt so isolated and in many ways it sat heavily on my mind at times. The world of men it seemed was enveloping me, Andrew's world and a world one day to be Jiemba's. My son was growing and although he was still a small child, I could see the richness which another man would bring to his eyes and his life. I recognized the dependence Jem built around Sean's strength and more than anything, I saw the glimpse of a future for Andrew and my small son. There were things I had not seen before. Jem needed a man in his life and it seemed at times to me that it was perhaps a need we shared.

After Jenna and Sean had left to return to the East Coast at the end of the week, the house seemed so quiet. Life went on along its normal paths. My work at the clinic absorbed me once more and my Mother and Aunts drew me back into our comfortable existence for many weeks. It was a safe world, though I would often think of Andrew and what it would be like to bring him into my life? I wondered about what role he would fill and I had reason to wonder, a reason that absorbed my thoughts more and more.

It was a call from Andrew that pulled me out of my comfort zone, a call that I was delighted to get, yet in some ways I could feel the breath of change shift around me. In the kitchen as I was sorting through the washing I found myself listening to the melody ringing softly in the air and it was a few moments before I recognized that it was the singing of the little mobile phone. That was enough to rattle me from my complacency anyway as I searched for where I had carelessly put it last.

"Hi..."

"Hey Ngaire. Finally!" Andrew's deeper laugh sang in my ears. "I was beginning to think you had left the phone in the car although Jen had said you had taken to keeping it in the kitchen."

"Andrew... Hi," I said softly, happy at the sound of his voice. "I have, I mean I do... but well, I guess I'm not so used to it as I thought," I said making apologies as I gathered my wits.

"You're going to have to use it more. But that's not why I am calling... Taipan asked me to ring you and make arrangements. .Jen and Sean were telling us about the child with the cleft lip problem and how you were hoping Ty could arrange something. Is it still something you need up your way?"

"Well yes. Yes it is. He hasn't got a cleft lip, but the palette. I haven't been back into the Lands but I know it's definitely something that still needs to be dealt with. Is he able to do anything?" I asked, excited that the child had not been forgotten and inordinately pleased that it seemed like something could be done.

"He says he needs to come up and make an assessment, without any records to go on it's very difficult but he does have a few ideas, he has an associate who may be able to help. Sean said that there was a guide, Billy Black, who could arrange something with the community or the child. If the Elders would prefer he is willing to visit the Community. He would choose to take Sean with him on such a visit as he's met Billy and they understand each other."

"Well I am sure something can be arranged, we are heavily into the 'Wet Season' up here but Billy has access to a chopper. I can contact Him... did Taipan say when he'd be available?"

I heard the pause in Andrew's voice, as he answered. "As soon as possible and... I was hoping I could do the trip up to see you? Ngaire I know it isn't what you wanted but would you consider it?"

"Yes."I answered without hesitation, smiling to myself. I knew that this was something that I had decided myself anyway.

"Well could you let me know when you decide?"

For a moment I frowned, not understanding his tone or words and then I realized... "Yes. I mean yes I would love you to come up for a visit."

"Oh... great then," he answered clearly happy. "Umm... then let me know when you get onto Billy Black and we can make arrangements."

"That's great Andrew. I am so pleased. Will Taipan want me to go with them do you think?"

"Don't know. He didn't say. I have just got into Brisbane but I am headed down to the Community, I can ask tonight and then get back to you. Or you could ring me? I am only going to be in the community for a day or so, or rather perhaps I can ring again as soon as I am back in the city at Jen's if you like?"

"That would be nice. I would like that," I answered, smiling at the thought.

"OK... I'm looking forward to seeing you Ngaire," he added suddenly.

"Me too."

Moments later he was gone and I was left holding his last words to myself. I hadn't known what to do, what to tell Andrew but I knew I was going to have to tell him something soon, if he came up to Katherine to visit then I knew that was the time.

The thought made me nervous and I wasn't quite sure how I was going to tell him at all, or even how he would take the news that I was pregnant. It had been a shock for me, but I accepted the responsibility of my pregnancy as unexpected as it was and as unplanned. At the thought of my child, my hand absently found the smallest of differences in my belly, resting there, as though comforting the small baby. He or she was going to be a part of my life, I knew that much. Regardless of whether Andrew was going to be a part of our lives, perhaps a more frequent part was something Andrew would have to decide himself.

I had been hoping that it wasn't news that I would be delivering over the phone. I had even considered flying into Brisbane to visit Jenna to tell them of my news, as well as having to decide how I would tell Andrew. Now, that wasn't necessary and I was glad that it had saved me that expense, emotionally and financially. Andrew was flying here and it would be something I would tell him during his visit when I found the opportunity.

Settling back to the task at hand, I thought about the baby and wondered how he would take the news. It would be nice to have him more regularly in my life, more regularly in Jem's life, but that was something we had to work out between us.

And if we didn't..? Well that too was always a possibility I accepted. Doing this on my own had never been a problem, but it would be nice to have my child's father around for them and I hoped, simply hoped, that this would be the case. The thought of destroying this life I had never even considered, it wasn't something that I could do and that was a simple truth.

I would ring the homestead where Billy worked tonight I decided. We could arrange for him to get back to me to see if it was possible to visit the Lands again soon. The sooner the better I knew because as my pregnancy progressed, it would become much more difficult to enter the Lands of the Mimi safely and the welfare of the baby with the cleft palette was often on my mind. It was something I would like to attend to as soon as possible before my body became too cumbersome and demands on my time became greater.

It was a week later that I was nervously awaiting the arrival of the men. Billy had arranged to meet them at the mine site where they would fly onto the Tablelands. Andrew I knew would be leaving Sean and Taipan with Billy and then driving down to Katherine. The men had decided that it was the most practical approach and that Sean had met Billy previously had helped a great deal.

They had flown in the day before and had camped out at the mine site the last night waiting on the weather and opportunity to get up onto the plateau in the calm of the morning, avoiding the afternoon build of often violent storms which swept the land. I wasn't quite sure what Andrew's plans were, whether he would meet the men after their trip into the Lands or not. He had simply said that he would drive into Katherine to see me.

That the land was deep in the wet season added an additional complication. The rivers were high and much of the low lands were isolated, cutting access to the tableland and the escarpment but I doubted this would stop the men. It never seemed to stop Billy, but then Billy never seemed to rely on vehicle access either, as a Shaman he knew how to move over the land lightly.

I knew he owned a much travelled and much used four wheel drive but it was more for the use of his wife and family on the Homestead, I rarely saw him travelling alone in his vehicle. He relied more heavily on the small homestead chopper particularly in the Wet, or another which was owned by the mining company, although I knew that the chopper was something which he would never allow into the gorge of the Mimi. He had always said that it was too dangerous to fly into the gorge and there was nowhere down in the gorge suited to landing safely. The passage along the river was kinder on the body, giving travellers into the Land time to adjust.

The men had made the arrangements between them and it seemed once Taipan had been able to speak to Billy, I was left out of the loop. I imagined that this was to be a quick visit, for Taipan to assess the child and not knowing just how much time Andrew would be able to spend in Katherine on his visit, held an edge of disappointment. I wondered how much opportunity I would have to tell Andrew of my news.

The morning had dragged on endlessly and I had been somewhat impatient at the clinic, something which I knew wasn't in anyone's best interest. But my work mates had been tolerant with me which was just as well. Jem too knew there was something going on, he wasn't used to moodiness on my part and as I had collected him from day care after lunch and headed home I tried not to be impatient with his chatter.

What I wasn't expecting was that Andrew would be at the house when I arrived, I had expected him later in the day perhaps even into the evening but as I turned into the street I didn't recognize the dusty bush vehicle parked up on the verge and it was only then that it occurred to me that he might be here already.

When I pulled into the drive, his tall, lean figure unfurled itself from his seat on the fence deep in the corner in the shade. He moved towards the car as both Jem and I climbed out. I could see he was carefully hesitant as his glance shifted between Jem and I.

"Hi Babe," he said softly, his eyes carefully measuring Jem's reaction. "... and you must be Mum's main man. Hi, I'm Andrew a friend of your Mum's and I have something for you."

Slowly he squatted to Jem's height and offered him a large plastic bag in which was a gift. I could see immediately what it was and relieved I smiled knowing how much my son would enjoy the thoughtful present. As Andrew waited, Jem glanced up at me hesitant, wondering if I would allow him to accept the gift and as I nodded slightly Jem made a reluctant move towards the waiting figure of the man he didn't know.

"Sean said you needed this. He helped me pick it out for you and told me to help you get lots of practice. He said you could be very good."

"Hi Andrew," I said pleased. "What do you say Jem?" I prompted hoping he would remember his manners.

Jem hesitated then stepped closer towards the taller figure now squatting to his height. "Thank you," he mumbled quickly taking the proffered gift.

In a short time the wrapping was discarded, though Andrew collected it absently as he once more stood having handed his gift over, seemingly pleased with Jem's obvious childish delight as he had all but forgotten about us.

Andrew's arrival on the scene and become more engrossed in the contents of the package. Pleased at what he had found he was eagerly now tearing at the light plastic netting keeping it together.

"Can I play with Tango...?" he demanded of me, happily gripping his new cricket bat and ball still contained in the now tattered mesh bag which was quickly being torn apart. Not waiting for an answer, content that my smile was enough, Jem headed off towards the back yard intent not so much on the bat at the moment but more on the ball. I could hear Tango dancing against the high picket gate with impatience; he knew we had arrived home.

Laughing at his antics, I was relieved at the impatience and thoughtless negligence of my son though normally I wouldn't have been and thanking

Andrew with my eyes I moved towards the house.

"Well that went down well," Andrew said under his breath as Jem answered Tango's dance at the gate, struggling with the catch.

"Yes. Thanks for that, he will love the gift," relieved, I grinned happily. "Come on in, I need a cup of tea."

Andrew glanced up into the skies overhead noting the afternoon storms gathering, knowing the short deluge they would bring to relieve the heat of the day. "Yeah... I could do with a cool drink too. So what have you been up to?" he added as we made our way through the front door, the sounds of Jem's laughter and Tango's efforts with the game letting us know what was happening in the back yard."

"The Clinic mostly. Did Sean and Taipan get into the camp OK?"

"Yeah. They caught up with Billy; they should be up on the tablelands by now I think. I should hear from them tomorrow or maybe the next day."

"Do they have a sat' phone?"

Knowing a few in the outback travelled with the expensive and cumbersome satellite phones which allowed them to better communicate in remote area's, I wondered if they would work in the gorge of the Mimi, and doubted their reliability.

"No. But they have something worked out I am sure," he answered smiling to himself. "Actually Taipan asked if I could set up a camp somewhere where I could get the vehicle close into the escarpment. He can contact me there and the guys will meet me when they are done."

"Oh, so you are only here for a few days?"

"I need to head out tomorrow, they will be looking for me in the arvo," he answered sobering suddenly. "I was going to ask if you and Jem would like to come into camp with me for the time it takes. I'm not sure what their plans are until they can assess what is needed. Can you get away?"

As I handed Andrew a glass of cold juice I considered the suggestion. It certainly wasn't what I expected but I knew that Jem would love the camp, he enjoyed getting into the bush and a chance to spend some time with Andrew without the distractions of work and those around us in Katherine had its appeal for me.

"We would need to take Tango along. I couldn't leave him with anyone." I qualified carefully, knowing what this could mean if Andrew had a prearranged place he needed to be.

"No worries," he answered grinning. "We can pick up a tent or a tarp in town, or is there one we can use, we won't need much bedding it's too hot. Plus we can get what supplies we need in town tomorrow."

"You have a set place where you will meet Sean and his brother?" I asked curious as I sat at the table, wondering if they had been up this way before.

This seemed to give him reason to smile which somehow annoyed me. "No. They can find us, don't worry about that." Then he changed the subject without warning. "You're looking good, I'm glad you decided to let me come and meet your son."

Inexplicably I blushed further annoyed as I felt the heat move into my skin. "I realized it could be a good thing..."

I would have said more as I knew I needed to talk to Andrew but at that moment, Jiemba suddenly raced through the back door, Tango hard on his heels heading straight for the sink I knew he was looking for a drink but he was barely able to reach the tap, so I moved to help him.

Tango in turn stopped in his path, then immediately headed for Andrew's legs under the table and reacquainted himself with his presence. I was surprised to see Tango's tail suddenly in swift movement and his attention light up as he looked up at Andrew.

"Hi boy," Andrew said pleasantly as he caressed and tickled his ears, surprising me with this welcome.

Jem however paid it scant attention and shot off through the house. "Come-on Tango..." he yelled in his boyish fashion, as though to let it be known just whose dog Tango was. Tango did not disappoint and followed him eagerly into his room immediately, now ignoring the petting he was getting from

Andrew.

"Don't make too big a mess in there Jem!" I yelled after them then returned my thoughts back to Andrew. "Jem will love a camp and I have some gear...What would you like for dinner? I can do sausages and salad."

Considering the pleased glimmer in his eyes I wondered what arrangements he hoped for and realizing he would be here overnight I jumped right into it deciding to approach the matter head on. "I hope you don't mind sleeping on the lounge, you're more than welcome," I added as I moved over to the fridge to check that I had everything available.

"Thanks that would be great."

I wanted to establish early the way it would be as I knew Jiemba needed time to settle to the reality of Andrew. It was important to me not to upset his sense of his place in my life and I figured Andrew would have to find his own way around this. I was inordinately glad that he so easily agreed.

The evening was enjoyable and with Andrew clearing up after dinner while I tried to settle a lively Jiemba down for the night. With Jem at last settled we relaxed, the telly turned low while we talked softly. Andrew had taken his place beside me and with his arm spread along the back of the lounge there was a gentle touch on my neck soothing my skin.

"How is work going?" I asked, enjoying the drift of his fingers immensely.

"Good. I've taken a bit of time off. I think that is what I like most about this job. I told them I needed a couple of week's break, maybe a month so they will get back to me around then."

"So what are you going to do, are you planning a holiday?"

"Yep," he grinned suddenly. "I'm on it."

I couldn't help but chuckle at the light in his eyes. He had such a pleasant way of teasing and as I settled into the lounge and the comfort of his presence I listened as he continued.

"What about you, can you get away for a few days, maybe longer?"

"Yes. I mostly work casually, I can manage a few days... maybe longer."

"Good then," he said softly as I watched his lips move to mine across the short space that separated us.

His kiss was gentle, exploring my lips and I almost became lost in their promise as he gathered me to his warmth, his hand at my waist. For a moment I could do little as I enjoyed his touch and then almost rudely I interrupted the intent of our bodies.

"Andrew I can't... not here," I whispered.

Immediately I felt his hands loosen their pressure and contented he sighed with a smile. "OK, I can understand that."

Easing himself into the comfort of the lounge we settled to chat with the low drone of whatever it was on the telly in the background. We chatted about the news, and the events of the week along with the antics of Jem. Somehow it all seemed so natural to share these things and I enjoyed having Andrew there to share them with. He in some ways was making this all so easy for us and I was glad, it seemed so much like the man I thought I knew and it gave me confidence.

When he began to fall asleep I brought out the spare bedding and helped him get comfortable. The lounge was barely long enough for him and when I later tried to settle in my room I found it difficult. I tossed about in my bedding and I knew why I had found it so difficult. I couldn't shift my thoughts from wondering what he would say when I told him of the baby. A part of me didn't want to tell him, didn't want to lose the friendship and trust between us. I wanted to enjoy that just a little longer before I would see the disappointment, perhaps even regret in his expression when I told him and I was tempted just to keep it to myself. I wanted to hold this fledgling relationship we had together as long as I could.

Much later I gave up trying to coax myself to sleep and crept out for a drink. I could hear his soft breathing as I passed on tip toes trying to move quietly about the room, not putting on the light in case it disturbed him.

On the way back to my room however, I found him propped up on his elbow watching me and I paused frowning when his voice stalled me.

"Having trouble sleeping?" he whispered softly. I grinned at his tone.

"Trying not to wake you."

"Well that isn't going to work, I am awake."

"I can see." Moving to the lounge I took a safe position sitting up on the arm-rest carelessly as I propped my feet onto the lounge seat and faced him in the dim light as he too sat up. "Wanna talk for a while?" I offered wondering if this was the time, wondering if I could tell him now?

"No." And I could hear the entertainment in his voice. "Would you like company in that room of yours?" he offered cheekily.

I bit my lip, not sure if this was what I wanted. It wasn't that I didn't want him with me, I didn't know if it was honest to use our relationship like this. Not when I knew what it was that I wanted to tell him. But as I dithered, Andrew didn't.

Climbing out from the light cover he moved over towards me and not waiting for the answer he slipped his arms around me, picked me up easily and brushed my mouth with the promise of his, moist sweet lips. Then he moved towards the room.

"Too late woman, you shouldn't hesitate over a question like that." Andrew chuckled as he nudged the door closed behind him.

"What about Jem?" I asked quietly as he reached the bed and settled us in a sure movement. I felt like a feather weight in his arms, even though I wasn't, but the heat of his body, his arms about me gave birth to a warm rush of promise sweeping aside any reservations I had. I forgot the questions, when his lips and hands dealt impatiently with the loose top I used as night wear.

"We can deal with that in the morning," he answered against my skin. His breath was a delicious sensation and I didn't want to think of any other problems, nor any questions. I wanted to simply enjoy the reality of having Andrew with me again as my body remembered the strength and the promise of his with delight.

THE EARTH LIGHTS

Andrew:

Waking up to the questioning eyes of a youngster wasn't something I was used to. It took me a moment to remember what was going on and I frowned at the immediate sight of Ngaires young son watching me while he pushed impatiently at my arm. The one comfortably wrapped around his mum as we shared our body heat in the aftermath of a rich memory which still hovered in my mind.

"Why are you in Mum's bed?" he demanded clearly annoyed.

As I struggled to gather my wits, instinctively I put my finger to my lips... signalling silence, checking that Ngaire still slept. I could feel the weight of her head resting on my arm, she was still soundly asleep and as I recognized Tango, watching behind Jem, I hoped he wasn't about to start barking or protesting too, while I tried to shuffle Ngaire carefully. Indicating to the attentive duo that I was getting up and that they should remain silent.

It took a minute to disentangle myself, a minute of time to worry over how I was going to deal with this and as I glanced towards Jem, carefully I eased myself off the bed, grabbing my shorts as I pointed towards the door and moved carefully as I struggled getting into my gear, making my way towards the other room.

Tango and Jem both watched me, none too pleased I could see but I had dealt with Tango before. Jiemba I wasn't so sure of, but he followed me at my signal despite his scowl. I was glad he hadn't just decided to climb in next to his mum once I had vacated the bed.

Closing the door quietly once we were all out of the bedroom, leaving Ngaire to her dreams, I decided the best thing to do was just ignore the first question. He was after all barely five if that, he wouldn't understand any realistic explanation. Maybe if I could distract him he might even forget his question.

"We'll let your Mum sleep... you want some breakfast?"

He watched me still with a look of uncertain petulance. He looked as though he might leave me to it and rejoin his mum. Certain I wasn't about to let him do that, I moved off towards the kitchen with a gesture of suggestion, hopefully flicking my fingers at Tango as I had seen Ngaire do a hundred times while I added. "I can do pancakes... wanna help?"

Jem moved to follow me, as did Tango but I knew the dog would go where Jem went. I was in no delusion that he was answering my flick of fingers but it helped somehow that it looked that he was.

It was a quiet and suspicious child who sat down at the small central table as I searched the cupboard for flour, eggs and milk, then getting a glass of milk and a can of instant chocolate powder with a spoon for him at the same time. It was all an attempt to give him something to do as I rustled up breakfast as quickly as I could manage. I wasn't going to wait so I worked impatiently. It didn't worry me knowing that the first pancakes would be crap, I could eat those. Maybe Tango would eat them, I wondered smiling at the thought.

"What do you think of the idea of camping for a couple of days?" I asked trying to coax a better mood out of the youngster.

Immediately I realised I had his attention as he shuffled in his seat, not sure if he wanted to look interested.

"Is Mum coming too?"

"Yeah... Tango too. We might even catch up with Sean and Ty his brother. They are in the bush now."

I could see him examining the idea. "Can we go fishing?" he asked suddenly, barely a whisper.

"Do you have some gear? A rod maybe? The water is too high to build good traps but maybe we will have time later in the camp."

"Mum got me a rod for my birthday. It's good, but I haven't used it much. I can catch fish though."

"Well then, I will have to get a line too. Maybe we can do that today and we can get in some fishing while we wait for the others to join us."

Having mixed up the batter I moved over to the now hot pan, I tested the heat with a knob of margarine and the first of the pancakes, and then turned it to a more gentle setting as they seared in the hot margarine'. I was extremely pleased Jem had decided to stay with me instead of waking his mum. He was an adventurous youngster I realized and I began to look forward to the next few days as we got to know each other better.

By the time Ngaire joined us much later into the morning, Jem and I were out in the yard playing with Tango as we tried to teach him to return the ball. The dog persisted in taking the ball to Jem and watching me suspiciously, anticipating that I would steal it from him, which was perfectly correct. It was an enjoyable game, even though chasing the dog around was exhausting and between Tango and Jem they had managed to make it something of a trial for me. I wasn't sure who was trying to train whom, to do exactly what? But at this point I didn't care.

I knew the kitchen was a disaster, but that didn't worry me either. At least Jem was now talking to me and when I caught sight of Ngaire, wrapped in her light dressing gown I immediately went over to join her, begging off the ball game.

"Hey mum, we're going camping." The youngster announced from his game, greeting her. My grin was by way of an apology to Ngaire for pre-empting her somewhat.

"Yes, we are," she agreed readily. "Have you cleaned your teeth?"

Jem's groan made me chuckle, but he stopped his game. "Come'n Tango." His tone was by way of a complaint as he swung towards his mum and the door.

"An' get dressed," she warned as he passed, then she looked at me laughing. "An' what about you?" she added.

"No mum." I answered back quickly, but was surprised at the dimming of her smile. "OK, I know I made a mess of the kitchen I'll clean it up," I added as I passed her.

"No. That's OK...thanks for letting me sleep in. It isn't very often I get the chance. I appreciate it."

Following me, together we surveyed the mess in the kitchen. "Yeah... he's a handful," I agreed as I looked over the kitchen and set about putting it to order as I glanced across to Ngaire trying to gauge her strange mood. "You want some of the left over's... Tango might eat them if not?"

"I might have one... Thank you."

Watching her polish off more than one though was great. I hadn't done so bad I decided and when Jem surfaced again, clean and dressed with Tango still at his heels, the dog happily ate the last of the pancakes.

It took the rest of the morning to organize ourselves. Ngaire worked mostly inside, gathering what she decided we would need while I checked over the gear in the small backyard storage shed. I loaded it into the dusty rental car as I sorted it. There was a large tarp I had found and a small tent which Jem had insisted on bringing for himself. Apparently it was a Christmas gift from his Nana, there was also an odd assortment of what he thought was all of his fishing gear.

I supplemented this at the store while Ngaire shopped for supplies and with more gear than I had ever taken on a camp, we headed out after a light early lunch, happy to be getting underway in time to set up camp before nightfall.

I knew Ty and Sean would be looking for me today and it was foremost in my thoughts that I had to pull together the camp early enough to get the marker fire going so that they would find me. It had not been in our plans to have Ngaire along, but this didn't worry me. I knew she was familiar with the ways of Shaman as did Sean. Taipan would recognize this too I was sure as Billy would have spoken of her knowledge. If anything, Ngaire's presence might be a good thing.

Once Ty had made an assessment of what could be done for the child, we could head back to Katherine. Then maybe Ngaire and I could get some time together with Jem. I hoped this would be the case as I wanted to get to understand the boy and find a place in his life, with his mum. For the moment we needed now to find a good overnight camp up as close as we could get to the escarpment given that the rivers were swollen and wait for the others to arrive.

I loved this part of the country even though it was fairly new to me. It had many similarities to the country in the Gulf which I had explored last year but it had a spirit of its own and a much richer land. It had a raw and wild character that in part was dry, but yet was fed by the Dreaming giving it a strong wild spirit seemingly renewed each year with the wet season. I could feel this was a land swept by the power of Namarrgon, the Lightning Man and there was something in that which answered my own spirit. The earth was accustomed to being flooded in the Wet and drained in the Dry and the land announced its seasons through the plants and animals. It was a bold and beautiful place of times long past. A place of the Dreaming I could feel it and it invigorated me.

Crossing the land in such a time was no easy feat. The rivers were fast and the ground often marked by the trails of others in deep ruts left gouged in the ground. It took six hours for us to find a suitable place close enough to the escarpment where Billy had indicated I should try to establish a camp, when the guys had made our plans a few days ago.

We had driven through the afternoons storm which had slowed us considerably and although I was pleased that I had managed to get the vehicle as close to the escarpment as I had, I knew it would still offer Ty and Sean enough of a challenge in finding it.

The first order of the day was to get the beacon fire going, then I could concern myself with setting up camp which was easy enough. I left Ngaire to organize Jem, once I had explained what I intended and once the fire was smoking steadily I set about stringing the large tarp between what trees and brush could offer by way of support in the promised heavy downpours that were to be expected in this season. It wasn't too difficult to find a branch support to act as a spine over which I draped the tarp and after due discussion I set about digging a small trench to divert any water run-off from the land in an attempt to keep the now sheltered area dry.

The only difficulty I had was when I suggested Jiemba put his tent up, with the help of Ngaire, under the shelter of the tarp. He wanted to set it up in the bush nearby but knowing the risk of foraging wildlife and the strength of the rain torrents, which could arrive as quickly as they departed, I insisted that the tent be set up under the shelter. Ngaire could see the simple practicalities of this and coaxed him to comply with gentle threats but it wasn't a happy lad who ended up doing as I had wanted, so I decided once we were set up,

I would spend some time trying to tease him back into a better humour. A swim in the shallower part of the river might be an option to distract him I figured.

We were camped on a high bit of land, a slow growing island between two arms of the river which were in steady and strong flow and the vehicle was parked behind us. Ngaire and Jem decided to head down to the run of water amongst the rocks to cool off from the stifling humidity of the day while I finished setting up the camp and reorganizing the small but steady camp fire, making sure it was visible from the skies. I didn't know if Ty and Sean would be in the skies yet, but I wanted to be sure, if they were, that they could find us.

When I joined the others it was to the welcome sight of Ngaire wrapped in a sodden sarong playing happily with young Jem who was frolicking naked, ditching my gear I joined them. Tango however had disdained our games and was sitting high and dry on the bank, watching the surrounding area attentively. I realized after a few minutes that this was something he was trained to do, a look out for his pack while they relaxed at play. Whenever I thought about it, it never ceased to amaze me how well the dog had been trained.

Ngaire and I had both checked for any mud slides which the croc's may have made but we were confident that there were none nearby. The bush smelt clean too and it wasn't likely that we were near any nests and we intended to stay well away from any deep water holes, though it was good to have the dog about.

Beautifully refreshing, the cool flow of the water was welcome as I let it wash over me, Jem was jumping about and balancing between us as we all set about building a series of small dams for our amusement in the flow of the water using leaves and sticks then I attempted to make small boats in a miniature race down the rapids.

It was just on dusk when I noticed the path of the two big eagle's overhead, spiralling in the air, their wing span breathtaking in its majesty. One darker and larger than the other whose white feathered expanse blazed along its belly, I recognized them and as I climbed to my feet, Ngaire too noticed the path of the magnificent birds.

"Aren't they beautiful, look Jem... at the eagle's. The white one is sea eagle, isn't it unusual to see the two different eagles in flight together?" she questioned, admiring the soar of both birds as they swept the sky overhead.

"No. They commonly fly together." I answered suddenly grinning. "I'll be back in a minute, just need to check the fire and see if the others are about."

Picking my way across the rocks I grabbed my gear and headed up towards the camp, turning back to Ngaire and Jem as I made the bank. "Come on up when you're ready, Taipan and Sean should be here soon and I'm sure Jem would like to catch up with Sean again."

Immediately Jiemba looked up. "Is Jenna gunna be here too?"

"No mate, just Sean and his big brother Ty." I called back to the youngster.

"We won't be long." Ngaire added. "It will be too dark soon anyway."

Heading back up into camp it wasn't long before I arrived at the clearing to find both Sean and Taipan just arriving into camp also, Ty headed straight for the fire to bank it as Sean moved to join me.

"Hey... This looks well organized. You have Ngaire with you?" he asked grinning, knowing I wasn't normally this organized or well equipped.

"Yes, and Jem. He is looking forward to seeing you though he's a bit put out Jen isn't with you."

"Yeah... they got on really well. You wouldn't have a couple of board shorts spare would you? We have to get into Katherine though I think we will leave it till the morning. You mind if we borrow the forbie?"

"No. Not unless you are planning on leaving us here stranded. What is going on?" I asked as I moved over towards my rucksack pleased to see the two of them and sorting through the mix of clothes which never managed to keep any order, I found what I wanted. Pulling out what I thought might be suitable gear, I handed Sean a pair and tossed another pair over to Ty. "You might need to find a belt or a tie or something on those" I added as Sean sized them up with humour. "They'll be a bit loose on your scrawny butt."

As the others pulled on the shorts I rustled around in the bag for a belt, coming up empty I gave up and joined them around the fire having donned my own gear, not wanting to be the only one running around in the raw.

"So what's happening?"

Ty looked up satisfied as he squatted near the fire and Sean hanging onto his shorts, found it more comfortable to sit. "I'm going in to see if I can contact someone I know. See if I can get them up here for a day or two to sort out the baby's problem. It isn't as severe as I feared, a relatively simple operation should fix it and it will make a great deal of difference."

"That's good news. Ngaire should be up soon, she is down at the river with Jem at the moment. Will you have trouble getting back up onto the plateau with someone in tow?"

"We shouldn't, we are meeting Billy hopefully the day after tomorrow, we can get hold of the chopper and he can fly us in. He's headed into the old mine site on foot now. We can do the repair on the baby's palate and then Billy can take us out again in the one day hopefully. I might get Tom to come up with Michael assuming that he can get away. I think the experience will be good for Tom and he can make sure Michael gets here OK, plus Tom should feel the strength of the Land, which we may need."

At a sound behind me I realized that Ngaire and Jem had joined us when Ty broke off suddenly. Turning to them, I watched as Jem's delight grew and he scrambled towards Sean.

"Hiya there little man," Sean greeted him pleased.

"I got the bat an' ball." The lad said happily. "Thanks."

"Me...! Don't thank me... it was Andrews idea when I told him how much you liked to play. I just helped him pick it out."

"Yeah well thanks anyway, mum said I should thank you. Anyway Tango likes it too though he doesn't share much."

After greeting the men, Ngaire busied herself organizing a simple one pot meal while Taipan acquainted himself with Jem, asking him about his home, including Ngaire in the conversation, we settled around the sheltered fire in companionable chatter after a short tropical downpour. The sudden dip of the sun as it dropped behind the horizon brought on the songs of the night, marking the beginning of the bush hunt for the nocturnal animals as we settled into the night around the camp.

Ngaire was at first quite reserved, with Taipan, but as the evening wore on she relaxed more and more. It was after dinner that she asked about the baby and what Ty had managed to assess and what was needed.

He went on to explain, conscious of her interest. "I have a mate, Michael, who should be able to help. I spoke to him before we headed up here and he was happy to come up and do something if I felt he'd be needed."

"Is he from your Community then?" she asked curious.

"No. He lives in Sydney, specialises in this sort of thing. I knew him at Uni, he isn't Indigenous but I don't think that'll be a problem. I've arranged for Billy to meet us and he will take us into the Land, given a day for his body to adjust we are hoping that he won't feel the transition, though Billy will be able to judge that. If there is a problem, then we will try and bring the child out, but stay as close as we can to the gorge. Michael can bring the equipment he needs, the operation shouldn't present too much of a problem and I wouldn't like to wait any longer. You were right, there is a risk to the child's hearing."

"I'm a bit worried about him, your friend... getting into the gorge. Will he cope?"

"Yeah I think so, he is quite capable and as I mentioned and I've already spoken to Billy about the difficulties, he will make a judgement call when they meet in a day or so. I'll get Tom to travel up with Michael; he can help with the gear and bring him up from Sydney. Michael was quite keen to help when I spoke to him and I have explained to him that it's an isolated community, though not quite everything." Ty grinned. "I would like you to assist him if you could though, gain some familiarity with the process, plus you can help the women. It would help the whole business. They're going to be a bit wary of Michael I think, particularly the women."

"Yes, of course. I have heard of Tom, that he's your younger brother isn't he? Jenna mentioned him once. It will be nice to meet him." Glancing then to me, Ngaire frowned. "Could you watch Jiemba for me if I'm to go with

Taipan, I don't want to take him into the Lands just yet? And we'll only be a day won't we?" she asked, her eyes travelling back to Ty seeking reassurance as he nodded.

"Yeah... shouldn't be a problem."

Ty added. "Sean can stay there too, with Tom we will be at our max. in the chopper, along with the gear and I would like Tom to come along. We can use his strengths in this business of getting Michael into the gorge."

Ngaire's expression spoke of her questions, but she wasn't quite sure if she should ask anything of Taipan. Her deference to him was a natural thing I realized, even from the point of view of the deference a nurse might show a doctor, quite aside from his community standing.

Taipan of course took it all in his stride and thought little off it, but I knew Ngaire would have questions for me later and I wondered if she would take the risk of asking while the others were away tomorrow.

The next day Sean and Taipan got away early leaving us to our plans. We had decided around the camp that Ngaire, Jem and I would make our way up onto the plateau and towards the Mimi's gorge where we could meet them. Ngaire had never used the land approach, but had travelled out over the plateau and would probably recognize many of the landmarks Taipan had explained to me. The trek should take us most of the day and as we set off to climb the escarpment from the wetlands and high onto the tablelands, once the others had left, we had to take a slow pace.

Leaving the camp still set up behind us we had decided to use it as a base on our return but it was a difficult and arduous climb up the escarpment, there were few access routes and as Jem tired I took him on my back which immediately attached Tango to my heels. We took with us a minimum of gear, carrying only Ngaire's travel pack which she managed and a few items I preferred to carry with me through the bush in my own small day pack. What we needed we could find around us and as we only planned on camping out for a short period it wasn't much of an issue.

Unable to make the distance we had planned; we set up a camp overnight in a valley on the tablelands that offered us some shelter. The nights were still quite warm once the afternoon storms had passed so bedding wasn't a problem we shared a ground sheet with Jem in between us under a tarp and so got a good night's rest.

By midday, the next day Ngaire recognized the landmarks of the gorge. It was well settled against the land line and it wasn't until you were practically upon the terse scar in the land that you realized the deep canyons of the gorge were before you.

From our vantage place high on the gorge wall, it looked an isolated and peaceful place as the three of us surveyed the Lands of the Mimi deep beneath our feet. Curious I squatted settling my hands into the earth to get the feel of the land and was surprised at the gentle hum I could feel as the Lands spoke to me. The Spirit strengths of the gorge held a strange song, though not one I didn't recognize as I assessed the ancient power of the land.

Stretching to my feet I looked around again, feeling Ngaires eyes on me, questioning me, a curiosity I ignored. "Over there I think. Let's see what that will be like as a camp." Pointing out the clustering face of rock perhaps ten minutes from where we stood along the cliffs dropping into the gorge, I knew it would offer us some shelter from the storms and together we made our way towards their shelter.

"The chopper usually lands just east of here, over there." Ngaire added, pointing out the general direction I nodded, seeing the open land which would be preferred. "We aren't far from the river here, maybe fifteen minutes to where you can get down into the gorge, this will be a good spot"

Jem trotted at my heel now looking for the promise of a ride, along with Tango who was never far from him, while Ngaire paced ahead. We were all tired and I didn't want to push the two of them any more than I had to. We had seen no sign of the others, though we hadn't expected to yet. Ngaire knew a few of the choppers preferred landing spots and she pointed out where a small creek cut down into the cliff face. I felt happier with our choice with the water being near.

A group of large boulders nearby, struggling to escape the grip of the earth offered a few good shelters and choosing one we set about organizing camp. We left Jem to construct the fire pit, knowing he would enjoy this important job, while I took on the collecting of larger pieces of wood which could be fed into the fire. Ngaire organized the bedding, softening the ground with an array of brush carefully chosen and positioned into a hollow over which she arranged the ground sheet.

We had sited the camp close enough to the small creek, taking advantage of the available fresh water which spilled down into the Gorge and as the evening began to settle in we relaxed around the small fire, very content with our choice tucked up into the overhang of the rock as we were.

"Tomorrow morning I think we will get some hunting in Jem... there should be some old man goanna around here, or maybe we could do some fishing." I promised, as we each enjoyed the simple pannikin of noodles Ngaire had prepared.

Jem looked up happily. "Can I catch him, the old man goanna?"

It was a teasing question I knew, and I smiled at the challenge. "Well let's see who gets him first."

The relationship between Jem and I had slipped easily into one of intermittent parenting though very occasionally he would break off and use his Mum to challenge me. Ngaire and I had spoken a great deal about this in the last days while we had walked. I appreciated how much leeway she was giving me and this more than anything persuaded me that she wanted me to adapt to the parenting role. Surprisingly it was something I was enjoying.

I liked the feel of this little family and I enjoyed the companionship and presence of Ngaire, I had even begun to feel accepted by Tango. I felt too that I had somehow found myself a family. It was one I had unwittingly collected and as I watched Ngaire and Jem tease each other and chatter around the fire I knew this was somewhere that I really wanted to be.

Part of me wanted to prove to her that I could do it, that I could earn my place as the man in her life. I could provide her and Jem with a life that they would enjoy, which could be comfortable and loving. It would be a life which I knew I too would be very happy with and for the first time I thought about just what it was I wanted.

I realized then that I was moving towards a reality that I had nurtured in the back of my mind for quite a while now and having found Ngaire I knew she was part of that picture. This woman I had chosen, now I could only hope that she had chosen me. I felt a strange possessiveness that I had never experienced before almost as though she was the other half of me, together we made a whole which completed me and I wanted the warm comfort that brought more than anything else in the world.

There were of course a million small problems we would have to deal with, the least of which was that we lived three thousand kilometres apart. Then again, I loved this land. I could feel it in my body, the way it embraced and welcomed me. Could I live here I wondered, find my place here amongst her family, her people. There was no reason why I couldn't spread my time between Katherine and the Community, no reason but finding a way to do so.

Perhaps it was time I spoke to her about it. Would it be something that she would be happy to accept I wondered, it was this thought that kept turning over in my mind throughout the night. With Jem snuggled in safely between us and Tango curled up at Ngaire's feet I wondered how I could go about approaching these questions. What would she say? How would she take such a proposition? It was with those questions uppermost in my thoughts that I let the night claim me.

The sounds of the distant thunder disturbed me and while I woke to the brilliant starlit night overhead, I could see the promise of the lightning and hear the roll of thunder off in the distance beyond where I knew the escarpment lay. Quietly I watched it, realizing that the storm wasn't headed our way but was feeding the low lands well to the south west, but the dance of the light and sound in the distant sky was something which was hard to draw my eyes away from. It dominated the landscape completely.

Carefully I eased myself up to better watch the spectacle, careful of Jem's tiny body curled against mine as he slept between his mum and I and tucking the light throw around him gently, I left the both of them sleeping as I decided to take the time to enjoy the night display of nature's power in the skies.

The camp fire was a bowl of grey ash and ember but it took little time to stir it to life as the sound of the distant thunder rolled around us. I loved this time, this noise, that was a promise of renewing the land. It was like talking to the Spirits somehow and the sheer energy which danced in the black skies held me captive, electrifying the air around me, it felt breathless. Life itself felt vivid, as bright as the brilliant display sweeping the sky off to the west.

I don't know how long it was that I sat by the fire, absorbed totally in the dance of lightning but when Ngaire seated herself quietly at my side I was surprised from my reverie.

"I love the storms in this season," she said softly, dragging my mind from its wanderings.

"Yeah, great isn't it. I hope I didn't wake you?"

"No. Tango is restless, his movements woke me."

Glancing over towards where the dog slept, I realized that the mutt was now curled carefully into Jiemba's back taking my own spot beside the child while Jem slept on blissfully. For some reason I found it funny and grinning I nodded.

"I think I have lost my spot. Ousted by a mutt... charming." I teased her.

Ngaire's soft chuckle soothed me but when she leant in towards my shoulder, resting her head there I fought the desire to take her into my arms, knowing we would probably disturb the sleeping duo who were barely a footfall from where we sat. Instead I slipped one arm around her and settled to watch the dance in the sky.

"Could you ever leave this do you think?" I questioned softly, conscious of the carriage of our voices.

Quiet, she considered the question. "I guess it depends on what for."

That bought a smile to my lips. She hadn't said no, could I persuade her I wondered. "It would mean you would have to move Jiemba away from his family. You would need to find a new job I guess, maybe take on some study if you like?"

Ngaire moved to gather my eyes steadily. "Just what are you asking Andrew?"

Drawing a breath, under the onslaught of her eyes I wondered that myself. "I'm not sure." Smiling at my own lack of understanding I went on. "Maybe I am asking you to come and live with me. In Brisbane I mean, though..." I shook my head uncertain myself, "It wouldn't be exactly that. I guess it would be living with Jenna really and I know she would love that. She gets lonely since Aine moved back to the Community and I am only there for a week at a time, then I am gone often for a month or more. Sean stays there with her but he prefers to be at the Community but doesn't like to leave her on her own..."

Her finger across my lips stopped me. "I can't afford to move Andrew," she said simply. "A lot of my work is voluntary and without the support of my family I could not afford..."

"No. I'm not asking you to do it on your own. Ngaire, I would look after you, and Jem, and Tango," adding the dog as a quick afterthought. "I have a room at Jenna's but I am sure I could arrange to take over the larger of the rooms which Ty and Aine rarely use and Jem can have my old room. I am sure Jenna would love the idea. I can ask if you like and as for moving, let me take care of that. We can just get some company in and deal with it. I want to do this Babe, seriously."

Tortured somewhat I watched as she chewed her lip and then she smiled. "Let me think about it," she promised softly. "I need to think about it, it's a big move and besides... there are things we really need to talk about."

"What things? I know it will take time to adjust, we have to settle Jem but it can be done."

Ngaire agreed, but I could see the doubt in her eyes. "You may not like being a Dad, the responsibility. It's a lot Andrew... what then?"

This I had not expected. I considered it for a while, the dancing light of the skies still overhead in a mystic display. Then I shrugged. "What bloke knows the answer to that? It's life, it happens." Turning back to her I smiled, trying to instil a confidence I knew I didn't feel. "Babe it just happens, we have families. I don't know how good a dad I will be but I know I enjoy having Jem around. An' I am sure sometimes he will drive me crazy but I seriously don't know. Tell me if you think I am being unreasonable. I'll listen to you,

I know that much. You more than anyone will know what Jem will accept."

The words sat between us for an age and then Ngaire stood slowly and held out her hand, I answered the invitation in her eyes with one of my own as I followed her movement, collecting her outstretched hand in mine as I joined her. I wasn't sure what she had in mind but as we moved away from the campfire I understood that she didn't wish to wake Jem.

The night was dark, though still crystal clear away from the small glow of the campfire. I hoped, just hoped I knew what her intent was. We moved towards the gorge, towards the small stream which presented a pleasant idea, it was after all still something of a sultry night. As alive as the air was with lightning, it was also warm and still. We were far enough away from the storm to not feel the brunt of any wind shift. Here on the tablelands we seemed to be almost on a platform built for viewing and the view was even more brilliant away from the small fire.

"I thought we could talk more freely away from the campfire, we really need to talk." Ngaire said dropping to the ground carefully, hopeful that I would join her. I did.

"We do? OK. But I know what I would rather do?" I suggested, as I moved to claim her lips, stretching her subtle body back against the sandy earth as she understood my meaning and giggled at the promise between us. It was a delicious promise fed by the electric feel of the air about us and the expanse of the land immeasurable between us and the rest of the world. It seemed we were all that mattered, all that counted and it was exhilarating.

Ngaire giggled again as my lips released hers, taking on a gentle tour of her skin. "This isn't quite the talking I had in mind," she teased me, though I didn't hear hesitancy in her voice and that fired my need of her. It was the promise of a seduction perhaps. A gentle game that was to be ours.

Quickly we moved to an intimacy which I had missed, had craved and the taste of her skin beneath my lips was a welcome meal in a wash of senses and power. I wanted to consume her, own her in a way that drove me crazy. Her body responded so sweetly to my touch, the small breathless sounds which tempered the air between us as I sought ways to make her senses, her body sing with mine. I gloried in every breathless gasp she made, each soft moan, as my mouth and hands tormented her gently.

Then unable to sustain the tension between us I moved over her quickly, wanting to claim her, bring us to the climax our bodies needed and as I brought her to me my hands dug deep into the earth beneath us, drawing the power I craved.

The strength I felt sweep through me was exhilarating and exhausting in the same way my thrusts became more urgent, too quickly urgent but I knew she was with me and as much as I wanted to take her into my arms, crush her to my body. I knew she too needed the release our bodies were driving towards so I needed to wait for the peak of our passion. Then it came, swift and heated as we shuddered, lost in our own ecstasy, individual, but sharing that which bound us together in that moment.

It was then that I noticed it, as the aftermath of the heat swept through my body, holding me helpless. I felt it, the heat about my hands, clinging to my fingers and as I emerged from my helplessness I struggled to contain the heated fluid that was light gathering round my fingers.

Ngaire had wrapped her arms around my chest and across my back as I lay over her, but now I could feel the loosening of her hold and the dance of her hands on my back, as in her own exhaustion she settled back slowly to feel the sweet afterglow of our passion.

There was nothing I could do. This wasn't going to go away and though the light dimmed as I separated my hands from the ground the fluid light clung to my fingers.

"Close your eyes." I begged breathless as she emerged from her own stupor.

"What?"

"Your eyes, close them." I demanded again softly.

"Andrew? What on earth..." then she saw it, saw the strange glow of light, coming not from the skies or the storm in the distance but gathering now much closer to us. Surprised she struggled beneath me, struggled to move my weight from over her and I had to move, shift my weight for fear of crushing her.

I moved my hands swiftly as I swung to sit up, not wanting her to focus but I knew, I understood the liquid light would stay with my fingers as I tried to gain balance, I shifted the light away from her amazed glance.

"What is it?" she demanded tersely as I swung my hands, putting my body between her and the sight I knew she wouldn't understand.

The liquid light clung to my fingers and I knew it wouldn't go, wouldn't shift until I dealt with it. "Don't be scared, it won't hurt you, just let me deal with it," I said quickly. I was impatient with her question, angry with myself and yet amazed that I had drawn this up at this time. I found my balance and knowing what to do I slowly bought my hands together, bringing some control to the fluid light like molasses on my fingers.

Ngaire shifted, better to see the spectacle, in a glance I could see she wasn't afraid, but fascinated. I felt relief wash over me as my hands found their position forming the union of light as I cupped my fingers together. I gathered strength from this union, the earth lights took their natural orbital form and then took on the aspect from liquid to air leaving the bind of my cupped fingers, the transition bringing the blinding glow of a orb which wanted its freedom from my fingers.

I released it when it took its form, letting it loose into the night and as I felt the weight of its knowledge within me, it stilled, hovering above us barely a hand-stretch away, waiting for me.

Then I turned to her. "Don't be afraid, it can't hurt you."

"What is it?" she demanded, fascinated. "Andrew... I have never seen it?"

"It's an Earth light, it's harmless. I use it to see where I can't go. It won't hurt you."

"But why... what is it doing here?" she demanded slightly breathless with amazement.

I gave a small chuckle. "Babe I don't know. It never comes to me unless I call it up but this time...I don't know... it came. It must be the land about us, the storm maybe. I know the storms enrich it but..." Shaking my head I glanced up at the waiting light, amazed that it had been drawn from the earth so easily.

"What does it do?" she asked amazed, "I mean does it just sit there, light up the dark or something?"

"No. No... it isn't that simple, it's connected to me. I can command it and it will seek out what I want to know."

"You can? I mean, how?" she asked fascinated.

I drew a breath, not sure how to explain what it was, this strange reality that was mine. "It's like... a minds eye. Perhaps that is the best way to explain it. Part of a gift I have is to draw it from the earth and have it complete a task, or a need. It's like... umm... an extension of me, like a tool in a way, one that I can command as though it's part of me. I can sense and see what it experiences. It's actually a lot of fun, but it isn't something I do for entertainment. It's a gift of Shaman Lore"

"I've never heard of such a thing, even amongst Shaman," she said softly.

"Yes you have, I am sure. They call it a Min Min light. At least that is what I was told people have named it."

Amazed she looked over at me, her mouth open in surprise which made me chuckle. "Wow..." she added breathlessly. "What... it can't stay there? What are you going to do about it?"

"I can send it out..., Jem... I can have it check on the camp, Watch."

I slowly drew a breath as I had been taught, shutting out the world around me, I sent the light on its way in a thought and opened my eyes in the split second to see the light whip off on a path towards the camp. With such a short distance to go it stopped within our sight, hovering again. I closed my eyes, seeing in my mind's eye the camp beneath the light's glow.

Jem lay still asleep but Tango had woken and was watching, restless, growing more restless by the second. He wasn't sure what to do about the strange light which hovered above him. He knew it was my spirit, in the blazing orb but yet he knew I wasn't there.

"Jem is still sleeping," I said, then as I smiled and looked up to Ngaire's amazed glance. "But Tango doesn't like the light. I will have to recall it before he begins to bark and wake Jem." Shutting my eyes, blocking out the distraction of her expression I recalled the Min Min light to me, opening my eyes in time for its arrival as it hovered once more nearby.

Ngaire laughed suddenly, "What a handy little beast that is."

"Yeah... it has its uses."

"But how long does it work for?"

"It will fade. It depends entirely on how strong it is. It feeds... draws its power from the earth around it and any lightning in the air. This one seems particularly strong," I added, feeling its strength about me. "It will fade eventually, and then vanish entirely."

"Wow... I can think of a million uses for it, least of which is a babysitter." Her grin made me laugh and then a thought occurred to me.

"Hang on..." I said quietly as I closed my eyes, blocking out the distraction of Ngaire at my side, her body still shimmering in the moonlight and the light cast from the Min Min glistening on the fine layer of moisture on her skin. It took a moment to empty my mind and then I cast the thought.

Opening my eyes I watched as the Min Min took off again, vanishing quickly into the night leaving barely a tail for our eyes to follow.

"Where's it gone?" Ngaire demanded.

Smiling I moved, once more towards her. My hand found the warmth of her skin at the nape of her neck while I leant in to kiss her, unable to resist the temptation she offered. The distraction was too sweet.

"I've sent it to find the others, it won't be back, it's too big a task but I will know when it has found them, if it does so before it dies."

"The others? You mean Sean and Taipan?"

"Mmm..." Settling her into my arms, I began once more to enjoy the promise between us. "They will be here soon, today or tomorrow and life will become complicated again," I said by way of a promise. "Let's just enjoy this moment hey?"

"Andrew?" she whispered becoming breathless.

"Hmm...?"

"That light, the Min Min. You aren't going to do that again are you?"

I chuckled against her skin, finding a punishing humour in the question. "No," I answered still amused. "I'll keep my hands out of the ground, I promise. I can think of other ways to keep them busy." My promise, suggested ways which my fingers followed. Hearing Ngaire's small quickly drawn breath was delightful and I revelled in her light giggle.

"Don't worry Honey. Now I know you can do this to me, I won't let you get away with it again," I said against her skin, laughing at my own loss of control as I once more became lost to the pleasure between us.

When I woke, it was well past the dawn and for a moment I just lay there looking over at the campfire where she was working. Both Ngaire and Jem were up and about the camp careful to be quiet and not disturb me, something which bought a contented smile to my lips. I was unused to others going out of their way to allow me the luxury of sound sleep and I liked it.

Simply watching her work about the camp fire also bought me a certain contentment. I found it difficult to believe she was my woman, difficult to understand that she chose so easily to be with me. I wasn't an easy person to love, I was too set in my ways, too ignorant of her needs and yet she fulfilled me. I would need to take more care of her I decided, make her realize how much she was coming to mean to me.

I couldn't resist a long stretch to welcome the morning, tightening most every muscle in my body. It was a delicious luxury, then enjoying the ease which followed I propped my head up to better watch her.

"Morning," she said softly

I grinned, remembering the night hours. "Morning yourself," I greeted her. "You been up and about long?"

Climbing off the bush bed, I once more stretched and then moved slowly over to join her, not wanting to disturb the sweetness of the morning.

"Only a few hours," she answered laughing at me in her own way.

"Hmmm... The Min Min kept my thoughts busy most of the night," I added by way of explanation for my apparent laziness.

Surprised she looked up at me. "How does that work?"

I shrugged. "It's like going on a journey, like a dream I guess. I see its path, where it ventures and I can still it and watch what goes on around me. Command it I guess, to go where I want it to explore. Not unlike you would do in the path of a dream."

Moving up behind her, I caught her within the circle of my arms and nuzzled her neck, kissing her lightly, greeting the day with a salute to the pleasures of the night we had shared. Then, I considered what had concerned me, distracted me, for a moment in the night hours.

"How are you this morning?"

"Fine... that's an odd question?"

"Mmmm... I am going to have to stop playing Russian roulette with our love life Babe."

Still, as she snuggled into the warmth of my arms wrapped about her I could feel her frown in her movement or lack of it. "How do you mean?" She asked softly.

"I mean... if I don't start being more careful or taking more care then we're gunna end up pregnant," I answered chuckling. "I have plenty of condom's I just keep forgetting to use them." I explained grinning.

I was surprised at her sudden stillness, and then she looked up at me, her expression indefinable. "Too late," she said softly.

Frowning, at first I thought what an odd answer and then it struck me. Surprised I suddenly released her trying to better read the thoughts in her eyes, her expression.

"It's too late Andrew. I'm already pregnant. I tried to tell you a couple of times but..."

I felt the blood drain from my face as my skin went cold, then flushed with a sudden heat and my heart stopped in that moment. "You're pregnant?" I asked inanely, it had to be the stupidest thing I had ever said.

Ngaire nodded, it was a simple answer which I understood in the confusion of my thoughts.

"Are you sure?"

Again she nodded.

I didn't know what to say. I just shook my head in denial of what I was hearing. My heart beat stepped up in panic while my mind simply went blank. That it wasn't possible kept going through my mind but I knew it was, it was very possible. I knew I had been careless but I never actually imagined there would be consequences. That they would be real?

Ngaire turned back to the fire quietly... too quietly before she went on. "I can raise the baby on my own Andrew. I'm prepared for that, it would be nice if you were involved but it's a choice you have to make."

"No!" Still somewhat stunned, unable to function properly I could think of little else to say. "No, this is our child. It's something we both have to deal with, I... I understand that." Struggling to bring the loose threads in my thoughts together I grabbed at any thought. "You will need to move to the East Coast, this is too far away."

"I haven't made that decision. I don't know if that is right for me," she protested after a moment. Once more a simple statement only this time it annoyed me for some reason and once more my blood ran oddly cold.

I sat heavily onto the log nearby, I needed to sit, needed to think but that wasn't easy and I struggled with it. "You're cutting me out of his life?"

That annoyed her, as much as it annoyed me. "No, I just haven't made up my mind. It's a big move away from my family, my friends. Away from what is my life here, I do have a life here Andrew and you want me to leave all that without any thought. And besides, it may not be a he! We don't know that yet."

This wasn't going well I suddenly realised. Why was I arguing, it was the last thing I wanted to do and as Jem burst into the camp with Tango on his heels he shattered my stupor as he demanded my attention.

"Are we going hunting now? I saw a wallaby, it wasn't very big but I bet we could catch it."

Seeing him, made me realise Jem was going to be a part of my family I drew a deep steadying breath as I struggled to take a grip on the day. I searched for a response, dragging my mind from what consumed it. "Yeah sure, though maybe we should go fishing, we won't need to walk so far. Sean and Ty should be here in a few hours, they aren't far away and we need to catch enough for everyone."

I climbed to my feet, knowing I needed to prepare the gear, I needed to move, to get my thoughts in order. "Can you give us a minute Jem, your Mum and I are just talking," I added, realizing suddenly also that there were things I hadn't said that needed to be said.

For a moment I just stood there in shock, watching the boy scoot off with a careless word of acknowledgement. I needed to say something but I was at a loss to know what. I needed time, time to wrap my head around this.

"Can we talk about this later? My head is all over the place. I don't want to argue with you... I don't know what I want actually. I can't think straight."

"Yeah sure," she answered almost carelessly. It was the careless tone that also shattered my inertia.

Stepping towards her I reached to bring her around to face me but instead I drew her into my arms, I needed to feel her close to me and as she too moved to shelter against my chest I held her tight, wrapping my arms around her a flood of emotion gripping me, washing through me.

"I'm sorry Babe," I said softly into her ear. "I'm being a pig. I don't want to argue, it's just the shock and all, give me some time to get used to the idea OK."

Her eyes were bright, too bright and I realized how much I may have hurt her. That was the last thing I wanted to do and now I wasn't even sure how to deal with that.

"I know. I knew it would be a shock, I just didn't know how to tell you."

Pulling her back into the shelter of my arms, I held her for a precious moment. "I think I like the idea?" I added amazed. I realised it was true as I said the words. "Just give me a bit of time and then we can talk about it again, forget what I have said. Well more how I have said it," I clarified. "We can work it out OK."

Ngaire nodded her head and rewarded me with the smallest of uncertain smiles as I continued.

"Well I had better get this kid sorted, if we are gunna eat tonight." Then I released her slowly.

"You'll make a good dad," Ngaire added.

"God I am glad you think so. The whole idea is bit of a bloody shock!"

To hear her chuckle felt like a reprieve, one I was intensely grateful for as I slowly set about organizing the lines and tackle. Fishing would at least give me time to work this out in my head, before I blew it again with Ngaire. I needed time, needed it badly before I opened my mouth again and well and truly put my foot in it.

THE ADVENTURE OF YOUTH

Tom:

The view from the small plane that had bought us from Darwin to the old mining camp had been brilliant, but this chopper was just the best. The land rolled beneath our feet offering huge expanses of wilderness, great lakes of shallow water and occasionally we would fly over small herds of buffalo and mobs of fleeing roo as they raced across the land. I couldn't take my eyes from the landscape. The few roads which carved their way through the bush were like veins, raw and vivid but it was the lack of people, the apparent complete absence of the mark of man which enthralled me. The contrast between the cities and this ancient landscape couldn't have been more defined.

Even Mike beside me was awe struck. He hadn't ventured into the outback before at all while at least I had some experience of it over the last few years. I had spent time with my brothers Ty and Sean as well as with Denis and his Dad John, up on the Tablelands of the Far North Coast and in the Channel Country. I understood in part the experience of the bush, the risks and the timelessness of the wilderness.

Mike however, now sitting at my side, was a city boy. Sydney was his stomping ground and when I had met up with him yesterday he had explained that he was looking forward to his first experience of the Northern Territory. For a moment I had wondered just what it was he was about to experience and how much he would realize was happening about him.

Though Ty's friend, Mike wasn't a Shaman, he just seemed like an ordinary guy but with learning, and knowledge well beyond my own, that was for sure. He had mentioned he had a practice in Sydney and that he mostly looked after kids, this was why he was sitting in the snug seat beside me as we made our way out over the wilderness below. I still wasn't sure why I had earned this seat, it had something to do with the Mimi People I knew. Perhaps because of John's links with the Mimi and my training which John was so much part of... just perhaps, this was why I was invited along. However although I had only heard some of the stories from the song-men, John had helped me with my Dreaming and his knowledge was now what I tried to recall. That we should visit the Mimi Lands when I had been with him, or any of their communities, had never even been suggested. I had thought it wasn't even a possibility but now Ty had said it was and I was more than a little amazed at this. I didn't see how it was possible for Ty to take me and not John, when John was a Featherfoot. I couldn't get my head around it..

Taipan had arranged it all, it was great to just get on the plane and have it take me to where ever it was I was headed. I'd been on a few planes in the last twenty four hours. The first was from Coffs Harbour to Sydney, then Sydney to Darwin where we had met up with Ty and Sean, who had been waiting for us at the airport.

The small plane out of Darwin was nothing compared to this. The chopper offered us so much more manoeuvrability and the view as we had flown up over the escarpment had been something else again.

It had all been so simple and I wondered how much Aine had been part of the arrangements. I knew she had spent a couple of hours on the internet at mum's and the phone calls had been fast and furious, but she was happy about the arrangements and between mum and Aine I had been on my way to Sydney to meet Mike before I had the chance to fully understand what it was I was supposed to do.

I knew that my eldest brother had something in mind I had no doubt but I wasn't quite sure what it was, nor was I about to complain. This was an adventure and I was keen to squeeze every ounce out of it that I could. A week off school offered its own rewards and I knew my mates would be wondering where I'd got to. Stuff like this just added to my reputation. I never really understood why girls found this stuff mysterious, after all they had their own mysteries to worry about, but it was fun avoiding their questions. The business of Shaman, even those still learning was no one else's business.

This chopper ride was just the last thing I had been expecting when I met the pilot Billy Black; I knew there was something the matter. It was the measure of the way he had looked at me, as though he was assessing me, I knew he had something to do with whatever it was that was going on. It was a worry the way he kept meeting my eyes in a silent question when I wasn't sure what the question was?

There was something about the way Billy Black had greeted Mike too, something that wasn't going well, I could see Ty had also noticed it. His look was almost quizzical at times though he had been friendly enough, even pleased to be catching up with his mate from Uni. Though something wasn't right and I wondered what it was.

I knew Mike was here on some medical thing, a job he had to do, something about an operation some kid needed which was why I was here as well it seemed. I had thought it might have been to tote gear. I may be younger than my brothers but I was solid, which gave me a look of more years than I had marked up, which was always handy at my age. Hopefully the only thing I had inherited from my Dad was my solid build..., well that and my Dreaming skills. I had been expecting to hike into the bush with gear but when it had been obvious we were boarding the chopper I knew there was more to it.

Sean had said something about Billy, but I had missed most of it, aside from what he had said earlier about going into the Lands of the Mimi. I would have to get Sean aside and find out about that. It was after all one place John had said he wouldn't take us, Denis and I, when I had first learnt of the Mimi people around the camp fire and I had asked if we could visit them. I had been surprised at John's reaction to that suggestion and even my mate Denis had scoffed at the idea.

Billy had something to do with the Mimi and he had the look of a Shaman about him. The way he had read me when we had been introduced which made me think he knew stuff. He reminded me of John, Denis's dad. I wasn't sure if I'd heard right though when Sean had said he was of the Mimi people; it didn't make sense with what I knew of them. I was sure John had said they were a Spirit people and yet it would seem that this wasn't the case. The only Mimi I had ever experienced where definitely in the Spirit World, yet Billy was certainly of our world. It wasn't making sense.

Thinking of Denis, I wondered what he'd make of this and in part I couldn't wait to tell him about it. Denis was like me, we were learning and I could see now on this trip, I was going to be on a learning curve which also could explain why Ty had arranged for me to come along. This time it would be with both my brothers, it seemed a long time since I had been walking with both of them.

My mind flipped to the first walkabout I had taken with Sean and Taipan. It seemed a world away now. My life had changed since then and thinking about it I couldn't believe how much it had changed. I no longer felt that I was a child, or even growing up from a boy to a man. I felt like I was a man, and at seventeen, nearly eighteen, I had no reason to think otherwise. I knew both Sean and Taipan would argue the point.

Ty still considered me a trial I knew, and that made me grin. There was something about annoying him that appealed to me, the same appeal that annoying Sean had, though Sean and I had a smoother relationship now. I could still annoy him but I was kinder about it of late, after all he had Jen to deal with now and she was enough to give him grey hairs at times.

Ty I wouldn't test in the same way. The consequences of doing so weren't something I wanted but I could stretch the point occasionally. Aine often found it funny the way I could wind Ty up, but he always came through and usually I learnt something, which was half the reason why I did it, though I don't know if Taipan had figured that out.

I had a lot of respect for my brothers, particularly Taipan. When I thought about it they were perhaps the men I most respected in my life. That I might be like them one day was what inspired me. I knew I had a long way to go yet and they were a hard act to follow too.

When the chopper banked suddenly, the first thing I did was search for the camp below. We seemed to be hovering over some narrow Gorge, like a scar in the land and I hoped Billy wasn't planning on landing inside the gorge. There were a few wider points, but it looked too narrow to safely manoeuvre through.

Then I saw it, the smoke from the small camp. Andrew was there and so was someone else, though I had no idea who she was. Maybe this was the girl there'd been talk of for some time, I had heard Jenna mention her a few times. Actually she wasn't unlike Jen and I knew Jen considered her a sister. She was maybe more solid in build, not bad looking, I thought as we settled to land. I knew Andrew was keen on her however, so there was no way I was going to get in his line of fire. Andrew and I were great friends and he had bailed me out of one or two scrapes in the past and kept it to himself. I wouldn't want to cross him or upset him, even if my life depended on it.

Billy bought the chopper down not far from the camp and began to wind the engine down as we all climbed out, grabbing for the gear that had been at our feet as the others came over to give us a hand.

"Hey... Good to see you made it before the storm," Andrew greeted us as he took hold of some of the gear and began to place it into a pile. His eyes glanced towards the distant angry skies which were threatening to engulf us. The humidity had hit us, it was like hitting a solid wall making me feel that all I wanted to do was to strip off and find a pool of water somewhere. It was worse than it had been in Darwin, though I wouldn't have thought it possible if anyone else had suggested this.

It didn't take long to off load the gear, then when Billy began to tie down the little chopper I knew he planned on staying. For some reason that made me extremely pleased. I liked him and would appreciate the opportunity to get to know him better. I had learnt over the years to look for the value of men in their eyes and face and I thought he was a man of considerable strength. The afternoon was growing late when we had finally settled and as I followed Andrew over with the last of the gear to where the camp had been set up against the rock, he called me over to introduce me to his woman.

"Tom, this is Ngaire and young Jem."

I nodded and smiled, taking a step towards the youngster but was immediately arrested by the low growl from the mutt at his heels. "An' that is Tango. He might let you closer later," Andrew added laughing as he turned away to greet the others.

Ngaire looked up, smiling also as Andrew turned back to the men, "We can put the gear over here in the shelter of the rock, it'll be drier I think. This storm isn't far off."

It didn't take long to sort us out, most important was the medical box and Mike took charge of that. Dinner was fish and some yams which someone had dug and I wondered who, though obviously Jem and Andrew had organized the fish. Jem was taking great pride in his achievement in catching that part of the dinner when the men praised him for it, I could see he was lapping it up.

Even Mike was impressed with the size of the catch, though he tended to take in more words than he put out. He was a strange sort of bloke, one of the quiet types who never let on what they were doing.

After dinner, once the storm had passed we sat around the fire listening and enjoying the companionship of the night Ty raised the issue of plans for tomorrow. It had been a good evening and although we were all content and growing sleepy after a full day, none of us wanted to retire before plans had been settled, aside from young Jem who had settled into a bush bed sheltered up against the rock some hours before.

Taipan deferred to Billy, his advice was obviously of prime consideration. It was as I listened that I realized he must be an Elder amongst the Mimi and it amazed me. Not only could I see him but I knew the others did, he was part of our world. In my experience the Mimi had always been a part of the Spirit World. How had this man become part of our world? Did they have many amongst them who could be part of both worlds I wondered?

"What are your thoughts Billy, in regards to tomorrow?"

Billy nodded; he had obviously been making his own assessments. "I'm thinking we will bring the baby out. There is a cave nearby which is cool. It will keep the flies away and it has the protection of the Dream Time Spirit."

Ty agreed, not questioning his assessment at all. "Then this is what we'll do. Mike, we can prepare the area. It will also mean Ngaire can assist you, as you know she has some nursing training."

Billy added. "The strongest amongst us are Andrew and Tom, I can guide them into the gorge tomorrow, but we will need to return with the child travelling by the Serpent's caves. It will be a difficult climb, I think that Andrew be best to carry the child. Perhaps Ngaire has a cloth to hold the little one, bind him to Andrew in the way of the women."

This afforded Billy some amusement, but his look was serious while Andrew instead looked confused.

Ngaire however smiled. "Yes, I have a long wrap which will work. It's simple Andrew," she said adding to his confusion. "I can show you later and the women will be able to help you as well."

"Why me? I don't know anything about babies!"

"Your Spirit's the strongest. You have the strength to protect the child," Billy answered simply. "In keeping him close to you, it will be safest for him. Tom also, will lend his strength. I can see that both of you are of the Land, Taipan did well to bring you."

"Billy understands who has the strength to move into the Lands, it's part of his sight," Taipan added then turning to Mike he continued. "It would be best to bring the baby here. The tribe has very strong beliefs about the risks of those entering the gorge and we don't wish to place you at risk. I hope you don't mind?"

"No. That's fine." Mike said, still a little confused. "...If we can find a suitable place, the cave?"

"It's well protected," Billy continued. "I can show you tomorrow at dawn, you can decide then. I think you'll find it's a good place."

The cave was ideal. Sheltered against a hill, perhaps a kilometre from where we were camped, it was at the edge of a small chasm amongst the trees and bushes which grew protected from the weather. As we inspected it early the following morning we realized that the only thing lacking was running water and as the men discussed the merits and problems it became obvious that this problem could easily be resolved

The cave had been used by the people in the past, the walls in part were decorated by hand stencils of ancient campers, but the predominant art work was of the serpent, winding its way along the roof of the cave. Within its depths the cave was cool and absent of the annoying flies which followed us endlessly outside. It was dark though and when I suggested a fire, Ty shook his head impatiently.

"We have a few good led lights that will work better, besides a fire will contaminate the air and destroy the art."

"Oh yeah..." I agreed grinning. "It was only a suggestion." After that I kept my mouth shut and let the others work out the details. Mike was fascinated with the ancient art and I knew he was somewhat disappointed not to be going into the gorge, however Ty had spoken at length to him about it, reassuring him that it would be best to take the path they had chosen which was to bring the baby to him. I could see that Mike had little inkling of Ty's true meaning. Mike was only worried about whether it was a convenient location and a suitable site.

By mid-morning Billy, Andrew and I were on our way and I was looking forward to getting down into the gorge. Little more had been said since the decision had been made that it would be Andrew and I who would accompany Billy. Once we were away from the camp, and clambering down a steep rocky bank a few kilometres from the camp into the deeply sheltered gorge I decided it was time I could chance a few more questions.

Billy was more forthcoming; he opened up a great deal as I questioned him about what he meant about the two of us being stronger. His answer was one of mutuality as though I should understand his meaning as a matter of course though I didn't tell him that a lot of this was new to me. It was only when Billy explained that he had a talent for feeling the spiritual strengths of men that I had any idea what he meant. I figured it was like my own sense of empathy in the feelings of others though it seemed he saw a man's strength in a coloured aura about them, as a matter of course while I was still learning to pay attention to these things. These talents didn't grow unless you paid attention to them.

"There's a warmth about you both which talks to the earth, that is what I can see. The Doctor, Mike... he can't enter the lands, he has no spirit link with the earth, so it's best the baby is brought to him. You and Andrew must not leave the side of the baby. You'll both need to be there when the Doctor works, me too. So the baby can borrow our strengths"

"What will happen if we leave?" I had to ask.

"The child will not be able to sustain the strength needed to survive outside the gorge, he is too young, his spirit, his presence will fade. The cave will help, but you must also stay and lend your strength to the little one. He needs to remain close to us as we can feed his strengths with our own and that will sustain him."

"This warmth you see...?" I began, curious.

Billy added. "Taipan has said you are a young Featherfoot but you're still in training. They have strong links with the Mimi, this is why you have their strength, it's perhaps a strength we share. But Andrew? I don't know." Billy's glance once more assessed Andrew, while Andrew shrugged.

"Perhaps it's the Land, I feel a link to this land." Andrew offered then smiling added. "It's caused a few problems, I draw the Koolrari lights, the Min Min lights of the earth come to me, it's my training, but I thought it was mostly in the Gulf country, not so it seems."

"You are a Shaman of the Serpent, but perhaps you have business with Namarrgon the lightning man, more so than you realize? It's often the way of the Shaman of the Serpent when they are in this land. Even though you are not a Banman of this land you still carry the strengths the land gives you. Perhaps it's that you belong here."

"Maybe, it was unexpected but I can feel the oneness about me Billy, I expect you are right. My histories and those of my fathers are chequered"

The water of Freezing Gorge was welcome after our trek but when we entered through the submerged cavern we were swept into the Mimi Lands by a current, it was as though we had entered a world apart from any other.

Waiting for us were children, it seemed like a dozen or more and as Billy led the way along a path which wound through the gorge, the kids followed us running ahead eagerly, I was amazed at how simple it had been to get here. Billy had mentioned the strings of beads he could use but it seemed neither Andrew or I needed them.

It seemed nothing complicated about it, though Ty had said that what would seem easy to me would be impossible for others and it wasn't the first time I had realized this.

Since my time in Cooktown where I first realized I could see the ghosts, or the Spirit Men, I had become accustomed to making judgements about those who I could see around me. I had learnt to ignore some people about me, mainly those who I suspected were not of my world.

I knew now that not everyone about me was of my world and that I could see the men who were of the Spirit World was something I was still learning to deal with.

The Spirit men or ghosts were worse in some places, more than others and I had learnt to block out a great deal and pay close attention to only certain things. I had come to consider this, the gift of mine, as something of a curse of the Featherfoot Lore.

John had shown me this peace and I was getting better at it. This was my path to my own sanity and sense of security in my world and it was the only way I could get through the day. But here, the light was in some way brilliant and the children were active and alive and for the first time I realized that I could see no shadows, no Spirit men seemed to live here.

There seemed to be no one that could be part of the Spirit world, none that were Spirit children and this reality fascinated me. It was like discovering a world of peace where no shadows lurked, no crossing of the worlds. The fabric of the Lands of the Mimi was clear of Spirits and Shadows and in some ways more a reality than my own world and the realization was daunting and inviting in one.

Moving up beside Andrew I asked in a low tone. "Can you feel it?"

"Feel what?"

"The clarity, the crispness of the gorge, it's like a reality that is more real somehow."

Andrew frowned, he knew of my ability to see the Spirits and he was someone I could talk to about it freely. He was part of my knowledge and he also had taught me a great deal about the ways of the Shaman.

"I feel a certain type of warmth in the Land, though it's a striking light. I don't know how to answer you Tom; we need to ask Taipan I think, if it worries you. Do you see any Spirit men or anything odd?"

"No; I can see nothing odd at all. Not even any spirit Shadows at all. It's all really normal. Maybe that might be best to talk to Ty. I guess it can wait."

But the clarity of the people around me, even the light in the air was peaceful. I knew we would be here only for a short time, time long enough to collect the baby, then we would need to return to the tablelands, but we would be back. We hoped to keep the child away for the shortest possible time and as such I wanted to take in as much as possible

When we reached the main camp we could see there had been preparation for our arrival, Billy indicated the quite substantial bush hut amongst the trees and it was towards that we headed.

The light babble of women's voices around us announced our arrival as we seemed to attract a lot of attention. It was a wise old bloke of some strength who emerged from the hut to greet us. His bearing marked him as an Elder and leader amongst his people and immediately I adopted a subservient position. I would in no way challenge this man I knew. I preferred it if he barely noticed me.

"Adoni," began Billy as he indicated our presence. "The Shaman have come for the child, is he ready?"

"Yes..." and glancing over at others just emerging from the hut behind the Elder I watched as three women moved out from the shelter. Only one met our eyes bravely and I realized what a trial this must be for them. "Toora, the child," the man who Billy had spoken to, said without preamble

Toora, undeniably the mother of the baby moved reluctantly towards Billy who carefully took the child, then turned to Andrew as he unwound the long, broad sash strung about his shoulders and chest. It was still damp from the water but would now provide a cool nest for the tiny baby in the growing heat. Indicating that the women should fashion the tie about Andrew to their own satisfaction, Billy encouraged them in their dialect which was completely alien to me.

The women though, understood and knowing what was needed soon had the child bound securely to Andrew's chest, supported by one of his arms. He looked anything but comfortable with the important burden he now held. It took him a moment to find a comfortable position for the baby against his chest and he looked ridiculously large against the tiny burden. Smiling at the awkward sight as he struggled to accommodate the child I stepped forward, I couldn't help but take the opportunity to check on the baby myself.

A young woman noticing my interest deferred to my curiosity, stepping back, encouraged me and I felt the thrill of being someone important to them. Cooing came naturally as I had often played with Debbie when she had been small. Thinking of my sister I slipped easily into the role now asked of me and grinning I acknowledged the delight of the women.

Billy talking to the women in their language seemed to be reassuring them. Andrew too began to relax with his small burden and tried to convey to the hovering Toora that he would take care with his special burden. He would return her precious bundle to her soon.

Billy turned to me, indicating the young woman at his side. "Loonea asks to accompany us, but I have said no. I think her interest is more in Andrew and you, than anything else," he added with amusement.

Amused myself at the thought I grinned across at the young woman, winking playfully much to her delight, though Billy looked perhaps less than amused at that. "Taipan would not be pleased of your interest," he warned me with a carefully considered tone. I thought it was something of a warning which I found odd despite the humour I could also see.

Surprised I shrugged, though I understood his rationale. We were after all guests in their land and I guess it was careless on my part but it was meant in more fun than seriousness, surely they understood that, I thought to myself. She was certainly an attractive woman, perhaps older than me with a mature body which excited my senses. It was the interest in her eyes that captured mine and this interest gave birth to an adventurous curiosity which I would have loved the time to feed. But my line of thought was cut short.

"Let's go." Billy said suddenly, interrupting my thoughts. "It will take us some time to make our way up onto the tablelands again."

Immediately he set off, his pace brisk from the start and we left the camp without any pause. It took only a moment to catch up with Andrew as we followed Billy along the path. He set a fast pace and as we travelled swiftly across the ground still following the river, I attempted to talk.

"What did you think of the girl, the hot one?" I asked interested.

After a short pause Andrew countered, "You have a lot of trouble keeping your mind on the job don't you?"

Surprised at his serious response I shrugged. It wasn't like Andrew to be so taciturn. "Well... yeah. Come on... you can't say you didn't notice her."

Still cradling the child in the sling about his chest you could see that he wasn't sure about leaving the light weight to the support of the cloth alone. Though itt seemed to me to be secure enough but Andrew fidgeted and again checked on the small mite nestled against his arm completely ignoring my question.

"Has it occurred to you that one thing leads to another? You won't be back this way again Tom, your interest can serve no good here."

"Geeze... it's just a comment. What has got into your shorts?"

"Nothing... just forget it," he answered shortly quickening his pace suddenly.

I had said something that had irritated him... that was for sure. Though for the life of me I couldn't see what it was that had got up his nose. It wasn't like we hadn't had similar conversations a thousand times.

For the next half hour both Billy and Andrew kept up a challenging pace so it was a relief to reach what looked to be the end of the gorge. Billy continued right up to the face of the cliff and I watched as he called to the Spirit of the rock, a chant in his own dialect though I was familiar with the purpose of the respect being accorded.

Asking permission to enter what I could see was a low cave, where the river flowed steadily, I realized that this was where we needed to pass. Satisfied that due respect had been paid I was somewhat relieved when he hauled a small craft from the hide near the edge of the bank. I had wondered how we would manage with the child if we were to make a crossing like the entrance we had made to the gorge. It wasn't as though we could simply go swimming with a baby but the sight of the canoe resolved the issue and it was a relief.

The light canoe, now heavy with our weight, followed the flow of the water and although we needed to take care as the ceiling swept close, the broad expanse of the cavernous lake drew us unexpectedly into a cavern lit softly by the light spilling over the edge of the lake.

That it was a place of the Spirit was undeniable, I could feel the life force of the guardian of the cave and frowning at Billy in the dim light, he must have sensed my question. The same question echoed in Andrew's eyes. Andrew had grown amazingly still, observant and oddly tense and I realized this had little to do with the bundle in his arm.

"It's the Unggur Serpent that guards the cave, the serpent of the Banman. She will allow no intruders, it's only the Shaman or Banman that may pass and ensure the passage of others. She keeps the Mimi people safe in their world. This is her place."

"I have been here before." Andrew said suddenly, he looked tensely at Billy, "I know this place, it's my Dreaming."

Billy nodded, understanding his words, though they confused me. I doubted Andrew had ever travelled this way.

"I can feel your strength, you know this place. It welcomes you; no harm will come to you, you who are a gatekeeper." Billy answered. As the steady flow swept us to the very edge of the pool, it seemed that we risked spilling down the rock face along with the cascade of water falling from the lake. Billy however stepped out onto a ledge and guiding the craft, he secured it, indicating we also should step out and make our way over to the very edge of the cavern.

There, in the dim light I could see a thick vine of a sort that offered a handhold; it followed the line down the dimly lit spillway.

"Take care, use the handhold as a guide and hold tight. There is an old man croc' at the bottom of the spill," he warned, as joining us Billy stepped ahead to lead the way.

It seemed to me that he placed absolute trust in what was a damp and slippery vine. Andrew stepped ahead of me, travelling between us as I followed, he was careful of his precious burden. He tested each foot fall on the slope of the spillway, keeping close to the wall where the best foot purchase seemed to be.

About two thirds of the way down I watched as Billy stepped onto what seemed to be an island of space which was clear ground in the surrounding bush and then he disappeared. It was a path that took you away from the spillway and following Andrew I was more than pleased to step onto surer ground and away from the water and the threat of the pool where the croc' was undoubtedly waiting for a lunch and the thought made my skin spike, it wasn't going to be me!

We were out, and ahead was a path that I was more than relieved to tread. The remainder of the journey seemed only a matter of time and soon we were arriving at the designated cave out on the plateau where the others waited.

Andrew was relieved to see Ngaire and I watched as she carefully helped him shed his burden of both cloth and baby.

"See, I can do this. I didn't drop him once," he told her, amusement in his words and while Ngaire smiled she was more than happy to unwrap the infant who immediately protested the loss of its cosy cocoon.

"There, there little one," she crooned, taking him through into the cave where we both followed conscious of Billy's warning to stay close by.

Inside the cave had been prepared and at our arrival it flooded suddenly with light from the two powerful led light torches which had been positioned beside a covered table. Mike waited, he wore a brilliant crisp light covering which I realized was a disposable gown, it looked incongruous against the setting of sand stone and rock and as Sean helped with fastening a mask about his face, Ngaire lay the tiny baby carefully on the table and began to prepare the child for the operation.

Watching the procedure was one of the most difficult things I had ever done and in the end I couldn't watch it anymore. Of necessity I stood back, as did Andrew, Sean and Billy while Ngaire had the task of managing the child. Mike worked quickly assisted by Taipan and for the first time I really appreciated the solid skills of my eldest brother. The procedure seemed endless but finally Mike stood back obviously happy with the outcome and as the others sprang to life, Ngaire once more wrapped the child against the coolness of the cave.

It was done and as Ngaire nursed the child Andrew and I hovered close by, conscious of the others who were headed into the fresh air outside. Now we only had to return the baby and once more I wondered what Billy had planned.

He wasted no time in organizing us; he was conscious that the baby was growing more fractious the longer he spent away from his mother. He carefully checked the child, as did Mike, then satisfied it was decided it was safe enough for us to return the child. With the baby still under the effects of a light local sedative, Ngaire and Billy helped wrap the child against Andrew's chest once more as he went through the plans on how to get back into the gorge.

"Make your way back to the cave of Unggur and the Serpent will allow you to pass through to the community. I need to take the Doctor to meet his flight before nightfall. Wait down in the gorge for me to return. Adoni will welcome your return and be glad of the opportunity to thank you. It will be too late for you to return tonight, I can bring you out tomorrow."

Andrew looked concerned though and as Ngaire finished tucking the somewhat restless child close against his chest he added, "It's a good hour to return to the gorge, I don't think the baby will settle for that long. Would it be possible for Ngaire to come also? I'm not sure I can manage a screaming baby and the climb up to the cave will be a difficult one."

Billy's concern was obvious but he considered the problem then nodded. "Yes, it might be a good thing. Ngaire can also advise Toora about the care of the baby and Andrew can lead the way into the gorge. Tom also is strong enough to pacify the Serpent; Ngaire has passed that way many times. But..."

Turning to Ngaire however he paused for a moment in reflection, "Your colour is not good girl. I will need to use the stones to help you in the Lands. Take care and go as slowly as you can, it will give your body more time to adjust."

Retrieving what looked to be strings of shiny beads, I watched confused as Billy wound them around her ankles and wrists, settling them carefully against her skin, I guessed it had something to do with the transition into the Lands of the Mimi. A transition for some reason Ngaire was going to have trouble with. So it was Andrew, Ngaire and I who set out with the baby a short time later, leaving Ty and Sean to see the others off and keep an eye on Jiemba. Jem wasn't at all put out by the absence of his mum. Having the full attention of Sean seemed to settle him and it was an excited kid, looking very much forward to a promised hunt with Sean who we left behind at the camp.

It was late in the afternoon when we reached the path to the spillway and with the passing of the afternoon storm it had held us up even more. The baby was becoming very unsettled and at one point Andrew had given the small package over to the care of Ngaire to calm him, but the baby was still restless so she decided that she would continue to carry the baby as we approached the rock slide where the water spilled from the gorge of the Mimi.

Andrew agreed readily, he would be better able to protect them both from accident unhampered by the constraints of the baby and he looked pleased to place the restless child in Ngaire's care. She was better able to sooth the baby, the gentle note in her voice being one that seemed to relax the little thing.

Carefully the small bundle was bound to Ngaire in the fashion she directed, Andrew who would lead the way in the climb up the slide, further secured Ngaire to himself using a long strip torn from her sash, then he went ahead. I helped her with her footing where I could, while I followed closely behind. It was a slow and difficult climb up the slippery spillway and seemed to take forever but Andrew set on a slow and sure pace upward, keeping close to Ngaire and often hovering over her and the baby leaving little for me to do but follow impatiently.

Pleased to finally reach the top we took a moment to rest in the cooling dampness of the cavern while Andrew retrieved the canoe from where it had been tied. The baby was unsettled and upset and was quickly growing more so. While Ngaire tried to calm the baby with small amounts of water it soon became apparent that the sooner we reached the Community, the better off we would be.

I can't describe the relief we felt when we moved out from beneath the cavern overhang to find his mother Toora and others of the Community waiting at the water's edge. Immediately Toora took the child and amazingly within minutes the baby was quiet, happy for a feed from his mum and the echoes of the infants wailing ceased as quickly as they had begun.

Andrew though was more concerned with Ngaire for some reason; he kept her close as they quietly followed the others as the last of the light began to dull the evening sky.

The Community camp was alive with people, the women had been preparing a meal and it became obvious that the men had been on a hunt. While Ngaire followed Toora and the other women to see the child settled, Andrew and I joined those around the camp pit.

Adoni was there with a few other Elders, there seemed to be more men about the camp than I had seen on our last visit, but then that had been such a quick visit and I guessed that the community had gathered together now at the end of the day.

It was Andrew who spoke to the others, as contented I listened quietly trying to pick up snippets of conversations and stories amongst the men and sometimes the women. Their dialect was very different to ours, though occasionally I could make out words. As the night moved on it became more difficult as the women began to chatter after the meal, particularly when Ngaire rejoined us bringing with her a posse of women who also settled about the fire and joined in.

The strain on her face Andrew noticed immediately and concerned he settled her at his side. One of the older women bought her something in a bowl which she drank readily, not having eaten much and soon Andrew had her resting beside him while the night moved steadily towards the quieter hours.

The circle of those gathering around the camp grew and I guessed many had come in from the huts scattered amongst small clearings along the path that we had noticed when we first arrived. It was interesting to hear the stories of the men and women, those which I could work out from the broken English many used, though I was pleased by the presence of Loonea, who seemed to stay close by. I found her English was better than the others, as was one of the men, Derain who was something of a song-man and good with stories so while our understanding of each other wasn't always clear it was certainly offering some entertainment.

Derain was older than me by some years, though he couldn't tell me exactly what his age was, it seemed it was something that was of little meaning to them. He had two children but what amazed me was that the eldest was several years old, which meant that he would have been my age, if not younger when the little girl had been born.

I soon realized, as he pointed out one of his wives, that she was much older than he and it appeared she had come to him from a brother who was no longer amongst the community. He had a much younger wife also who he spoke about and she had been his choice, they too had a child though neither were present at the camp.

I couldn't imagine what it would have been like to have such responsibilities and as I relayed my curiosity, Derain found my interest amusing. When he mentioned Jenna though I found I was drawn more into his world. It was when he realized Jenna was part of my life, as my elder brother's woman, that Derain became more animated. To him this seemed to mean that she also was part of my life and how fortunate I was to have such a woman as Jen in my world. Amazed at his outlook I could do little to dissuade him from his imaginings and when I tried to explain how Sean and I had nearly come to blows over Jen, he found it even more amusing.

Loonea too, was entertained by my outlook and as the night wore on she became friendlier, offering something I was beginning to understand, something which seemed in their world to be completely acceptable. As many wandered away from the camp fire others settled into the night, content to sleep by the comfort of the dying embers, she made it very clear that the invitation in her eyes was more than just a flirtation. When she stood inviting me, I followed her lead readily away from the company of others the thrill of possibilities inviting.

Entering the dark of the night afforded by the bush about us, she quietly led me towards the clear flow of water. Though older than me, my height and bulk gave me an advantage, I wondered if she knew or even guessed that there would be a number of years between us. Did she even care I wondered as she slowed her pace and held out her hand inviting me to move closer to her. For just a moment I wondered what Taipan would say and then I didn't give a damn. Surely he would understand my position, this woman was something else, and clearly this wasn't anything of an unusual step to take in her community.

I had always been the leader, initiating the play between girls and myself, but now this was different. Clearly this was something she was in control of and I found it oddly exciting that I had given over control of the situation to a woman. Making my own thoughts clear I pulled my t-shirt quickly over my head, tossed it aside, my eyes never leaving off questioning hers, hopeful that I hadn't read this wrong.

I didn't want to get it wrong; I didn't want to be offensive but a small smile which played around her mouth at my actions made it more than clear that this was something we were both wanting. I enjoyed the thrill that surged through my body as I reached for her. Sex was rarely as simple as this and it intrigued me that it could be this way.

Laughing softly she stepped back, her eyes scolding me as she turned away. It was a playful ploy and I found it amusing.

"Tooomtom..."

At first I froze at the familiarity of what had been my childhood name, the name my father had used, but her giggle then released me. The inflection she gave to my name was unusual, the single vowel sound drawled and I grinned at the differences. Most of the women wore little, this was the summer tropics and I had become accustomed to the women's bare breasts in this isolated community. Some wore their skirt knotted at their hips if they wore anything at all, while others tied the loose woven fabric gathered about their breasts, still others would knot the sarong like a dress at their shoulders. Loonea wore hers around her hips. She had a wholesome female shape and the way she wore her garment accentuated the tight curve of her waist and her full breasts. I had found her delightfully distracting throughout the evening, but now, I just wanted to feel the warmth of her skin in my hands.

Laughing I stepped up to her grabbed her arm and pulled her to me. My strength was much greater than hers and her quite playful attempts at resisting me were a game, the interest in her eyes was my invitation. I was growing impatient; I just wanted to kiss her soundly for the now, though my body had other ideas and it was pretty apparent.

As her lips met mine I felt immediately the promise beneath my hands and it fired my body. She could use her lips in a way I had not felt before; my own kiss seemed almost childish so I let her lead. I learnt quickly and the response of my body was immediate as her lips met mine and my fingers trailed down her body.

The heat of her against me was almost burning, but slipping my arms around her I pulled her closer into me, crushing her as she laughed when my hands explored her body. Our lips released each other then mine dropped restlessly against the soft skin of her neck and shoulder. It was delicious, we needed no words. This was about a driven passion, there was a need to release our bodies to their own demands and for the first time I understood a purely animal drive as it swept through me.

My hands impatiently sort out the warmth of the skin beneath her sarong then finding the touch of her naked thigh and buttocks I pulled her closer to me. I almost lifted her from the ground as she giggled and wrapped a leg around me. Sinking to my knees I took her with me laying her onto the sandy ground.

She was as impatient as I with my clothes but when she touched me, I couldn't help but groan at the fire her fingers brought. It was now, this moment that I felt my most inexperienced. But to find pleasure in her body was all consuming. I was driven as I felt the fullness of her breast in my hands. I brought these to my lips impatiently, hungry for her.

She knew what she was doing and she accommodated me despite being disappointed that I couldn't even slow the drive I felt to possess her. I tried, I struggled but she wasn't a placid lover and her own energy acting with mine made it impossible. I had never had a woman who was such a participant in sex and it fascinated me. She moved in a way that drove me on and made it impossible for me to have any control. So all too quickly the shudder of our passion gripped me and I surrendered myself to it.

While I lay spent over her I tried to gather my wits, she was still and patiently she waited though I wasn't sure why. Kissing her gently I eased my weight from her once my urgent need to thrust had settled and my power spent but her eyes watched me attentively in a way that I didn't understand. I could feel her attention, as well as see the curious light reflected in her eyes.

I needed a moment; time to recover after being so swiftly spent so I lay back onto the sandy ground drawing deep breaths as we rested. She turned to me and said something softly in her dialect, it was a question but I didn't know what she meant so I smiled while she waited.

After a time she reached for my hand, she took my fingers in her mouth surprising me, though it was a gentle kind of game. She then lay back and drew my fingers to the silky softness of her thighs, then her inner lips. With her hand over mine she directed my touch, explaining again something in her dialect. I frowned but her much smaller hand was insistent as it directed mine with a careful weight as she opened her legs to my touch and then I thought I understood. It was fascinating,

It wasn't over, I may have had my time but she wanted hers and she wasn't about to let me be selfish. I didn't understand much about women but I realized that perhaps I had always been a bit selfish. No girls had ever complained or even insisted on anything like this. In fact I had always thought that the girls I had been with had gained their satisfaction in my own and now, now I wondered if this really had been the case. Loonea was no girl, she was an experienced woman and she obviously knew what she wanted. I found myself wondering if all girls felt this way, could I really have been so ignorant.

I leant towards her fascinated as she continued directing my touch, her hand over mine, the pressure of her fingers over mine changed subtly until I could feel something I had not felt before. I had never bothered to explore the secrets of women, I knew the anatomy but this was different. I could feel subtle changes in the silken skin of her body and I could hear the subtle movement in the depth of her breathing as her body moved into my gentle touch, her excitement touched me and as she moved her hips into the growing pressure of my fingers, I realized an amazing truth. There was much more to this than I had ever previously thought, how could I have been so ignorant I wondered, the question echoing through my mind.

Suddenly I really wanted to be part of this, I wanted to participate and explore more of her mystery. Dropping my lips to her breast I teased her nipple hopeful of her attention, a distraction with my mouth, the pressure of my tongue exploring the hardened mound so to feel her move towards me with a soft groan was like music to my ears, it delighted me, calling to my body.

The small node beneath my fingers was swelling and gaining its own form and while I had found this small secret of a woman's body before, I had never really understood its place in a woman's sexuality. The silken skin around the small bud engorged, becoming harder and she suddenly pushed my fingers away from the mound and dipped her own into the pool of her body, drawing two of my fingers, deep into the warmth of her then dragging our fingers back over the engorged skin, we brought liquid fire to that little magical mound as she groaned again with shortened breaths. Then impatiently she pushed my fingers away, taking control over her own pleasure. She was obviously impatient with my inexperience.

I wanted this, I wanted so much to know what was happening and yet I didn't know how to become part of her pleasure without annoying her. It was a torrid path for her and I began to feel the strain of her body now warm and moist and my own body was answering her need. Then Loonea took control for both of us. Reaching for me, certain of her own need she ran her hand over my own swelling erection before she pushed me back and moved to mount me, straddling me, she left no part for me to play. She was warm; her body heated against mine, the slippery silk of her thighs engulfed me leaving me suddenly breathless as I gripped her thighs, not wanting her to move from me.

I had no control, she directed our dance but I reached up, cupping her breasts in my hands, running my thumbs over her nipples in a gentle tease at first, but then she pressed the weight of my hand to her breast and I understood that it wasn't gentleness she wanted. I tried to control the pressure I used on her breasts. It was the only way I could feel any control in any part of what was happening. Quickly though, I was again losing any control as my body coiled to embrace its release, it seemed every muscle tensed as the sexual heat burnt through me.

Then suddenly the dance changed and my body took hold of hers in an urgent way which I had never experienced before. Her body gripped the swelling of mine and the pleasure was almost excruciating as I used my strength, what strength I could gather to shift her weight beneath mine with an impatient movement. I was driven to have her beneath me, I was swamped by a passion that was overwhelming in its force and I could do nothing but give into it.

I was as impatient as she, it was an incredibly urgent drive that gripped us both. The release when it came knocked the breath from me and as the fire burnt through me it seemed to torch her as well. I had never known sex could be like this and I realized what I had felt before was a shadow, an undeniable pleasure but a shadow of something that was truly magnificent.

I collapsed into the heat of her exhaustion then slowly, carefully after a scarce moment to gather my wits, I rolled off her and to her side, as I was unable to support my own weight steadily. I knew I didn't want to crush her but it took time to control my breathing, gather my wits and deal with the reality of what had happened to me. My body was heated, sweated, sated and replete and now flooded with languid warmth that felt great. Loonea too was quiet and breathless but I felt her stretch beside me as she released the weight of my body and shifted the moisture pooling between our skins.

When she giggled suddenly, I turned to her curious. She was relaxed and the smile lit her eyes even in the heat of the night about us then she reached again for my fingers and lifting them to her lips, kissed them.

"Tooomtom, you learn... yes?"

I grinned back, at the strange use of my name, at the languid delight of my body and nodded, shifting her again against my side slowly helping to settle her. My thoughts drifted with her words. Yes I had learnt but it wasn't a lesson I was going to forget easily, in this moment I didn't want to let this woman go. I wanted to hold her close, smell the heated scent of her skin still mingling with the sweat of mine. Wrapping my body around hers I could feel the exhaustion of the night envelope me. The thrill of my discoveries tormented my thoughts, whispering a promise in my mind as I held this strange woman. She was a lover like no other I had known, I didn't want to let her go. It was like being held in the arms of the Earth Mother and it lulled me into a deep and peaceful sleep.

When the morning broke I became conscious of her heat, her subtle scent as we lay together. She was awake and looked to have been watching me for some time so I smiled, not sure if her curiosity was something I wanted to invite. I was afraid to measure my youth against her experience and in the scrutiny of the morning there might be revealed more than I wanted her to know.

"So young," she said softly, two small words that alarmed me immediately.

"No," My voice was gruff, and I cleared my throat impatiently, unsettled. Loonea however merely smiled as she turned still in my arms.

"Your women, not show you well."

Surprised, I wondered what she meant but curious I shifted about to better watch her, hopefully to see the meaning behind her words.

"You teach me well," I answered, smiling, trying to convey my pleasure. The pleasure I had found in her. "You're very beautiful," I added in a contented tone.

This seemed to please her though she moved to sit up, turning to watch me. "Today I show you well. You come?"

"Come? Where?"

"To a special place... in your world. A place for Banman to learn of their women."

Frowning I wondered what she meant but her smile disarmed my questions as she continued.

"The women have such a place. You will come, you will understand. We walk together."

"Today?"

Loonea nodded, "Now... we eat as we walk. First, wash."

It didn't take long to understand what she had meant. The cold water soon had me alert and Loonea was delightfully and playfully attentive to my needs. I think I would have followed her anywhere and as we headed out towards where I knew the Unggur's caves were I wondered what it was she planned.

She knew a lot about the land and true to her word she fed me along the way, encouraging me to eat the crisp water plants and bush fruits she found as we walked.

When we arrived at the low entrance to the spillway I hesitated. For the first time I thought of Andrew and Ngaire back at the community, they would probably be wondering where I was. Then I realized they would head out when Billy arrived back. I had every confidence that they would realize I would return to our main camp. I had every confidence that my delayed return would not be an issue. I was after all a secondary concern in this business. That I had found such a distraction, a woman such as Loonea would sit well with my brothers I was sure. Besides, it was no one's business but my own, what we had come for was finished with and this was time-out for the moment.

Loonea waited for me expectantly at the edge of where the water slipped beneath the rock-face and I realized she intended us to cross the Unggur Serpents Lake. For a moment I hesitated, if I took the canoe which I knew was banked nearby then Andrew and Ngaire would not be able to use it so instead, after scarcely a thought I stepped into the water.

I had watched Billy sing to the Serpent Spirit but I didn't know the song. That it was important I do this, I didn't doubt, so carefully I moved towards the overhang and begun to hum a tune I had heard Taipan sing and called to the Sprits asking my own permissions. I had learnt some of mum's tribal language so I thought perhaps if I used this to ask permission to pass, it would suffice. Language wasn't part of the Serpents Lore, it was merely something we used. It was the intent in our spirit that interested the Serpent and my intent was passive so I waited then when I was sure that peace was settled about me, I held out my hand to Loonea, expecting her to follow me.

Loonea though, wasn't so sure, I could see. I signalled her to follow, brooking no argument and was half surprised to see her come readily. I only hoped I was as confident as I thought I should be.

I had never met the Serpent of the Dreaming and doubted she would disturb me anyway. I didn't doubt she existed, I had seen evidence enough but she wasn't part of my physical experience and I didn't think she would even bother with me.

The water was chilly under the rock overhang and as I steadily stroked my way into the dim light of the cavern I knew Loonea followed close behind me so I turned to encourage her. It wasn't overly deep and in places I could feel a foothold against the sandy bottom which was skirted with smooth stone. For some reason this gave me confidence and I began to enjoy the whole experience of what seemed to be braving the Spirits. I could do this I realized, and it added to my strength in some way.

The current gently pulled us along and soon we were approaching the spillway edge so my feet began to seek the ledge I knew to be there and sure enough, I soon found it. Pulling myself from the water as I found the foot hold I turned, grinning at my success as I reached to help Loonea onto the ledge.

It was then that I saw it, the rippled advance in the water as it snaked towards us and as Loonea swung in the direction of my startled glance she screamed in a babble of sound and began to scramble suddenly terrified, grabbing for my hand, for my arm... any part of me she could reach.

"Shit!... Quick..." Grabbing her I hauled her onto the ledge as I watched the approach of the rippling stream cutting its way through the otherwise calm of the pool and I hauled her to me, knowing that there weren't many places to which we could escape. Our only option was to head for the edge of the cavern pool where the rope was, so pushing her recklessly ahead of me in that direction as in a step I swung back to face whatever it was, knowing we could not both reach the safety outside of the waters grasp in time to escape the Serpents advance. This was my fault and I had above everything else to protect her.

I had to embrace this. How many times had my brothers told me that fear was my greatest enemy. I didn't even have my bush knife, I had nothing and in an instant I realized how stupid I had been. I used the only weapons I had, I began to sing, knowing the timbre and the gentle vibrations of my song would be something the Serpent would feel, it was an instinctive defence.

It was a defence that worked! The Serpent slowed, her approach no longer swift as it had been and then oddly it stilled. Realizing it was the vibrations of my song, my voice that it could feel I sank my hands into the water, dipped lower beneath the surface, still singing a song softly, deeply, almost humming, I was using the walls of my chest as a means to carry the sound.

The sudden stillness of the water worried me though, it could mean that the

Serpent had slipped deeper below the surface and as I listened to the sound of Loonea reaching the caverns edge, the sound of her splashing subsiding I wondered if I could use this time now to escape the water myself.

Then I saw its shadow, a sleek glint of dark grey moving beneath the water towards where I was now crouched humming fast with restricted breaths that were edged with fear. It wasn't headed directly for me but seemed to aim for behind me which alarmed me, my muscles constrained by fear or curiosity, I'm not sure which... I watched as the dark snake like form circled barely centimetres from the rock-shelf bottom which I crouched on. It swept around me in a arc... twisting to form a circle, to loop its body around me.

This wasn't an attack I realized as it maintained a distance but its speed increased and I could barely follow its sleek head as the waters grew strangely warmer around me. I could feel its intent, sense its ambiguity in that it meant no harm now and I was filled with a strange sense of peace and good will that somehow fed and warmed me.

Then suddenly... it departed, more swiftly than it had arrived, it left with a movement of water fast enough to create a current of its own then the chill flow of the cavern waters began to claim my body again.

Amazed, yet shocked, I looked over at Loonea who had her back pressed up against the cavern wall her face full of fright and wonder as the water around us once more returned to its calm pool, spilling contentedly over the rock face, as though nothing had happened.

I laughed, still shocked. My laughter was breaking the spell of mystery born of this sacred place which had settled about us. My laughter shattered the eerie silence along with the sound of water spilling over the rim of the pool and into the forest ahead and below.

Then, my body still shaking, I climbed to my feet and stepped carefully over towards her. I still felt the warmth of the Serpent in some way, I felt strong and invigorated. I felt welcome, strangely I felt part of the cavern and as any fear I had dissipated. It was lost in the strange feelings being born inside me. I reached her then as though nothing had happened directing her ahead of me, signalling towards the rope on the path ahead. Loonea looked at me strangely and then almost reverent of the cavern, the Serpent and the confidence of my steps, she was careful to do exactly as I indicated in motioning her ahead of me. She said nothing, and for the first time since being with her I felt totally in control. Fleetingly I wondered if this was how Taipan often felt, and Sean... did they too feel this sense of powerful control.

When I had watched Andrew, without hesitation, tie Ngaire to him when we had climbed up this spillway only yesterday, neither Ngaire or I had questioned him. He was in control and we simply had obeyed. It was a heady sense I was feeling and while I knew it wouldn't last I revelled in it. I knew that the minute Loonea touched me, the minute I felt her small hand on my body I would not hold this control but it was a wonderful thing while it lasted. I felt like a God now, I felt strong, able to achieve whatever I wanted, it felt good. For the first time I felt the full measure of manhood even though it was something that was soon to leave me, perhaps it was an initiation of a sort.

It was a birth into a world that was a promise of the future, a realization of the man I could be.

THE ADVENTURE OF MAN

Taipan:

It was well after the afternoon storm had passed, the very edge of dusk, it would be only a short time until the sun dropped below the horizon and while the storm had cooled the earth, the humidity was again settling into the evening. Soon it would be a pleasant heat and stirring the fire I watched as Sean and Jiemba sat in the shelter of the rock-face with the dog.

I had enjoyed spending the day with Jiemba and Sean. The hunting had been fun and now I watched as Sean showed young Jiemba how to temper and heat a spear in the fire. Straightening and strengthening it as we had spent the day strengthening Jem. The boy was a delight, curious and game as a snake. Ngaire had done well with her son and he had a quiet presence about himself which was edged with the impatience of one so young. He was a great kid and we would miss him, hopefully though we would see more of him over the years.

It had been a good business this. By now the baby would be back with his mother and I knew well the difference we had made in his life yesterday. But the men were late back, I had expected them earlier but maybe Billy had been delayed by something. He had set out early this morning to bring Andrew, Tom and Ngaire out of the gorge. I understood the delay, Adoni would have wanted to thank them but he also would understand my anxiety over Tom. He was strong, but he was at an impressionable age. Maybe this was the problem? The men of the gorge would have more maturity than Tom at the same age. I hoped it wasn't going to be a problem and he hadn't involved himself in something daft.

The opportunity for Tom had been too great to pass up. The Featherfoot links with the Mimi were a strange bind, both transitioned between worlds easily but it was something I had little experience of, it wasn't my Dreaming. The chance to expose Tom to such an experience as this was exceptional, even John wasn't able to do such a thing for him. This meeting with Billy Black had been extraordinary and I had a great deal to thank Ngaire for. It would help resolve many of the difficult questions that plagued Tom, questions I didn't always have answers for. I hoped he would begin to understand the tenacious links the Mimi had with our world as they were half way between the world of the Spirits, and that of our own.

A sudden movement at the edge of the camp brought me quickly to my feet as I watched Andrew and Ngaire come into view. Ngaire looked ill and immediately I moved to meet them, her colour was almost grey.

"What's happened?"

"Ty... Hang on I just want to get Ngaire settled." Andrew said impatiently, as he led her over to the rock-face where Jiemba was immediately aware of his mother's discomfort.

"Mum?"

"It's OK Bub... I just need a rest that's all, it was a long walk and I'm hot," she reassured her son as she settled on the camp rug. Andrew hovered close while Jem handed her his canteen of water.

Tango too came over to greet her, I could see even he was concerned though he allowed me access to her readily as I helped Andrew.

Her cheeks were flushed against her grey colour and her breathing was shallow, she was obviously in discomfit. Dehydration was always a issue in the tropics and I checked her carefully, my mind filling with questions.

"It's OK really, I just need to rest. It's just a headache... I get them occasionally. I have tablets for them. Andrew can you get them please, they're in my pack in the side pouch."

As he moved off I looked at her concerned. "Your blood pressure is through the roof," I said softly, measuring the pound of her heart under my fingertips.

"Yes. I know. Billy wanted me to leave the gorge as soon as possible this morning, but we have been delayed, it's been a slow walk. I don't know if we should have left so soon."

"Hmmm... I'm glad of that. Do you know what it is?"

Ngaire hesitated and then as Andrew arrived bringing with him some tablets it was obvious he had heard the question.

"Ngaire is pregnant," he said simply. "I want to get her out of here as soon as possible as the gorge seems to have a bad effect on her. When Billy gets back, he can fly us out."

"Andrew... it isn't necessary," she protested impatiently. "I'll be fine in a while I just need to rest is all."

"Babe... I'm taking you home as soon as I can."

Ngaire sighed impatiently, "You're being silly" she began but I cut her off.

"No. I agree with Andrew, you need to rest and a long car trip, not to mention the trek across the tableland is out of the question."

The stern look I gave her silenced her and she had to agree with me, to insist otherwise was foolish and she knew it.

"How far is Billy and Tom behind you?" I asked Andrew, turning to him as I noted Ngaire gave up the argument and closed her eyes to calm herself.

"We don't know. That is the other thing. Tom's gone missing. Billy had an idea where he might have gone and went off after him. He is with one of the women, one of Adoni's wives. It seems it's some kind of thank you business, he will be able to tell you more I'm sure."

"A thank you?" Impatiently I held my temper. Tom was something of a trial at times, he constantly managed to get himself into scrapes and usually with women involved. This wasn't good news, "One of Adoni's women?" I questioned suddenly realizing this could be a disaster.

"Yes, but it hasn't caused offence." Andrew reassured me, knowing what my concerns were. "It seems they have Adoni's blessing, whatever it is. I found his shirt down by the water this morning and it was in some way significant to Adoni. He looked rather pleased, too pleased if anything."

Struggling with the meaning of this, I slowly stood. My glance once more checking Ngaire who looked to be at last recovering her colour somewhat, her breathing was also improved.

"What has he done this time?" Sean asked as he joined us, humour in his voice. "I assume that Tom is in trouble... he isn't here."

"I need to talk to Billy. God I am going to strangle that boy one day," I threatened half heartedly.

Her voice tentative, Ngaire interrupted us. "I'm sorry Taipan but I think I know what is going on. The Mimi are probably wanting to build links with Tom. Billy thinks he has strength or he wouldn't have taken him into the gorge without using the stones. He seems to have a link with the people and they would know this, sense it. They don't mean him any harm I am sure they probably simply want to... well hope to encourage him or maybe just to thank him in some way. I am sure Adoni would not allow any harm to come to him, as he would be grateful for your help and not want to endanger your friendship."

I hesitated at her words knowing she was likely right, Adoni would not want to insult us but then Ngaire didn't understand Tom's real strengths. My eyes moved to Andrew, he would understand my concerns I knew and he would also better understand Ngaire's knowledge.

Reading the look in my eyes easily Andrew turned back to his woman. "Babe, Tom is like Billy and we are sure Billy has recognized this. Would you trust him to return Tom to us, knowing that?"

Surprised, Ngaire was at first silent as she took this in, "Like Billy? You mean he is a Banman, a Mimi Banman?"

"No, he is of the Featherfoot Lore, but he moves easily through their world as they are the same."

Ngaire frowned, "But..."confused she stopped and tried to understand, to read the knowledge in my eyes. Then she shook her head answering us both. "I have known Billy for years and he is honest, a good man but he also is of the Mimi people. I know he will look after Tom but... but his loyalties are with the Mimi. They are his family."

"Then we will go after them," I added with decision. I couldn't afford to risk Tom's future and I knew Sean would agree with me. "Andrew, can you help?"

It took barely a minute for the question to register and as it did so I could see the decisions Andrew was making. He stood up and moved quietly towards the low burning embers of the fire, so I knew then the answer to my question almost immediately. I also understood that Ngaire wasn't ignorant of Andrew's strengths and this made my own decisions and reservations easier.

Andrew settled cross-legged near the fire, his concentration clear and steady and as he sunk his fingers into the ground at his side I squatted down beside Ngaire, sending her a reassuring smile, but she was calm and I was sure she had seen this before. It gave me confidence to see, though this wasn't so common a sight for her that she could hold back from the curiosity and uncertainty I could read in her eyes.

The liquid light when he drew it from the ground moved up over Andrew's fingers clinging strangely to his hands. The light was drawn like a fluid from the earth; it coated his hands moving up from the sandy earth like viscous thickened oil which had a life force of its own. Then when Andrew felt ready having gathered the light he lifted his fingers from the earth, and bringing them almost together he moulded the liquid light to a soft glow which slowly grew in strength forming the orb. It was beautiful to watch, magnificent, and I took some pride in his achievement.

Then as he spoke to the light through his thoughts, Andrew released it to the darkening skies where it hovered for a moment as though taking in its surroundings and assessing its place, then it moved. It moved swiftly, then suddenly stopped hovering for a moment as though waiting to see its intended path.

Sean had already stripped off his shirt and was preparing to remove the rest of his gear when I joined him. My mind was on Tom, my thoughts following the Min Min light trying to link to its path and it wasn't until I leapt to the skies moments later, knowing Sean was at my side also fast entering transition that I could feel the orbs strength and pull. Once over the escarpment of the gorge, I remembered Ngaire. For a split second I faltered but then instinct took over and the thought was lost as I twisted towards the now singing orb as it swept past me and Sean, on its path up the gorge.

I knew Andrew could deal with Ngaire. Surely as a healer, having lived with a Shaman she would understand also she would not be without her own secrets. My only thought now was to track Tom and it was to this purpose that Andrew had given birth to the Min Min light. Its path would be steady so we could follow it with confidence. He couldn't be too far away I knew and as Sean and I swept along following the path of the Min Min I felt confident that we would find Tom before the night was over. Tom would have some serious explaining to do I decided as I settled into the flow of the air about me as we trailed the Min Min guide.

The shift between the humidity of the ground and the swift cool currents of the air was invigorating. With sharpened sight it didn't take long to focus on small changes in the landscape, the smoke of a fire, the mark of a trail, the feel of moist air along our bodies as we flew above lands which were a honeycomb of water traps. The Min Min swept suddenly towards the earth to follow the path of a small gorge which at first seemed dry but pools of water opened up with the green touch of forest, then I saw the origin of the smoke trail in a fire.

The Min Min guide suddenly slowed, stopping beside the cliff-face it glowed deeply as though drawing a breath, then suddenly died. It had found its quarry, Andrew would know, as did we that Tom was there. With a sweep we turned to the last place the Min Min had been, which was at an undercut. Tracks and movement could be discerned but the cave that could be seen ahead wasn't my choice of habitat and my spirit creature would not entertain the confined space. I recognized the signs though, the subtle message of the rocks. I would not enter such a place I knew for more reasons than the obvious, it was a place for ceremony and I didn't have the time to read clearly the taboo's, instead I swept towards the light trail of smoke by the waters path, Sean was in my slipstream not far behind me and he was allowing me the choices and was content to follow in my wake.

I recognized Billy immediately I arrived at the perch high in the gum tree then it was a simple drop to the ground, transition heating and directing the flow of my body as I landed. Sean used a more direct approach though I found him at my side also sweeping through transition as I stood to face the man. Billy also stood as he set his simple meal aside and rose to meet us. He wasn't surprised at our arrival I noted, though he seemed more alarmed.

Deciding to take the direct approach I faced Billy. "Tom is nearby, we know where he is. What is going on Billy, you'd know I would come after my young brother," I asked steadily, neither anger nor accusation tempering my simple question. I wanted an explanation or an understanding of what was obviously intentional.

"Taipan," he answered simply in acknowledgement, turning to me standing tall, with authority. "Tom has chosen his place here; Adoni wishes simply to welcome him. He is free to leave at any time though it's our hope he stays. If not, then we will help him along his path and welcome his return."

"He doesn't understand the ways of the Mimi. He doesn't realize the consequences of his choices but he will have the freedom to choose." I raised my own voice as I demanded Tom's freedom, my eyes met Sean's, who was standing at my side, then went back to Billy, challenging him. He would feel the strength of our brotherhood. Billy would understand we would fight for Tom's freedom whatever the cost. The Mimi hadn't bought his loyalties, others had a rightful claim. As his family, his skin, we would still protect him. "No one... no woman will make these choices for him," I added forcefully.

The breath Billy drew told me more; it told me that he knew I had read his intent and the intent of the Mimi Elders in offering a woman to a young man. I watched as the man measured my own authority and asked, "If he chooses to stay, you will challenge him?"

"He will not choose to stay... In our Community where Tom belongs such liaisons are no longer governed by the Elders. Your offering has value but no binds for Tom. He is too young in our world, there is a great deal ahead of him and he knows this," I answered simply. Then at sounds of movement nearby I cut off what was in my mind to say. It would serve no purpose to say it now.

"Ty...?" The three of us turned to the couple as they approached us along the narrow path. Tom and the woman moved with confidence towards us though Tom I could see was surprised to find Billy. Equally surprised he looked to Sean confused... "Hey... We're on our way back guys. I hope you didn't think I wasn't coming… sorry for being so late but... well I was busy..."

His grin was on the edge of apologetic which was as close to an apology as we were going to get. I realized he had no idea that the choices he made had consequences. Tom had no understanding that the world he moved through was very different from the one he knew. I had failed to make him conscious of these differences and perhaps his choices were in part my fault. With difficulty I struggled with my irritation at both myself and Tom.

"We'll talk about this later, Ngaire is ill and we need to get her back," I said tersely. "We were expecting you by midday."

"Ill?" Even Billy was disconcerted by this

"Yes, her blood pressure is up and I'm concerned for the baby."

"The baby... but it was fine yesterday," Tom commented.

"Not the child from the community..."

Sean cut me off, answering Tom's question. "Ngaire's baby... Ngaire's having a baby and this trip hasn't been good for her. Andrew is going mad with the news and with her feeling sick. So Bucco', we have to get back right now... and Billy..."

"Billy..." I interrupted, "We need you to fly her out as soon as possible. We can deal with this other business at another time should we need to."

Billy nodded in agreement and immediately moved to douse the fire as I took in the woman at Tom's side for the first time. She was silent; she had dropped her glance and was compliant with those around her. I wondered what level of complicity she had in this business.

"Tom, we need you back at camp."

"Yeah sure.... Umm...I guess I can get Loonea back to the gorge?"

Billy stood interrupting us as he broke into his dialect, speaking to the woman. Immediately she reacted, not even affording Tom a glance she turned back along the path they had just come. She left his side without a word.

Tom, clearly shocked, moved to stop her.

"Tom... no..."

"But Ty... what...?"

"Let her go, she will know her way back to the gorge. The woman is fine."

"No. I'll stay with her... seriously I can't just let her find..."

"Tom let her go," I said tersely as I watched the struggle he was having obeying me. "She's Adoni's wife, you have to let her go."

Clearly shocked yet again, Tom moved to say something, then still confused looked to the figure which was disappearing down the track from where they had just come. "But... no... I mean she didn't say...I never..."

"We'll talk about it later." I added firmly, reassuring him. "Billy will you be able to get him back to camp?"

But Sean forestalled me, "I can go with them. It's OK Ty, I could do with the walk, I've been babysitting all day and I am ready for a stretch," he added humorously.

Billy nodded his expression again inscrutable. "We hope you can visit us again Taipan, Sean. Adoni and the Mimi owe your people a considerable debt in this business."

I knew he meant no animosity, I knew he was sincere in his hope and yet I could still feel my anger at his complicity in this business, and it edge my words. "We will return," I said, knowing it to be true but just who, or when would be a question for the future.

Turning away my sudden glance warned Tom, I had not finished with him and then I stepped back lent down to my crouch wanting now to leave them, and called the heat along my body. It was just moments before I felt the shift of the night winds across my body and my thoughts were torn as I took to the wind.

It was exactly what I had feared and it could well be a strong lesson for young Tom, but then I felt the humour of it touch my thoughts. My younger brother certainly knew ways to test me and I wasn't about to take it easy on him. If nothing else... this was going to be a hard lesson for him but it was one he was going to have to deal with. He had made choices and the chances were he was about to learn something important in all this. There were consequences that we may well have to deal with in years to come. I would be back or one of us would, of that I was certain.

Sitting around the camp fire an hour later, having returned to camp, I waited on the others arrival. I hadn't decided on how much to tell Tom, he needed to know but I needed to judge carefully how to tell him, how much to tell him and how much to leave for him to discover. His youth would make this a difficult task.

I was torn with the need to protect him and my anger at his lack of comprehension. How much could I really expect him to understand? He was after all barely eighteen, still at school, still without a lot of experience but yet if he remained ignorant the consequences were unacceptable.

As I chewed over the dilemma Andrew joined me. We hadn't had the opportunity to talk aside from my assurance that we had found Tom and that the others were on their way back to camp. That really was all Andrew had been interested in, his concern for Ngaire clouded everything else, yet I hadn't even spoken about that. That too was beyond time.

"How is she?" I asked, understanding his concern and in part sharing it.

"She's asleep now, once Jiemba finally settled, so did she."

"You're worried," I added needlessly. "You have need to be, blood pressure problems so early are not a good thing Andrew. Watch her carefully as she needs to be under a doctor's care."

"I thought as much." Sighing, we both watched the fire light dance. In some way it was comforting. It drew our eyes and somehow soothed you. Then Andrew added. "I want this baby; I mean... it was a shock at first and I think... well I was an arse about it, but... the thought of Ngaire carrying my son... Ty... that is an amazing thing, I never realized... how much..."

I grinned, "Yeah it's amazing. Are you going to stay around here to look after her do you think?"

Surprised he looked up and then thought about it. "I could I guess, but I would rather keep working. You need things for a baby you know... something else I never really thought about. I mean I haven't got enough capital to do what I want yet, but I can get it if I keep working. The pay is good but it means being away a lot."

"Maybe that's a good thing. You both need time to adjust."

"Yeah... yeah you could be right. It's hard to know what is more important. The business between Ngaire and I, or... well the baby, the kids. What would be best for both?"

"That is easy, it's the children you need to look out for. You and Ngaire, your relationship will always be changing, developing, growing. But kids, they have only ten years in their childhood to grow, and be who they will be and they need as much support as you can give them in that time. After that they begin to take on their own choices and they will look for those they trust to help them. To take that time away from children...it can never be regained, childhood is precious."

Those thoughts sat with us in the night air around the camp. It was a clear night, the skies were brilliant with no hint of the afternoon storms, there was nothing quite like the skies of the outback and the Centre. They were beyond description I decided after a time. As we sat we both considered the value of our own childhood. Andrew suddenly broke into my reverie, "You didn't say how you found Tom?"

I grinned, knowing the irony of this conversation. "Tom was with Adoni's woman, at a fertility cave. Though I don't know if he realized exactly what the place was to the women."

Andrew chuckled suddenly then swore softly, "Shit. I wondered about that?"

"Hmm... it's worth worrying over. I should have warned him but with everything else happening, I didn't."

"I knew. I mean I knew he was with her but I didn't think that it would be beyond the night. He isn't a kid Ty..."

"He isn't a man either. There is a lot he doesn't understand, I mean who understands these things at seventeen."

Andrew drew a breath... "You are talking to the wrong guy," he answered chuckling. "Who understands at any age? I don't even understand it now. You don't do you... until you arrive at that point."

"No you don't. I don't think I will tell Tom the whole story, but he does need to be aware of the chances, the risks of going into such communities as this. He should have been warned and I failed him in that."

"You can't take the blame for his actions Ty."

"Can't I? Yeah well... can you keep your ear to the ground? Ngaire might hear or even Billy. You seemed to get on well and perhaps you might be the first to hear if there's a child."

Andrew nodded, "Will you tell Tom, if there is I mean?"

I shook my head, "He is seventeen and she is not his. Perhaps when he's older, and if I need to, it may yet come to nothing'. Of course he could choose to come back one day... he might find out on his own. I guess it's a risk we take a hundred times when we are young... we give it less thought than we are giving it now?"

As Andrew laughed I couldn't help but grin and I thought about my own words, my own experience. How many times had I taken such a risk? My first months with Aine, the memory was sweet as I recalled easily what I had felt about pregnancy then. I had been more reckless in those first months than at any other time in my life. We were more careful now and in fact I wondered what Aine would think of Ngaire's pregnancy.

Aine had been spending more and more time amongst the women with young children and I knew her mind had been turning to thoughts of babies. I would have to consider our future, work at meeting the needs of a family. I had to find a way that would afford me the time to spend with a family and it wasn't so simply done I realized. Things were going to have to change soon if this was something we were going to move towards.

The others arrived soon after and it was clear that Billy had accepted that Tom would be leaving with us so it was a relief to see that it wasn't an issue then the night settled into its rest. The next morning Andrew, Ngaire and Jem, along with the dog harnessed into the central seat left early. Ngaire looked well and was happy, though irritated with my insistence that she fly out rather than make the long trek. Her irritation was something Andrew would have to deal with and the thought was in some way entertaining as I watched him settle her into the small chopper.

As for me, my thoughts were now on Tom as we began our walk back towards the edge of the escarpment, towards where we could drop down onto the low lands where the camp had been set up. I wondered how I was going to get through to Tom, without risking encouraging him to return to the Mimi Lands.

It was a beautiful land. The stone country was alive with the breath of Spirit and I knew there was much about me, more than I had the time to explore. I could feel the strength of the land as I passed and it strengthened my shadow.

In this season there was food aplenty and the animals moved mostly silent about us, resting in the growing heat of the day having filled their bellies at dawn, in the morning light. Once we tracked to the river, it was much easier and more pleasant to follow where the water flow had carved its way towards the escarpment and the three of us covered the ground quickly.

Having reached the escarpment edge by mid afternoon, we finally stopped to rest and look out over where we knew the wetlands camp to be that Andrew and Ngaire had put together. Tomorrow we would break camp and head back to Katherine then head south back home. Resting to draw a breath before the descent, I watched my younger brothers as they too took a moment to look out over the spread of land at our feet. Tom had kept to himself throughout the walk and I understood there was much on his mind. In so many ways he was inexperienced and experience wasn't always easy to gain.

"You've been quiet Tom, are you still thinking of the woman? What was her name... Lea, Leigh?"

He looked up unsure of my intent. "Loonea."

"Yes." I said more kindly. "You didn't realize she is Adoni's woman?"

"No. She never said... I never asked. I guess I should have."

"Hmm... No." Letting my eyes wander over the land at our feet I considered his position. "No Tom. I should have told you how it would be in such a community. There is no reason you would know, you haven't been to such a place before."

I could feel his frown, his lack of understanding and I was glad when Sean joined in the conversation.

"They're different to what we understand. They play by different rules bro."

"How do you mean?"

"Well..., they are a small community though I know it doesn't seem that way but they are. Where you have that, the Elders usually understand the risks and the business between men and women is closely watched, the marriage Lore is there to protect the community. We have become used to moving around a lot, meeting many different people but it isn't like that for them. When others come into their communities they understand the value these visitors have. It isn't uncommon to be offered a woman; it strengthens ties between clans and strengthens the whole community. The Mimi are very vulnerable in this way. Their communities have difficulty maintaining the old story lines which once linked them together. They would have normally used these to find partners once."

"You mean, Adoni offered me his woman? He would have known...?"

Sean smiled, understanding it fully. "Yep... I guess he is hoping for a son and if he gets one, he will be one happy bloke."

Shocked, Tom sat up. "What?"

Alarmed, I jumped in quickly. "It's not uncommon for such an offer, to be given with the hope of strengthening blood in the community. Tom, you can't expect the women of such communities to have everything available to them as our women do when it comes to birth control. You shouldn't expect it anyway... you govern your own choices."

"But, she never said. Oh... come on. Surely..."

"The reality is, Tom that was a fertility cave that you were taken to."

"No... no. Loonea told me, it was a place where the Banman... go. The women teach them how... about stuff."

"Perhaps you're right. But the progeny of their Shaman is very important to them, to the women, to the community. It ensures the survival and health of the community."

"Progeny? You mean kids?"

"Yes."

"But... but she's older, it was just a one night thing."

Sean hooted softly. "An' that makes a difference? No... Tom."

Stunned Tom swore softly. "You mean... Geeze...."

Clearly he didn't know how to deal with this and again I jumped in.

"What's done is done. The important thing is for you to remember who you are and where you belong. You can't change this now Tom and it may come to nothing but you need to be aware. As a Featherfoot, you will move amongst many communities, not all will move as easily as you do. Values are often different to yours. You need to remember this, remember who you are and where you belong in life, at least until you are old enough to decide what it is you want in life."

"John never explained... I never thought about this... it doesn't seem right."

I understood his confusion, though John would have no reason to tell him these things yet, if ever. His mentor amongst the Featherfoot wasn't his father, he was a teacher and he knew the value of visitors to such a community.

"This is business for your fathers, Tom I should have realized and spoken to you about it. John can teach you many things, take you many places but this is not his place. Billy Black is like you in many ways and the opportunity for him to lead you into the world of the Mimi was a rich experience for you. These people follow the old way and the giving of their women is not wrong for them, because the women are returned to them, they will have lost nothing and gained much."

"Billy is a Featherfoot?"

"No, but he moves through the worlds like a Featherfoot, in some ways he is a gatekeeper. He doesn't see Spirit Men but he is of the Mimi and they are a people closer to the Spirit Men. How did you find being in their lands?"

"I was going to ask you about that. I didn't see Spirit Men there, it was strange... like before when I was younger. Everyone was the same and they didn't move between the worlds... it was sort of comfortable."

"They do move between the worlds Tom, only in the Lands they are all of the same world, closer to the Spirit Men. To the Mimi people, it's us who are different. We have lost the ability to be close to our ancestors. They consider our people to be ignorant and unfortunate in their loss these days. Billy's place in the world of the Mimi is to judge who is able to cross into their world and not be harmed by the experience. It's only the Shaman who have not lost this ability in our world to be part of their Dreaming. Which is another reason why they so value their Banman."

"So those of the Spirit World are there in the Mimi Lands?"

"Yes. They move amongst them easily. They are them of their own community. You would see them easily, there would be little difference."

Frowning Tom struggled to take it in. "Who? Who wasn't a Mimi but of the Spirit Men?"

I shrugged knowing I couldn't answer that, "They would be fairly powerful, perhaps some of the Elders, perhaps even Adoni."

Tom struggled with his new knowledge throughout the rest of our time together in the Top End and as I watched him carefully, even on our return to the community, I could see about him a new wisdom. I knew he had learnt valuable lessons and I hoped that it would make him a stronger man. Sometimes I felt like the father he had lost, though this wasn't something I would choose.

As we returned back into the flow of things in the community, I realized that it had been a valuable time for Tom, indeed for all of us, but more than anything I bought back with me a new thread in my life. As I watched Aine around our home some days later my thoughts turned more to our own world and what we could bring it to.

THE WHISPER OF THE KOOLRARI

Ngaire:

Seeing Andrew settled into the pattern of our lives in Katherine during his visit bought with it a new realization, a promise perhaps and as wary as I had been of just such a thing, part of me had enjoyed his presence, I enjoyed the knowledge in his eyes and the nights we shared. It sometimes seemed to me that he was very much at home, very comfortable with the world around him and knowing he was of the Bama people I wondered how he had been so easily able to slip into my world.

Waking with his body curled around mine was a special delight and even Jem had become accustomed to finding Andrew in my bed. It was a strange relationship they shared. At times I thought my son enjoyed his presence when they would play and Andrew had a way about him which calmed Jem. Yet at other times I would find Jem brooding almost, though he never openly challenged Andrew. He was reluctant to challenge someone who had the power of the Shaman. It was an unknown quality, an unspoken reality one which wasn't challenged.

When the men had gone after Tom, when Andrew had raised the earth lights in front of young Jem, my first thoughts once I realized what was happening around us were for my young son. He didn't understand. He had never known his father well and had never spent any time amongst men so it had taken time for Jiemba to understand that the strengths of the Shaman were not the same as the strengths of the women he knew, his mothers and aunts who had been so much part of his world so far. It was hard for him to see that neither was greater than the other, that each had a place and his place was amongst men, not women. For the first time he was questioning his wold which had been the world of women up until now.

Andrew had spoken to us both once the others had departed and he had seen the look in Jem's eyes, the men taking to the skies had left Jem speechless. Andrew had at least settled Jem's excited questions, questions which gave rise to a world I realized my son was only just now finding.

I had become accustomed to many things in my life, living with shaman prepared me for many wonders and secrets and being a healer gave me access to knowledge. I had seen before the power of shape-shifters, I had treated the consequence of growing skills. In my opinion it was one of the most dangerous of skills as while the shape of spirit animals was taken, their natural instincts were not necessarily listened to. That took even more training and that training often came at a heavy cost for any unskilled Shaman.

I had met many Clever Men, who could do many things, those who held power over the weaknesses of others and who generally wielded such talents well, for if they didn't then their skills would desert them. The gifts of the Shaman were taken from them as easily as they were gifted. The Spirit Men were masters of who they would allow to wield such strengths.

I was familiar with those with the strong-eye, who saw and knew the Spirit Men in their own world and the power of the Miriru which was that of the Bardi men, Shaman, men such as Billy Black who understood the mystery of the stones. There were many things that the Shaman of the tribes could do, each had their own, often unique skills. I had heard of the earth lights, the strength of the Koolrari but never had I seen its power raised from the earth. More common amongst the Shaman I saw was the fire of Namarrgon, the man of lightning; his power came from the skies, not the earth.

To see such a power so simply wielded was awesome but in some ways it frightened me. The Koolrari was a dangerous skill and it had led many to their deaths, those who follow the promise of the Min Min light as it's often known. I didn't imagine that Andrew would draw such a power from the earth only to lead his friends to their deaths, but I knew it was possible. Only the Shaman who raised the Koolrari could command it and other than that it was a power unto itself, one which lived, served a need and then died.

I could see that it had raised many more questions in my young boy's mind as I watched Jem at play. He had been so young when his father had died, and he was still a young child beginning to understand that there was a world that wasn't tethered to his mother. To have knowledge of the ways of the Shaman, to see the path of the Banman in the world which was to be his, was a big step for someone barely five.

It had been reassuring to meet Sean and Taipan and their younger brother Tom. I realized that the men of Andrew's community could offer Jem the guidance of his Dreaming. They could guide him as he became a man and teach him about his blood skills as they had taught Tom. This way I would not lose my son to the Mimi. More than anything this was such a rich promise that it was difficult to separate my feelings for Andrew from the knowledge that he could give my son the learning that he needed.

I knew also that Jenna could always maintain the links, tell the stories and sing many of the songs which my son needed to help him grow. She was of the Sky people and they were slowly gathering her knowledge to themselves, they would not let her go so easily if ever she moved within their realm and decided to stay, in this the Mimi offered Sean and Jenna a threat. Sean was strong though and I was confident Jenna was safe within his reach.

Even if Andrew wasn't of the Banman Lore and the Lore of the Mimi people, he, Jenna and Sean could bring to Jiemba's life the knowledge of his blood and help with his training as a man.

Although Andrew's skills were very different from skills I was more familiar with, skills I had seen and experienced in my husband and in my time healing. He was a strong Shaman and his strength was a valuable thing.

I had heard of Shaman who could raise the earth lights, though I had never seen the same in anyone other than Andrew. I had heard of such a skill from the tribes of the Channel Country, the women had spoken of such abilities in their men and I had heard the stories, it had left me in awe even then.

It was comforting to know that as a father Andrew could ensure Jiemba's knowledge as he had so much to offer him in his community. It felt as though a huge weight of responsibility had been lifted from my shoulders as I considered the way my life was moving to join Andrew's, but still I knew the fear of drawing Jiemba away from the world of his people. Was I right to do this?

But then there was the child. As my fingers brushed the small changes in my belly I smiled at the thought of the baby. Andrew was more aware of the growing child and I grinned quietly at the memory of his fear in harming the child when we had settled the newness of the knowledge between us. When he had once more taken me in his arms and had wanted to make love but was afraid of harming his son I had laughed. It was such an innocent fear he had... innocent of the ways of women. In one so strong it was endearing to see his doubts and for some reason I loved him all the more for it.

He was so convinced it was a boy, so sure that this also made me smile. Perhaps he would have his way and Jem could enjoy the arrival of a brother, children of different worlds. For me though, I didn't care whether it was a boy or a girl. It was a child, our child, a child born of my growing love for Andrew and I wondered what the future held for us.

"Hi Babe, what's with the pensive look? How did it go at the doctors?"

He settled beside me on the back step as I was watching Jem, I enjoyed the warmth of his arrival while I tried to piece together an answer, "It went well, it was what I thought. Too much excitement, the Doctor wants me to take it easy, that's all," I turned my glance away; it was difficult to keep my thoughts and my fears, to myself.

"Then that's what we will do," he added concerned. "Have you given any thought to coming down to Brisbane? I can look after you better there and you heard what Jen had to say, she would love to have you in Brissy. I don't like you being here alone and coping on your own."

"That isn't true Andrew, my Mum is nearby and I have my Aunties, my family."

I watched as he once more struggled with the fabric of my loyalties. "You're not losing them Babe, your gaining a family, my family. Your Mum can be in Brisbane within hours of a call and Jenna... I know you two are close."

"Yes." Agreeing, I thought of my spirit sister and I recognized the longing that drew us together. Maybe Andrew was right, but I needed to be sure and the thought of leaving my family in Katherine frightened me. I would have preferred that these choices not be forced on me now. "Have you spoken to your Mum? Does she know...?"

Andrew shook his head and grinned. "I can't get on to her. But I will... there's no hurry. Maybe that is something we can do together when I take you to meet them. It's all the more reason for you to come to Brisbane."

"Mmm... yes." I agreed smiling. "But there's no hurry as you said."

Standing suddenly Andrew laughed, "Don't use that as an excuse woman. Come on, I'll start dinner if you help." Holding out his hand I took it in my own as he lovingly pulled me up from my comfortable seat.

"OK...I was thinking of lasagne."

"Sounds good... sounds easy..."

I loved the ease of our days together. It was something that had grown between us slowly but surely, though I knew it would end soon. Andrew was due back into Brisbane at the end of the week and I knew he wanted me to decide on my move before that, but I just couldn't.

In my heart I couldn't make the decision, I didn't know why and his disappointment at this was showing in every expression, every gesture he made in those last hours before he left.

I tortured myself trying to understand my hesitancy; I spent hours on the phone to Jenna trying to understand why, struggling to come to a decision I had to make. Jen's advice was simple, touched as it was with Andrew's disappointment as he had left Brisbane for another hitch on the rigs.

"Ngaire, why don't you just get on a plane... make the booking... come down if only for a few months. I know you need to be here and Andrew said he will get removalists to pack up the house. The removalists can do everything so you don't need to do a thing."

"It's not that Jen and there isn't a real lot to move. Most of it can go to my family, its only old stuff anyway. It's just the thought, the change... I don't know what it is...Besides, I have been told that a plane trip with the pregnancy it's not a good idea, something about my blood pressure. I would need to drive and then there is Tango and the car. It would need to be a road trip."

"Well if you are planning on driving I know Andrew would freak at that idea," she commented laughing.

"Yeah... I think he might. So maybe I need to wait till he gets back."

"Why do I get the feeling you're just delaying this?"

"I'm not really. I mean I know... I know what I have to do. I think I have decided that I need to be with Andrew but it's just... I don't know..." I finished confused. "I need a bit more time I guess, I just can't seem to make the decision."

"You know Andrew threatened to go up and drag you down don't you. He wasn't so kind when he was talking to Sean before he left.

The thought of Andrew raging at Sean made me smile and I could see him easily in my mind's eye. He wouldn't want to show me that side of himself I knew, not now. He had been so careful when he had been here but I wasn't deceived, I had seen flashes of the depths of his passions before.

"Yes... I know."

Trying to pin point the source of my indecision I sighed. It seemed impossible but whatever it was, it was keeping me undecided. "Let me think on it a bit more. I know I should be there. Maybe I will just get in the car and drive down. Maybe just for a few months... I don't know?"

"Well don't do anything rash without telling us. OK? Look I have to scoot, I have a class in an hour and I need to prepare. I'll ring you later tonight."

"Ok Jen. Thanks, it helps to talk to you... you're a great friend."

"Well just take care of yourself... We can work something out."

Talking to Jen had again left me restless though I knew it was what I needed. I needed to work through my doubts and I knew this was helping. I only hoped I could come to a decision soon for all our sakes because this was fast becoming a trial and an issue.

It was in the quiet of the night as I lay letting the Dreaming wash through my thoughts and my hopes that I came to understand what it was that kept doubts threading through my mind. I had understood my man, my husband so well. Understood his ways, his gifts and from where he had travelled throughout his life. Andrew however was so very different in every way from what I had known.

I was of the desert, the hard stone country while Andrew had grown up amongst the forests. Our worlds were a life time of experiences apart. Could

I survive in the big towns and cities I wondered. What of our child? What of Jiemba? Could I move them to a life amongst the trees, with the rain and damp of the southern temperate forests such a contrast to the searing heat and cutting cold of the desert and the dry rocky plains and tablelands. The world and lands of the Mimi, the stories and spirit songs of the rocks and water holes, would they ever come to know these things as well as they should.

It was then I knew that I needed to seek advice, seek out the wisdom of my mothers and with that thought came the peace of sleep. It was settled in my mind and I knew what I had to do, tomorrow I would prepare for my journey. It was a journey which was hopefully towards my future, one with Andrew and the children.

The peace I felt as I moved about my morning preparing Jem for his day spoke of the rightness of my decision. There was a great deal to do, the first of which was to tell others of my plans and my intent. Jenna, I knew would also need to be told and it was with that in mind that I rang her once I had dropped Jem off at his day care, then I called into the Centre to talk with the Director of the clinic.

"Hi Jen, I have decided," I announced pre-emptively, pleased to have caught her on the phone before she had left for class.

"And...?"

Laughing I answered, "I am coming down, and leaving soon. I have even begun to pack up the kitchen."

"Ngaire that is wonderful. To be honest I have started organizing the rooms down here... it will be great to have you here and Jem can enrol into school or day care or whatever. It will be so much easier to manage a new bub... and so much fun! Ohhh... I can't begin to tell you how pleased I am..."

"Yes, I know I can hear it," I chuckled happily. "I figure I can leave by the weekend and maybe take a week or so to travel the distance, what is it... 3,000 klm? There is someone I would like to see along the way so it may take a day or more extra..."

"Travel... you're driving! But you can't do that trip on your own?"

"Of course I can, I've travelled through the Outback before Jen, I understand the things I need... it's no big deal..."

"No, I can't let you do that. Andrew would never forgive me. Can't you wait until he gets back, it will only be four or five weeks and then he can do it with you? He even said as much..."

"Jen I can't. There is someone I want to see along the way. They live around Boulia in Outback Queensland and... Well, it just wouldn't be right to drag Andrew along."

"Not right? I don't understand... it's not another bloke is it?"

"Oh, nothing like that! I mean, well it's one of my Aunts, she is really quite old and well... well, I want to talk to her is all."

"Is that all? Then what is the problem? Ngaire... I really can't see that there is one... I mean Andrew is OK with oldies...?"

"No, you don't understand. I want... well I want to talk to her about Andrew and I can't do that while he's there," I added chuckling. "Can I...?"

"Oh. I see."

"Yes... it just wouldn't work. Seriously, I will be fine."

"No... no! I really can't buy that. Look, how about I come with you... I could hop a flight, you could pick me up in Darwin and then we could head off. It could be fun... I could do it."

"I can't ask you to do that Jen, besides Sean wouldn't allow it I am sure..."

"Aghh... don't be silly. Sean wouldn't stop me but I guess I would have to tell him or I will be in trouble again."

"Well there is no way you are coming without him knowing," I threatened, though hearing the mischief in her voice had me smiling. "What about your classes... you can't just drop everything."

"No he would be fine with it, I know just how to tell him," she said with a small giggle. "I can do catch up with class, there are no real performances I need to be here for in the next weeks. As for Sean, he's headed out home soon anyway. Taipan has asked him to go back for a while, seems Tom has got himself into some strife again and the men are going to sort it out."

"Nothing serious I hope?"

"No. I don't think so, something about too much partying. Drinking I think... they'll sort him out. He is building his own place in the valley and it's something of a man-cave at the moment. Dianne, his Mum, refuses to go there. Says no good would come of her interfering, that it's for the men to rein him in. You should have heard what Sean had to say."

"You know I would love to have you along, that would be great. I really would love that. Do you seriously think you can organize it?"

"Leave it with me, I'll ring you tonight, it will be all done and dusted by then I am sure. It's not as though we don't know what we are doing is it? How hard can it be to stay on the tar... seriously?"

That I planned to call in and visit Aunt Darri gave my family much satisfaction. She lived in an isolated part of the country, too distant for many of the family to visit regularly but it was a place she preferred to live, happily at one with her memories and in what was her country.

Darri had been married to a man of the Channel Country forever and they had spent much of their lives living off their land. As age had overtaken them they had built a shanty about forty kilometres from the Outback isolation of the Queensland town of Boulia. She lived in the dry bush near one of the many water bores in the area and that was where they had been settled for a number of years, and even after her man had died she had chosen to stay on. She was a woman of the old ways, one who welcomed the family about her and yet valued her time with only her mother country to keep her company.

I had last visited a number of years ago as a young woman, before Jem had become a part of my life. It was at a time when I had needed the company of my aunt and my new husband had taken me into the region so we had made our visit part of our travels.

What drew me to her more than anything was that she knew well the Lore of the land. She was one of the wisest of the women I knew and I felt assured that she would be able to tell me more of the man I was tying my life to. Darri knew about the Koolrari, the earth lights, it had been a skill her old man had known and I knew that she would be able to help me to understand if what I was doing was the right thing.

When I picked Jenna up from the airport in Darwin a little less than a week later it was with great excitement of the travel ahead of us. The weather was beginning to cool as we moved towards the desert winter which made travel and camping out much more comfortable. The season of storms had passed and the land was rich with the growth of green and the colours of the outback.

Saying my goodbye to my family in Katherine had been hard. Farewelling friends and family had left my heart heavy but it was a new beginning and I felt the excitement and warmth of what I hoped was the right decision. My world was changing and I had begun to welcome it.

We travelled with a minimum of baggage; it had been easier than I had thought to leave my life behind me. The house had been packed up, a lot of things were spread around the family. I wanted to travel as light as I could and with the knowledge that Jen welcomed me to what was an already well equipped home, it was easy to let go of so many things. I had kept only my personal possessions and my medical kit with me. I freighted the rest I had chosen to keep, along with Jem's things, in a freight pod which Jen had organized and which would be in Brisbane waiting for me.

I wasn't sure if Andrew knew of my decision yet as I had been unable to contact him, but by the time we reached Brisbane I felt I would have time to settle into my new life before he was expected back from rotation. Sean had promised to keep him informed when he could, so I knew he would soon know of the decision I had made and it would make the settling into the house with Jen and Andrew that much easier.

Jen hadn't said how she had managed to convince Sean to allow her to come but I looked forward to hearing the details as we stowed her duffle bag and headed out along the tar road south to meet the junction where we would head east towards the Queensland border.

It was a long and tedious drive but we aimed to travel between 300-500 klm a day across the flat landscape, which was relieved only by the pockets of bush and other travellers and the long freight trains that rode beside the thin strip of tar with us. We soon settled into a travel routine, making camp each night on the dusty lay-bays and road camps.

The country around here had its own brand of beauty, it was hard, dry and real, but what I loved most were the nights where the land was blanketed with a brilliant sky. It was an endless expanse of land with broad and quiet horizons; the sounds of the bush animals were around us, reassuring us that we weren't the only creatures on the earth. I loved the camp fire the most, it was a link with a world that danced and seemed timeless beyond the shadows of the night outside the rim of fire light.

We were left mostly to ourselves but we didn't feel the need for company, though our fellow travellers and campers where we found them, which was rare enough, were friendly and companionable. I knew as Tango was so very protective in any new environment that we would have little trouble and each evening he and Jem slipped into the way of gathering wood for the camp fire as soon as we arrived into a suitable camp site, while Jenna and I set up.

We travelled with a serviceable old tent that I had picked up in Katherine; it was big enough for the four of us. Tango took to guarding the entrance, protective to the last and while we looked forward to reaching the few larger towns and settlements we mostly kept to ourselves preferring to camp bush-side.

I also enjoyed the opportunity to chatter to Jenna, and chatter we did. It was a wonderful entertainment to be able to swap stories and trade experiences. It drew us closer together as sisters in spirit if not in fact and even when we took the opportunity to ring Dianne, Sean's mother, at near every given public phone we passed it was a delightful trip. Our mobile connections were patchy at the best and that in itself became an entertainment as Dianne thought our trip was such a challenge for the men to accept that she delighted in telling us all about it. I even think she took to torturing Sean with the details with the short text messages Jenna sent.

Our mobile phones were mostly useless as we had known they would be and few were the times we could pick up a signal for many hundreds of kilometres at a time. However when we passed through Mount Isa our phones rang non-stop with messages, so much so that we were forced to stop. Taking the opportunity to camp at the local camping grounds overnight, we could not only stock up on supplies, but also attend to the business of reassuring Sean by calling, and Andrew by message that we were all fine and travelling well.

Taking the development road south towards Boulia from Mt Isa we headed out the next day, only a day away from Aunt Darri and as we drew closer I tried to explain to both Jen and Jiemba what we would likely find.

"I should warn you that Darri might be the sweetest of old Aunts but she is far from helpless," I said having a hard time explaining my meaning. "So Jem, you had better be on your best behaviour and do as she says. You show her respect son and she will welcome you with open arms."

"Is she very old?" he asked, curious about my unusual tone.

"She is. She knew your father you know and she will look for him in your ways."

Jiemba's silence was telling. He understood what I was trying to say. I didn't often speak of his father and when I did he knew it was with purpose.

As we turned off onto the track that led us deep into the country around us, I felt the excitement of meeting once more with my Aunty. Jenna had been full of questions and I was pleased to answer those I could. We would enjoy this visit I knew, just as I knew Darri would welcome us with the enthusiasm in her bright eyes and broad smile, this she did when she stood in the dust from the car as we pulled up.

The shanty had changed little. It was a rough made tin structure supported by bush wood with a beaten and brushed sacking floor in the single room that served both as a bedroom, lounge and kitchen. The bush around the shanty looked strangled and desperate with scarce greenery to soften the tortured limbs of the trees. We could see where Darri had struggled with the land to raise a few vegetables and the old tin water tank which lurched drunkenly beside the house drew birds and ants to a secure supply of water.

But it wasn't the shanty we had come to see; it was the lively old wrinkled worn woman who stood pleased as punch to welcome us to her dusty and crusty little shanty. Enveloped in a bear hug which warmed my soul I revelled in the pleasure of finding her so well, not apparently much older than when I had last seen her.

"Ahh.. Ngaire, how much you have grown. My you're a woman now and you were such a young thing last I seen ya', she chuckled, tucking me tightly to her and then finally releasing me from the warmth of her rag apron and bosom. "And this must be Mindindi, I know lots of you child... it's good to meet you and this young fella' Jiemba...?"

Bending she drew Jem to her, her careful hands running over his thick curly hair and stroking the planes of his face, coming to rest on his shoulders as he stood transfixed by the brilliant flash of her eyes. "You're such a good strong boy!" Shaking her head I could see the moisture glitter in her eyes as I realized that Jen was herself recovering from shock, the shock of hearing her Spirit name on the lips of such a wizened old woman.

"Jen, Darri would know Yoonda well..." I tried to explain.

"Ahh... Yoonda. How's she by the way? Have you seen her... that old man of hers... crotchety old bugga'," Darri added grinning as she led us towards a small but well used camp fire sheltered under a roof of iron that had something of a ragged lean, the area serving as an outdoor kitchen which caught the cooling breezes on the hottest of days.

Jen recovering answered. "Yes... she was good when I saw her; it was ohh... maybe a little over a year ago..."

"Good, good... t'is good to hear little Mindindi. T'is good you'n Ngaire have found each other. This is a good thing, for both you. It's right, the old people are happy an' you bring much to those around you both. But that is not why you're here?" she finished smiling.

"No Aunty. It isn't, but there is a lot to talk about we can do that later. Tell me how you have been?" I insisted. I wanted to hear any news of the family and I knew my mother and aunts would never forgive me if I didn't bring them news when I next spoke to them. There was much to talk about and a great deal to laugh about as I told Darri of the family's news over the light campfire meal we helped prepare, a meal of simple damper and tea with syrup and we talked of many things long into the evening.

Jiemba was soundly sleeping with Tango guarding the doorway of the tent we had put up near the fire. The moon was high in the skies, flooding the camp with the light of the stars when I got around to mentioning Andrew.

"He is a good man Aunty, a man I could be very happy with but I am also little bit scared of him," I said quietly slipping easily into the colloquialisms Aunt Darri would understand the easiest.

"He frighten you? You silly girl, he sounds just what you're needing in life now. It's right way. Thinking you done right-thing in being with him. It's good way business with this man."

"I think so too," I agreed. "But he's a Clever Man of the Earth lights and I don't understand, I don't know this way. He follows a path different to my own and I ... I wonder? This is why I wanted to come to see you, to talk to you; perhaps you can help me to understand."

"The Koolrari? But this is a good thing girl!"

"I know, but ... it frightens me. I have heard of the debil light and how it can destroy you. Andrew trusts it so much, he follows its ways and it... well it frightens me. I am afraid for Jiemba... I don't understand what he will be taught."

"No... no girl. It isn't that way. The debil light, only part of our histories here. Elsewhere it's very different. Well mostly different way," she clarified strangely. "You understand, what you have heard of earth light is not always right way. Different way story to be told and when you little kiddie we tell you to keep you proper safe and teach you to protect you."

"How can you be so sure this will not lead Jem to be afraid of what he should learn, to be a man?"

"Your Andrew is good man, he not teach such a thing the wrong way. But, you girl must let men's business be. You need to understand or it'll be you that leads that kiddie of yours into a fear. This skill that your man has, marks him as a strong man and you respect that girl!."

"But haven't we always been warned about the debil debil light? The stories we were told... as children. Aunty, they were a warning?"

"They are real, but you were kiddies then. You don't understand what we were saying. Here, around these parts the debil debil lights are the mark of murder and can lead the whitefella' into their death, but it's not always the way. The blackfella knows these things. The whitefella don't know right-way things the blackfella know."

"I've something I will show you tomorrow, something you should see to understand... but let me tell you story first of the debil debil light that lives around these parts, about which you know. It would be good I think if you were visiting the place, the Min Min place in town, in Boulia when you pass through that way. They have some old photo' you can show your boy there. Help you too, help you at the museum place and it tells the white man's stories, also good to hear. Young Jem will enjoy that too I think," she added as she went on. "You can tell him the truth of it though... the blackfella truth."

"This country wasn't then as now you know." Darri said settling into the story she wanted to tell and pleased for the tale. I made myself comfortable and noticed that Jenna did also, listening carefully as Aunty continued.

"It was very different and lot changes, for good mostly but once was a very different way. The debil debil light that lives around here is from the things of a long time-go and that is the one I tell you about. Years ago the blackfella had to fight-lot to live and the whitefella he had to fight too but they couldn't live without the blackfella and the blackfella liked to live his life blackfella way. They didn't understand each other and there was much that was wrong-way business. But the blackfella he's not so stupid... there are many ways."

"There was once an old pub around here you know, not far from here that was a real bad place for all men. The pub boss would make his own grog and it wasn't always good grog. It real gut-rot it was, and the stockmen and station mobs..., they would fight. Oh they could fight real hard way... I remember my grandmother telling me much of what went on at that pub place when she was just a littlen like Jem and then the place, she burnt down. Your grandmother she was just your age maybe, it was cursed place, a real proper bad place."

"What went on at that old Min Min pub though wasn't a good thing. It was well known in the country about, its reputation bad... real bad and men murdered for their station money and for their women too. They buried lots out the back of that old place, they even had their own place to bury them and when it was a blackfella', well the mob would dig 'em up and bury them proper, like the old way."

"Did the station blackfella's get wages then? To buy grog?" Jen asked, knowing it wasn't very likely in the early years of the Colony."

"Ohh sometimes but mostly not, but they fed the kids and their women whitefella food and got blankets and clothes and 'backy and there was ways to get grog, but it was the pretty black girls they would fight over. It was a blackfella, a magic man of the Koolrari whose spirit now haunts the place. It's only since the whitefellas came and began the killing that the Min Min light, the Debil Debil light of this Clever Man travels about the district. He doesn't much like the whitefella I think," she added grinning.

"They killed him? Why?" I asked

"It might be that he killed himself, took to drinking he did. He still looks for his woman the old people says, rises up from the earth where they bury the men. Don't know what he would do if he ever found her?" she added further, still chuckling. "Maybe give her a right good beating, or maybe she would do it to him... Silly bugga that he been."

I smiled, to hear Darri talk of the old people and the old stories." But Darri you're not old are you?"

Darri laughed along, knowing I was teasing her. "Nahh... I'm not old. Still a good few years in me yet, but I tell you the story it's true... I can prove it to you. It's the old men of magic that they buried in the dirt out the back of that wicked place, the old pub. The old people even dug him up and moved him... but still he haunts the road and the stations abouts here."

"Ohhh... go on. How can you be sure? I mean I don't doubt it could be true but..." shaking my head I wondered how she could be sure of such a thing.

"I can. I still have the old book, the bible that was your old mothers, lots of greats I think. The one that the woman 'longa-boss gave her, it's in there. Someone saved it. I'll show you when I find it in the morning... dig it out I will."

"What does it say?" Jenna asked intrigued.

"It's the story of the magic man that lived around this way, from the newspaper sheet it is. They called him Jimmy but that not his name, I remember what they say... couldn't write down his name. He was at the old Brighton Downs place until he killed that whitefella and they took him long-way sunrise way to lock him up in Brisbane. That fella he wanted Jimmy's woman and her kiddie so Jimmy chopped him and he was sent to long-away whitefella place in gaol."

"They didn't hang him? That is a wonder?" I added.

"No. They didn't like it when the boss Judge in Rockhampton said it was good business, he deserved it did the whitefella and they only lock Jimmy up for little while. That whitefella Judge, he said that if the whitefella lives like a blackfella then he should live by our law too. If the whitefella takes a pretty gin, then he should live by the blackfella law.

When Jimmy got back to his country here they got him in the end. Killed 'im good at that pub but the whitefella law not much law for blackfella, no one matter. So Jimmy now sends out the Koolrari an search for his woman and he good-scares the whitefella's. It's the debil debil light that they tell of."

"This old stockman, Jimmy, he was a Shaman?" Jen asked very much wrapped up in the story.

"Yes... a good man, a clever man. His woman was young and fine pretty woman they say. Only the whitefella thinks that he owns her whitefella way. I think she was known by whitefella name Lizzie, the whitefella' always gave them another name in those days. They couldn't say the right names. She was of my family and when Jimmy was sent away she tried to follow him but I don't know what became of her and the kiddie she had with her."

"So the Koolrari is not always a promise of death. You think then that it's not a bad thing Darri that I am with Andrew? I worry that he is not of Jiemba's people. Maybe the Mimi Banman will come for Jiemba one day?"

Her look was warm and knowing. "It's a good thing, Andrew is good strong man, I have seen this in my Dreaming, there is strength about you protecting you Ngaire. I had wondered what it was but I can see now... it's your man."

Then for a moment she was quiet as I felt she moved through my thoughts, feeding my strength as I added, trying to explain. "I was afraid for Jiemba, to take him away from the world that was his fathers. I wondered if I was doing the right thing?"

"Jiemba, that boy of yours, he is fine. There is a strong Spirit Man who looks out for him also. The man, I have heard of him, the Spirit Men speak of him and he is known by his name Moonggun. It's a strong good name and Jiemba will always feel his strength."

For some reason I felt the pressure of tears gather in the back of my eyes... something about the Spirit Man Darri spoke of shook my heart and while I knew not to ask more of Jiemba's Spirit shadow, the one that would guide him through his Dreaming, I found instead a need to share in a happiness.

"Aunty, I am going to have a baby. Andrew's child and it has torn me apart to know that the baby may need also the Lore of Andrews people, as much as Jiemba's need is for his own people."

Darri smiled, "I know. It's a fine child who will be strong and happy. You are building a fine life for your children, girl. You should not worry over these things, you have chosen well."

Reaching for her hand I couldn't help but share the light pressure of my fingers on her dark skin. For some reason I felt the relief of confidence, my fears which had silently haunted my thoughts vanished and as I drew a deep freeing breath, Darri moved struggling slowly to her feet.

"It's time, I should get some rest. My old body isn't made for long camp nights anymore."

"Thank you Aunty, you have helped me a lot. I'm so pleased that I came to see you."

"Perhaps this be the last time I think. I am glad you came girl, it's good to see you and your young Jiemba," she said softly.

"Don't say that! We will be back, I have to bring Andrew to meet you... perhaps after the baby..."

Darri just nodded and smiled, "P'haps."

The next morning as we prepared to leave, Darri joined us carrying a dusty and somewhat tattered and aged bible which she held open to reveal a news paper clipping. Jenna was fascinated to read the faded clipping and while I stowed the last of the gear, she read parts aloud.

"It says 1887 and his name was Jimmy, no surname but he had a mate Billy. I wonder why they always gave them such common names?" she asked chuckling. "Absolutely no imagination I think?"

I had to smile at her quip as she continued, "Says here... look it was over his woman. Seems the white stockman tried to stop them from leaving, he wanted her back and tried to take her from Jimmy or force him back to the station, I guess he figured if he had the husband then he could have the wife... Daft idea."

"There is another clipping also," Darri pointed out as Jen flipped to the next page.

"Oh look...I'll be damned," she muttered as she scanned the clippings in amazement. "Hmph... they did gaol him, sent him all the way to Brisbane after he killed the white bloke. But I guess he came back hey?"

"Yes, it's like I said. An' he is still here haunting the whitefella's, looking for his woman," Aunty added.

"But the child..." flicking back to the first clipping, Jenna frowned. "Says the child was a half-caste, which means it wasn't Jimmy's. It must have been what's-his-names... William Bayles. That's almost Andrews Surname... only it's spelt different, his mum's name is Bales."

"Could be it's his great grandad, maybe a couple of greats," Aunty added. "In those days though, it would have been thought to be Jimmy's boy. He was after all her old-way husband. Maybe if blood follows blood and this man of Ngaire's has the skills of the Koolrari then that's what become of Lizzie and the kiddie," Darri shrugged as we both stared at her amazed by her statement.

"Do you think so?" I asked somewhat shocked.

Aunty shrugged. "We will never know. It would take the wise Elders to decide I am thinking. But the Koolrari is not a skill of the Bama people, they follow the ways of the Lightning Man or the Rainbow Serpent, their magic doesn't come from the earth an' rocks as with our people. Their power comes from the sky people, the Lightning Men and the water serpents. If the man of yours, Andrew, draws his magic from the earth then his blood is not of the Bama people. He would more know the ways of the caverns and the secret things of the Earth."

"Can I tell these things to the Shaman?" Jenna asked suddenly. "I mean, there is a strong Karadji in our community who would appreciate this knowledge Aunty, and I know others would enjoy the storytelling of such a thing, it's a good story."

Darri just nodded. "This is knowledge that such a man would need to know I am thinking. Also the kiddies should enjoy to hear the telling," she said softly then she hugged Jen happily and moved, enveloping me once more in her arms, holding me in what was a bruising hold before she suddenly released me. "I will look for you. Tell your man of my place in your life and I will look forward to meeting him."

"I will Aunty. I promise."

It wasn't far to reach Boulia and there we spent much of the morning in the Min Min Centre where the story of the Min Min lights, the whitefella's version unfolded. It wasn't so different from what we had heard but it did help us to understand and most importantly, Jem enjoyed it tremendously as did we.

After a light snack we headed around to the museum where we found the old photographs of the warriors which fascinated Jem but what drew me were the displays of an ancient sea. This was a sea which helped form the greatest artesian aquifer in the world, the Great Artesian Basin. On display also were the bones of water monsters which once swam in the ancient inland oceans of our land, many so different from those I had seen in pictures from the Northern Hemisphere and I wondered why I had never been taught of my own land and its ancient creatures.

The discoveries of our last few days on the road kept us entertained for the rest of the journey and we took time to seek out the evidence of an ancient world along the way. Learning a great deal of the mega fauna which had foraged on our land before man had ever stepped foot. Jiemba was fascinated and by the time we arrived into Brisbane he was full of the world of dinosaurs and mega monsters. Something for which we, Jen and I were grateful though I doubt Tango fully understood all that he was being told.

We were exhausted after the long trip across the land and it was good to arrive into Brisbane to Sean's welcome. Jenna was pleased that he had travelled up from the community to welcome us back though Sean, delighted to have Jen back within his reach looked to read me the riot act about taking her on such a trek across the continent. Jenna though would have none of it and while I worked to settle a tired little man to a bed which Sean had already prepared, I could hear the teasing she gave her man and began to understand with some amusement something of the volatile relationship they both shared.

Settling into what was now my own room; I appreciated the touches of welcome which Jen had taken care to arrange before her departure to meet me. I could find nothing of Taipan and his woman that could remind me that I had taken their room. Jen had also insisted that there was no need for me to worry over the board as Andrew had arranged it all in preparation for my arrival, even before I had decided to come, as Jen had furnished the room in fresh linens. But what most impressed me was the comfortable rocking chair that she had insisted on for my use and it was this more than anything else that welcomed me to my new home.

It was difficult to wait for Andrew's arrival, though I knew it was only a short time away. Time I filled with organizing Jem into early school and finding my way around my new home.

Promise of Life

Andrew:

Hearing of the arrival of the girls safely into Brisbane was something of a relief. Sean had been sure to make certain I heard the news. It was just like Ngaire to think lightly of such a trip and I had been sorely torn when I had heard they had undertaken the journey across country and deep into the desert region of the Northern Territory and Outback Queensland.

It reminded me too much of when Jenna had taken off into the northern tropics with that nutter Warren and for the first time I could appreciate the fears that must have tortured Sean at the time. The bloody women were going to have to learn not to put us through this sort of thing. My anger had cooled a great deal however when I heard they had managed the trip without mishap and as the days until my return into Brisbane had slipped by, my temper had become lost to the thoughts of Ngaire, even Jem and the mutt Tango, settling into the house in Brisbane and waiting for my current hitch to come to an end.

I wished she had waited for me, allowed me to help her move, but then that was also just like her not to. I knew she wasn't used to being with a partner, I understood that she had been managing alone for years, but still that didn't make me any the less concerned for her. Things would have to change, but change slowly I guessed. We could begin when I hit Brisbane, she would have to allow me some measure of responsibility and for the first time I wondered if this was what blokes meant when they spoke about their women running wild.

I had grand plans about how we were going to work our lives together. Plans about the talks we were going to have, the things we were going to do and plan, but all that went out the window when I saw her. I knew immediately that there was no chance of me getting it all my own way, I didn't even want to. It was all lost to the bright depth of her eyes and I felt my grand ideas slipping away like dropping a jacket on the floor, as I dropped my duffle bag when I stepped through the front doorway and Ngaire emerged from the lounge room where she had been waiting for me.

"Hi Babe," was all I got out before she met my open arms, I straightened and chuckled at her enthusiasm when she kissed me, her welcome warmth stretched against my length.

"You should have rung... told me when your flight got in."

"No point. I can just as easy catch a taxi." Lowering her slowly I glanced over at Sean and Jen now also in the lounge room doorway, "Hi you two. It's good to be back."

In the confusion that followed, the jumble of voices and questions and the warmth of the dinner, my eyes followed her. She looked just beautiful, I had forgotten how beautiful, and she glowed. I figured it was true about pregnant women as Ngaire simply glowed with health and life.

Jiemba too was welcoming though quiet, careful to stay out of the way, and Tango just followed Jem about. My arrival seemed to be nothing to either of them.

It was odd to see the rearrangement of my old room when I helped Ngaire put Jem to bed. Really odd, though the room looked good. It was when I dumped my bag into what had been Ty and Aines room that it was really brought home to me. It was much later in the evening when the others had decided to hit the sack, and for the first time I had moved towards the bedroom with her. Ngaire was here... here to stay I hoped and this was our room, a place where we could be together.

Surprised I watched as she without thought, unzipped my duffle bag and started to sort through the tumble of dirty clothes, odd socks and what nots.

"I've left you all the right side of the drawers and there is heaps of room in the cupboard. I moved all of your jackets and things already..."

Laughing suddenly, I stopped her as I caught her arm on her way back to the drawers with a handful of things, this was driving me crazy. Pulling her around to me as I sat on the edge of the bed I held her, grinning at the strangeness of it all, my hands firmly about her hips.

"Will you stay still for a minute," I chuckled indicating my gear on the bed. "You don't have to do this, I can do this..."

"No it's OK. I don't mind... really."

"I do," I cut in.

My thumbs played over the planes of her hips, held between my larger hands, measuring the small bump, I stopped. I hadn't noticed it before but there was a larger bump, larger than ever and surprised I looked up at her, held as she was now between my legs. She was wearing a loose cottony top and jeans and restlessly I slipped my hands up under the top to her waist, my thumbs still moving to feel the differences, but now brushing over her skin.

"It's just a little bump," she said flushing suddenly as her hand covered mine and I struggled to understand the reality.

"It's a bump," I said fascinated. "Come here..."

Ngaire giggled uncertain as I shifted her across my leg, letting her fall to the bed and impatiently pushed the fabric of her shirt out of the way of my fingers against her belly. She didn't protest as I slipped the button of her jeans and tackling the zip, pushed them aside. My much larger hand spread out over the small mound of her belly as I grinned, noticing, feeling, the small firm shape there.

"There is a baby in there," I said, somewhat densely. Trying to convince myself more than her, I was sure.

"There is," she answered with a light chuckle. "What did you expect?"

"I don't know. I... guess I never thought of that side of it." Holding my hand still, stretched almost flat over the small mound of her belly, I looked up. "Can you feel it?"

Ngaire shook her head, smiling. "Not yet, soon though."

Dropping my lips suddenly to the planes of her belly, tasting the sweetness of her skin, I kissed the promise of our child. Then I stretched up beside her, settling myself as I impatiently tugged at her top trying to free her of it.

Ngaire just laughed then sitting up suddenly pulled it up over her head, tossing it aside with the jumble of my clothes from the duffle bag. But then suddenly she climbed off the bed and stood facing me, laughing. Disappointed, I knew I wanted her back here, back on the bed with me and as I again reached for her she instead, slipped from my fingers.

"Jarmies!" she protested again, still grinning. "You're not going to bed in your clothes, get changed! You're just like Jem," she accused me, clearly teasing I was sure.

In a second I was off the bed, pulling my shirt over my head and dealing with my dacks, "We aren't going to need jarmies... come back here."

It didn't take long to settle back on the bed, the duffle bag and clothing tipped impatiently to the floor and with Ngaire firmly back in my arms giggling I began the slow exploration of her skin, the warmth of her body and the subtle and delightful changes I found. There were so many small changes... the fullness of her breast, new and intriguing, even the subtle scent I thought was different. She was passionate, warm and responsive, more so than she had ever been and I delighted in her softness.

I wondered how I could have been so bloody fortunate, if felt good, it was right, and I wanted so much for it to never change, never go away. I wanted it always to be like this, never to alter. As our bodies moved together, towards a rich reward, I came to understand for the first time how two people could be bound together. Nothing could compare with what I was feeling, experiencing now. There was absolutely nothing which I had found or could imagine that could come close to the feelings I had for this woman of mine. I knew then, that she owned me and I would never let her go.

Much later as we lay together, our bodies sated and replete I wondered again at the peace I felt, the completeness .Then drifting my fingers gently over her still damp body I wondered how I was going to show her how I felt, what was there that I could say... it seemed beyond simple words.

"Will you marry me Ngaire?" I said softly. It just came out, an expression of the contentment and passion that filled me. I hadn't even thought about it, I didn't even have a ring.

She turned to me and smiled, lifting a finger to trail along my chin.

"Why?"

I grinned. Realizing just how unprepared I was for this question. "God... I don't know. I want to make sure you're mine I guess." Then suddenly I frowned... this wasn't a good reason I realized. "I think I am in love with you," I said suddenly, quickly trying to make amends realizing this was something I hadn't said, I had just wanted to secure her to me. I was being possessive and as I recognized it I wondered where it had arisen from.

"You think?"

"No... no I mean I am... I am sure this is what I feel Babe. I don't want us ever to be apart, don't ever leave me."

The silence between us was suddenly becoming excruciating and I wished I had planned this better. I should have waited... been better prepared.

Then, she suddenly snuggled into me, shifting her head to my chest, tucked into my side. I couldn't see her expression anymore and it suddenly worried me.

"No Andrew. I don't think I want to get married... not at all."

"Why not?" I asked confused, even a bit disappointed.

"Why?"

Drawing another breath I frowned again. I wasn't expecting this. "I don't know? Why do you usually get married?"

I felt her smile against my chest. "I never worked that out." she said softly. "How about we just wait till we can work out why we should get married. I mean it isn't like it's something we do, I don't think my mum ever married my dad... I never asked them actually. Besides, we're together now and I don't plan on going anywhere different."

"Hmm..." I was confused. Now wasn't the time to tell her that my parents were not married either, not in the manner the Government or a Church would see clearly. Though my grandmother was, she married once in a church but it hadn't worked out and I knew she had left him not long after. Then I wondered why I had even asked Ngaire. "OK," I said softly. "Then how about we go to the bank tomorrow and sort out that stuff."

Again I felt her smile. After a moment she looked up at me, challenge in her eyes. "Are you after my money?"

Surprised I frowned. "You have money?"

She chuckled softly before answering, "No."

Then I grinned. "Will you be serious for a minute, all I want is to make sure you have money to live on, you need stuff. The baby needs stuff. We can arrange a card for you on my account."

"Oh... so you're trying to give me money. I have some, I'm on a support pension."

"Yeah... about that. You really need to cancel that. I can look after you and Jem. And the baby too..."

"You don't have to," she said softly.

"Babe... I get a good wage OK. Look, how about I match the pension to begin with and we start an account or something. It will be just the same, only it will come from me... you can manage it how you like."

For a moment she was silent as she thought it over. "You don't have to do this you know. But I am rather flattered that you want to."

"Yes I do. It's for me as much as you. We're a couple and I want it to stay that way. We are living together Babe and I want it to be this way. Besides it will be so much easier you know. You can do all the wife stuff". I added chuckling.

It seemed forever that the moment was drawn out while she considered my suggestion.

"OK." she said suddenly. "We can try that. I can let the pension people know this week."

The relief I felt flooded through me was as unexpected as it was rewarding. I wanted this. I wanted to provide all I could for Ngaire, Jem and the baby. "Good. That is settled then,"

"Anything else?" she suddenly asked softly, teasing almost.

"No. I don't think so?" then something occurred to me. "Yes. We will get you a card on my credit account, so you can pay the bills. That will make it easier for me too. I have a hard time keeping track of these things. Don't spend all my money though," I threatened half heartedly. "I'm trying to pull together enough money for a place."

"You sure you want to do this then? I mean I could stay on the pension. It's not like you're here all the time."

"No. We do this. Babe... I don't want the government paying for my kids when I can."

Ngaire wrapped her arm back around my chest and snuggled, something I enjoyed immensely. Then she quipped almost cheekily, "I'm going to be a kept woman I guess."

Chuckling, I appreciated the irony of having Ngaire dependant on me, on what I could provide for us. I even liked the terms she had given, though nothing on this earth would persuade me to tell her that, and it was with that thought I drifted into sleep. I was more contented than I had ever thought I could be.

When I woke the next morning, it took a moment for me to remember where I was, and then as it came to me I wondered where Ngaire had got to. It was later in the morning than I was accustomed to and as I climbed out of bed I found myself a pair of jeans, I could hear the noise in the kitchen. It seemed I was the only one who had slept in.

Everyone was around the small central table, aside from Ngaire who was still doing toast for Jem and as I helped myself to milk from the fridge then gathered up a couple of eggs she forestalled me, taking them from me with every expectation I would let her.

I did.

"How would you like these?"

"Scrambled would be great. Thanks"

I watched as she set about preparing breakfast, amused as she cut the crusts from my bread, setting it on the side of the plate as she handed me my breakfast minutes later. Picking the toast up I considered it, then glanced across at Sean who unable to restrain himself laughed out loud drawing everyone's attention.

Ngaire frowned, and it wasn't until she glanced up at me still holding up my toast that she looked at me confused...

"What?"

I grinned at her confusion. "I like my crusts," I said simply.

"Oh for goodness sake," she scolded somewhat startled as she grabbed the toast from my fingers impatiently and put it on Jem's plate. Flushing unexpectedly she turned back to the counter top, popping another couple of pieces of bread into the toaster quickly.

I climbed to my feet, moved to reach over her and grabbed the fingers of crust she had cut away popping them into my mouth as she looked up at me apologetically.

"Stop it!" she threatened softly, trying not to grin. "I just didn't think."

Returning to the table, I couldn't help but chuckle at her embarrassment as I winked at Jiemba who sat there trying to work out what was going on that had caused Sean so much amusement.

Breakfast was good when I got it all, and I admitted to myself that it was something again having Ngaire around doing these small things for us as a family. She wasn't so amused herself when I mentioned what I had planned for the day.

"Once we get back from the Bank, how long do you think it will take to organize some gear?"

"For what?" she asked obviously confused.

"To head out; if we get away by lunch, we can be in Nimbin for dinner."

"Nimbin? Andrew I can't just waffle off to Nimbin, Jem has school today. And I planned to get up to the Council office to register Tango and there are other things I need to do."

"I thought we could head south to the community so you can meet everyone? I would rather Jem come, but if you don't want him too then..." Shrugging I continued. "Jenna an Sean can watch him for a coupl'a days."

As I suggested it, I turned to them both in question.

Sean shrugged, "I guess so, Jen has class but she will be home by four and I can hang around."

"Andrew no!" Ngaire cut in and then turned to Sean. "I won't impose on Jen or you, Jiemba is my concern and Andrew... you don't just leave him with someone so cavalierly. I can't believe you expect to be able to."

"It's not like he would mind Ngaire, he is used to staying with your Mum when you're not there."

"Andrew!" she said in a tone that surprised even me. "Jem is only just getting used to his life down here I won't leave him at the moment. Besides, it would be impractical to take him down to Nimbin, he's still adjusting to Brisbane and his school's still new to him. He doesn't need to be dragged away again for another long trip." Then adding as she moved to gather the breakfast dishes she dismissed the lad. "Jem, go get ready and I'll be in soon."

I realized then that this was more a ploy to further discussion as Jiemba climbed down from the chair with a purpose, calling Tango as he left. This was a discussion she didn't want young Jem around for and I had been lacking in sensitivity.

"I wish you would tell me about your plans earlier. It's important that Jem see we are in agreement. We can't go off willy nilly on a trip for days on end without planning. Not for a while anyway. Jem needs to settle in, at his age he needs to feel secure."

"I can't see what the problem is. I think your being over protective. Jem's fine, he loves Sean and Jenna. He would love to spend time with them I am sure."

"That may be the case but he's not Jenna and Sean's responsibility. He is mine, Jen is not a babysitter on hand when we want to do something."

"It's OK Ngaire..." Jen said almost apologetically only to be cut off.

"No it's not! You have college and Andrew has to understand that Jem is our responsibility not yours and Sean's."

"Look I understand that," I protested.

"No you don't. If you did you wouldn't have suggested this without checking first. You didn't even ask, you just assumed Jen would want to babysit..."

Shrugging, I surrendered. I could see I wasn't going to win this as Ngaire became more and more passionate in every passing minute. "I'm sorry if you thought that..."

"It wasn't a thought Andrew. You just announced we were going and Jem was going to be looked after by someone else..."

"Well I'm sorry," I said, standing myself now. "Yeah... well you are right I did think you would want to come down to meet my family. I'm sorry; I shouldn't have assumed you'd want to do that." I could feel myself growing angry and defensive. I wasn't sure why so I stopped myself before I said something I didn't mean and instead just drew a deep steadying breath. She was being infuriating and I couldn't understand it. This shouldn't be so difficult surely.

Ngaire turned away angry herself I could see and as Jenna slipped from the table and Sean moved to join her, neither wanting to be around for an argument, I acknowledged that maybe I had been thoughtless.

"Look I don't want to argue with you..." I added as the others left.

"Well then you shouldn't have assumed we could just drop everything and do what you wanted to do..."

"OK. If that is what you want then we won't go..."

"Andrew it's not about what I want," she protested turning to me shaking her head. "We have responsibilities with Jiemba, you can't just take off without working these things out and you can't just dump your responsibilities on whoever you think will be able to deal with them when it suits you."

"Well it's been months since I have seen my family and I told them I would be down this month, I promised them Ngaire..."

"Well then you go. I can't, I have Jem to sort out."

My anger flashed, I felt almost as though I had been deserted and that Ngaire had no intention or even desire to get to know my family. I know I used too much force to push the chair back in under the table, enough force to vent my anger and my frustration at the difficulties in what should'ave been a simple road trip.

"OK. If that is how you want it?" I said still infuriated.

Uncertain of my mood, Ngaire flashed her glance at me and in her look of surprise I felt my anger melt.

"That's how it will have to be. I can't just go off and leave Jem and he can't just take time off at the drop of a hat, it's too soon for him," she said not unreasonably and suddenly I felt like a petulant child, something which I knew I hated the minute the sensation overtook me.

"OK." I said uncertain. Then turning away in my confusion I left the kitchen. By the time I reached the bedroom my anger was renewing itself. While I understood why Ngaire felt the way she did, I didn't see the reason for it. I didn't much like the idea that I had been judged as wanting, not knowing how a parent would think and of not understanding the needs of a child.

I felt confused and inadequate and grabbing at my duffle bag, still on the floor I emptied it onto the still rumpled bed and began to pick out the few things I would need for a couple of days. I didn't wait for Ngaire, she had already said that she had things to do and soon after packing, I washed and changed for the day, irritation growing within me. Then I was out the door, stowing the bag in the boot as I headed off leaving Ngaire to deal with Jiemba, having noticed them preparing for the day at school, unconcerned with what I was up to.

There were things I needed to do and now was as good a time as ever. That the bank was still closed and I had a good forty five minutes to kill before they opened didn't help my mood and I spent the time wandering the shopping centre trying to convince myself I had a purpose and had been justified in my actions.

By the time I'd collected the forms I would need I was in a better temper, so much so that when I passed the florist I decided that I had been a pain and was going to have to make an effort to make amends.

The bunch of flowers were all natives, they even looked impressive and when I got back to the house I was disappointed to find that Ngaire wasn't at home, in fact no one was. Not sure what to do I sat around for an hour then decided that this could take all day, it was time I didn't want to waste so digging out some note paper I put the forms on the table along with a short apologetic note to Ngaire. It didn't take too long to find a big enough jug to put the flowers in and I used this to anchor the papers and note to the table top and feeling better for my efforts I headed out for the long drive to Nimbin. Accepting that Ngaire wouldn't be making the trip this time.

It was going to be a long and lonely drive, not one I had been planning on but there was nothing for it. If I didn't leave today then I would only have the one full day and I needed at least two to catch up with everyone. I knew I had a round of training and assessment and I wanted to give myself enough time to spend with Ngaire and Jem before I had to head out to the rigs again. I was sure I could sort this all out with Ngaire when I got back The space apart would give us both time to calm down and consider things.

During the hours of driving I came to see that I had not considered Jiemba's needs, that she was right in that. It must be difficult for a youngster to adapt to the way their parents lives changed and moulded their own experience. It was a big thing to uproot him from everything he had known, then put him into a world that would be not only different, but confusing and new.

I also realized that Tango would be like a security blanket for the lad and also that he couldn't go to school with him. Jiemba was on his own there. I should have foreseen the trial that would be. I also knew that I had taken Jenna's compliance for granted, that was something that I would not do again. Once more she had been right, I hadn't considered my responsibilities properly and at that point I wished I could turn around, drive back to Brisbane to tell Ngaire that she had been right. That didn't solve the problem for me though, in being where I said I would be, then perhaps it was a good thing that Ngaire and Jem weren't with me. I hadn't been forthcoming with my mother and maybe she too needed time to adjust to the idea of my woman and my own family taking first place in my life.

It was time I told my family all about her, Jiemba and the coming baby. They knew I had a serious interest in a woman but I hadn't elaborated and it was high time that I did. It could only be painful for Ngaire to sit through such a discussion with mum. It had been way too long since I had sat down and spoken to my mum who also looked to me to be a role model for the younger kids. I had been pretty much wrapped up in my own life and Ngaire's, so it was time that this was set to rights. Yes... perhaps it was good that I took the opportunity to sort that out before I bought Ngaire home, it would smooth the way.

The community was just as I remembered it, some things just never changed. It was growing dark when I arrived and parking the car I headed out down to mums place. There were the usual group of mothers around the fire pit, it seemed that it was going to be a quiet night at the main camp and I wondered where the younger group were gathering these days. I suspected that it was over at Tom's place, from what Sean had said that was where the young Shaman had been hanging out.

There had been something of a ruckus only recently when they had been caught with an attempt at a homebrew and Tom had suffered the consequences. It had helped that the group had kept it amongst themselves. That wasn't too serious as we had dealt with a similar incident once before when a boy's night had got out of hand. That brew had been confiscated but still, they had managed to anger Taipan and that was bad enough.

What the young men were up to now was something I could check up on while I was here, as they saw me as more with them than above them. Tom was a handful and I knew Ty struggled to keep tabs on him without being over-bearing, he was like any sixteen or seventeen year old. He was a smart kid, though his brains seemed to get him into trouble rather than keep him out of it, I thought as I reached the house.

Mum was glad to see me and I soon had the whole family around me, it helped that it was dinner time and it was good to see how they had all grown. When I mentioned Ngaire, the look on mum's face was almost embarrassing and I wished that Ngaire had been here to see it. As I spoke of Jiemba, I knew that I had pressed just about every maternal button my mum had. I had nothing to worry about when it came to welcoming Ngaire and young Jem into the family.

Mum was full of questions, eager for any scrap of information I could come up with and wanting more, but once the youngsters had headed to bed it was as we sat around the small crowded lounge room that I decided it was time to mention the baby.

"There's something else I should tell you too," I started, knowing that I was going to get a reaction to this news and hoping that it was going to be as positive as my other news had been.

"What? You done something you shouldn't 'ave son?"

I grinned, "Yeah... you could say that." Leaning forward I drew out the suspense; I had a good idea how this news was going to be received. "Ngaire and I.., we're having a baby, he should be here just before Christmas."

"What! You come to tell me I'm gunna be a grandmother twice?"

I nodded grinning at the sudden light in her eyes. This was something she had spoken of often, since I had been of age and I could see in her eyes, it was something she had been waiting for.

"Well it's about time boy!" she announced delighted. "You bring her down here, we can't have her up there all on her own. She has no family up there hey? They would want her with us...you hear me Andrew!"

"Yeah I hear you mum, but it's not that easy, she needs to be in Brisbane where she is with Jenna. They are very close, Spirit Sisters. They knew each other before time. I have only just persuaded her to move to Brisbane from the Territory."

"You say? Well... that is good thing hey. Jenna, she is a good girl. Young Sean, he has to look after her, and you... you have to look after your girl. Took you long enough to find her... I thought you would end up with another one from here. You better look after this one."

"I will Mum," I reassured her. "Perhaps I will bring her down when the baby is closer but give her time to adjust. Let me bring her down to you when she is ready, OK. I will have plenty of time up by then and I plan to spend a few months at home when the baby comes."

"That's a good thing young man. Yes, a good thing. You will be a good

Dad," she added smiling. "You bring her here. I will fix up your room for you again, or you can have the verandah room it will be quieter out there with the baby, and it's bigger."

Knowing my younger brother had taken over my old room I nodded in agreement. There would be things I would need to do out in the verandah room. It was still a little exposed and it would need refurbishing, that was something I could start on. A couple of pieces of furniture and another bed at least, then there was the question of Jiemba I had to solve. We might be able to put a temporary cot in with the other kids, I would have to have a look and make a decision.

"Thanks, I can fix it up, I have a few months and Jiemba will need a bed. The next time I'm down I will bring some stuff. Actually I might doss out there tonight if that is OK?"

"Yeah... you go right ahead. The young one, when he comes he can sleep in with your brother, in his room there. I have a sleeping bag in the cupboard that I was going to give away you can use that tonight, save going back up to the car. There's a camp cot out there already just move the stuff off it and you'll be alright."

It wasn't a very comfortable night, and as I lay awake listening to the sounds of the house I made plans for what I could do with the room. It wasn't ideal, it was small and almost airless. There was no way I would consider it as a permanent base for us. In the end I decided that we would stay in Brisbane until I could decide on where I wanted to buy a place, or build one. I loved Mum, but Ngaire would find this house cramped I felt.

Living with Mum would do while we waited for the baby, but it wasn't going to work for very long. It was something I would have to give thought to. Maybe when Jenna finished her course this year, Ngaire and I could take over the lease of the house in Brisbane. It was a viable proposition and I could talk to Taipan or Sean about that. It was something else to think about as I finally drifted off to sleep.

The next day I called around to see Taipan and caught up with all the community news. Aine was full of questions about how Jen was doing and what I could tell her about Ngaire. I realized that Ty had already told Aine about the baby, and I understood that there was little that Aine and Ty didn't share. Perhaps that was something else I was going to have to get used to with Ngaire.

Ty also filled me in on what Tom and the other Shaman of his group had been up to and it was with this in mind that I headed over to see how the building on Toms place was progressing. It was a slow process, made slower by the constant flow of Tom's friends through the house.

Once the 'A' frame had got to the stage of being weather proof it seemed to have come to a halt but Taipan was hopeful that the colder weather would spur his younger brother on once again.

It was good to catch up with the younger men, it was like revisiting old times when I settled into an evening of eating and drinking a home-brew of ginger beer which some of the girls had set down a while ago, and which they had now bought out as we sat around the camp fire. I was set on trying to convince Tom it was time to consider getting on with the building and finishing the large fire place he had planned in the initial stages. Most of the outer work had been done and it just needed to have a few safety issues seen to before winter would make sitting outside at night too cold an experience.

I could understand why the kids were drawn to this place. The company was amiable and both the Shaman and their women seemed at home there. It seemed to have something which the other huts didn't offer. The young women had taken to organizing a kitchen of a sorts, and I was surprised at the ease with which they pulled together to organise something to eat, as it seemed haphazard.

Some of the older men mixed amongst the group and I guessed that this was more Taipan's doing than Tom's but it was a good thing. It kept the younger guys in line but still gave them the leeway to have a good time. The place had a good feel about it and as I settled more into the night, having caught up with some of my old mates I soon realized why the main camp had been surrendered to the mothers and younger teens. Why would the older ones want to compete for the camp when they could come here?

The evening took on a party feel and as a few bought out the guitars and someone began to tap the sticks I slipped readily into the ease of friends around the fire and the memory of good nights spent with mates and their girls which I realized I had missed over the past year. It was like slipping into old ways and I settled in to enjoy the dance, the talk and the night.

When I opened my eyes the following day there was a feeling about it which I was sure I had experienced before and the realization sent fingers of alarm through me, stirring my stomach. The sun was high and the surroundings vaguely familiar though it took a moment to recollect just where I was. Then I froze.

Lifting my head gingerly I looked around. My head pounded and I felt oddly woozy, hung over and disorientated, which given that I hadn't been at a solid nights drinking didn't make sense. When I found the thick glossy head of dark hair, streaked with brilliant red colour on the pillow beside me I frowned and alarm bells really began their noisy clamour in my head. A clamour that wasn't at all welcome.

Easing myself up I tried to gather my wits as I sat amid the tangle of sheets and bed covers, wondering what the hell had happened. It seemed pretty obvious, the room was a mess and clothes were scattered around everywhere. Realizing just where I was, I looked down again at the girl and didn't understand how I had got here, indeed I didn't want to understand just what the hell I was doing here and as I moved to sit heavily on the side of the bed getting ready to get out of here as fast as I could manage it, I saw that Carley was beginning to stir.

Reaching for my jeans on the floor was a mistake as a sickening dizziness hit me, whatever it was I had drunk was an evil mix and this was going to be no short hangover I realized, as I gripped the sides of the mattress trying to still my heaving stomach and quieten the pounding in my head.

"Are you going?" The question dribbled across the bed as I gingerly turned my head towards her.

"Yeah... I don't know what the hell I am doing here," I answered thoughtlessly.

"Mmm... You don't remember?" she said with a short laugh.

Dropping my pounding head into my hands I thought about it, trying to call forward memories and then I glanced across at her. "Yeah... I remember. I'm sorry..."

"What for?" she mumbled as she turned around. "We had a good time; it isn't as though we haven't been here before you know." Her smile held threads of pleasure, tinged as it was with the apathy of the acceptance that it meant little to her what her current boyfriend thought about her dalliance with me. I didn't doubt that she had a steady boyfriend of a sorts, it had always been Carley's way to grab at pleasure where she could find it.

Carley was an attractive woman and as my eyes ran over her exposed breasts, firm and shapely I grew impatient with my memories of their weight and taste as these emerged from the fog of the night we had just spent together. We had been here before, we had enjoyed each other's company often when I had returned to the community in past times, but now it was different. I should not be back here I knew that without a shadow of doubt.

"This shouldn't be happening Carley. There is someone else..."

She shrugged, "Obviously not too serious a relationship." She quipped smiling. "Come back to bed and stop whining."

Pulling the tangled sheets aside, she invited me back into her arms; the sight of her shapely body tormented me. I knew where we had gone last night, I knew the pleasure we could share, but I also knew that what I wanted was Ngaire lying in the bed with me and this wasn't Ngaire. Carley smelt very different, tasted very different and even the passion we shared was very, very different. Carley was a poor substitute in every way. It was the memory of Ngaire which bought me to my feet. I didn't want to be here.

"I'm going Carley. I shouldn't even be here. I don't know why I am here at all?"

Carefully I reached again for my jeans, collecting what gear I could see and struggling to deal with it and my head as I dismissed Carley from my thoughts. I refused to deal with this, I didn't want to think about something that should never have happened.

"Well that wasn't what you said last night."

I stalled then, frowning I glanced across at her as I was pulling on my shoes. "I told you I had a woman in Brisbane..."

"Yes. You did, you also told me we had some good times. I thought, no I knew it was what you wanted or you wouldn't be back here without her."

The conversation was vaguely familiar and as I considered what I could remember, I finished with the shoes. "It isn't going to happen Carley. This was a mistake, I'm sorry."

"Yeah whatever," she quipped, stretching back out on the bed. "See you around Andy."

Annoyed at the use of the pet name she had given me I stood, knowing that I never wanted to hear that nickname again. I knew she continued to watch me as I stepped over towards the window. The look in her eyes felt like the eyes of a cat measuring the speed of a mouse.

"You're not going out the window?" she challenged suddenly, lifting her head from the pillow surprised and chuckling.

"Yep!" As I straddled the sill, I looked back at her. She was quite pretty, stretched out on the bed as she was with a fine sheen on her dark skin still alluring with its thin veil of passion evident in her eyes. I could appreciate the subtle curves of her body, the weight and fall of her breasts, the tussled disorder of her hair as it moved about her, but I felt little. While my body responded, my senses were numb, I was still reeling from the after effects of the night, I was feeling ill enough for me to ignore its demands easily. These were after effects I shouldn't have I felt, but that I did have and it made me annoyed with myself more than anything else. I hated that my body even responded to the sight of Carley. That seemed the worst betrayal of all to me now. Not only betraying Ngaire, but myself as well.

As I ducked through the window I heard her careless laughter, it was almost dismissive which didn't anger me. I felt like a fool, I had risked everything with a really bad decision to be with her. I couldn't understand why I had made such a decision but the long walk back towards Tom's was enough to help iron out the worst creases of my hangover.

When I was able to empty my stomach of whatever it was that was turning it constantly over, I felt much better. The cold water from the creek helped a great deal and taking my time I stopped often in an attempt to bring order to my thoughts as I walked back along the path.

I couldn't afford to let Ngaire know about this I realized, our relationship was unsteady enough without this added stress, so I had to find out who else knew, and what if anything I could do to head off any idle talk. I knew I couldn't trust Carley to rein in any gossip but hopefully I could put enough time and distance between us that it would not be an issue. It was a hope that I nurtured for most of the day.

At Tom's, the place still showed the remains of the night before and as penance I began to clear up a bit, knowing that there was still a few of the guys sleeping inside. I watched indifferently as they emerged to greet the day. Some stayed for a scratched breakfast while others left as soon as they felt able.

It was just after lunch that Tom turned up around the fire pit, where a few of the guys had stirred the embers and were toasting bread scraps from a loaf someone had found in the kitchen. Butter though was in short supply so we made do with thick layers of jam that had been found in the crates that were the pantry.

"What a night hey?" Tom commented as he tucked into heavily burnt toast.

I looked up not wanting to get too involved in the conversation, content to just listen to the impressions of the others.

Few were concerned with who had ended up where, and even fewer bothered to enquire and as the afternoon drew on I became more confident that I had at least been discreet. I began to hope that my choices would not have been obvious enough to be noticed and as my fears faded I found I could join in the flowing conversations more easily. It was forgotten, over with and hopefully would not ever be revisited. Ngaire would never know and I wanted to keep it that way.

In the weeks and months that followed, life became surprisingly easy. I don't know whether it was because I was much more tolerant and more aware of Jem's needs and how to cope with them, or whether it was because Ngaire seemed to easily slip into creating a order to the pattern of our lives, heading off anything that she thought might cause a problem.

We came to discussing most things at night. I loved the moments where she would join me in bed and curl up to talk about whatever it was in the day that she felt needed my attention. The ease of our relationship was probably helped by the reality of my absence for weeks on end, topped with my return and the firm knowledge that we only had so many days before the next contract began.

Work knew that I was planning an extended period of leave with the birth of the baby and it was with this in mind that I was kept in steady employment on the rigs. This helped with training and the move up the hierarchy of authority so it was with ease that I moved through life on the offshore rigs and as our savings grew we began to talk about where we would live and what it was we wanted for our future.

One thing we never discussed though was our trip down to Nimbin together, though we talked of perhaps living there. For me I avoided the entire suggestion of a visit for the time being. I wanted to put as much distance in time between Ngaire and the community for as long as I could. I didn't want to ever have to deal with the risk of Ngaire discovering my indiscretion and time would give me distance from this risk.

It was all relatively easy to arrange and as I explained that I needed to work on preparing our room at Mum's, this gave me reason to undertake an occasional quick and bustled visit to that end. It was a visit that usually coincided with Sean's own return when I was on rotation.

These were visits which were over almost before they had begun, usually with a clear purpose that was attended to quickly not only because I needed to but because I wanted to.

I wanted to prepare the room for Ngaire and I wanted it to be ready. I really wanted to ease Ngaire, Jem and the baby into my family, but I was afraid of what she might learn. I would give anything not to disappoint her again.

I didn't doubt Ngaire knew that I had enjoyed past relationships, she was aware that she would meet some of my old girlfriends amongst those in the community. I realized quite early that there were few secrets between Jenna and Ngaire. I hoped in the back of my mind that time would confuse the issue, but I couldn't keep our planned visit at a distance for ever.

During one of my absences out on the rig, Ngaire and my mum had managed to get together when Sean had brought her up from the community on one of his runs to see Jen. Mum had stayed for a week and they had got on together really well, something which I had expected. She had complained though that she had just about given up on my bringing Ngaire and Jiemba down for the promised visit and that she was out of patience with my delays. She wasn't sure whether it was of my or Ngaire's making so had decided to take the initiative into her own hands.

What had come out of the trip though was Ngaire's desire to be in the community and with my family when the baby was due. This I think was something which was supported by Jen, who would be returning herself to the community at the end of her course so between the three of them the women had arranged for the move down to Nimbin so that the baby could be born amongst family.

The business of birth was strictly a woman's affair and I felt helpless to interfere in any way. Ngaire would do as she chose and I would fight for her right to make whatever choices she made. Once the women had settled on their plan I gave in to them and put notice in to work of my intent which gave me a clear cut off day, which would see us arrive and settled before Jenna's course came to an end and before the babies arrival. It was arranged for me to return on contract when I felt we were ready to take up our lives in Brisbane again.

When I thought about my son, the reality of him and the promise of his birth I was often overwhelmed, uncertain about a reality which I didn't understand. I felt the only thing I could do, the only way I could contribute was to make sure of the security of our future and this meant saving and working towards a life with Ngaire and our growing family. My own father had been an absent dad, one who returned to the family three or four times a year. It was my mothers and aunts who were the core of my family.

Each time I returned home though, rediscovering the mysteries of the pregnancy had become the most entertaining and inspiring reality. Ngaire's growing belly was a fascination for me, it was something I loved to revisit and wonder over. Feeling the movement of our child against my hand at night was a delight I looked forward to and my world became wholly consumed with the promise of his arrival.

Sean and I had always been close but he had difficulty in understanding my preoccupation with the baby so instead I shared my enthusiasm with young Jem. Jem and I had discovered something of a closer relationship, one shared with Tango. Each time I return home I would plan a special outing just for the men, me, Jiemba and Tango. If Sean was there he would be included, however the women were strictly forbidden, much to Jiemba's delight and together we would plan carefully each adventure.

This could be anything from fishing, to kayaking along the Brisbane River or any one of its tributaries. Bushwalking was a favourite as it usually involved a night in the bush though hunting was another and we made use of much of the forest lands and forestry area's in the South East Corner of the state. We ventured out around Brisbane and Ipswich, and as far afield as Toowoomba and the Darling Downs as well as the Moreton Bay Islands which usually involved fishing or crabbing.

On a hunt our prey was usually wild pig though wallabies were equally as available and the farmers often welcomed this measure of skilled population control. On the Downs though we would often track the wild dog packs and thin out the threat to both men and wildlife though this was more a control measure than a food supply but it was more satisfying.

Ngaire seemed to cope well with her pregnancy and the growing baby seemed healthy, things were going well. So when it finally became time to consider our extended stay down south in the community, we began to pack and prepare for the event with some enthusiasm. I was looking forward to the opportunity to spend more time with Ngaire and young Jem, and as the birth was getting closer I enjoyed sharing with Ngaire something that we both were looking forward to.

Even young Jem was excited but I think that had more to do with spending time with new friends. He seemed little touched in some ways by the promised arrival of a brother, or sister as Ngaire kept insisting, though a little girl seemed a distant possibility to me as we undertook the move and I began to focus on settling in and helping prepare for the birth of the baby.

CHILDREN OF THE SPIRIT

Taipan:

The table was cluttered, it seemed overfull of things I didn't necessarily enjoy doing. It was the paper work; the paper which helped put in order the things which were demanded of me. Aine usually collected the correspondence and invoices and harangued me into attending to these periodically. Her attention had made it easier, but not necessarily any more pleasant a task. Tired of the demands, I looked up to let the scene on the apron of green between the house and the forests lighten my mood. It had been a restless few months for me, for some reason my attention was no longer on the demands of the community and I wondered about that as I watched Aine and smiled, contentment edging out my irritation.

The sight of Aine, playing with the youngsters bought pleasure to my morning, as tedious as the morning was being. She loved being with the young kids and had even mooted starting a kindergarten or early day care group for the mothers, but the letter she had received yesterday had laid her dreams aside for the time being.

Karyn wasn't doing so well. She was Aine's elder sister who was married to an offensive husband, Brad. I had met them the Christmas before last and I wondered what there was that Aine had not told me. She would not have liked detailing everything which had occurred between them I knew. There would be things she would not have told me, but I would give her time to come to terms with these things herself. I knew she would tell me in time and I could give her that time.

Shuffling the accounts around I again considered the group of women on the lawn, shaded now from the morning sun as it was before the heat rose high in the forest canopy. They were a play group of sorts brought together to amuse the youngest of the children in the community and I knew both Aine and Ngaire encouraged the mums to gather regularly about the house. Today they had chosen the small lawn area and despite the noise it was a pleasant scene to work to, something I was surprisingly enjoying.

Andrew, I knew, was down giving Tom a hand not that they would get too much done. Tom still had not reined in his mates and it always took time to move them along before any real work could be done on his place. It still surprised me how much time Andrew had for the young Shaman. He enjoyed the challenge and he moved well amongst the group, better than I had of late in fact and it had made the demands on my time more manageable.

Ngaire too had settled in with the women since their recent arrival from Brisbane and some of the elder women had taken her under their wings, Gran included. Perhaps it was her young son Jem who encouraged them with his open and friendly acceptance of so many aunts in his world though I thought it had more to do with Aine's efforts to help Ngaire make friends amongst the women. Ngaire's dog Tango rarely left her youngster alone and while the kids accepted the mutt, the mums were more wary. Tango was more devoted to young Jem than he was to Ngaire it seemed to me at times as the dog had become almost Jiemba's shadow. If we saw the mutt we knew that Jem was close by.

I watched the swollen figure of Ngaire now lounging somewhat uncomfortably on the rug and my smile broke again. Andrew I knew still had difficulty understanding that it was his baby that she carried and I had often caught the look of amazed wonder when he caught sight of her swollen belly. Ngaire seemed now to be the centre of his attention and I guessed it had a lot to do with being away so much but now, they had more time together, he would grow more at ease with the coming promise of the baby.

It wasn't so much that he couldn't accept the thought but that he was unsure about how to deal with the new arrival, unsure of himself more than anything else. The way in which he protected her was enough to tell me he would not be an absent father and I hoped that this would be the reality.

Children needed both parents about. As our world was changing and customs of the past didn't always mesh well with the present, it was a bigger world now. Andrew and his woman seemed more settled here though, less troubled and definitely more balanced and happier. With both parents around willing to help kids cope with life and its lessons was now the best way. This wasn't always possible unfortunately but at least family could help in our community, and that was a good thing.

The housing they were in wasn't ideal for a new baby. Ngaire and young Jem were staying with Andrew's mother, with Jem sharing a room with Andrew's youngest brother and while it was a help I knew, once the new baby arrived it would be more cramped. This knowledge fed my thoughts and edged my sense of the future. I valued Andrew's presence amongst the Shaman; he was a sobering influence on what was becoming an increasing problem, one centred around Tom.

While I had encouraged Tom's independence, I wondered if it was a good thing now. The house he was building was becoming more and more a problem for the Elders. They were concerned about the influence the Shaman had over the young women. The small female group that more often than not hung around where the young men gathered down at the house. The Elders felt they were no longer under the direct influence of the older core of the Women's Council while they spent time out in this valley. It wasn't a situation the women Elder's liked and I was at a loss to know what to do about it.

I couldn't forbid the mix of the group, it wasn't my place, any more than I could control who Tom encouraged to spend time with him. Andrew's acceptance in the group was a huge plus in this situation and I knew they felt the effects of his influence. I had been at pains to explain this to the Council only recently. I hoped things would settle down some when I had done with arrangements to have Tom up in Far North Queensland, once he finished with secondary school. It was only a few short weeks away now and in that time I could have found my footing up there myself, which reminded me I still had to talk to Aine.

Andrew was home now for an extended holiday period to await the birth of the baby, so he would be around to keep an eye on things. I knew he wasn't sure of what to expect, not sure of what he could do. I could imagine such a feeling and wondered how I would cope with Aine and the prospect of a birth and its necessary process. I doubt I would cope well with the risks, the attendant pain and discomfit that she would need to endure to bring our child into the world. It amazed me that there were so many children when I gave it some thought, though I had no need to worry over that. Aine had no immediate plans that I knew of and there was a great deal I still had to do without the demands of children to slow me down.

Absently I thought of my younger siblings. Josh and Deb were still under Dianne's control but my younger brother Allan was beginning to break out and spend more time in the bush with others his age. He had gone through his first initiation well and had proven to be something of a serious character, settling into the community quietly over the last two years or so, unlike Tom who had raised something of a storm. Though he hadn't decided on a path, I knew he leant towards the skills of the Shaman and it was just a matter of wait and see if that was the path he would be accepted into. He had plenty of time. At only fourteen it could be a year or so before he would possibly show any talent and I wasn't entirely sure what to look for. If I knew more of the Featherfoot, I would better understand the signs.

Aine I knew would very much love to return to Sydney for a few years, I only had to hear her voice when she was able to phone her sister when we got into town, or when we dropped in to see Dianne and she took the opportunity to phone.

Shuffling suddenly through the papers in front of me on the table I found what I was looking for. It didn't take long to collect together the invoices and while my thoughts were clear I ran my eyes down their tally and began to write out the cheques and authorise payment. The house on the Wanny would benefit from the works I had arranged, it would be good to have that concluded. I would need to contact the agent and ask him to complete a final inspection for me though I was hesitant to put it onto the rental market. It was something which could wait I decided, at least until after the Christmas season was over and the work was complete.

It may well be that Aine's sister Karyn could be offered the residence if she ever got away from that dog she had married. It would help I knew, but it was an isolated location and I wondered at its suitability without the support of a man to help her. I knew how difficult it had been for my own mother, Dianne, to manage children in a relatively isolated location without that support.

Sean and Jenna would be arriving back into the community soon too. Jen had finished her course and wanted to bring the skills she had learnt into the community. She was keen to start up a centre for the kids and sitting back I considered the plan. I had organized a draft plan of the community hall which would sit in the corner of the clearing down from the entrance to the access track which ran along the creek. It was my way of giving back to the community and the idea had been well received by the Council.

It could serve the community in many ways, not just as a studio for performance and art but it could double as a day care house at a pinch and would provide a sheltered area for gatherings bringing the community closer into the Shamans valley. We needed something which was open, yet comfortable and had settled on an unusual design suited to the site. The Elders would be supporting its development and many in the community saw its advantages fortunately, so the building would go ahead in the New Year.

The house in Brisbane had been let already, Andrew was keen but he planned on a good few months in the community so I had left it in the hands of a local agent and now it was only a matter of days before Sean and Jenna arrived. I knew Ngaire was looking forward to Jenna's arrival and once more I considered the problem of Andrew and Ngaire, I was sure there was something I could do there and tapping the pencil I held against the table I again considered the problem.

It had been too long since Aine and I had managed to get away from the demands of the community but I had already suggested a run north to the Council, though I had not mentioned it yet to Aine. The Elders had been in agreement as there were matters I needed to attend to up near Cooktown and then there was the problem of Tom.

The ongoing saga of Tom, I considered all that was inherent in the thought of his training and managing the worst of the scrapes he got himself into. He was adventurous, that much was certain and constraining the worst of his adventures, particularly where girls were concerned was an ongoing battle. He had a collection of young girls who continued to feed his ego though with his graduation at hand this would thin out his posse' of followers I was sure. He had no interest in further studies and I wasn't about to allow him to do little with his time, a sure recipe for disaster.

That Tom managed to get along well with the other Shaman was a good thing, more positive than his female following and I wondered not for the first time if it had more to do with the rumour of his initiation into the circle of the sorcerers which added to the attraction or the mystery. It had never been confirmed to the community to my knowledge, that wasn't our way, but the question was perhaps more intriguing than the reality. He was rightly proud of the markings on his upper arm which he had earned, a thin line of scarring which marked the initiate, but his training I knew had a long way yet to go and it was nearly time for the next step. It was a step that would remove him from the influence of his friends for some months, a step which had set in motion my own disquiet.

The talents of the Featherfoot were secretive and highly selective skills and I knew Tom would soon need to head north again to spend more time with John and the other Featherfoot. It was a complex matter and we were still working through them. There was much to be discussed and the problems were compounded by the absence of his father and his clan knowledge. It was something we had to work around and not without some difficulty.

His experiences with Billy Black had served him well and I knew that John was keen to hear more about what Tom had learnt, he wanted to peel back the knowledge to enhance his own understanding. Of that I had no doubt but then that he was willing to take on Tom's training at all was something of a grace for Tom. John could only enrich Toms skills, build on his knowledge and that could make a fine sorcerer of my younger brother.

This was a big deal to John and I wanted to discover more myself about his plans and aspirations for young Tom. I knew Tom's talents with his strong-eye, his ability to see the Spirit World meshing with ours marked him in the world of the Featherfoot as a Shaman to be watched carefully. I also knew that John's son, Denis had talent, he had the ability to see over distance and to read men in the manner that Shaman spoke of with some interest and I wondered at the power of the two young men together.

"You look deep in thought."

Startled I looked up into Aines beautiful eyes, there was the light of interest and curiosity there and it warmed my thoughts.

"Kitten… just thinking about things," I answered smiling, glad of the interruption. Reaching for her I brought her to my lap taking time out in a pleasant dalliance, a teasing play that could divert me easily and often with a welcome consequence. I never ceased to marvel at what the warmth of her closeness could do to me, as it did now when I savoured the sweet scent of her skin.

"Hmm…" she commented, picking at the papers scattered on the table top.

"These are the papers for the community hall. I'm so glad the Council decided to go ahead with the project."

"Yep. It will keep the teachers and natural leaders among us. All we need is the support of the community to use these talents. Jen will be a great asset in this as will Sean. Even Ngaire has suggested a children's clinic and play group."

"Oh. I hadn't heard, she has kept that bit quiet."

"I think she is waiting till after the new baby has settled before she raises the idea."

"Yes, she will need somewhere to escape; Andrew's place is so crowded. It's really too small for them and the family as well though they don't complain. I think Andrew's mum is just pleased to have Ngaire with them at this time."

"I think you're right. I have an idea though, I have been playing with it for a while but I'm not sure how you will like it. I know you want to go down to your sister, Karyn's. This idea would make that hard, you wouldn't be able to do both."

Aine turned her eyes on me. She knew as well as I that I found it difficult to argue my position over hers under the flash of her eyes and I tried to conceal my smile. Of late I had learnt to also used what advantage I could muster and a steady look from me, one with a trusting depth, I found that I could hopefully match and even counter her challenge. It was a silent duel of our eyes we participated in and it was often amusing. When she grinned suddenly and dropped her glance I knew immediately her mood was softening towards anything I might add so I took my chance.

"I would like to travel north for perhaps a month or two, maybe even three? Would you come with me?"

"North? Up to John and Marnie's? The wet season will be with us soon. It's not a good time. Is there a reason why you would choose now?"

"I do have to see John... yes. But I also have other Council business. Sean and Jen will be back in the community soon and I know Jen is looking forward to learning more of the Wandjin from Ngaire. Gran too is looking forward to revisiting some of the women's stories of her people; it has been too many years for her. It's also time I got to know John better as I need to understand his influence over Tom, and perhaps even Allan for that matter and a few months up that way wouldn't go astray."

"Are you planning on tenting it through the wet season?"

"Are you considering joining me?" I asked hopeful. "I could organize a camper trailer if you are. It would be high, dry and easy to manage if we need to head into the forest and we could also rent something in Cooktown for a while, we don't have to tent it all the time. Would that tempt you?"

Aine chewed her bottom lip and my mood grew hopeful.

"Would it have a kitchen built in? I know you like a fire and so do I, but we need to be practical and with the wet, a fire is not always practical. Or maybe we should get a little caravan?"

"No, a caravan can't go easily where we'll be going. It would have to be a camper trailer or perhaps a roof top tent though a trailer would be more versatile especially if we are going to be in it for months."

"One with a built-in hard floor. The type that stands on its own... above the ground on feet things?" Aine added with the edge of excitement in her voice.

"We'll be gone for maybe two months, longer if we get flooded in. What about your sister?"

The sigh was drawn and I watched the frown build. "Karyn has left Brad, it's that awful time... they say the first few months are the worst. I don't think I could cope with the anger that they will be swimming in. This would give me a good excuse not to participate," Aine answered almost regretfully but with a conviction. "She said that Dad was helping, which is something."

"I don't want you down there without me Kitten. Come with me into the wilderness, it will be much more enjoyable."

"What about your work here?"

"Hmm... and we are back to where we started," I said grinning. "I have been debating asking Sean and Andrew to pick up the reins for a while. Andrew is more than able to train the Shaman and guide them and Sean, well he can certainly hold things together in a business sense. It isn't as though it will be for too long. He would even make a fine Karadji if the Council would accept him. With the prospect of gaining Jenna's talents they just might. It would be a tough call between the two of them."

"The Karadji?" Aine asked surprised. "But what would that mean for us?"

"For us Kitten, it would mean less responsibility. Think about it. It's a prospect that has certain advantages for us. But it's just a possibility, for the moment I should head north and see to this business. What do you think of inviting Andrew and Ngaire to use our rooms while we're gone? It will help keep those spiders you love off the ceiling."

Aine's sigh was deep once again, though for different reasons. She had no love of the bush creatures who tried to move into the house, although she had come to accept some invaders. The miniature bats which found their way into the cupboards and dark places, the huntsmen and daddy long-legged spiders who felt they had land rights along the high ceilings regardless of how often they were swept away.

I could see the suggestion shifting around in her thoughts and she found it a pleasing idea I realized, as I watched a small smile play around her lips with softness reflected in her eyes while she contemplated some aspect of the idea.

"Yes. That's a good idea," She announced suddenly. "It could work all around and it would be easier when the baby comes."

I grinned, drawing her lips to mine slowly, exploring them, enjoying the taste of her mouth and the soft skin of her ear.

Aine giggled and squirmed in my hold. "Oh no..." she whispered still laughing. "Tell me more... when are you planning on leaving?"

Chuckling I lifted my head. I loved the sound of her laughter it always made me smile. "Hmm... maybe a week or so. We can pick a trailer up in Brisbane, I've been talking to the importers and I am happy with what they have available. We could make sure the house in Brisbane is cleared and head out from there. The new tenants move in after the New Year, I have the agent taking it over in four weeks and Sean is bringing down the last of Andrew and Ngaire's things. That will give us time to equip the trailer with what we will need."

"You have thought this out haven't you?" She said challenging me.

"Yes. Guilty I am. I was hoping you would decide to come with me and I had to figure out how to make it happen."

"Mmm… I will have to let Karyn know, and we will need to make a list…"

I watched as Aine set about her self-appointed tasks, and I was glad to leave the table for a scavenge through the kitchen for a light feed. It was a good outcome and suddenly I could feel the excitement of a new adventure, a new path perhaps. The prospect was well worth considering as I set about making the plans in my head about things I would need to attend to.

The track over to Tom's hut had become well worn when we reached the fork where the track the Shaman used joined ours. As I paced along it, nearing the hut, I wondered when it would be that Tom would find the constant presence of his friends cumbersome. The young men had turned the hut into something of a meeting place, it was larger and more accommodating than other huts and shacks around the community.

Tom's place had an inbuilt fireplace now which was something of an advantage in a rain forest, keeping the inside of the house drier and more comfortable.

I was confident that the day would come when he would draw the line and it was just a matter of maturity that would come with time. It would be good to get him away from the community for a bit, give him time to reflect on things and now that his studies in his senior year was only weeks away from being complete, I would have to give it some serious thought.

I had hoped Dianne would frequent the hut more often than she had. But then, a mother's constant presence in her son's home wasn't ideal. Traditionally mothers had little to do with their sons need to tread the path to becoming a man. Dianne was also in some dither about his status as an initiate Featherfoot. It was an unknown element in her life and in part I understood her reservations. Most people feared the Featherfoot and it wasn't a Lore we were familiar with, this was enough to put her off from upsetting the balance of his training and the growth of his independence.

As I approached, I noticed that a few of the young men were gathered on the verandah and amongst them were young Allan and a few friends. Acknowledging them with pleasant surprise I continued on into the hut I decided that it would be a good thing if Allan spent more time with Tom. The experience of the responsibility of a younger brother around could be positive and they would have more in common with any skills Allan might develop since they shared the same father.

The house was still essentially one large space with an 'A' frame structure overhead, the ceiling height made it initially appear less space than it actually was. Tom had installed a small rough kitchen area in the corner, off to the side of the over-large fireplace but I noticed that the structure of the mezzanine overhead trimmed the area visually and gave it more character. They had only got as far as the floor joists so it was going to take time to finish it.

A few friends were lounging around the odd assortment of old lounge chairs and sofas and I saw Andrew off to the side. Tom was perched on the small low table and while he smiled he continued with the conversation as he knew that I was here to see Andrew who had climbed to his feet and headed over to join me.

"Hey. Nuthing wrong?" Andrew asked, by way of greeting.

"No. The women are fine, having one of their mornings up at the house. I've escaped. You have a minute?"

"Yeah sure."

Andrew signalled to Tom that he was leaving then joined me at the door and we made our way back towards the path.

"Aine and I have decided we are going up North for a few months and I wanted to suggest something to you."

"Yeah sure, shoot. You know I am happy to help out where I can."

"Yes, well that too," I added with a grin. "Sean will be able to handle much of the business end and I am hoping you both can keep an eye on the Shaman. I realize it's something you do already and it's been a great help. When the baby comes though you may have less time?"

"Ngaire says the same thing strangely enough. I can't figure out how much harder it could be with two of us to look after just one little tiger."

I shrugged, "Women seem to manage. The Elders are willing to help as well with the Shaman, they will do what they can but it takes a certain measure of acceptance. You have the confidence of the group and that's not to be devalued."

"Thanks Ty. It's something I enjoy and while I am not in a contract on the rigs for the next few months, it will be a pleasure."

"There is another thing. Both Aine and I would like to ask if you might like to move into our rooms while we are gone. I expect our absence to be well into February next year and it could be much longer, though I haven't told Aine that, so don't mention it will you? I will keep you in the loop and having someone staying in the rooms will help keep the bush life at bay."

Immediately I could see the pleasure that idea gave Andrew as his grin widened. "That would be welcome. Thanks..., from both of us. I know Ngaire is feeling the close quarters and with the baby due soon enough... I think it's why she spends so much time at your place, plus she and Aine seem to have a lot in common. It would have to be just great for everyone, particularly with Jenna coming back; I know Ngaire will be tickled pink."

"I thought it might help. With Sean and Jenna in the other rooms, the girls will be happy for the close quarters as well I think. Plus having you and Sean in the same house will give the community some continuity. We expect to leave as soon as Sean and Jenna arrive, which should be any day now. We have some things to attend to in Brisbane and then we'll head north."

"Ty thanks. Really... Ngaire will be over the moon and it will give Jem more space too."

"Yeah, there is that small guest room that Jem can use. I don't imagine Jenna will want it."

"No," Andrew agreed knowing as well as I did that it had become something of a store room in the past year when Jen and Sean had been in residence and Tom no longer used the room at all. "There is the problem of Tango, he is used to being with Ngaire and Jem though I could try and keep him out of the house if you prefer. I know it has caused a problem with my mum at times."

"Tango is fine, just keep him out of the top bedrooms, otherwise I have no problem with him being in the lower lounge room with Jem. I know Ngaire keeps him well groomed."

When we reached the house I could see Andrew wanted to waste no time telling Ngaire about his news so I left him to return to clearing what was left of the paperwork. I hoped that Aine had managed to sort it again for me. I wasn't disappointed, she had and I was grateful for the order she had bought to the mess I had made as I settled myself once more to the task. I needed to get through this lot and then get into town before the evening, so I sank into the neat pile once again scattering the papers over the desk as I dealt with them. Once Sean arrived back I would be pleased to hand the management over to him for a few months and take the time out to spend with Aine, which was well overdue. We would have time together; it was something we didn't seem to get much of for ourselves lately.

Hours later, returning from my business in town, I walked back along the track towards home. I found myself enjoying the shift of light into the evening while I reconsidered our plans. I would miss the valley, miss the family and the community but wondered what the Far North Queensland forests would hold for us. It was a life closer to nature, one where we would be more subject to the vagaries of climate, the extremes of heat and the deep troughs of the wet season. There was something about the promise that called to me and I wondered if it had anything to do with my father's blood, which I knew at times ran restlessly through my veins.

Meeting up with my father nearly two years ago now had stirred me. I had never before been so unsettled though it had taken time to understand just what it was. I hadn't at first realized just why I was so restless. I had lived so much that was the way of my mother's people that I now found myself intrigued by my father's world. I had put my restlessness down to wanting to know more of my father's country and this had been a sense that had crept up on me since meeting him and my half brother. It was a restlessness of which I hadn't spoken about to anyone, not even Aine. It was a restlessness which had surprised me as much as it had left me with an odd sense of disquiet.

As I approached the house I was pleased to see the soft glow of flickering light, rather than the harsher glare of electricity. Candles suited my mood, it would be just like Aine to notice such a small thing as this and use it to welcome me back to the house. So it was with a quicker step that I dismissed my thoughts and headed inside.

What I found surprised me. Aine had scattered a few solid candles about the room and even though the evening wasn't chill, she had lit the fire and in front of it had arranged a picnic of a sorts. She was obviously planning something and while I welcomed the thought, I delighted in the mystery that I knew was going to unfold. She was up to something, it was a game we often enjoyed playing and I never quite knew what to expect.

Shrugging off my light jacket I dropped it around the back of the chair, kicking off my shoes as well, not wanting to track the forest mud into the house. That was something she was constantly nagging me about but which now made me smile as I oddly remembered it for once. There was a bottle of wine and a couple of glasses on the low table with an assortment of food set aside in front of the fire, so that was where I headed. I freed the cork and announcing my presence I poured us both a glass then reached for some of the finger snacks which she had carefully arranged on a few plates.

The sound of the cork bought her out as I had hoped it would. I glanced up as she reached the steps from the upper landing and momentarily froze.

Aine wore the simplest of kaftans. It was made of a very light fabric and it flowed around her like water allowing me to see every movement of her body. My throat went dry at the sight, stilled I watched as she came down the steps. Within seconds she had folded her body onto the floor next to mine as I lounged up against the sofa, smiling at what I was sure was my delighted expression.

"Gee-zus… what have I done wrong... or right?" I whispered a little hoarsely as I reached for my glass again.

With a small giggle she bit her lip in a way that I loved, showing the indecision of her thoughts. "Nothing really."

"Nothing really, tells me, there is something. Not that I'm complaining..."

Aine smiled and settled more relaxed, reaching for her own glass. "I just wanted to celebrate a new... well a beginning I guess. I saw Dianne earlier, Sean and Jen will be here tomorrow and if we're leaving in a few days as we hope, then this will be the last night we have alone in the house for a long time, won't it?"

"Yeah I guess." Reaching for her, I laid my hand on her neck, my thumb lightly brushing the soft skin of her cheek. I appreciated moments like these with this lovely woman, who I still had trouble believing was mine. "I love you... you know that," I said softly as she leant in towards me, smiling at my words.

Kissing me gently she released my lips as my response deepened, hopeful. It was then I knew she wanted to talk, this conversation had just begun and I grinned acknowledging it.

"I thought we could talk about moving north... and other things. You never talk about Far North Queensland at all you know, it's a mystery. Secret Men's business, I don't know a lot about what you really do up there?"

"Nor should you," I chided her grinning. "But there are some things we can talk about, depends on what you want to know?"

Again she chewed her lower lip. "Mmm... Maybe I will save that one when I know what I want to learn," she countered. Then she grinned, suddenly sitting to prop her head on her bent knees as she wrapped her arms about them and looked up at me impishly.

"You are making me very nervous," I said softly laughing. I loved the soft curve of her body in the muted dancing light around us, her body curled as it was into itself and enhancing her gentle shape, the womanly curves that moved in the thin fabric of her dress. I drew a breath cooling my thoughts; I knew there was something behind this. "Can you just spit it out... whatever it's on your mind?" I teased on a chuckle.

Aine smiled and sighed deeply as she straightened again. "You know me too well, it isn't fair."

"Aine...?" I threatened, wondering now just how serious this was.

"Don't get all serious on me," she countered. "I don't want that..."

"Then tell me."

Again she sighed. "It's not that serious. I was just thinking, maybe it's time we thought about babies, having children ourselves... do you think?"

"Babies...? This is what is on your mind?" Grinning I reached for her, drawing her to me, "Babies are a lifelong commitment Kitten but we can talk about it if you like."

"Oh I am over talking," she said suddenly as she slipped out of my grasp and instead settled between my legs facing my frown. Her cool fingers slipped carefully up the front of my shirt, tracing the planes of my chest evocatively as she spoke, her smile threading through her words. "I've spoken to the women, talked to Ngaire, even Jen and I think it's time."

"Were you going to talk to me?"

"Yep. I am now," she said softly. "But you see you are a different kettle of fish. You're stubborn, opinionated and very, very sure of yourself so you require special handling." As she said the words softly she chuckled, her eyes glinted strangely, challenging me and I couldn't help but grin at her.

"Do I?" I laughed.

"Oh yeah...; You see you have decided already but you just don't know it."

"I have?"

"Yep."

Aine slipped her hands up the sides of my chest, pulling my shirt up and I knew she intended it to be gone, so I worked with her at what was a delightful game, one that was making it hard to concentrate on what she was saying. I was sure that this was her intent and while it scraped on my nerves, making me wary. I couldn't deny her the game, a game I loved.

"What have I decided?" I challenged. "Having babies is not high on my priority list you know... but I think it might be different for you."

"Yep," she said tossing my shirt aside. "You see... I have learnt a lot about you over the last year or two. You take your responsibilities seriously. You get all involved in the community, in Sean, Tom, Jenna, Dianne... the list is endless and it's all about caring for the people who are close to you."

"You left yourself out," I corrected her.

"No. No I didn't. You see, I don't belong to you... everyone thinks I am the Karadji's woman and I have lived a life where I am well... joined to you." The small grin took the sting out of her words, but I knew what she said was true. I knew also between us it was subtly different, perhaps she had not seen this and at the thought my confidence faltered momentarily. It was important to me that she understood that she was the other half of my world, not just the woman I had chosen as a wife.

"It's not entirely..."

"True? Mmm," she said, knowing the end of what I had intended to say. Then she flashed me her brilliant smile and I relaxed. "It's good to see you know that." She added, her fingers drifting down to my jeans playing restlessly with the button there. "You see, you belong to me. It's you who are mine," and with that she kissed me softly, then dodged away from my lips. She obviously wasn't finished and now she had my full attention, she continued, her voice almost a sweet song.

"I've been watching you and you are getting restless. It's time for a change, you were right to see it and going north is a good thing. Even Gran has noted your restlessness you know."

"She has?" This surprised me, but Aine obviously found it no surprise.

"Hmm... and going north, even though you plan for only a few months, is the beginning... a change. You tell me you are going for Tom, for Jen, even maybe for Allan and Josh, and even Deb. But now I tell you we are going for us."

"We are?" I countered intrigued.

"Yep." Aine moved to snuggle into my chest, delighting me. This was good, a great place to be and I reached for her happily but although she came to me readily she sat so she could still watch my reactions to her soft spoken words, her silken sheath settling about her. She was intent on what she was saying, her eyes were laughing as they warned me she wasn't finished when my hand gently took to caressing the warmth of her skin through the light fabric. It was then that I noticed the small circular amulet around her neck, it was the fertility charm given to her by Dianne some time ago, the one she had set aside. I knew that if Dianne had seen it, if others had seen it, then it had also been discussed a great deal amongst the women. The Karadji's woman was hoping for a child, smiling I knew beyond doubt she was serious.

"Jen and Sean get here tomorrow... and tonight is our last night alone in the house so you are going to make a decision in your own mind. You see, I am going off the pill. It's time for babies, our babies. It's time for us and we can go north together and learn what we need to, take our time about it. I know you have been renovating the place on the Wanny, Dianne's old place and when we are ready we could go back to there."

"You think so... do you?" I questioned, enjoying her mood.

"Yes?" Her answer was a question. She sat still for the moment and waited for my answer.

"We could," I suggested, knowing that what I was suggesting meant that we leave the community if only for a few years. Knowing that with children she meant for us to be away from the community where my focus was distracted, or she would not be planning on moving to the Wanny and going back to Sydney. "I won't give up the house here." I warned softly. "This will always be our home."

Aine smiled, "No. I'm not asking that of you. It would be good to come back, even stay for a time but Ty... I need you to choose life with me and our children. I need your full attention for a while, maybe a few years while our babies are young. I want us to build the tight unit that is our family with the extensions that are part of our family. Your brothers, your mum, the

Elders group, my sister even. But what is important is us, and I want to give our babies that grounding without the distractions of everyone else, without the distractions of the community and you playing dad to everyone. I want this time for us alone."

Surprised at her insight I laughed then suddenly realized she had thought this through a great deal, that she might need this time and I had to recognize her needs. Her eyes were intent on me and I was forced to rethink. "You think I play dad to everyone?" I shook my head, not sure of her perception on this one point.

"I know you do. You can't deny it, it's part of who you are, but I need you to be there only for our babies for a while. That is if we have any...?" she qualified suddenly.

"We haven't decided on that yet," I teased, knowing I had to seriously consider her words.

"Hmm... You haven't decided. I have, Ty... so the choice is yours. If you decide that you also want babies then..." shrugging she continued, her eyes playful. "You can stop using condoms, because as I said, I'm giving up the pill. I have decided."

My mind filled with all the possibilities, and impossibilities. Was I ready for the responsibility and demands of babies and a young family I wondered?

I was surprised at the impact her words were having on my emotions, on my thoughts and as I held her to me I tried to examine what I was feeling. This was her way of joining our lives together irrevocably, I understood that. We would share the future of children well into our old age, beyond our own ties to each other. It was a commitment I felt very comfortable with, however what would such a commitment demand of me? I needed to consider this. I needed to be fair to my children, to our children. They would be my first consideration in everything I did. I never wanted to bring my children into a world where I wasn't a primary force in their lives, I knew the cost of absent fathers and it wasn't a price I would ask my own kids to pay.

It had been a long times since I felt such confusion, such indecision, it went against everything I had sorted in my mind, future plans, directions in the community, in the family. Then I realized Aine was talking about another family, hers and mine. I had foolishly not accounted this in my plans for the future. I had assumed that if it happened then it would make little impact on the pattern of our lives and we would continue on here together with the support of the community around us, but this discounted her own family. Her thoughts and concepts of a small nuclear family tossed the whole pattern into disarray yet strangely it felt as though it had settled something in my core that had been unsettled

"Leaving here for a few years wasn't quite what I had in mind," I warned. "If we did that it would mean we would keep the links with the community, I would always do that and we would return often. When I said that we could go away for a few months, I didn't mean break ties completely Kitten. I meant we could live up north for a while and then come back..., back here. I had thought this would always be our home."

"I know you thought that. We can come back in a few years but I would like to break away for a few years and take on building our lives together with children, children we can focus completely on while they are very young. It's something I want very much to do just for a few years. This is what I want for us. I don't want to have to share you at all for a while and here, sharing you, sharing your attention with others is our life. Please try to understand what I'm asking."

"I didn't know you felt this way?" Surprised I considered her words even though I knew them to have an element of truth. "Kitten, living here... it's what I do. It's what I have trained for and I don't know if I want to give it up. Give up the community, my family?"

"I'm not asking you to give up your family Ty... I love them too. What I am asking for is for us to have the same opportunity to build a family together. For us to explore all we can be together and for the opportunity for us to grow without the constraints of the Community and the direct responsibilities you take on."

"My responsibilities are part of who I am Kitten. I don't mind them; they are what my life is."

"Exactly!" she said suddenly, totally confusing me now. "They are part of your life, not our life or the lives of our babies. Especially not the lives of our babies, they are entitled to have you to themselves for a while don't you think?"

"These things aren't mutually exclusive you know."

Aine sighed deeply, and then settled back into resting against my shoulder. "You're not understanding me," she added softly.

"Kitten... I am trying to."

"I know."

Restless as she was, I struggled to understand. "OK. I can see you mean what you say, but I can't grasp it. I guess I need time to think about it. We have these few months ahead of us... so maybe we can talk it through?"

"Yes. I guess, but I mean it Ty."

Again I frowned. I was either not understanding or I was missing something here. "What?"

"Children," she said, sitting up suddenly. "I mean it. I want to have our baby and I am going off the pill. It's up to you now, the choice is yours. The responsibility of it... it's no longer mine."

"That sounds awfully like blackmail Kitten."

"Why? Because I choose not to continue to swallow doses of hormones on a monotonously regular basis and alter my whole physical and emotional cycle so you don't have to use condoms?"

Surprised I saw the threat of anger flash in her eyes and I was forced to consider her position. She was deadly serious about this and I had to acknowledge I was on shaky ground here. She had given up her life for mine; it was a life that had become ours in the community, so perhaps now I needed to consider what she had given up. Perhaps she needed to claim some part of her life again. Maybe this was what was driving her passions at this moment?

"You're right," I said suddenly, capitulating. "OK. It's beyond time for me to take some responsibility, I agree with that."

I watched carefully as her anger mellowed slowly and again I searched for the meaning behind her strange mood. Perhaps it was time we considered just ourselves and our plans and as I waited for her to calm, I saw the gamut of emotions pass through her lively eyes.

"Kitten OK, you just might be right. Maybe we need time for just us, let's explore that, just that... for a while. But maybe we don't need to move to Sydney; maybe we can work it out here. Would you consider that?"

Aine chewed her lip again, and I couldn't help but smile.

"Yes. I guess so, but I am not saying yes to it. What I am saying is yes... I will consider it. Just like you too need to consider having a family. Our family," she clarified.

"Good then. I can hold off on letting the house on the Wanny river. There are a few more things that need to be seen too anyway. We can keep that option open for a while... Let's just see how it pans out?"

Shifting suddenly, back into my arms I felt a flood of relief sweep through me as I gathered her up against my chest and was delighted when she slipped her arms around me. She was calm, the woman I understood was back and I felt I had made it through a mine field of emotions.

"I do love you Ty... please choose our family, our babies... me," she said softly.

With a small groan I gently shifted her to the rug, feeling with humour the silken ropes of an emotional ambush, as bringing her body beneath my own I sheltered her within my arms and I so much wanted to reclaim her. Make sure she was still mine, even in this strange mood she was apparently lost to. My lips found hers, punishing her for her doubts and challenges, promising anything, to be close to her. I felt the emotion of my need for her sweep through me and thought to myself that I would never truly understand this woman in my life. She was the woman who was my life and as my lips began the tour of her skin that I loved to travel, as my touch explored the shape and heat of her I knew I could never risk losing her.

I was going to have to work to understand her needs, it was a confusing world of emotion and drives which I had little clue about. But by everything

I knew, I was going to try.

"How can you doubt that I would choose you Kitten?" I whispered, my smile brushing the soft skin of her breast. "Though... do I need to get a rubber?" I asked chuckling as looking down at her cheekily.

"Oh no," she answered laughing, equally as challenging. "You don't have to do that at all...if you don't want."

Suddenly I started to laugh, a soft sound which grew as I realized the irony of her words. "You are going to be the death of me Kitten," I warned still chuckling... "But it's going to be a pleasant demise I think."

Instead it was a birth, the birth of what felt like a new path through our lives so my thoughts and dreams had a different edge to them. Somehow things had changed and I wasn't quite sure in what way. It felt like I had shaken off a weight but it should have been that I had accepted another. Though oddly it wasn't and I wondered at it as our passion for each other was reborn.

The thought of having children with Aine held a certain deep pleasure which teased me as much as it pleased me. I was beginning to realize that perhaps this was what our life was about and the thought of being a father, having a child that was as much part of me as it was part of Aine, was a sweet thought. My body thrilled to the idea surprisingly and the thought of leaving Aine's arms in search of a condom seemed to me now to be a ridiculous suggestion.

PAST AND PRESENT

Aine:

Packing stuff had never been a love of mine and as I cast my eyes over the collection of cardboard boxes, slowly making their way down to the storage area under the house I wondered how I'd managed to acquire such a huge amount. I thought I'd always confined us largely to our rooms but I'd gathered so much which had been scattered about the house, and now it seemed the boxes just multiplied. Even Ty had been surprised at the number of boxes I managed to pack when he had taken them down to storage in preparation for vacating the room for Andrew and Ngaire.

I could hear Jen and Ngaire laughing in the lower lounge room, as the sound tripped around the house it made me smile to know that they drew so much pleasure from each other's company, it was a good thing that Ngaire and Andrew would be staying in these rooms. Thoughts of their new baby, due so soon plucked at my heart strings, I would be away for the birth but I'd hear all about it I was sure. It seemed this was all I thought about now, even my dreams were filled with babies and children and I knew it was making me restless.

Sealing up the box I was working on finally, I moved over to the small desk where I kept my papers, letters and books. I wasn't looking forward to this task, sorting through letters and papers, choosing what to throw out and what to keep was going to be a tiresome task. Opening the file drawer restlessly I considered the vertical files and then with annoyance, I gathered up a handful of files and irritated I layered them deep into the box. I didn't even open them. I couldn't be bothered with it. Taipan could help me with these at another time I decided.

As each of the files had the same fate, my mood lifted somewhat but when I reached the back most files I paused. These were my truly personal files; they contained many frivolous, personal letters collected over the last years. There were also projects begun and often not finished, attempts to order our lives which sometimes failed, but brought some semblance of order none the less. These I took the time to glance through and that afforded me an impatient humour as I scanned each of the plans, the notes and drawings I'd done, some many months ago

When I came to a series of carbon sketches I stopped. I'd done these a while ago now and still they bothered me. They were threads of dreams, my attempt to order the confusion of thought, though I'd forgotten this particular series. These were some of the very early sketches I had made and with curiosity I gathered them up together, setting the file into the box but I took those over to my sketch folder. These could join the others, they belonged together and I should consider them as a group. I didn't consider myself an artist but I did gain pleasure from the simple line sketches. That was, what art for me, was really all about I thought quietly to myself.

I had taken to sketching my thoughts, my dreams and it gave me a great deal of satisfaction to bring a type of order this way. It was almost like a hobby, an amusement that I shared with young Debbie, where we would indulge ourselves when we could. The others found it entertaining, particularly Deb's sketches. We never quite knew what she was going to come out with and it was always entertaining. She no longer talked about her invisible friend. Jep it seemed had slipped into the shadows of her childhood, particularly now as she had started school, he no longer accompanied her about at all it appeared.

I found some amusement in the fact that while Deb had apparently lost her invisible friend, Tom who had always been so intolerant of that invisible friend, now was learning to deal with the world of Spirit men intruding into his own. Taipan rarely spoke of Tom's vision and it was mostly what I had gathered from the women and in particular from Debbie and Dianne. Surprisingly a lot of my misinformation also came via the younger girls, it had taken some time for Tom to learn to be discrete and unfortunately he had gained a reputation for frightening the young girls. That was before Ty had managed to rein in his antics.

Finally locating the portfolio of sketches, I opened it to add the others in my hand, then noticed the similarities of the subject. They were strikingly odd, so sinking to the floor I spread the sketches out about me and considered them. They weren't exactly the same, many were different but they had similarities, in particular it was like looking at a series of sketches of the same area and surprised I began to arrange them.

What struck me as odd was the ones of water. There was a narrow creek running through a tortured gorge, one scattered with native bush and rock.

It wasn't as tropical as the bush which covered the ground that I was accustomed to, as the land was more patchy. The sketches were rough and often the crudeness of them made me smile but they had symmetry about them. The bend of the river was the same in several of the drawings; the hill structure was the same except that it was drawn from different angles, drawn from different positions.

These were landscapes drawn from my dreams over the last twelve months, though now I could see that they were of the same subject, they might even be the same area. Views drawn that were strikingly similar and I had thought they were abstract places, more a collection of terrains and activities but when grouped together it was as though I was drawing the same gorge and it was a small amazement to me.

Very few of the sketches had people in them, most had been added on prompting from Deb but now I could see that these people too had similarities in their features. I was hopeless at drawing faces, but mostly these were figures, simple in structure. They were engaged in swimming or cooking or at play, but it struck me that the figures had a symmetry also. There were simple figures of a man and a woman, I had thought they reflected Ty and me but now I wasn't so sure, it just didn't seem right, so I decided that they were just fanciful figures. There was about them a sense of difference however and I wondered at it. Then I realized one or two of the sketches had a child in them but then, that was fanciful too. Deb would have insisted on that I was sure, or she had inspired it in my sketch.

I'd become accustomed to viewing Deb's drawings with a flow of movement, almost like a series in each set and curious I now scattered the drawings in a form, a plan, and I could see the beginnings of a tale, a story almost. Some of the drawings were done in crayons, others in carbon and others watery sketches done in pencil and coloured with Deb's water colours but even the ones done months apart had a sameness. As I shifted the sketches about I could see the likenesses and links found in what could be a panorama and that too surprised me.

At a noise from the door I suddenly looked up as Jen knocked.

"Wan'a cuppa? We are just about to have some afternoon tea."

Quickly gathering the sketches together I smiled welcoming the intrusion into my unsettling thoughts. "I would love some, I need a break believe me. I am beginning to see things," I added with a chuckle.

"Good then. I have just put the jug on, come down when you're ready."

Alone again, I slipped the sketches and drawings into the folio and set it aside for later. I was being fanciful I decided. I really needed that cuppa.

I enjoyed the company of Ngaire and Jen and sitting around the small round table we talked freely. Ngaire had spent most of her time with Andrew and his family when she had first got here and I hadn't wanted to intrude, though Andrew had bought her to the house often and we had enjoyed some great conversations. We were building a firm friendship and I welcomed that.

In the last few days she had been quite different in her openness towards me and I felt the full warmth of our friendship growing. I guessed it had something to do with the few years between us, and asking them to use our rooms while we were gone for what could be months, if not years, had helped bridge any reservations.

I liked the idea that Jen could be on hand and offer Ngaire the help she would need when the baby came and I was glad that we could do this for them both. Their friendship was so strong, they were really more like close sisters than just friends. It also gave me the sense that maybe Ty would seriously consider leaving the community for some time with such an arrangement in place, I was hopeful.

Watching Ngaire negotiate the discomfit of her swollen belly was both endearing and frustrating. I envied her the promise of the baby though I felt secure in the thought that it would be an experience I would share someday soon. I loved that thought. More and more I was looking forward to a child of our own, a small package of love that was Taipan's and mine and I knew it was something I wanted more than anything else that we could share. I didn't expect Ty to understand my growing need for a child, I don't know if I even understood it myself but as the promise grew I knew it was becoming more and more of an obsession and there seemed little I could do about it.

It had been with me for months now and having spoken of it finally, seemed to have set my thoughts and hopes free. I wanted so much to hold our baby in my arms. It was as though my heart ached for the warmth and sweet wetness of a child with Taipan's eyes perhaps, the hair lightened by my colouring, fingers and toes so tiny and the want to snuggle a baby within my arms was irresistible.

"Do you have everything you need for the baby?" I asked of Ngaire, curious as we sat around the table enjoying light snacks and easy company, as I tried to drag my mind back to what the others were saying.

"Mostly, we have left of lot of things on lay-by in Lismore though Andrew wants to bring it home now we have more room. We really appreciate you letting us stay here, it will make such a difference," Ngaire said as her hand once more moved to the impatient, yet entertaining movement of her belly. She was soothing the baby, and we all enjoyed the small intrusion.

"I'm glad someone will be here while we're gone. The room seems to lack something when no one is in it for a few weeks. I haven't worked out whether it's the spiders moving in or the stillness of the air but it seems somehow to suffer from loneliness. Fanciful hey?" I chuckled.

"Well I will look after it, I promise."

"It's going to be great having you stay; I can help with the baby. I can't wait... even Sean is looking forward to it, though he has threatened me about getting clucky," Jen added then pulling a face she sighed. "Though I guess he is right... so you will just have to put up with me helping."

Both Ngaire and I smiled at the playful mischief in Jenna's expression. She was way too young to be wanting a baby I was sure, Ngaire and I both agreed on this.. But Jen would be herself and Sean would have to deal with her enthusiasms. I even believed that he could manage to control the worst of her mischief in the end.

"Well Ty and I hope to get away tomorrow. We are just about packed up and it will be good to get off to Brissy though I'm sorry to be missing the birth of bub... make sure you let us know when that happens and you will have to send us lots of pictures when he or she comes along. Do you have any clues about the sex?"

Ngaire smiled, "No. Not really, I never went for the scan though they did schedule it in Brisbane but..." shrugging she continued. "I don't want to know really... I know it sounds silly but I hate doctor's appointments. It isn't as though I haven't done this before."

"Andrew mentioned they were pretty annoyed with you at the hospital," Jen added.

"Yeah... I'm not sure I want a hospital birth, but I may have to anyway. Depends on how things go I guess. I had a bit of trouble when Jiemba was born and they're worried about that. We will see how it goes."

Concerned I looked up, I hadn't known she had difficulties, no one had mentioned it though Ngaire kept much to herself. I'd assumed Jen and she shared many confidences but that this was news to Jenna too.

"It's not too serious...?"

"No. Nothing I don't understand. It'll be fine... really. Don't worry," she reassured us. "It's just normal stuff to expect."

"Well I am hoping it's a little girl." Jenna interjected enthusiastically. "Then that will be a pigeon pair, besides little girls seem so sweet... and you can dress them up so cute, not like boys at all."

"Andrew still thinks it's a boy. He can't seem to get it into his head that it might be a girl. I guess he is used to having Jem around and the alternative is an unknown," Ngaire suggested chuckling to herself happily.

"Well it'll be delightful either way," I suggested. "As long as bubz is healthy that is the main thing."

As we sat discussing the merits of the sexes and the hopes surrounding the baby I noticed the arrival of a small group of young women, they were Jenna's friends. So standing, I moved to open the wide glass doors, welcoming them.

Since Ngaire had been visiting often in the last weeks, we'd become accustomed to the gathering of women, encouraging them but with Jen's return I could see that we would be also enjoying the company of the younger women and girls.

It was a good thing that Ty and I were going to be away for some months I thought to myself silently somewhat amused. I knew he valued his privacy. It seemed to be part of his nature and I wondered how he would cope with the constant visits of women about the house which would be now inevitable with the arrival of the baby and Jen being in residence. Perhaps this was also why he'd decided to head north for a few months until things once again had settled down. Maybe this too would encourage him to extend our absence.

These were four of Jenna's young friends who I knew reasonably well, amongst them Judy and Carley and as they arrived I decided to leave them to enjoy each other's company so instead of joining them I settled on the sofa in the lounge to finish my coffee. Settling to browsing through the magazine someone had left on the table while the young women gathered in the kitchen and around the dining table greeting each other.

Ngaire also moved to allow the girls room, shifting out of their way and settling into the corner of the table as she watched the chatter between them, although she listened companionably as Jen greeted her friends. It was within a circle of friends which I thought she perhaps didn't feel entirely part of, having had more to do with the older group of women in the past weeks.

It was a comfortable, even noisy group and as I watched the companionship between the women I noticed the subtle reactions amongst them. Judy was clearly the driving force, she was perhaps the eldest; though Carley was an interesting character who clearly enjoyed the companionship of the others even though she now also sat at the table. It was this that made me aware of the subtle exclusion of Ngaire from the chattering group.

Carley was the most extrovert amongst the women and I guessed something of a leader also though I wasn't entirely sure that would be a good choice. The closest of Jenna's friends she also often wielded the most influence over Jen and I knew Sean had little patience with that influence. I had heard Taipan and Sean both express subtle frustrations with Carly at times, though they largely left Jenna to manage her own friendships. It made me wonder just what it was that they had to complain about.

I had little to do with Carley or Judy but I could clearly see that Jenna had a long standing friendship with both and it seemed very comfortable as I watched Jen chattering with Judy and the others in the kitchen area. Yet it was when Ngaire suddenly stood, her demeanour very quiet and yet abrupt that I also stopped to observe what was going on.

Realizing there was something wrong, I watched her quickly leave almost unobserved by the others, slipping out of the door without comment. She seemed calm, but determined to leave and Jen had not noticed, surrounded as she was by some of her friends at the kitchen bench.

Carley, on the other hand watched Ngaire's departure with an expression which could only be described as one laced with malice. That expression was soon hidden, but it hadn't escaped me and surprised I watched as the girl turned back to the others standing to join them. Obviously pleased about something which had been said between her and Ngaire she now seemed quite confident and little perturbed.

It had only been five minutes between their arrival and Ngaire's departure so I stood myself and moved towards the exit, Carley shot me a quick look, one knowing that I had observed whatever it was that had occurred.

Whatever her thoughts, they were soon masked as I dismissed her and headed out to find Ngaire. Something was obviously not right and I wasn't going to allow the minx to get away with whatever she had said that had caused Ngaire to depart so pre-emptively.

"Ngaire... wait up!" I called once outside, crossing the small open area as she reached the lower path at the edge of the clearing. She obviously heard me as she glanced back at me, but she continued to move into the forest as though sheltering from the attention of the company where she then waited while I hurried to join her just inside the shadows of the trees.

"What's going on?" I demanded in a gentle tone as I reached her.

"It's nothing." I could clearly see this wasn't the case, she was obviously troubled and concerned, I followed her as she stepped ahead, intent as she was on leaving.

"No you're upset, what did Carley say?" I reached out to slow her progress and as she turned to me I could see the disturbed look in her eyes. "Come on..." I coaxed now concerned, "She clearly said something to upset you..."

"Yes she did... but it's OK. I guess I should have realized... but... I just didn't think about it."

"What?"

"Well... about Andrew. I mean I never thought about it, but he must have had girlfriends here..." she said hesitantly. "I realized that but I didn't think it was something I would have to deal with."

"What on earth are you talking about... girlfriends?" Confused I wondered what it could've been that had been said."

"Carley... It was something she said. She, well she said that the baby... my baby... should have been hers. That I was just lucky to get away with it."

"Away with it..? What on earth...?"

"It's just that she said it should have been her. That they should..."

"Oh good grief. What rubbish!" I spat finally grasping the gist of what had been said. "How dare she! Ngaire you're not listening to her are you...?" I demanded exasperated.

Hesitantly Ngaire turned to me, her eyes clearly growing over-bright as she considered her own words, a sad realization in their depth. "She could be right... I never thought, it never occurred to me," she added quietly.

"Well I think it's absolutely rubbish. I have never known Andrew and Carley to be that friendly. I mean, maybe once ages ago when they were younger... I mean Andrew has never been that interested in Carley and if he was even ever interested it was... was years ago."

Clearly confused she frowned, "That isn't what Carley suggested. She said... meant that they were quite close..."

"What...Carley and Andrew? Rubbish! I don't believe it. Look I've lived here for two years and I have never thought that those two were ever involved. I would have noticed I am sure. Andrew has been away for most of the last year anyway. I think she is just stirring trouble... seriously Ngaire. Carley is a mischief maker, she is overly sure of herself... it's all in her head I am sure. You should take whatever she said with a grain of salt." Ngaire looked upset, clearly she was still unsure.

"Yes... just ask Jen, she would know. Even Andrew..."

"I can't ask him something like that." Ngaire protested. "It would be awful... what if...?"

"Then, Jenna. Look I am sure there is nothing to it. Just ignore the girl; she is just a trouble maker. Whatever she said... you don't go saying things like that to someone who is about to have a baby any day. What was the girl thinking... clearly she is hoping to stir up trouble."

Frowning, Ngaire scrubbed the moisture from her eyes with her fingers... her thoughts were obviously in turmoil as she cradled her belly then continued her way hesitantly down the track.

"I don't know? I'm not sure Aine... she sounded so uncertain."

"Well I am," I countered. "Look... what difference does it make? You can't seriously listen to her? Andrew loves you, even without the baby.... I mean I saw what he was like when he got back from Far North Queensland even before you found out you were pregnant. You should have seen him.... really Ngaire you would have no doubts," I coaxed confidently.

Surprised she caught my eye. "Before?"

"Yes... before..." I confirmed laughing. "Ngaire he was almost beside himself, and he couldn't even remember your..." Stopping myself suddenly I realized what I was about to say, realized it wasn't perhaps the best bit of information to impart at this point. "... well he didn't know how to contact you," I amended quickly. "He was livid with himself for not getting a phone number or something... Don't let this silly little girl get under your skin. She is just trouble making... He... he would never have taken her seriously."

She suddenly smiled, uncertainty still in her eyes but I could see that she was considering what I could tell her.

"I hope you're right Aine... I really do."

"Of course I am."

"Maybe I should ask him... maybe after the baby..."

"And you think he is going to tell you he wants to be with that nasty little kid rather than you? I seriously doubt it," I reassured her confidently. "You're not to listen to her... Look you need to tell Jen what it is she has said... let Jenna deal with her. If anyone knows if there is anything then it would be Jenna. If you're going to ask anyone, then it should be her."

Ngaire nodded. She was at least seeing the sense of my argument and I hoped that Jenna would do what was right to stop this stupid friend of hers. I decided then that I could say something to make sure she would... I couldn't allow that girl to work so much damage.

I left Ngaire at Andrew's parent's house not long after; glad that there was no one at home and knowing she was going to rest. I hoped it wouldn't be long before Andrew's mother got back. It was growing too close to dinner time and I only hoped that she would get enough time to rest.

I decided that I'd find Ty and tell him what had happened. He would be somewhere about the main camp, perhaps down at Granny's and as I headed off in that direction I tried to work out what it could have been that had driven Carley to suggest such things to Ngaire.

It then occurred to me that drawing Taipan into this situation would not perhaps be in my own interests. I was trying to ease Ty away from the unending concerns of the community, perhaps I should talk to Sean, or even Andrew. Surely he would be concerned about what some silly chit had said to Ngaire to upset her and as I considered what would be best to do I wondered where the men would be.

One thing I did know was that I wanted this business to be addressed before we left tomorrow. I couldn't bear the thought of Carley undermining Ngaire's position and if it meant that Carley would be asked not to call at the house, then that I could do.

With a determined step I suddenly turned back towards Tom's place. I had rarely gone to Tom's and I knew it was going to cause something of a commotion. However if this was all going to be part of the message Carley would get, then she should know that this is where I stood. It was something I would not allow.

As the Karadji's woman I understood the authority I could wield amongst the community, but I had never had need to exercise it before this, but now I would. I knew that Taipan hoped that Andrew would step up and help guide the Shaman in his absence and in this Ngaire would need the strength to support him. Some little twit of a girl wasn't going to be allowed to undermine either Andrew or Ngaire like this and she was about to learn a keen lesson.

I was beyond angry with the girl and I knew I would have little patience in dealing with her myself. Perhaps any messages should come from Andrew and the more I thought about it, the more determined my step was towards Tom's place. I could feel the confident warmth of a decision well made settle in my belly.

A HAND OF FATE

Andrew:

Sitting outside with a small group of the young initiates as we exercised a few of the basic principles of the Shaman's Lore was always something I enjoyed. The young men were often eager and open to exploring the demands of such a life, and exploring the possibilities. It wasn't only about what skills they could hone but about their approach to a way of life, their commitment to protect and help each other and the members of the community and those about them, as well as looking at their own personal growth and to help them structure a plan for their future.

They needed to be solid core members for their own families. Their women would need to know they were protected from the price paid by the Shaman. This was a price which was theirs alone; they would need to protect the families they may build and understanding this was essential.

I wanted to foster a sense of responsibility, of self worth and self respect which were often the most difficult of tenets to learn and as I explored each of the young shamans concept of themselves I carefully tried to draw them out. Tried to get them to reveal their thoughts and hopes and show the others by example how to nurture this in each other.

It was the sudden distraction in the attention of the young men about me which caused me to follow their line of sight and when I realized it was Aine who was headed over towards us, her eyes intent on me, my own confidence faltered and without thought I found myself on my feet.

Aine never came here, it was unheard of and that alone silenced the group as we watched her approach.

I didn't wait, breaking from the group I made my way towards her alarmed at the concern shown in her face.

"Is everything OK?"

"Andrew..." she said, greeting me with a fleeting smile which vanished as soon as it was born. "Yes, Ngaire is fine. I just wanted to talk to you about something...something I think you need to be aware of?"

Breathing suddenly, I realized I had been holding my breath. "Good... you had me worried there for a while," I countered smiling in relief, a relief I didn't quite fully feel.

"No. Ngaire is OK... well sort of. She is... upset. That is what I wanted to talk to you about."

"Upset? What happened?" A hundred possibilities ran suddenly through my mind and I struggled to still them while Aine continued.

"One of the girls said something... something that upset her. Carley..."

My throat went dry, I had been dreading this, but I had convinced myself I was being irrationally over concerned. It was months ago now and I had thought, hoped, that my relationship with Carley had evaporated... as it should have. I wished it had never been but I couldn't say this... so instead I said. "Carley...? I don't understand. What happened?"

For what seemed like an eternity Aine's look was steady and then she frowned. "You tell me?"

That had to be the one question I didn't want to hear as I looked into the honest clarity of Aine's eyes. I couldn't lie, but then I couldn't tell her the truth. It was impossible so then I decided to take an emotional stand. It was the only defence I really had.

"Nothing happened. Carley and I are nothing... Aine for Christ sake what did she say?"

"Well I don't know exactly what was said," Aine countered after a moment then continued, her gaze searching mine carefully. "Ngaire is upset, she is uncertain and she doesn't need to feel like this, not now. Andrew you have to reassure her."

"Of course, where is she?"

"She is back at your place, I told her to rest. Andrew look... I thought I knew what Ngaire meant to you... but you didn't...? There isn't anything in what Carley might have said is there, I mean you haven't been... well cheating on Ngaire... not now?"

"No!" It came out thick with fear, an automatic denial, but I knew... I knew it wasn't entirely true and with a frustrated sigh which followed my words I gave vent to my doubts. Doubts which Aine read correctly I realized. "I mean no! But there was a time... Aine I swear it was nothing, it should never have happened. It was stupid, I drank too much... I don't know why... how I ended up... I can't tell her Aine, I can't tell Ngaire this." My plea was a question and I even heard the doubt in my own voice. I wanted reassurance... I just wanted it all to go away as I tripped over my words I hoped that in confessing, it perhaps would.

Silently Aine watched me as I tortured myself with the knowledge that what had happened all those months ago should never have happened, that such a thing would hurt Ngaire. Something I would have done anything to avoid, how was I going to convince her of this? And I knew... I knew that if I couldn't convince Aine then there was no chance I could convince Ngaire... not now.

"Aine it's nothing. It meant nothing. I hated myself as soon as I realized... Look I know that is no excuse but what can I do...? It happened and at the time... I mean I told her. Carley knew it was nothing." Then at the hurt in Aines eyes the lie came easily. "It was before... long before I knew about the baby. Seriously...I can't risk this Aine; I can't risk losing Ngaire... Jem; Not now! Not with the baby due any day. Ngaire and I are building something here, something that is special and I am not going to risk that... ever."

I watched fearful, as Aine chewed her lip unsure. It was an uncertainty that was eating away at me, gnawing at my fear that Ngaire would judge me harshly for a stupid drunken mistake.

"Then you can't tell her. Not yet," she said softly shaking her head. "She is way too vulnerable now, too uncertain herself. She feels there is something but she thinks it might have been years ago, you need to reassure her now. She needs you Andrew and well... I won't say anything. Not now, not until after the baby is here and then only if she asks. I can't lie Andrew but I can avoid confirming what she suspects anyway, even if what she thinks was something that happened a long time ago."

"That's all I want. Thanks... I can deal with that and I promise I will be honest with her. But there was never anything between Carley and me apart from... well from circumstance. There is nothing there Aine. Ngaire is my life... and the kids... the kids are it. I would never hurt her knowingly. It will never happen and so help me if Carley goes near her again I will throttle her, so help me! I mean it!"

"No. Don't do anything, it will just make Ngaire think there is something more to this. I will have a talk to Jenna and she can deal with Carley I think."

"Jenna? God... do you have to tell her? I mean she might say something one day... she and Ngaire are so close. Let me deal with Carley, it would be best. She won't ever do this again I swear."

"No. That's a stupid idea... look let me talk with her instead. I can just ask her not to come around to the house. I mean she deliberately set out to upset Ngaire so that is reason enough, I doubt she even knew that you and Ngaire were moving into our place, Jen hasn't seen her since she's been back so it's understandable, it's possible. I expect she will be a bit put out by that information," Aine suggested softly, a small smile of reassurance peeping out amongst the disappointment.

"OK. Thanks Aine... really, thanks. Look I better go and find Ngaire... I have to sort this out, I can't let her worry over this," I said wanting to reassure myself that she was alright.

Aine nodded and glanced up towards the group of young men still gathered about the fire pit. "I left her at your mum's. Sorry to drop this on you right now, but you should deal with it immediately. You're right about that, but please be careful with her, with what you say."

"Yes I know. I would never hurt her Aine... seriously. She means the world to me."

"Yes... well make sure you don't hurt her."

"I won't... this was a mistake that happened before everything. It won't happen again... it should never have happened."

"Yeah well...; it's easy to say that now." Aine warned softly, disappointment still apparent in her tone as I turned away. It was that tone which tethered my thoughts and hopes to being able to fix this; it was a tone I never wanted to hear. I had to deal with this now and I wanted it never to come up again I decided, as I made my way to find Ngaire. She had become to mean everything to me, Ngaire and Jem were my world and the baby would make our little family all that more secure. This... what had happened between Carley and I was of so little meaning to me, it was something which was just simply so stupid a thing for me to have done; meant nothing to me in my world.

I didn't know what I was going to say to her, or even what I would find but I had to find her. The drive to make sure she was OK, to make sure I could fix this was very strong. Part of me wanted to seek out Carley, to throttle her and I struggled to contain this emotion and suppress it. Carley was nothing and I would give her no hold over my thoughts. I hoped I would never see the girl again though I knew I would. But to me she would no longer exist, no other woman would. It was Ngaire and our kids who were the focus of my life and I wanted it no other way.

The walk back to mum's place seemed incredibly long but when I got there it seemed I was carrying my stomach in my hands. The house was full of noise and that seemed to make it worse. Most of the racket was coming from the lounge room and kitchen and I realized that the youngest of the kids, Jem included, were rioting. They were playing some game which involved bouncing off the furniture by the sound of it and as Mum yelled demanding they take their game outside as Ngaire was trying to rest, I detoured to our room, my glance catching my mother's when I passed the lounge doorway.

Ngaire was lying on the bed quietly, the room in the same disarray I had left it early in the day as I had tried to gather my gear together for our move over to Sean's. Some of my gear was still strewn around boxes but I could see it had been moved. I hoped Ngaire hadn't attempted to pack it into some order. It wasn't something she should have been doing and impatiently I berated myself for my thoughtlessness in leaving it, as I closed the door softly, trying to drown out the noise from the lounge room.

Moving quietly over to the bed I sat on its edge wondering if she was asleep though it seemed impossible with the noise about the house. As I gently placed my hand on her hip she turned to me, she had been crying I saw and the knowledge churned my gut.

"Babe... Aine said you were upset. Talk to me..."

Shaking her head she stretched a hand to her brow and tightened her lips as though to seal in whatever she had heard, to silence her thoughts as she cut me from her sight.

I too shook my head, denying whatever it was. I didn't care what it was I just wanted it to go away. "You OK?" I said instead, softly, worried about her strained look.

Again she shook her head then slowly turned back to the small window. I knew from experience that the scene out that window was a place where she could lose her thoughts to the bush outside.

"It's not true Babe... I have never been close to Carley. She's nothing to me..."

"Don't!" Ngaire demanded softly. "It's not that... I don't care. I don't want to talk about it anyway... not now."

"Babe... What can I say...?"

"Nothing," she whispered. "Really Andrew I don't want to talk about it now. I just feel a little sick... and tired. I just need to rest a bit."

The sense of helplessness that washed over me was unleashing my emotions but I sat there and thought of all the things I could say... things she didn't want to hear. In that moment, I think I hated Carley... hated myself... hated what I was doing to my beautiful woman then helplessly I moved, I stretched out on the bed and gathered Ngaire into my arms curling her back into me.

At first she was stiff and unbending but then she moved into my arms, resting her head against the nook of my shoulder and as I gathered her closer, the weight of my hand sought the mound of her belly carefully, gently lending her the heat of my hand as I stroked her and our child carefully.

I felt her tension slip away and was grateful for that as I soothed her thoughts with a gentle breath on her ear.

"I love you Babe, please... please let us..."

"Andrew don't," she said suddenly, with some impatience. Not turning, nor tensing... it was as though she wanted to deny me a voice and I felt the sting of her words. "I don't want to talk about it now. Not now... just shut up or go away."

Biting off my words, my thoughts, I forced myself to silence again, dampening down the agony of not knowing how to soothe her, not being allowed to wipe away her fears. While a dozen protests gathered in my mouth I forced them to be quiet. "OK," was all I said.

For an age we simply lay there together and after a while I felt the softness of her weight as she must have slept. My arm went numb and after a time my body ached, but it was nothing. I needed her to rest, to lose the anger she had with me and for that I would have lain there for an eternity.

Deep into the night she moved, restlessly and I felt the blood rush back along my limb as I carefully slipped my arm out from under her and eased myself up. Covering her with the blanket, I watched her carefully for a moment. The dim moonlight bathed the shape of her as she breathed, her breath was even and light and that reassured me. Easing off the bed I silently stretched my aching muscles. It was late into the evening and I was starving but it was a small price to pay to see her sleep so peacefully.

Silently I left the room as there was something I wanted now to do. Something I needed to do and after spending hours trying to find a way to make this go away I headed for the kitchen to wake myself properly with a sluice of water from the kitchen taps then as I ate a vegemite sandwich I considered what I needed to achieve.

When I stepped out into the night my one thought was to put an end to this torment of Ngaire's, she would never need to go through this again. Not while I had the means to stop it.

I wanted to find Carley... needed to find her. It would be a simple task, it wouldn't even require much effort and once I was into the shadow of the night, away from the house, I knelt and dug my fingers deep into the silt at the edge of the road and watched as the earth lights oozed up about them.

Here, the earth lights were not as strong as in the dry Outback but I had known that this would be the way. The country was all wrong but I knew I could draw the lights none the less. As I watched the subtle glow gather I felt it when I had gained what strength I could garner from the earth in these mountains. Wollumbin was a place of power, but it was the power of the Serpent, not that of the Lightening Man but what power there was, I gathered to my fingers.

The earth lights glowed about my fingers like a brilliant molasses and as I harnessed its power I bought the strength of the Min Min orb to life, marrying its form and giving it direction. As it left me there was no hesitation. It wasn't the brilliant glow of the open country but a more subtle hallowed light and at first it hesitated, then split the night and in my minds eye I watched its path

It knew where it was going and quickly I tried to follow it, tried to slow it so that I might keep up and harnessing it to me carefully we made our way through the bush. The Min Min orb didn't follow a path, its flight was direct but I could see as I scrambled after it that it was headed towards Tom's. While this wasn't ideal I had little patience for the havoc I might create when the light reached its quarry. If anything, I would teach some the strength of discretion even though I was now flaunting that tenet of the Shaman myself, in drawing this Spirit power to my own cause.

The orb seemed to sense my feelings, my mood; it was as though it stayed just ahead of me. I met no one, which was a good thing and as we neared Tom's I was grateful that for once there seemed to be no one about. Then the hour was late and I had hoped that the others would have left.

The fire-pit still smoked and there was a flicker of light in the cabin, candles I guessed. It was too warm for a fire and as I approached, the Min Min orb slowed, stilled and gathered its light around the door as it slowly began to die. It had found its quarry.

Its death wasn't to my purpose though and with my growing anger I flicked it back to life. I hadn't known I could do this, but then I hadn't known I could tether the orb either and I allowed my anger to harness and feed its power. It was an instinctive thought and it was like the orb was alive, part of my very existence.

When I opened the door I stood still for a moment, allowing my eyes to search the room and then I saw them, it was simple... Carley screamed suddenly when she saw the strange orb and scrambled to her feet. I wondered at that, though my frown couldn't be seen as the orb gathered its strength behind me, fed by my anger, casting my shape into relief I realized as Tom too... stood, clearly disconcerted.

"What did you say to her?" I spat in demand of the now cowering girl. I let my fury spit my words at her as she scrambled for something to protect herself with; anything would have done if seemed. I felt my anger flame anew as I watched her and the light of the Min Min crackled behind me, she was clearly badly frightened and that bought me some satisfaction.

Carley backed behind the larger shape of Tom and I could feel her fear. It calmed me somehow and I watched as Tom took a defensive stand in front of her, I wondered if he realized it was me.

As I waited for her answer my eyes took in the sight of them clearly now. They had been engaged in a moment together, Tom was naked and what I could see of Carley, she too was wearing little, though she had some garment gathered protectively in front of her.

"Nothing... I didn't say anything..." she whimpered. She must have realized who I was. "She's lying..." she added defensively.

"That would be hard," I spat impatient with her excuse, but I was surprisingly calm now in the face of her obvious fear of me. "As she didn't say anything at all, but you have hurt her Carley... hurt her with your malice and what is more, that is what you intended!"

Stepping lightly inside the door I felt the power of a chasing predator, having cornered its prey and it amazed me as it shifted through me. But I also felt the power of the Min Min orb behind me, again begin to flicker a death and I stopped its death with my silent thought once more. I held its dying strength a moment longer to my purpose then holding up my hand I drew it to me. It was as though in holding a glowing orb I could use it to my purpose and I wasn't about to dismiss its strength, or its threat.

"Andrew... hold up..." Tom said urgently. "What the hell are you doing?"

"What am I doing?" I asked, not an unreasonable question I thought to myself as I considered the circumstances and slowly stepped further into the room with the orb still about my hand. It was likely that Tom knew little of this business I realized as I moved towards them. "Your little girlfriend has been trying to injure Ngaire... Not just Ngaire but Ngaire and our child," I said heavily, drawing the knowledge of Carley's attack on Ngaire from the depth of my own condemnation, emotions which threaded through my words.

"What?" he countered confused.

"What manner of malice did you use Carley... what lies did you tell?" I demanded my anger firing again as I considered my words. "Did you tell Tom that you slept with me... what... barely nine months ago? Did you tell him that you spiked my drink... just what was it that you did Carley?"

"You drank it!" she spat from behind the shelter of Toms back... "It wasn't all me... you chose to drink it... it was just a party for Christ-sake. A bit of fun, you don't have to get all high and mighty about it. It was harmless, it couldn't hurt you... it was a bit of fun!"

"You slept with Andrew?" Tom said suddenly in the oddest tone, almost disbelief... "Geezus Carley... even I knew about Ngaire then. Andrew's my mate! Can't you keep your legs together for anyone?" he demanded clearly affronted.

"Don't you dare say that to me!" Carley spat. "Can't you keep it in your pants?" she countered savagely, in an equally derogative tone as they glared at each other, momentarily forgetting the threat of my presence.

"Enough!" I roared angrily, the orb in my hands sparking; that was something which surprised me as much as them. I was uninterested in their relationship; all that concerned me was Ngaire. "I don't give a shit what you two do... but let me tell you something Carley... you go anywhere near Ngaire, or Jem.. or the baby again, and I will take this bloody great light globe here and shove it down your lying throat girl. Is that clear?" I demanded. "You will not go near the Karadji's house, you will not even talk to Ngaire... nor even look at her sideways...I don't care if you're friends with Jen, you will say nothing; do nothing... stay away from my woman!"

Suddenly the globe in my hand died... it was as though someone had flicked a switch. Surprised, I started and then quickly recovered. I wasn't about to backtrack on this. I stood my ground and glared across at her. "Now if I were you I would get the hell out of here while you still can."

I said it with anger still flicking in my eyes, I watched as she gathered up her things and hastily made for the door... she circled around me carefully and made a quick dash for the swinging exit.

Both Tom and I watched her as she left quickly and in that time I wondered if I had overplayed my cards, but it felt good and I cherished that feeling, feeding it. Though once she had left, once I still stood there watching the door close crookedly between us I felt the feeling of satisfaction leave also.

"Look... I didn't know," Tom said suddenly, surprising me. He drew my attention from my own reverie and I was forced to consider what to do about his presence. I guessed I owed him an explanation of a sort. "Honestly Andrew I had no idea she did anything to Ngaire..."

"It's done," I said, cutting him off. "It's over..." I added with a sigh as I turned to him.

For the first time I saw Tom as he struggled into his dacks with difficulty. He was a man, I could no longer see him as a child. It was odd. I had known he was fooling around with Carley; it had been going on for ages, off one moment, on the next but that she could be so cruel I hadn't known. I realized then that Tom had not known that part of Carley either.

"It's not entirely her fault, I am at fault here too... she couldn't have hurt Ngaire without me, without my participation. Maybe I've put too much blame on her but ... but whatever it was she said to Ngaire... it's costing me dearly. She shouldn't have done that."

"Bloody hell... I mean I would be angry too... In... in your place I mean."

"I'm angrier with myself," I said as I felt the tension leave my body, slowly I felt the flood of relief and acceptance. I was very much at blame here as well. "I've hurt someone... someone who I would never ever want to hurt." I finished regretting the reality.

"Yeah. I can see... but, I didn't know... I mean that light. It was a weapon...

I didn't think...?"

Surprised I looked up, realizing what perhaps he had perceived. "No, it isn't a weapon. I just wanted it to appear like that. I had to have something that would scare her... frighten her and keep her away from Ngaire," I explained carefully. "I have probably done a lot of damage, doing what I did, but I needed something..."

Tom looked at me; I could see he was confused. "You mean it wouldn't hurt anyone?"

"No. It can't do that, it's only a tool of the Shaman, not a weapon. The worst it can do is scare you into doing something stupid."

Tom released a tight breath, a small smile building around his mouth. "You scared the shit out of her... and me; coming in the way you did."

"Yeah... I meant to," I agreed somewhat relieved that I hadn't destroyed the friendship I had with Tom. "You want to be careful with that one Tom, if she has you by the short and curlies, she will mince you. You aren't the only string in her bow, you do realize that don't you?"

"Yeah... I know... but hey," he grinned suddenly. "She ain't the only string in mine either."

Shaking my head I considered him, I considered his youth once more. "Not so many years ago I would have appreciated that. It changes you know... life changes us."

"You're beginning to sound like Ty," he countered quickly and I took that in the spirit of a warning, not to lecture him. It wasn't my place.

"Yeah well, maybe Ty is right in a lot of things."

"Yeah... it don't make it easier to hear," he added chuckling hesitantly now. "You want a beer... I have a stash, it's light but it's not too bad."

I looked across at him as he walked over to the esky near the fire place I had helped him build, and watched as he reached for two bottles then he stretched, offering me one.

I took it. Even though I knew it wasn't what I should have done. I would have to talk to him about that stash... but for now...

The tension in the room began to shift, abate as we talked. It was good to talk to someone, good to exorcise my guilt and in this way I could find a way back to Ngaire and our little family. Today would be a new beginning and when the dawn broke I made my way quietly back to my Mum's place.

Ngaire was up when I got there though it was just past dawn when I walked into the bedroom. I froze at the sight of her perched on the bed attending to the boxes I had left the day before; her glance was fearless but hesitant at my arrival.

"Hi Babe... I will take those over today. If you want... unless... if you would rather I stay here and you go over...?"

"No," she smiled. A smile that lit her eyes and the light in her eyes had the thread of forgiveness, a wary emotion as she looked up at me. She put her hand to her belly and eased the discomfit in a way that tore my heart, I found myself holding my breath as she added. "It's OK. I was just a bit upset, it was unexpected I think. I... I believe you that there was nothing Andrew. I have to believe that. I was maybe expecting too much, I should have realized you would have had relationships amongst the women. But I didn't expect..." Ngaire shook her head still uncertain of what had occurred and why it had happened.

"Babe there is nothing," I said quickly, moving across the bed towards her. "She won't come near you again. Look, I'm not blameless..."

But putting her finger's quickly up to still my words she silenced me. "I don't want to hear Andrew," she said softly but with a conviction that surprised me. "I don't want to hear it. Maybe another time but not now... not now please."

Gathering her into the circle of my arms I bit off the words that I would have said. "OK... OK Babe, if that is what you want that is all that counts."

It wasn't about me now, I realized in the days that followed and if what I felt was an uneasy guilt then I could live with that because Ngaire didn't want to know. She simply didn't want to face the truth of what might have happened, she didn't dwell on the possibilities in the days that followed. I was grateful that she chose this path, grateful that she wouldn't hear of my duplicity, my stupidity and part of me hoped that it would just go away.

I found it hard to fool myself though and I was aware that Ngaire was quieter, careful in her movements as though she had somehow become more fragile than she had been before. I felt responsible for that but there was nothing she would have allowed me to do about it.

Jiemba settled into the small room off the lounge room, though we had a hard time keeping him there. He much preferred the noise of my mother's place and while my mum welcomed him, she despaired about Tango his mutt, his constant companion, wondering if he would ever get used to staying outside of the house.

The space in Taipan and Aine's old rooms was a welcome relief from the confinements of my old room, and watching Ngaire ease into its comfort and gather all the things for the baby around us, I knew I would have to make plans for our own place.

I had raised the prospect of buying or building a house with Ngaire. I had saved more than enough funds for us to choose where we would like to live and I hoped to move on an investment, our first home, as soon as practical, but Ngaire would not be drawn out on such a plan.

After a time, I came to think it was because of the companionship she found with Jenna and having Jenna about was a boon. It was Jen who coaxed Ngaire into smiling so readily again after she had spoken to her, as women do, then the soft light I so loved in her eyes returned, especially when her eyes were turned on me.

We saw nothing of Carley, nor Judy for that matter. Though other of Jen's friends dropped in occasionally, they rarely stayed long. I wouldn't have noticed it except for the strange way they treated me now and I wondered about that. It was a sudden switch in the manner I was treated which concerned me, particularly the younger women. Sean joked that it was due to my pending status as a dad. I never told him about the night I had threatened Carley with the koolrari light, nor did Aine mention it. It was a secret we kept.

Where the young women had once before been subtly flirtatious and even dismissing, they were now almost hesitant, though Ngaire as well as Jen seemed to enjoy their light friendships, so I wondered if it had more to do with the respect they had for her. I doubted I would ever understand the minds of women, but I cared even less as I watched Ngaire grow closer to delivering our baby, we were looking forward to the welcome arrival of our son.

At times Ngaire seemed to glow with health, and at others she was drawn and tired, the pregnancy weighing heavily on her. Night time was the time I loved the best. Then I could draw her into the circle of my arms and explore the movement and reality of the promise of our baby.

Those were times when I could lay and watch her breathing, drawing slow and steady breaths when she was relaxed and seemingly content and if the baby was restless I could put the weight of my hand to her belly and still him. I could keep him from waking her too much when he would move towards the warmth of my palm, it was a beautiful thing.

I had taken to bringing the car down to the house, along the narrow road in readiness for when it was time to go to the hospital. It had taken ages, but Jen, Sean and I had convinced her to be prepared to go to the hospital instead of the home birth she had been considering. The little sturdy vehicle of hers soon claimed a regular spot along the narrow track. It was a good thing that there was no one who lived further along the road than us, as there was no room to fit another car along the track. There was barely enough room to turn the little forester and soon Ngaire could not fit comfortably behind the wheel.

Then one night, she woke me. At first I didn't understand the importance of what she was trying to tell me, but when I did... it was like being pushed off a balcony.

"Andrew... Andrew... are you awake?"

"Mmm..." I shifted to reach her, gather her to me and settle the heat of my hand on her belly as I did to calm our son.

"Andrew. Wake up."

"Hmm... I am awake."

"I'm in..." It was her sharply indrawn breath that woke me. Suddenly I was wide awake.

"What!"

But I already knew what and in a moment I was out of bed and struggling to gather my wits together as I realized how tense she was in that moment. "Breathe Baby... breathe carefully," I coaxed concerned that she had stopped breathing. But when I heard the labour of her breath, I too released my breath.

"I'll get the car." I said quietly, seemingly in control, as I desperately tried to reassure her that I was ready and able to help, though I felt anything but.

"We already have the car Andrew... I just need my bag," she said as she finally began to breathe normally and eased herself up to the side of the bed, smiling, she reassured me. "My bag... it's behind the door."

"Oh. Yes... OK. How is it?"

"We have plenty of time; they're about fifteen minutes apart." Gingerly she stood and reached for her dressing gown. "I didn't want to wake you until I was sure..."

"Damn it Ngaire we spoke about this," I scolded and then stopped. This wasn't the time. "OK... OK let's just go. Before it starts again... here let me help."

I knew she was impatient with me but I could have danced her out the door. It was time... even I could see that we had to pause to allow another contraction to pass before we reached the car. Jen had heard us and had surfaced from her own room as we reached the door. She looked more concerned than I and that worried me... but I couldn't afford to be worried. We had a good half an hour drive ahead of us and my son was going to be born today... or tonight. I didn't know which, but as the woman I loved strained, unable to... or unwilling to move, for the moment I forgot all about the promise of my son, and worried instead about the woman in my life.

It was time and I had no idea how hard it was going to be.

A GIFT

Jenna:

Waiting was the most difficult thing I had ever done and it didn't help that I was sick to my stomach. I couldn't have slept even if I had wanted to though Sean managed it, sprawled on the sofa, inexplicably he was soon unconscious and it annoyed me beyond words.

At first I tried to ignore his snoring, it wasn't too loud just loud enough to annoy me and I was tempted to just empty a glass of water over his head.

Instead I decided on checking the room. I remade the bed for Ngaire and Andrew and checked that all was in readiness in the bassinet we had fussed over almost every day for the last few weeks, moving the soft, golden brown teddy around, changing the covers and rearranging them. We had talked often about the dream of the small bundle that would inhabit the tiny bed. I don't know why I rearranged it now, because I knew it would be a few days at the very least till the bassinet had an occupant. But it soothed me.

Then I made myself a hot chocolate and perched up on the back of the sofa watching Sean sleep. I took the time to contemplate this night, wondering what Ngaire was going through. I wanted to know and didn't want to know. We wanted to go to the hospital but Ngaire would have none of that. She wanted us to stay here and watch out for Jem, who wasn't even here now, it seemed such a waste. He preferred to stay over at Andrew's old place and quite often we allowed him to do that. He had made friends and preferred them to our company, but tonight... tonight I would insist on him staying home. Well not actually tonight... tomorrow night. He could visit with his brother or sister in the hospital, see his Mum. It was a lovely thought.

The night deepened into the small hours of the morning and eventually I joined Sean, curling up beside him and as I slipped into sleep he was unaware of my movement. It was a strange night, a strange sense, it was as though I could feel the tension about me, I could feel the sudden burn and that pain, the pain of the burn in my head was when I screamed. I couldn't have done anything else

"Bloody hell!" I felt Sean jump beside me, suddenly awake, as I was shockingly awake. The pain in my head was excruciating as the sharpness of it hit me... and then as suddenly as it hit, it vanished!

Stunned, having jumped up, I quickly hit the floor. The impact was shocking. Hurting and confused I looked about unsure as I could feel Sean's hands as he tried to find me in the dark, as he tried to grab for me.

"Jen... God you scared the bejeezus out of me," he said shocked, scrambling to reach me, quieten me. "Baby what's wrong? God don't do that again..." he said clearly shaken as having found me he slipped to the floor at my side.

"Sean...!" I cried, afraid... terribly afraid for some reason and then he gathered me into his chest.

"What's wrong...? Jen look at me... it's only a dream..."

"No... no... Something's wrong…!"

"No. Baby... it's a dream..." I watched as he shook his head trying to reassure me, humour me but still strung out I shook my head denying his confidence. The weight of his hands stroking my hair, fighting to soothe me, helped to still me. Sean was here... it was a dream ... it had to be...

"Oh God... I have this horrible feeling Sean... no... something's wrong?"

"Shhh... settle down Baby... settle down. It was just a dream. It's OK. I am here... OK. Look we can talk about it. Just settle down first." He scrambled quickly and I suddenly found myself enveloped in the heat of his body as he cuddled me to his chest.

Forcing myself to be quiet, stilling the throb of my heartbeat, I drew long breaths. For some reason I wanted to cry and I struggled with the flow of tears. It was a helpless struggle and as the tears tripped over my lids I tried to wipe them away before Sean could notice them.

Then as he noticed the dampness on my fingers he too was silent, he forced me to face him. Pushing at me suddenly, I could see his expression was confused; the disquiet in his eyes upset me more now than my own tears that I was fighting to control.

"Jen... Baby what's wrong?" he whispered.

"I don't know..." and then the tears again threatened to flow. "There is something wrong... oh God Sean what if it's Ngaire?"

"No. No... no... Baby she is OK. Look don't think about it for now, there's nothing we can do. It's OK. She'll be OK... she is in good hands." Gathering me back against his chest he tried to soothe me again. "It's OK. It can't be Ngaire... she's fine. Surely... really she is fine," he whispered softly but I heard the hesitation in his voice... He wasn't sure.

I didn't believe him. I couldn't force my heart to believe him, so instead I curled into a ball in his lap and we began what seemed to be the longest hours of our life. It may have been only a few hours... but it seemed to be many more, too many hours. Dawn arrived, then the brightness of the day; and still we sat on the floor with a sense of dread which kept us there.

Once the fingers of bright light began to stretch into the room, telling us it was well into the morning, Sean moved and picking me up easily he settled me into the depth of the sofa. Fearfully I put a pillow where his warmth had been and without a word I watched as he moved off to our room.

He wasn't long, barely time enough to wash and change, so when he came back out he moved over to the lounge and braced himself as though for a blow.

"Jen, do you want to get dressed? I'll take you up to the hospital. I can't stand this much longer."

Immediately I was up off the lounge. It would only take me a few minutes and as I moved swiftly towards our room to change I suddenly froze. I had heard the slam of a door high on the road, a door that could only be Ngaire's car.

When Andrew stepped into the upper landing moments later I knew immediately there was something wrong. I could see it in his face and as he looked at me, tortured, I began to move towards him slowly and before I knew it I was crushed against his chest as I felt the heaving of what was his inexplicable grief.

"Jen she's gone... she died. God she died... you don't die any more ... no one dies. God why did it have to be her... why..! Why her...?" he cried, his heart breaking as he poured his grief out over us. I felt Sean... felt the heat of his body as he caught me, gathered me up against him when my legs lost the strength to support me.

"Dead... she is dead?" I said... suddenly fighting Sean's arms. "No... no... she isn't!" I screamed at him.

"Shh.. baby..."

"No you don't understand... she can't be... you said she was OK. Andrew....? What...? Why....? How?"

He just shook his head as Sean half dragged him, half carried me to where we could find support. I found myself back on the lounge with Andrew to one side and again I reached for him, sheltering him as he seemed to shatter in my arms. Sean held us together, stopped us from both shattering.

Brokenly I heard how she had suddenly just gone... left him. They said it was an aneurism in her head, her blood pressure had gone through the roof, then she was gone. There had been all the confusion of an emergency caesarean operation and the baby had been born. She had been dragged from her mother's belly with a swiftness and cruelty that had saved her life... one life beginning, as one had slipped away. She had never known her mother, never been held in her arms.

The hardest thing, aside from struggling with the reality that my friend, my soul mate, was no longer here with us, was watching Andrew's heartbreaking grief. I didn't think it would ever end but it did. When he began to quieten and still, I too drew the same deep breaths of relief. It was a moment of relief from the pain as I felt the numbness invade.

I must have slept because when I woke up it was to the dullness of the afternoon, I was in the room Sean and I shared. I was deeply buried into the warmth of the feather doonah, the heat was growing stifling but I didn't care.... I didn't want to wake, didn't want to move. Not yet. If I moved then I would have to face it all again and I didn't want to do that. If I stayed here, maybe it would prove to be a dream... a nightmare, so I stayed there for what seemed another eternity.

I heard when Sean stepped into the room, heard his light tread as he moved across towards me, then he gathered me up. I was crying and hadn't realized it but Sean lent me his strength as he held me against him and allowed me to dampen his shirt. Use it to dry my nose, he didn't care about it.

"Shh... Jen. I know. I know," he said, trying to soothe me. "I've rung Ty and Aine, and left a message and I spoke to her mum. It's all taken care of... Andrew and I are going in to the hospital tomorrow... shh... Baby."

"Andrew? How is he? I asked after a time when once more the tears passed and a numbness began to settle on me.

Sean just shook his head, "He is with Jiemba... they have gone into the forest to look for Tango, he has gone to ground but Andrew will find him."

"Tango? Oh I never thought of Tango," I said fearfully.

"The dog will be OK."

"Jem? How is Jem?"

Again Sean shook his head. "I don't know if he understands. I think he does... Andrew is talking to him."

For a moment I moved back into the warmth of Sean, I lost myself in the strength of him, and then as my mind settled I once more suddenly looked up.

"What about the baby?"

Sean smiled inexplicably, "She is fine, a healthy little girl. They will keep her at the hospital for a few days. I took a run into see her, check on her. Andrew was too much of a mess and he slept for hours but I wanted to find out how she was. You've been asleep all day yourself Baby."

I bit my lip hard... I couldn't ask... couldn't bring myself to, and I felt the hot sting of tears gather once again as Sean shifted me back into his arms.

"She looks just like her mum," he added softly. "She has the most amazing head of curls and she is so tiny." At that, I couldn't stop the tears and as Sean once more tried to soothe me I struggled with my loss... our loss. Struggled with the knowledge of Jem's loss and Andrew's, would the pain ever ease I wondered.

It did however; it eased as we moved through the days and the following weeks. Watching Andrew lead Jem through those early days was terribly difficult. Jem stayed with him almost constantly and when he was unable to be with Andrew, he stayed by Sean's side or sat by himself in the lounge, stroking Tango's coat for hours. At first he said nothing, did nothing but curl occasionally into the dogs coat and sleep.

Some mornings we would wake and we would find him curled up into Sean's back, or into his side and if he wasn't there, he would be with Andrew. He didn't sleep in his own bed for nights on end and it wasn't so much Jem, but Tango who was less tolerant of being shoved or kicked during the night and I became accustomed to his low warning growl when Sean moved to dislodge him from the centre of the bed to make room for himself or Jem.

The funeral was the worst, and the Elders organized a smoking ceremony to help the community, to help us and as we passed through the scent of the smoke I felt keenly the loss of my friend. It was time though, time to let her go. She would never be far from my heart; I knew my Spirit once more would walk with hers in the shadows.

It was the day of the smoking ceremony that Andrew bought little Yindi home. To me she was a precious bundle, someone with whom I could share my own grief and the opportunity to hold her, bathe and feed her. Her constant demands were what helped me most. Sean had been right, she was so tiny yet she was a normal weight. Her hair was brown, strong but lighter than her mothers and it fell about her head in a riot of curls, each day it seemed to grow stronger and more difficult to contain.

Often she made me laugh as she would nestle into my arms seeking her bottle and it was a battle between me and Andrew when it came time to look after her. Andrew took to carrying her as he moved about the house. I would often see him with her lying along his forearm or held sleeping against his chest. He seemed to gain comfort from her closeness and his expression would soften, the sadness would leave his eyes while he held her. I didn't have the heart to take her away or scold him for taking her from her bassinet yet again.

He took her each night and tended to her needs during the lonely hours, he would not share this time with me even though he often looked tired and drawn. No one moved the bassinet from where it had been placed, no one wanted to. It was as though this was our one concession in our loss. Other than this we all struggled to find a way around the constant reminder of the loss of little Yindi's mum. We never said her name, the time had passed to call her to us in this way and it helped me to realize the loss of her and learn to cope with it.

I spoke little to Andrew other than what was needed to get through the day. He didn't seem to want to talk but it was the sadness in his eyes which often tripped my own grief. The only time he was apart from little Yindi was when he was with Jiemba. I treasured these hours with the beautiful little bundle of sweet smells and growing awareness. Weeks had gone by, weeks where we silently waited for something, anything to break the pain of the day.

Aine and Taipan had finally got the messages we had sent and had decided to continue on their trip north. They could have done little, though Aine often would message me asking after little Yindi, Jem and Andrew and I answered where I could. I would have loved her to be here but it wasn't necessary. She too would compete for Yindi's times so I was loathe to even suggest it. Quietly I moved about the house doing the things that often reminded me of what I had lost, but as we moved through those early days, the memories took on a sad sweetness of their own.

It was some time later when I was working in the kitchen I saw again the flash of Andrew's smile. He was playing with Yindi, teasing her cheek with his finger when she suddenly started to gurgle at him, surprising him. His smile was like the break of the day and smiling myself I moved towards them. It was such a precious moment, one to be gathered and remembered.

He sat on the lounge with Yindi stretched out on the small soft blanket. Holding one of her tiny feet in his much larger hand as he carefully rubbed the soft pudding sole of her foot and she wrestled with the constraint she could feel in his grip, making him smile all the more to himself. It was such a private and gentle moment between them that it made me smile.

It was an odd sight, though I had become used to seeing him holding his little daughter. Seeing her lost within a blanket he would often become impatient with it and remove her from it, even though I complained about it.

But now, against her tiny size he looked strangely gargantuan, it was a sight I had never thought to see and as he cooed to his small loose bundle my heart melted.

Dropping down to the floor beside them I joined in the game, one of touch and sound that seemed so easily to entertain her.

"She is beautiful isn't she," I said softly chuckling at her sudden attention.

"Yeah. She has her mum's temper," he said, the words left hanging in the air for a moment before I had the strength to scatter them.

"Have you decided what you are going to do?" I said softly after a moment, knowing that he had spoken to the family in the Territory, fearful that it would mean that he would send Yindi to them and I did not want to face the possibility of losing her.

"No. Not really." Drawing a sigh he pursed his lips, "I am thinking I will need to take the kids up, to at the least, meet their family. Her Nan wants to meet her and I can't deny her that."

The very thought emptied my soul and tore at me. "You're not going to leave them there are you?"

"I don't know what to do. Yindi? No... Yindi will stay with me but I can't... the thought of Jem... away from us..."

"You can't separate them Andrew... it's not what... You can't!"

"I want Jem to stay with me, me and Yindi, but I need to be sure it's what he wants. I need to talk to the family... if I can work with them... sort it out."

"We could come with you?"

"No," shaking his head he continued. "They need to know I can care for the kids, having someone with me doesn't give them that message. But... but I do need your help Jen, yours and Sean's." The question in his voice was deep and anguished. "I need to decide what to do and there will be times when I can't be here with them. Yindi needs a foster mum and I can't be here all the time. I can't lose her too."

"Of course we are here. We've talked about it, Sean and I, we will always be here. You can leave them with us, but they need you. You will always be their dad." Holding my breath for a moment I then continued. "I would love to be their foster mum, Jem would be happiest here with you and Sean, and Yindi... Yindi would be a delight. I feel like she's already part of our family. Sean and me ... and you! You and Jem... and even bloody Tango!"

Andrew smiled, kissing his daughter's foot and in that act, there seemed to be an answer, an agreement. Though he couldn't have spoken the words just then and I understood that. After a time he looked up. "You have your lives; I really shouldn't ask this of you."

"Nonsense! There is nothing more important than the children," then I grinned. "Besides, it will keep Sean from worrying that I will want babies of my own." With that I laughed, knowing the irony of the statement. "I guess he figures sharing Yindi and Jem will keep me busy enough."

I knew Andrew watched me, assessing my commitment and as my eyes met his I could see he in part understood how I felt about the little bundle between us. I didn't know how to explain my feelings for Yindi, she was such a tiny little thing with her glorious riot of curls and ready smile. It was as though she was meant to be with me, with Sean and I, and with Andrew and Jem. She had so easily become a part of our lives, she owned us and we were all willing captives.

"It's decided then," he said after a while, relief palpable in the air. "I'll take the kids up to the Territory, to see their Nan and see what can be worked out. Either way, no matter what, Yindi will stay with me. Have you met her, Jem's Nan?"

"No. No I didn't. How about you?"

Andrew sighed, taking a moment... one that worried me. "Yes. She's OK but too old, too tired perhaps. I couldn't leave the kids there, that would never happen but she won't want to lose Jem. Maybe I can work something out. I want Jiemba to stay with me and I will fight for that. It's the way it was meant to be."

"You know that... that well... a life with the Mimi while he is so young wasn't what was planned for Jiemba."

"Yep, I know and it's not what it will be. I won't let that happen. When he is older and more able to choose, that will be time enough."

The moment stretched and after a time, Andrew again smiled reassuring me. Yindi will always stay with me Jen. I have made sure of that, but... Jem... the thought disturbs me as I don't know what his father's family may have planned for him."

"Well you can only go and see them. I could never imagine that his Nan and the family would be unreasonable."

"I think I can give him a better life. Do you think they will let me?"

I thought about it for a moment then smiled. "Yes... surely. How could they separate them?" Though neither of us were sure.

 Some weeks later when it was time to see Andrew and the two kids off to Brisbane, where they would travel onto Darwin, I held my heart once more in my mouth as Sean and I watched them depart for what was inevitably a long trip.

He looked a strange sight as he packed the car. He saw no difficulty in travelling with the kids and it amazed me. He simply had Yindi in her sling which he wore around his chest. It was one he had found in the shops which he felt comfortable wearing. The baby supplies he carried with him, he packed into a duffle bag along with his own gear while Jem travelled with his own bag, a small one he could carry.

That Jiemba mimicked Andrew was amusing, both of them doted on the little package. Andrew barely seemed to notice the burden around his shoulders and chest as he moved with complete ease. He never considered it an imposition, so much so that others often would not realize he had a baby buried within the simple sling, though his hand often moved to steady the sling, or soothe the bundle with little conscious thought. Yindi seemed to love her position against her Dad's heart and when she was her most fractious it was Andrew who would take her and soothe her with ease.

Over the weeks he thought nothing of feeding her, changing her nappies; though washing her tiny clothes had no part of his regime and I despaired of his practice of simply disposing of anything that he deemed too soiled. He kept a ready supply of cotton knit baby suits, they were as readily available as her tiny disposable nappies and it was these that she lived in.

Sean and Andrew couldn't understand my want to dress her into what they considered frilly and unnecessarily fussy clothes, and though Andrew tolerated my persistence, he wouldn't encourage it and certainly didn't follow my example. It worked well while she was so tiny; she slept most of the time and waking only to spend an hour or two at most seeking attention. I wondered how he would cope with Yindi when she was demanding more of his time. But that was yet to be seen.

As Andrew prepared to leave with Jem and Yindi I was torn. I didn't want to let them go and while Sean, Tango and I stood and watched them drive off down the narrow track I had to hold tight to the rope harness I had on the dog. As far as I knew, he had never been separated from those he loved before and we weren't quite sure how he was going to cope.

I was certain if Taipan had known we now intended to keep Tango locked in the house, he would have something to say about it, but there was no other way we could think of to keep the dog happy with a semblance of familiarity about him. As it was he strained and barked furiously and I found Sean had to take control of the rope which was increasingly difficult to hold.

A STEP INTO THE PAST

Andrew:

It was a long drive, one I would need to break at least once to feed Yindi but for the moment she was settled into the baby capsule harnessed into the back seat with Jem and they were travelling well. I had deliberately booked a late afternoon flight from Brisbane and planned at least one night in a motel in Darwin. I figured that this would give me time to organize transport down to Katherine, settle the kids, and give them a good night's sleep.

Travelling with two kids had its complications but that Jem was old enough to understand what was going on made it much easier. He had been quiet since the loss of his mum and he had become possessive of both Sean and I and little Yindi. We didn't mind, however he felt the loss of Tango's company and that worried me some, he said so little. He seemed to think he had to bear up under the strain of it all. I would rather he let loose so I could deal with his anger and his sense of loss. Maybe once he settled around his Nan and his Mum's people who he knew well, it would help him to adjust, though I found myself worrying once again about whether he would ever really adjust to losing someone so close, at such a young age. The worst of such a long drive was that it gave me time to think; which was something I didn't really want or need to do.

When we finally reached the airport hours later I booked the car into long term parking, then I realized Yindi had managed to build up enough ammo' in her nappy to smell badly. I had changed her at her last feed which was over an hour ago and the smell told me she had managed to fill her nappy again anyway.

We didn't travel with additional luggage, only my duffel bag and Jem's backpack so there was no need to book luggage into the cargo hold. The last thing I needed was more gear to manage and I couldn't see the need for it anyway. Travelling light had always suited me and despite Jen's best efforts I had offloaded most of the gear she had insisted I carry. She would have found that pile by now I thought to myself grinning and I bet Sean was now dealing with an ear full from her. I was sure that I hadn't heard the last of it. But for now I wasn't there so I wasn't overly concerned. Jen would catch up with me eventually and I could deal with it then.

Strapping Yindi to me in her simple sling, I carefully swung my bag over my shoulder and took hold of Jem's hand as we made our way into the terminal. I wasn't going to bother overmuch about changing her nappy right now, I could do that in the parent room where it would be simpler. I was sure I had seen one on the boarding deck, now I just needed to get through security and as I tucked our boarding pass into my jacket I headed off towards the security gates reassuring Jiemba that the bathroom wasn't far away.

It was passing through the security scanners that they stopped me. My bag had already gone through with ease, as had Jem's and I frowned irritated at the delay as I backed up when the guard signalled me.

"Could you put your tote through the scanner." He said tersely.

"It's not a bag mate... it's my kid."

Jem had gone through ahead of me and was waiting at the other side with a security woman who fortunately realized that he was with me, she stood with him to one side, carefully watching those stepping through. The male guard indicated the bag slung over my shoulder and across my chest, he must have decided I hadn't understood him.

"That, needs to go through the scanner," he said, indicating Yindi's sling with a nod of his head.

"Not bloody likely," I said almost laughing at the suggestion and as another guard moved up beside me anticipating trouble, he at least realized his colleague's mistake.

Yindi had fallen back to sleep despite her smell and as I pulled the cloth aside to show the curious guard that I wasn't joking, I challenged him with my eyes.

"You want me to wake her up?" I said my voice not too kind. Instead the guard indicated I should step through the scanner, clearly not sure whether he should smile or frown, he was more than happy to see me on the other side of the security, and out of his hair.

After the others had checked the canvas sling with some curiosity and gone over me carefully with the wand, the woman took a moment to check over the sling across my chest again, making sure it only held what I had shown them. That it also held a few nappies I had tucked into the bottom caused another round of probing but I think they took a distinct dislike to the whole idea that I had the baby with me, or perhaps it was the smell that upset them. I didn't care about what they thought, Jem was getting restless and I knew we needed to get to the restroom, but there was no hurrying this lot I had decided impatiently as I tolerated their security checks.

That was when the drug scanner bloke indicated I could step to the side. He was more polite, more accepting and the process went off without a hitch and with a smile. Yindi however was now getting restless and as I headed up the elevator to the departure deck I was attracting way too much attention and that was something which I wasn't overly happy about.

I had planned to feed my little possum as we had taxied out and I knew I had a good hour and a half before the plane departed so heading for the parents lounge seemed a good idea.

It was occupied, and I hadn't realized it would be so compact. The lack of space was made worse by a woman with a stroller which was parked alongside the basin and a couple of kids, who seemed to be playing in one of the two toilets. I had figured weeks ago that people were not accustomed to seeing men with babies slung about them in carry slings, nor were parent rooms always openly welcoming for fathers. I also knew that there was something in the way I carried Yindi that disconcerted people and I hadn't quite decided if it was that I had Yindi with me, or the manner in which I carried her, but it worked for me and seemed of little account anyway.

However when the woman noted my entrance, towing Jem with me and trying to comfort what was now a crying baby, she gathered her kids and made room in the compact area... something I was eternally grateful for. Yindi was in full voice, which was rare enough for her and I guessed she hadn't thought much of the security guards probing and I joined her in that sentiment. It may have been a necessary evil, but it had proved an annoying inconvenience.

Dumping the bag I found what I wanted in its depths then I eased the sling off my shoulders. Jem made for the loo and as I unwrapped and began to strip Yindi off, I became aware of the other woman's attention. Yindi had managed to make a mile long streak in what was in her nappy and there was no saving the jumpsuit so while I ditched the lot in the bin. I laughed at the little minx as she screamed and struggled now naked as I tried to calm her and clean her up at the same time. I looked around for anything that I could use. The only thing I could see was the canister of paper towelling which was just out of my reach.

There wasn't a great deal other than this, so deciding that water was the best solution I eased her up into my hands laying her along my arm on her belly. Then I ran the tap which was suspended in an arc over the basin I tested the water as she bellowed her protest then satisfied with the temperature, I ran her tiny length under the flow of warm water. At first it shocked her but after a few seconds of squealing she settled to enjoy the sensation of warm water running over her back and little body.

"Jem... could you get me some of those paper towel things."

Jem was quick. He liked hearing Yindi protest even less than I did but the woman with the now mesmerised kids was quicker.

"Can I help...? I have some wipes..." she said moving across with the first offering of paper and the oddest smile on her face.

"Thanks... but I just need to dry her off. She has really done her duds."

Laying Yindi on the collection of paper towels I tore one of her nappies in half and using that mopped her dry as best I could. Then I laid her against my chest trying to soothe her while I arranged her fresh nappy and got another little terry suit ready, jigging her all the time, hoping to soothe her screams while I shot the woman a reassuring grin. She looked as though she wanted to rescue Yindi, but there was really no need, I could do this.

Within minutes I had her dry, dressed and somewhat calmer and almost ready for the sling, Jem hovering as he kicked our bags out of the way of the other kids, he waited patiently..

"You managed that well... how old is she if you don't mind me asking? She is just gorgeous, what an amazing head of lovely hair," the woman commented, obviously enchanted as most people tended to be for some reason. But I couldn't deny I felt a stab of pride in my little bundle.

Uncertain, I looked up. I didn't mind her idle curiosity but mostly I wasn't accustomed to comment. "About six or eight weeks now I think," I answered as I carefully positioned her back in her sling, settling her weight comfortably back about my shoulders and against my chest. Yindi was more settled and I hoped she would go back to sleep. I considered simply giving her a snack and pre-empting her feed in favour of some extended quiet time. Anything would be better than have her screaming her protest while we waited to board the plane.

"Umm... umm... can I help you with anything?" the woman asked unsure as I bent to go through the bag again looking for her bottle while I supported her against me with my arm and hand. All I needed was to add some of the formula powder and heat the bottle in the microwave I could see behind the woman. Dianne had showed me this nifty trick the other week when I had been in town with her for her medical checks and I had Yindi with me when feed time had come around. Most cafes seem to have microwaves and I'd decided it was simpler to do this than chase boiled water when I needed it. The bottle in the thermal pouch needed refilling and reheating too, so as I found the bottle of pre-boiled water I set this up on the bench also and grinned across at the woman.

As I shook the powder from its pre-measured container into the bottles now with their water measure I answered her. "If you could just give these a round in the microwave, it would be great thanks." I wasn't at all sure I could work out how to use the microwave and the woman was standing right in front of it.

She took the bottles off me and I watched, still soothing my little minx, as the woman found the master switch for the microwave oven which they had hidden on the wall. So it wasn't long before the bottles were both heated. I asked if she would give the bottle for the thermal jacket an extra shot while I tested the other and began to settle Yindi with an aperitif.

"You manage her very well. I can rinse the jumpsuit for you if you like."

Chuckling I shook my head. "No thanks."

Tossing the thermal bottle into the bag, I zipped it up and tucked the other bottle into the sling when Yindi gave it up. It was then that I noticed the woman's confused and concerned look. She looked unwilling to give up the jumpsuit I had ditched in the bin so I decided to explain. "I don't do washing. Not that anyway... you're welcome to it."

"Oh no... no, I didn't mean..." she said surprisingly embarrassed as she again dropped the little suit into the bin. Gathering her couple of kids and the pram, she made for the door and holding it for me, I ushered Jem out while I carefully hoisted the bag to my shoulder again.

"Thanks for your help anyway," I added. Wondering what she was thinking as I rubbed Yindi's back lightly, soothing her through the stiff canvas cotton of the sling. She was settling again and I was grateful.

"You're welcome," she said as she turned away almost reluctantly, but I knew the kids kept an eye on us as we headed down to the gate where I wanted to wait. In part I had come to realize that little babies attract a lot of attention but it never ceased to surprise me that women in particular would speak so readily to someone who had a tiny baby with them.

It was something I was still getting used to and as Jem waited, and then slipped his hand into mine confidently, I wondered if I would ever really get used to this whole Dad thing. It had seemed so simple thinking about it, but the reality was somewhat different. Though I guess it was really no different than the experiences every bloke had taking on a family and as I absently eased Yindi's back, I thought that I would want little more than the opportunity to raise my own kids.

The plane trip went off surprisingly well. The hostess had given Jem some colouring books and suggested she stow my shoulder tote in the overhead locker. That was when she realized I had Yindi tucked away in it and embarrassed she apologised. After that it seemed all the hostesses wanted to do was make sure Yindi and Jem were both comfortable and happy.

Yindi on the other hand simply wanted to sleep after I filled her belly and eased her wind. Her small mewing cry went barely noticed and I got used to the smiles and curiosity of the passengers around me.

It was an odd sensation this attention and even though I felt a certain pride in my little bundle, thoughts kept me pensive, though I struggled to push these to the back of my mind as I encouraged Jem in his colouring. It was going to be difficult meeting Jem's family and I wasn't looking forward to the memories it would invoke.

They knew we were coming but I had been unable to reach them for the past week. Old Nan had said that they were going bush and that they would let me know where they were. I wasn't sure how they were going to do this, but they knew our flight details and that we would be getting into Darwin tonight. They would have worked something out I was sure and it remained to be seen what it was. I had a plan and I was going to stay with that. They knew what my plans were and they could sort out the rest.

The whole question was resolved as soon as we stepped into the arrivals hall. We were the last through, I had never understood people who hurry to stand in the aisles of a plane while anyone with half a brain would be content to sit and wait till the aisles had cleared, so we were the last off. It saved risking some idiot knocking my precious bundle by accident and made it much easier to manage Jem and our bags.

As soon as we got through the doors Jem broke into a run on catching sight of Billy Black, who was standing boldly in our path and the path of anyone else who had taken their time to get off the plane.

"Uncle Billy!" he screeched and in a flying leap he was crushed into Billy's welcome arms as they both laughed. I had never witnessed Jem's enthusiasm for his family and seeing it here gave me a taste of foreboding. Doubts rang through my mind as I gripped the older man's hand in greeting.

"Billy. It's good to see you again."

"Andrew, likewise." It was a moment before he went on, a moment where we shared a loss. "It's a sad business, but I am glad you came." He set Jem down carefully and fondly caressed his head in a way that told me they shared a strong bond. "And this one, he has grown so much in the past year, you're a weight boy. What have they been feeding you, hey?"

Nodding, enjoying the joy in Jem's look, he looked up at me. "But we can talk of this later, I have the truck outside. I had better move it before the policemen do... do you have much gear?"

"Only what we carry, but tonight I would like to stay in a motel. Settle the kids, you didn't plan on travelling did you?"

"Well yes... but that can wait if you want. Maybe overnight in the city isn't so bad if that's what you want," he agreed reluctantly.

"It is. Jiemba has travelled a long way today, he needs a good night's sleep, and so do I."

"Well then. We'd better find something then." Turning to Jem, Billy picked him up readily again laughing, but his glance across at me sought my approval and my disquiet settled somewhat as I nodded.

"Somewhere on the way out of town would be good," I added as we made our way out of the terminal.

"I have family, not far out of town... perhaps we could go there?" Billy suggested.

"No. This one is on me, thanks anyway I appreciate the offer but I would be happier with our own arrangements. Perhaps another time Billy, when the kids are less tired."

Yindi stirred suddenly and stretched, perhaps disturbed by the sudden heat and humidity still in the air despite the cool of night having settled in. The movement within the pouch strung around my shoulders attracted Billy's attention and he stopped suddenly.

"You have the little girl with you?" he asked almost incredulously.

Grinning I nodded, my hand instinctively moving to help settle the little possum as she wriggled in her pouch. "Yes. She stays with me, she is ours hey Jem?" Jiemba smiled, wrapping his arms about Billy's shoulders he leaned in checking on her, satisfying Billy's disconcerted curiosity also.

"Well I'll be dammed!" Billy said grinning. "The old women will be pleased. They didn't think you would bring her. You never said."

"I didn't? I meant to. To be honest I never thought to leave her behind."

"Well old Nan will be pleased. She is in camp, expecting only Jiemba, they are preparing for your arrival. The camp is only a couple of hours down the track, it won't take long... are you sure you want to stay tonight here in the city?"

"Yeah mate. I am sure. It will be easier travelling in the morning with the kids after they've had a quiet night."

"Well OK then... we had better get a move on and find a place hey?" Billy suggested as though he had thought of it all along and we made our way towards the dusty old four wheeler parked illegally on the verge.

The place we found on the edge of town was a large caravan park, and the cabins were clean and quiet. Shaded by the abundant gardens and trees it looked pleasant enough and I could feel the cooler shift of the air through the undergrowth.

The furniture was strictly utilitarian and I offered Billy the use of the second bedroom in the cabin while I took the main one with the kids. Yindi was easily settled after I had given her a basin wash, dressed her in her nappy only and created a nest of soft towels for her. She settled into one of the larger drawers of the lowboy in my room. This I removed and it now sat neatly beside the double bed on the two small bedside tables pushed together. She was soon fed and out like a light in the barmy air, which served to help settle her.

Jem on the other hand had decided on a riotous time in the bath of cool water and Billy seemed to take delight in amusing him while I set out a dinner of chicken and chips with a tub of coleslaw we had bought at the local takeaway.

As I listened to the noise coming from the bathroom I wondered at the connection between Billy and young Jiemba. It wasn't something that we had ever spoken of and I wished now I knew more of the family links. It would serve me well to explore these before I trampled in gung-ho and announced my intention of keeping the kids together. It was still what I intended but there were ways of going about it without causing ill feeling and disagreement. I wanted to preserve Jem's links with his family, but I wanted also to keep him at my side for his sake and for the sake of our small family. I could see now that it wasn't going to be an easy task. I hadn't planned on dealing with the men of his family and it seemed that Billy was to be counted amongst them. It was something I was going to have to explore carefully.

The trip the next morning took us well into the bush along dusty tracks with the occasional river bed crossing, but true to his word it took us just over three hours and when we arrived at the camp it was obvious we were expected. The women were the first to greet us and wasted little time in wanting to take Yindi from my care once they realized I had her with me. Reluctant to give her up I waited until I recognized old nan, one of the few women I had met before and who was insistent that it was her place to take the baby. Jem took no time in cuddling others who I didn't recognize, but it was obvious he did. I realized he was once more in his element and in no time was off with some of the children his age while the women were adjusting to the novelty of Yindi's unexpected presence.

Billy on the other hand drew me away towards where some of the men were gathering in the shade. It was a bush camp and it could be seen that they had been there a few days at least. No wonder I had been unable to contact anyone I thought with amusement.

"The women will want to prepare a baby smoking for your girl," Billy advised, watching as the women settled nearby closer to the campfire as they cooed over the little package. She was soon stripped of any covering, which allowed the air to move around her little limbs and I watched carefully, reluctant to let either of the kids out of my sight. Jem though, showed no reluctance to be off with the gang of kids. He certainly seemed as happy here as I had seen him with his friends in the community, he appeared to have no trouble settling in either environment and I was glad to see his sadness set aside so readily.

"I guess they know what they're doing?" I said with reservations as I glanced back towards Yindi, a comment which made Billy laugh deeply.

"Yeah, they're women. Come on, we need to see to this business of Jiemba."

Immediately Billy had my attention and with a nod we moved over to the gathering of men. I figured they must be representative of those concerned and as I gauged the mood of the men sitting where Billy was leading me, I tried to put aside my immediate concern with Yindi and concentrate more on what was going on with Jem. I felt I was going to have to battle to keep my boy with me and until I could feel confident, I wasn't giving an inch.

Billy introduced me and gripping the ready hand of each man I realized this wasn't going to be a simple matter. In this business the men would speak with consideration, the conversation could take time as words were carefully measured. First I had to establish who these men were and turning to Billy I tried to convey this to him. In turn he introduced the relationship each man had with Jiemba and I soon realized I had a posse of males who were not going to be keen on releasing Jem to my care. I was someone they considered to be an outsider; I wasn't part of their family.

It was a complex issue and I expressed my respect by asking if I could speak to each man in turn. As due respect was accorded to the men with the closest interest in my boy, our talks begun. These talks were to take us well into the night before I felt they had even begun.

I discovered it wasn't an entirely difficult process settling Jiemba's future once the ceremony of smoking for the children had begun the next day and we were able to enjoy the ceremony of dance together. I had much in common with the family and the issue of Jem's future was visited often amongst the men and quietly amongst the women when given the chance.

It was a friendly camp though, one for families and as the kids returned throughout the day to the clear swimming hole below the camp, I was able to easily keep an eye on both Jem and Yindi.

When darkness fell, the kids settled down on a large tarpaulin away from the fire, to sleep in a huddle. They were close enough to the fire to occasionally get the benefit of the smoke haze which helped to protect them from insects. While the adults mostly settled about the camp, some on blankets and a few had the comfort of a camp mattress.

The fires burnt throughout the night, and it seemed that more than one billy of water was in constant supply, replenished regularly. It was late in the night when I had taken the opportunity again to refill Yindi's bottles with freshly boiled water. I had made a habit of preparing at least three bottles, once during the morning, and again during the evening. Jen had been regular in this practice and it was one I found definitely convenient. It meant that at any time I could retrieve a bottle and simply add the powdered formula measure, needing only to find a means to heat the milk again if the water had cooled.

Late into the evening Yindi had ended up with one of the younger women. They had fashioned a basket for her from woven grasses and reeds which made carrying her and passing her around a simple thing. So when she was passed around she was much less disturbed. She was now stirring though as she looked for her feed and as I retrieved her bottle from where I had dropped it into the billy of water to cool, I wandered over to where she lay. The woman realizing my intent sat up smiling a welcome.

"Has she been good?" I asked, careful not to disturb those around us as I squatted down beside them both then I moved to take my little possum up, forestalling the woman's attempt to reach for the warm bottle. "I have missed her," I explained with a smile as I ignored the proffered hand.

"She's a good baby," the young woman whispered. "She has someone to care for her back at your home?"

The question was a simple one and I smiled as I sat and settled the little possum in the crook of my arm, popping the bottle easily into her eager mouth. "Yes, she has many mothers and a father who will not be happy if she is away from him," I said by way of an explanation. It was an explanation I intended that she should hear clearly.

"You have good kids," she agreed carefully. "Mine is over there, I have only one and he is nearly as old as Jiemba. They are good friends, they play well, they're like brothers."

The invitation in her voice was clear and I smiled, but my attention went to Yindi by way of answer. I hoped the woman would understand my subtle rejection. She was an attractive woman, young and gentle and at another time I might have considered myself lucky she was making the suggestion that her eyes were making, but it was beyond my ability to allow someone to become close to me yet. I wasn't ready to let my memories fade so easily and I hoped she understood.

Yindi broke off before finishing her feed, her belly full of wind no doubt and failing to tempt her to take more I gave up for the moment. I found it easy to chuckle at the sated little mite as I moved her to my shoulder and tried to get her to give up her wind. The woman watched me and suddenly I felt the weight of her amused curiosity.

"You're a good man," she said softly, the invitation still there I realized as I thought about her words.

I grinned, not sure what to say. "I am a jealous man," I answered in a tone not entirely inviting as I heard the soft belch of wind and began to resettle Yindi back to finish the remainder of her bottle. I couldn't help the smile of pleasure over my success getting the wind out of the mite, and my smile extended to the woman, a smile which I hoped perhaps softened the warning in my words, that I wasn't looking for a woman.

"You're a Clever Man, I have heard," she added with care.

"The women speak too much I think," I countered amused. "It will be a long time before I look for another woman I'm afraid. I don't think I could easily share my children, or my time."

This time, my message was clear and I felt the withdrawal of her immediate interest. Though determined she now reached for Yindi and the bottle I still had balanced to her mouth. "Here, let me settle her for you, you need to rest. Tomorrow the men plan that you should dance with them."

"The women do talk too much," I said again chuckling, and then a thought occurred to me. "Tell me...?" I added curious, tempering the volume of my voice to almost a whisper, conscious of those trying to sleep close by. "What do they say? I don't want my boy to leave my care. What have you heard?"

Shooting me a glance as she settled Yindi and continued to feed her, she considered how to answer me. I knew it wasn't entirely fair of me to ask my question, but I wanted to gauge what the family thought and I couldn't pass up the opportunity I now had to discover the mood of the women.

"It's not only the boy that we look to keep with us," she said quietly and immediately I felt the tension in my stomach.

"Yindi will not be staying, she is mine and she will remain mine," I warned, determined.

The woman shot me a small grin, which seemed almost amused. "They know this. But if they keep the father, then they know they have also the son and the little one," she offered softly now, her eyes taking in little Yindi before they returned to me." It's you they want, more so than the boy at this time. The women have talked of little else for this past week. It's why there are so many of us here. Perhaps you will choose one of the women to help you with the kids."

Surprised at her words I looked around the camp. "They have gone to such lengths?" I questioned surprised still, it seemed almost incredible to me. I had not even considered such a thing, and to hear it, came as something of a surprise but it went a long way towards explaining the things which had been said to me, and why I had the constant attention of the young women.

"Billy has spoken a lot about the strengths you would bring to us, you move easily amongst our people, walk easily in the Lands. You also have powerful men you count as your friends. These things are of great value to us and the men would do a lot to keep them at hand. So would the women I think."

Her words were something I had not considered and still somewhat surprised, I wondered at them, though I could not help but feel flattered. "My family is not here, but I know it's Jem's country and it's true, I do feel at peace in this land... but..." Shrugging I wasn't sure how to explain to her how I would not turn my back on my own world it was a world I knew, it owned me.

"Home is always the place you were born to," she agreed, understanding me. "But for women, we often leave our home and make a place for our children somewhere that is not our own. Maybe men need to learn this also," she offered with some subtly.

She finished Yindi's feed, then carefully put her on her lap, propping her gently and worked to massage her back, extracting an indelicate reply that had me smiling again. Then carefully she settled her into her woven cradle with small cooing sounds to sooth her.

"We would love to see more of you, and the children Andrew. Perhaps you can find a way that would be best for everyone. I would be happy to help to look out for the kids. I could look after your camp or your place and help until you are ready to begin your life again. That would be good for us both I think. If I can help in any way...?"

"Thanks. You have given me something to consider, I had not thought about many of the things you have said, it has been helpful talking to you. But I have a place and someone who loves the kids and asks nothing. I have good friends." I reassured her conscious of her carefully worded suggestion, one which I knew was offered with the best of intentions.

With a smile I left her, my mind turning over her words. As I settled closer by the fire I found it hard to sleep as the thoughts churned around my mind. These were thoughts which tangled easily as I looked for a means to an end, searching to find a solution to the question of the kids and their happiness. There had to be a way but I would have to gauge if it would work for all of us, for the families the kids and me. This is what filled my mind as I drifted off to sleep under the brilliant blanket of stars overhead.

During the next day Yindi was coated in a paste of the fine ash of a tree used in particular for the baby smoking ceremony, an ash that I knew not only would serve to protect her from bad Spirits, but also protect her from bugs and as the younger women were given the task of feeding her and tending to her needs throughout the day, I was left to the important business of men.

I was content to let the women take control, though I made sure that they understood that Yindi was mine and I would not be giving her up to the women of the clan. That made the old women laugh as they thought at first I was joking. I wasn't, and they soon realized I meant it by the stern threat in my eyes.

Not sure of what they were saying in dialect amongst themselves I did however become aware that there was some plot to find me a suitable wife. I didn't even entertain the idea and dismissed it out of hand, but being forewarned is being forearmed and even though I was aware some ,that younger women were attending to anything I might need, it wasn't a prospect I encouraged.

Billy on the other hand seemed to encourage them, while our conversations with the men over Jem continued. I knew I was gaining ground when Billy suggested the prospect of me joining the men in ceremony apart from the women. There was something afoot and loathe to discourage him I agreed. It took some time before I realized exactly what I had agreed to do.

With the advice of the woman during the night still teasing me I decided that the best person to talk to would be Billy, so it was when the men gathered together for a small hunting party to feed the camp that I volunteered to join them. I had nowhere near the experience the other men had when it came to hunting but I knew I could throw a spear accurately but when I realized it was fish we were going after, I was glad of what experience I did have.

Joking with Billy, I commented that I was more accustomed to hunting on the shelves of the supermarkets and home cupboards than in the wild, though fishing with a spear wasn't completely a hit and miss affair and I found that the group of men I was with, took delight in tormenting me. Their mark was true and swift while mine was less practiced, but the hunt was good and I very much enjoyed the time away with the men.

It was while we were resting beside the river, before returning to the camp that I thought to raise the questions foremost in my mind. The talks were going well, though most of the men were of the opinion that Jiemba would be better off with his mother's family, they were ready to consider that separating Yindi and her brother wasn't the best idea. Many of them felt, because of this, that Yindi too would be better off with the women but this was a point I wasn't prepared to negotiate on.

We had taken the opportunity to visit the spiritual places known to men. I had listened carefully to the stories told of the paintings, to the recount of past deeds and good hunts. They were spiritual tales with many varied facets and I came to appreciate the talent of the song-men, those who kept the knowledge of the clan and family alive for others to hear. Walking with the men was something I enjoyed and it gave me time to think.

That I wanted to keep Yindi with me, and Jiemba also, was a point that many of the men didn't share. They didn't quite understand my position. Many of the men felt that my place should be more traditional. Some had even suggested that I might have a woman in my community that I had interest in and this was the problem. We had hit a point of impasse and it consistently was being raised and reprised.

Settling beside Billy as he prepared a fish for a sand bake, a reward before we returned our catch to the camp, I raised the issue yet again.

"I want to get your thoughts on an idea I have, one that may serve us all well." I offered tentatively, gaining his attention. At his nod I considered again how best to phrase my words. "The kids, as you know are very important to me but I know they are important to the family also. Perhaps there is a way that all of us can be a part of their lives. A way that Jem can learn a great deal about his family and what is his history."

"Go on," Billy said with a nod. "He is like my son. He deserves much that you can't give him Andrew, he belongs here with family."

I measured the words seriously. Billy had never spoken with such commitment, now was the time to offer what I felt I could. "I know you have many men who are fortunate to be sons. I too would like to count you as a father amongst my family," I suggested steadily

Billy sat back, carefully measuring the strength of my words, and then slowly he smiled. A broad grin welcomed my suggestion and I felt the relief flood through me.

"You would be like a son to me?" he said carefully, "I would like that."

"It's something that I would be honoured for you to think on. It means a great deal to me that you are pleased."

The idea settled about us as we examined it and welcomed the prospect together. It was a good plan, one with a good outcome and as I thought about taking Billy as my father, he too considered taking me as his son.

After a time he stood to his feet quickly. I followed and he called to the other men by the pool. Billy was quick, and eager to share the bond we had agreed so easily to build with the others. It was something of a achievement he obviously felt. It was an exultant moment and the others moved about to greet me and welcome my acceptance into the family. Billy beamed proudly, as happy as if his woman had just given birth. It was a pride I shared.

This was to be my family now and things would be sorted with greater ease. I was glad beyond relief that Billy had recognised the solution so easily at hand. We had bridged an important impasse and the sense of sharing I felt with those around me gave me the courage I might need in years to come.

The hunt we had planned to accompany the celebration of what was an already important gathering, now turned into one of greater import. The whole mood of the camp changed as the news spread on our return and I understood the acceptance I was now experiencing amongst the families around me. I knew the importance of what had come about and how it changed their very concept of Jiemba and myself as father and son as they settled and discussed my new relationship with each person in camp.

Billy understood in part, my world. He knew and understood the gifts I could bring to his people, his family and I understood well the gifts they now gave me. No one would question his right and his decision to adopt me as his son and I would continue to give him the respect a son would give to his father. What we had exchanged was a promise, a gift for our futures; it was an exchange that could not be broken easily. I had not found myself a wife as they had hoped, but I had become part of their family and that suited me better.

That night I danced amongst the men, with pride and the celebration went well into the evening. There was no longer the issue of Jiemba, it had been resolved to everyone's satisfaction and they knew that he would be as much part of their lives as would Yindi and I, and in that spirit I was welcomed by them.

I was reintroduced to those who had thought to merely come to observe and to be part of what had been initially just a show of strength and hope of the family. I was now one of them and I couldn't have been more pleased with that outcome. The Elders present discussed my place in the family and clan at length and accorded me my place in their camp. In a moment of decision I had inherited amongst the traditional groups within the family, fathers and uncles, mothers and wives in the manner that was as ancient as the lands around us. I held a relationship to each person in camp and they went out of their way to welcome me and the kids.

The young women, particularly those who were accounted as my possible wives, knew that this wasn't a time for what was in their minds. Yet Billy and the men made much of any glances I incidentally made or small conversations I had with the women. It was an amusing pastime on my part. As I had no need of a wife and now was the time for celebration. It was the newness of it and the need of others to learn more about me and what manner of man they had accepted into their family on the word and judgement of Billy Black my new father.

In all we spent a week with our new family as Billy took delight in the important business of welcoming me. Yindi barely missed me when I had need to be away, nor did Jem, but I missed them. When it came time to leave I did so with a sense of belonging and the promise to return soon.

Billy, amongst my fathers, was to prepare an important ceremony for me but first there were things he needed to do, one of which was to share the news of my acceptance amongst them, with others who were not there in camp. As he dropped me and the kids off in Darwin I knew I would return soon, it was important and it was an arrangement I would not miss.

My learning was to begin; it was a learning that would take me into the world of the Mimi as one of Billy Black's sons. It was the beginning of a ceremony and journey that I was looking forward to. It bought such a sense of contentment, as much as an eagerness in me, that I knew without doubt that I had made the right decision..

My own father had been absent most of my life and Billy Black was a man who commanded respect, he was a man I could aspire to be like. He was a fitting Grandfather for Jiemba and Yindi and this place was now his right. When I returned in the following months on my own, to be amongst the men and take my initiation, I would learn more of the family I had chosen to join and the ways of the people who had accepted me.

I knew this was no simple matter, that there was much to learn but without my chosen woman at my side, this was the next best thing. I was happy with the direction of my life and the people I had gathered around me. Sean was as a brother to me and Jen was like a little sister. Both, I knew wanted to be part of Jiemba and Yindi's life as did Billy. There was room for all, with people such as these around me I felt I had built for my kids the firm foundation of a future, a good life, it was one to be pleased with.

I thought of what I had lost to gain such a family around me and I knew I would have changed it all just for the chance to live with the woman who should have shared my life, but that was never going to be. Instead I held onto what I had been offered and I prepared to move forward.

MOONGGUN OF THE STONE COUNTRY

Aine:

The letter from Jen was just what I needed, it was long, chatty and full of good news and while it gave me a sense of home sickness, it also distracted me. It had been some ten months since we had left the community and news of little Yindi and Jem was very welcome but what had surprised me more was what she had to tell me of Andrew.

I studied the small photo of Yindi and Jem. They looked absolutely adorable, sitting on the lounge with Jiemba determined not to allow Yindi to slip from his hold despite her struggles. Even in the static photo I could see the lively movement of them both. Yindi's dark curls were almost dancing on their own as they laughed together. It was hard to believe she had grown so much in ten months, now she was worming her way across the floor and would soon be up on her hands and knees in the next months.

Jiemba had also settled into school and his first year was now almost over. He had made friends easily but he was beginning to get into the mischief that was expected of a six year old. Tango, ever-faithful Tango had attached himself to Yindi, now persistently refusing to leave her side in Jem's daily absence, though he was constantly at Jiemba's heel after school. He had taken to waiting expectantly at the car park for the youngsters to return from school each day, while Yindi was napping. Jenna couldn't work out how he knew the time of day but when it was time for the kids to arrive, Tango could be found faithfully waiting for the school bus to arrive bringing the kids back home.

I had to laugh when I read how the faithful mutt would seek Jenna out during the day and bark furiously if Yindi woke and Jenna did not attend to her immediately. Even Sean found that funny, though it seemed that the ongoing battle between Sean and Tango on centre bed rights wasn't as amusing to him, as it was to Jenna. From that I judged that they had lost the battle in keeping Tango from the bedrooms which was a battle I half expected that they would lose and one I hoped Taipan would not hear of.

Andrew had returned to the Northern Territory after his initial visit there to see Jiemba's family and had then spent nearly six weeks away from the community almost immediately after.

What had concerned Jenna most after that second visit away was that he had come back in some ways changed but she had yet to decide in what ways the ceremony had changed him. The only thing she could see was that he had grown in some manner that was also as difficult to grasp as it was to get him to talk about. He was the same, yet he seemed to smile less, except when he was with the children. A seriousness had become very much part of his character and it was one which kept secrets she felt.

Yindi was the only one with whom he truly lowered his guard and it was only when he was with her that the gentleness she knew he was capable of returned to his eyes. It wasn't that he was colder, only more guarded. Jen wasn't sure that she liked the new Andrew overly much, in some ways he scared her but she wouldn't allow him to alienate himself from the community and she worked hard at coaxing him in remaining involved with the young men. Tom was a great help in this and while Sean and Andrew often found themselves involved with the younger Shaman, Tom made sure they knew of any mischief that was afoot, mostly because he was in the thick of it inevitably.

She also spoke of finding the small quartz stones Andrew had placed in the base of little Yindi's cot beneath the mattress. When she had asked him about them, reluctant to move them without his knowledge, he had asked that she leave them be, in a manner in which she could not question. The maban stones were given with the power to protect Yindi in his absence and Andrew didn't want them disturbed.

He also scared people in other ways. The women of the community had begun to stop visiting when Andrew was home, something Jenna had just noticed. When she'd questioned them about it, it became apparent that there had been a great deal of talk about which she had been unaware. It was talk from which she was excluded. This had surprised her and she'd decided to pay more attention to exactly what was going on around her.

On the outside, it had all seemed the same at first. Andrew had returned to his work on the rigs only in the last three months, though now it seemed he was less keen to sign on for a long hitch. He preferred to spend time with the kids, or with the Shaman. It was when she commented on his recent return from Northern Queensland, where we also were, that I thought I had misread her letter, and settled back to reread the page.

The heat in the last weeks had once more begun to build as we approached the wet season and the frill-necked lizard had come out of hibernation some weeks ago to announce the imminent arrival of the rain. It wasn't so much the threat of the wet or the attendant heat which bothered me, it was the humidity. Ty had installed a slow moving rotor fan overhead in the rafters and its constant motion kept the air cooler under the shelter here than elsewhere. It was driven by a few solar panels which in turn fed the batteries and allowed us limited power, enough to run a few lights and the fan. It was a neat and efficient system which rarely required the booster of the generator to maintain it.

We had given up on the camper trailer in the last months though at first it had served us well as our only accommodation, but now we found we preferred the open aspect of the large circular shelter Ty and John had built. It was a simple bush structure they'd put together some months ago, one which we had added to constantly expanding its scope and comfort. Now that we had included platform flooring and some simple insect screening which rolled up and down like a blind, it was much more comfortable than the camper trailer. It was more open, airy and convenient.

Only one short wall length was fully covered in, this was to shelter us from any storms moving in, the same wall also protected the wood and stone cooking bench which housed a gas cooker Ty had built-in for me to work at. The rest of the structure was open and in many ways exposed to the forest but it bothered us little. This wasn't the suburbs and there were many, many miles of forest around us on these Traditional Lands which offered us more privacy than I had ever known.

We slept where ever we happened to drag the bedding at the time, it was entirely dependent on the weather as we now found we preferred the centre position under the entire structure which was directly under the new fan. This all required little effort on our part to move the bedding, and during the day it offered us a padded lounging area as well, one where we could sprawl comfortably. Our furniture was spartan, all we needed other than the bedding was a small work table by the kitchen and a few crates turned on their sides that we used for storage.

Taipan had fashioned a cooler from a crate lined with a fine metal mesh and draped with hessian. It was made the same way as the old koolgardie safes. It needed only to have the hessian kept damp during the day, which I did by a drip tray kept full with water.

It never ceased to fascinate me how it managed to keep the drinks and our foods cooler, though as a rule we kept little that would need cooling. We still had the small twelve volt fridge freezer which lived in the cruiser, running off its own battery supply though we had become accustomed to rarely using it at all. It remained in the cruiser so we used it when we travelled rather than any other time. Our koolgardie safe was more about insect and ant control than anything else, standing in its own small moat of water as it did.

I don't know if I could live like this forever and I wasn't sure how I would fare throughout the cyclone season, but it was certainly convenient for the time being and what had begun as a temporary camp was growing with a sense of extended permanence about it.

With the addition of a few large plastic kegs for water storage which was topped up by the now regular afternoon storms, it was easy to manage our water supply and we rarely had to tote water up from the main creek. I often kept our drinks in these kegs also, that way they were much cooler. We kept a huge solid teapot permanently filled with water as our water heater when needed and with a bush shower, and in the heat of the day it was often more comfortable just to wash in the creek or opt for a cold shower. Slowly the place gained a sense of order that was comforting.

The old teapot was used to also warm the water for the shower bucket which hung in the exposed shower area though more often than not I preferred a cool shower, to help shift the heat of the day. Often we would wander down to the river near the main house and sit in the cool of the water holes whenever the humidity got too oppressive.

As inconvenient as it looked, I actually loved the open shower. With only Ty and me there, showering in the exposed surrounding bush behind a screen of sticks and grasses I had played at weaving together was entertaining at least. The movement of free air around me was delicious and the song of the forest was always a delight to listen to.

What I truly loved the most was the wildlife that would visit us throughout the day and night. We had become part of their world and to me they were a constant delight. The possums would scour the kitchen area each night, looking for scraps which we may have inadvertently left about, the bush turkeys and hens I could hear foraging through the undergrowth before they appeared on the edge of the camp and it seemed we had been accepted by the forest.

I loved to discover small wallabies who would often feed from my hand if I was quiet enough, there were also lizards that would sneak about, trying so hard to become part of their surroundings, they were like children in an endless game of hide and seek. We'd learnt early to secure all our food, to seal everything into containers. It was only the possums who gave us any grief with their dexterous fingers and curious minds. I found it hard not to feed the mums who would arrive with their babies on their backs looking for scraps. Although Ty often would try to discourage me, I knew he enjoyed their visits as much as I and so they continued to come adding a wonderful flavour to our days.

John and Marnie were not far away, perhaps five hundred metres along the bush path though we more often were at their place than they were at ours. When we had first taken up their invitation to stay on the property John had suggested we build a camp nearby. We had been happy to accept the offer knowing that any structure we might build would probably be used by others over the years. That was if it survived the cyclone season and so it had been a happy build which seemed to endlessly grow and change.

The arrangements had suited us all well and I'd come to very much enjoy the company of Marnie. She was much older than I, more my parent's generation than mine but she was like a mother to everyone and I'd learnt a great deal about living in the bush from both her and Ty. It was fun and a wonderful adventure in many ways.

Ty of course loved the life, he loved the freedom it offered him and he had come to enjoy the community here. Though we both knew we weren't going to be part of the community forever, they still had become family. In the months we had been here I had seen a change in Taipan, he had shed the mantle of responsibility which he had so often worn back at Nimbin and now, it seemed to me that he'd found a newer and fresher sense of freedom.

I often teased him that it was like a honeymoon, one that we hadn't been able to take before and while that amused him it also helped us both find a sense of a new beginning, one which we were both enjoying a great deal.

"Any news?"

Startled I looked up as he stepped up onto the low platform, aware that he had broken sharply into my reverie, his smile apologetic, yet teasing and relaxed as it often was these days.

"Oh... Don't sneak up like that!" I warned, half serious.

"I'm not sneaking," he chuckled as he stepped over towards me then he eased himself onto the central area where I was lounging under the fan. "You're a million miles away. So what does your sister say? Marnie mentioned that she picked up some mail from home for you."

"Oh it's not from Karyn, it's from Jen."

"Jen? She never writes, what has brought this on?"

I chuckled understanding his sentiment, knowing how much I had complained about just that issue. "I haven't read it all yet," I answered as I sat up and began to gather the pages about me.

"Good grief" Ty said laughing now as he took in the scattered sheets. "She's written a book by the look of it. Here let me have a couple... Share with me woman!"

As he grabbed for a few sheets I snatched them back, warning him with a scolding look. "Wait for your own mail... I haven't even read it all yet," I said with a laugh. Moving them securely out of his reach he chuckled at my quick tempered petulance. In the end I shot him an apologetic grimace. He would know I meant to allow him to read my letter, but first I was going to read it and he'd have to wait.

Sighing, he stretched back into the comfort of the bedding and then settled to watch me, a grin across his face. He knew that would annoy me but I refused to be drawn and as I struggled to ignore him I couldn't help but cast him an occasional look, one he caught every time.

As I tried to read the letter, I found it nearly impossible to give it the attention it deserved and again I frowned at what I was reading.

"Has Andrew been up this way lately? Jen says he has."

"Andrew...yes, yes he has..." Ty answered after a moment almost reluctantly.

"And you didn't tell me!" I demanded, both surprised and somewhat stunned as I glared across at him, the letter suddenly no longer holding my attention.

Taipan shrugged, almost apologetic, "I told him you'd be annoyed he didn't call in. It was all about Men's Business Kitten, they were pushed for time, he came up with Tom and a few others. They only had a couple of weeks and had a lot to do."

"Tom too?" I added, not only annoyed now but upset. "When was this?"

"A few weeks ago now," carefully Ty propped himself up, his eyes wary.

Suddenly furious at him I moved, I had to move... If I hadn't moved, I would have hit him, I was sure. I couldn't believe that he would think that their visit was something that wouldn't interest me.

"You didn't tell me! You could have mentioned it Ty." I yelled at him, beyond furious now as his admission sank in. I stood there and an odd sense of deep hurt swept through me, then I flung the letter at him, scattering the pages, completely upset and very angry. "How can you NOT mention it!" I demanded.

Taipan quickly climbed to his feet as I swung myself away from him angrily, ignoring the scattered sheets of news, careless even of them, he quickly stepped towards me and while I moved to take a step back and evade him, but he grabbed my wrist. I knew what he was going to do and I struggled but I wasn't quick enough.

I hated how he could do this to me, he was quick and I was angry, furiously angry and I rarely got this way with him but on the rare occasion that I did, his response had always been the same. Holding me tightly from behind he had wrapped his arms about me, restraining me, holding me firmly to his chest as I at first struggled furious and then finally realizing the futility of it

I stilled, breathing deeply, fighting to calm myself I waited, patiently.

"Let me go," I ground out between gritted teeth my anger seething, knowing what he was waiting for.

"No."

"Ty I am warning you…" I spat equally determined as I again struggled against the steel bands of his arms

"No Kitten, not till you calm down. I know you want to fight, I know you are angry with me and I am not going to have you take off in a temper into the night…"

"It's not dark!" I spat ill tempered.

"It nearly is, and its feeding time out there and you're liable to run into something that can hurt you. You know that. Plus in twenty minutes it will be pitch black. Just calm down, I don't want to go hunting for you at night if I don't have to."

Agitated I drew a deep breath, fighting against his arms, his strength. "How can you not tell me?" I demanded hurt and allowing him to hear the threads of pain.

"Moonggun asked me not to," he answered quickly, too quickly and it was his quickly drawn breath, the breath held a long moment; a moment which I could feel as he held me against him keeping me silent. What else wasn't he telling me?

"Who the hell is Moonggun that he should tell you your business?" I demanded suddenly alert to something, though not sure of what.

As I waited my mind searched for a possible answer. Ty's answer was so long in coming that I had plenty of time to wonder what the hell was going on.

"I can't talk about this Aine," he said carefully after a time, in a whisper.

"Who the hell is he Ty?" I demanded annoyed again, though I could feel my anger waning. "Who is he to say that my family, our family can't visit?"

I could feel his fight within himself. I felt it in his stillness, in his tight breath and in the sudden ease of his hold, though he didn't release me. By then I had lost the will to struggle, now I wanted answers and I was focused on a stranger, a man who it appeared had a say in our family business and I had no idea who he was.

"He is a Spirit Man of the Rocks, he is powerful and he is strong and I need to respect that, this is purely the business of men" Taipan said carefully.

I knew I had been told only what I would have been allowed to know. This was men's business and I wouldn't be told much more. I also knew that there were times of important ceremonies when Men would disdain the presence of women, I understood that. As I considered what his words could mean I calmed, maybe I was being unreasonable.

Ty must have felt the calming of my mood as he eased the pressure of his arms around me, allowing me to turn easily within the circle of his arms and confront him.

"Why do you need to listen to this man?" I asked curious. "You have never needed to consider such a thing before?"

"Kitten…" Ty shook his head as he released me. "I have always had to consider others in this business they have just never had the power to upset you," He explained. "Tom will be back for a visit soon, he and Denis are heading back up this way and I hope he will spend more time up here for a while. He was sorry not to be able to call in and say hi when he was here."

"Were they at John and Marnie's?"

"No Kitten. Do you think Marnie would have kept such a thing quiet? John had more to do with the visit than I, it was very much Mimi business, very much related to the training of the boys and initiations."

Capturing my hand he led us back slowly to where we had been lounging, before I had lost my temper. "So you didn't have a lot to do with it?"

"I think you would have noticed if I had?"

I bit my lip, he was right. I would have noticed his absence and the pattern of his days hadn't changed. Sometimes he was home and there would be the mens affairs, others he was with the men or working with others, sometimes gone for a day or two but rarely more without telling me about it. He always told me when he planned to be away overnight as he disliked the idea of me here on my own for any extended period of time beyond the day.

I couldn't recall a time recently where he had been gone for perhaps longer than a night so it had to have been a ceremony which hadn't involved him and yet it had involved Tom, and this Moonggun and that in itself was odd. At times when he was away he would arrange for me to stay with Marnie and I could return to our camp during the day if I chose. It was an arrangement that suited us all but it had been a good few months since that had been necessary.

"Have you met this bloke before, the bossy one?" I asked suddenly.

Strangely, Ty smiled and then glanced up at me as I settled back beside him. "Kitten…"

"Yeah… yeah I know," I answered impatiently. "Well If I run into this guy, I am gunna have something to say," I warned. "It was a good thing you used his Spirit name…"

"Kitten enough…" Pulling me towards him Ty used an old ruse to silence me as he tipped me over and I squealed in protest, knowing what he was up to. When his lips released mine and began a slow tour trying to capture my attention, I struggled against the promise, squirming against his intent, trying not to laugh.

"This is not going to get you off the hook or out of cooking dinner you know." I threatened. "It's your turn…"

"I did it last night," Ty suddenly protested chuckling, his attention now diverted.

"No you didn't. Last night you flipped the chops…that was all you did."

"Well that is cooking isn't it?"

"No. Not unless you start the dinner as well. Then sort out the salad… all you did was flip the chops you cheat."

"Hmm…Dinner hey?" he considered the prospect. We took turns in these small chores and although I would often take his turn if he'd been busy throughout the day, tonight I was in no mood to do so.

"Yep… You better get started, we are nearly out of light and I have a letter to read… after you have crumpled it all," I finished protesting as he eased himself up. I looked around searching for the scattered pages.

"How does jaffles sound?"

"Nice." I answered smiling as I began to gather the scattered sheets, trying to bring some order back to Jenna's letter. Smiling to myself at the tone in his voice, which I was determined to ignore, I knew I would be helping him, though he was going to have to wait until I was ready. I was still annoyed with him for his silence.

Later in the evening, well after dinner when we were once more lounging relaxed under the single light, Ty reading his book. I once again found myself recaptured by Jen's words when I was surprised again to come across another reference to the Mimi people, only this time Jen spoke of the Mimi of the Stone lands in the Territory.

"Have you heard from Taipan that Andrew has been adopted by Jiemba's people? He is now counted among the Banman of the Wandjin and was initiated into their Lore months ago. A lot of the women of the community are now a little afraid of him. I wondered if it was because of the new scar's he wears, it could also be because he has a new knowledge in his eyes and a crooked smile he has developed, as though half of him is no longer amused. His thoughts are often elsewhere, except when he's playing with the kids and particular little Yindi. It's only then that I see the old Andrew peep through and we miss him, it has never been the same…"

At that point I had to stop, there was something upsetting about Jen's words and I could read no more tonight. They brought to mind words which I didn't want to hear, memories and sadness as I thought of little Yindi and Jem and how they had coped with the loss of their mother and how it had changed Andrews world, the very path of his life it seemed. Added to that now was the knowledge that it was also leading him away from us and I wondered how he was truly coping.

I knew Sean had grown a great deal outside the shadow of Ty, something even Ty had commented on and I wondered if it had been the same for Andrew. Outside the shadow of the community was Andrew experiencing the same growth? Is this perhaps what his newly forged links with the Wandjin people gave him? Were these links with the people of the stone country now going to draw him away from us?

Folding Jen's letter carefully I set it aside till tomorrow when I could read it over more carefully again with ease. It only took a few seconds to settle the light netting and bedding about us and Taipan also set his book aside to help, then gathered me into his arms for the night.

As he killed the light I turned to him, suddenly realizing something, "You didn't tell me about Andrew either, Jen says he has been adopted by the Wandjin mob, Jiemba's people."

"Hmm… sorry Kitten, I did mean to tell you that. Is it important? I didn't think it would be a big thing for you?"

"No I guess not," I said softy. "It's just Andrew is a good friend and I hate it that we may see less of him over time. Will it make a big difference to the kids do you think?"

Ty considered the question before he answered. "I think, if anything it will keep the kids around longer. I know Jen and Sean would miss those two kids if Andrew decided to move to the Territory but that's not his plan."

"Have you spoken to him about it?" I asked curious.

"Yes, I have. His links with the Mimi and the Wandjina were built because he didn't want to give Jiemba up. Now he will have the skills to teach Jem what he needs to know of his people. He can better protect Jem, and Yindi. It was a good thing for all of them."

"I guess." I agreed softly, now seeing the sense in such a decision. "Will it take him away much, do you think?"

Again I knew Ty weighed my words. "Yes, perhaps a few months a year. But it costs him less than if he were to face losing Jem. Now the kids will remain together and he knows this."

"Were these the people you met when you were up there last year?"

"Yep... the very same. I know his adopted father, Billy Black and I trust him, Andrew is in good hands. He will learn a great deal from the men there. It will not only serve Jiemba well, but Tom also."

"Tom?" I questioned, surprised.

"Hmm... The Mimi are close to the Wandjin mob and their Lore is akin to the Featherfoot Kitten. I have told you this before. Tom's spending a great deal of time with Andrew; I believe he has found in him a mentor though John is concerned it draws Tom too close to the Mimi. He has spoken about bringing Tom up to this part of the world. The Featherfoot want to do more in his training."

"Well yes. But I never thought the two... well I never considered them connected beyond association."

"The worlds are connected in a number of ways... not one of them is on their own, or a law unto themselves. Now go to sleep, we can talk about this again another time," he answered softly, a breath in my ear.

In my world, there was one place where I felt safe, one place where everything about my world was secure, it held a pattern of familiarity and nothing was able to threaten me. Within the circle of Taipan's arms I knew a sense of being protected which I had never found anywhere else. He was my haven, and my rock and he knew it.

Within the circle of his arms I knew my thoughts, my dreams could take me anywhere, I was fearless there. As long as I could touch him, feel his warmth and hear his heart beat. Even if it were only my feet which would chance on the heat of his throughout the night I knew I was safe.

My dreams did often take me to places where I knew I hadn't been before and to revisit those which were familiar to me. Even if this familiarity was only a sense I felt and there were places such as this in my Dreaming where I knew I hadn't been and yet I also knew my way around the same place, I knew what to expect. I had often thought that this sense of the familiar came from knowing that Ty was with me. Even in my dreams.

My favourite place for my Spirit to wander was the gorge of my sketches and I had become as familiar with this place over the months and years. Now I felt I knew this gorge intimately. Within time, my time, it had become very real to me. The creek, the shadow of the hills which fed the gorge, even the cast of the afternoon shade across the land was familiar.

I had given up trying to draw the features I saw in my Dreaming, I had accumulated many sketches and I knew that they didn't help me now. Ever since I had begun to hear the song in the gorge, a woman's song, I knew that I no longer needed the sketches. The song could draw me back so easily now as I knew it so well.

At first, the song had fascinated me. It was a soft echo which breathed the spirit of the gorge and it made me think that it was sung by the Spirit women of this place. Then, over time, I realized that it wasn't other than the song of one woman. I had discovered this at the same time I had found the deep pool of the gorge. Now this had become one of my favourite places within the pattern of my Dreaming and I would visit here often.

I had not found the woman of the song; I never actually expected to find her. My Dreaming wasn't of that nature but I understood her presence and her song had become like a conversation between us. She had become someone who greeted me often now and I felt her presence like I would feel the presence of a friend.

Tonight she was with me and as we moved about the deep pool of the gorge I understood her. I could hear her soft song on the air though tonight it had purpose and I wondered at that. There were many things which I had wondered about over the months, things which I had become aware of but which had caused me no reason to question what was in my Dreaming, I merely accepted the knowledge that it was something that would be revealed in time. Tonight though the woman was trying to show me something, reveal some part of her world which had escaped me.

I had come to understand that the woman lived here in the gorge. It was a knowledge that I carried with me and I knew that she didn't live alone though this awareness never bothered me either and I never had cause to question it. Why would I? It was the way that women lived, more often with a partner than not and it raised no concern for either of us.

Tonight there was something different about my dream though. It was as if tonight we were waiting for something and as she spoke of this in her song, I too, settled to the wait. The expectation was of something which I didn't understand, yet I knew it was important. It was something the woman had waited a long time for and her anticipation fed my own. It was like a promise shared.

Waiting wasn't a difficult thing to do, there was a great deal to entertain us and we had enjoyed these small amusements for many months. These were amusements of the spirit, a sense of joy and one of play and as we shared these things about the deep sandy pool I wondered what it was we were waiting for. Well into the night the moment finally came when we both knew that what we had been waiting for was with us, it came upon me with something of a surprise.

Men were not part of my Dreaming except for when they were a presence of which I became aware. I knew when Ty joined my Dreaming, though it didn't happen too often. We had our own paths to the world of the Dreaming Spirits. Of course the Dreaming wasn't quite like a dream, or even a fantasy. Dreaming was also different for men and women. For a woman, men were often part of what was merely a dream, but their Dreaming was different from a dream. For men it was a journey Ty had said and yet for women it was an experience.

So when I felt the shadow of a man, one other than Taipan I was shocked. That I felt this presence was more than enough to shock me but that I could see his shadow in the deep blue waters of the pool and to watch as it emerged to the light was even more shocking.

I knew immediately that the woman of the song knew this man. I knew immediately also that I should remain calm, after all she must have called him to this place I decided. But it was as I heard her whisper his name in her song that I truly became frozen, my instincts screaming my protest and even my acute annoyance.

Moonggun emerged slowly from the water, it was though he was part of the liquid that was life and hope in this country and while he had no solid form, no defined features I knew he was a man. I saw the deep ceremonial markings across his gut that marked him a powerful being and for the first time I wondered how his shadow had come to be here.

His presence wasn't yet a solid thing and I felt that he had come a great distance, that he had followed the Spirit paths known only to a very few and as I watched his shadow take form for the first time I became afraid. I didn't understand this and I wasn't entirely sure that I wanted to.

As my fear began to wake me I knew he reached out, tried to stop my flight but my passage was too swift and I knew then that he only had limited power to intrude on my Dreaming. Even that frightened me enough to shake me from the Dreaming and deliver me swiftly back to wake in the shelter of Taipan's arms.

I woke suddenly with a start, and a quick drawn breath but the shock of being instantly awake left my heart pounding. Ty must have felt my shock, heard my heart as he suddenly stirred, drawing me more deeply into his arms.

"Did you wake with a jump...?" he mumbled sleepily almost amused. "Bad dream?"

For a moment I was still, fighting to gather my thoughts and calm the pace of my heart. It was a pace also that Ty must have just noticed as he felt my disquiet and turned to me.

"You OK?" he asked again, more awake now though sleep still deepened his words.

"Yes, I just had a shock that's all," I said trying to reassure him, my voice a whisper in the night.

Easing him-self up more to better see me in the newly breaking light of the very early dawn I could just see his frown, "A shock? What sort of shock?"

Not sure now if it was a shock, not even sure that it wasn't a dream or even something of a nightmare. I struggled to make sense of it all.

"I don't know... maybe it was just a bad dream."

"Hmm..." he agreed after a moment, his eyes never leaving mine.

He must have decided I was OK as I felt the heat of his hand travel gently over me.

"You awake now?" he whispered softly as his lips caressed my ear, my neck, and I turned into his chest happily. Pleased for something other than my dream to distract me.

Stretching up against him I enjoyed the heat of his body, the solid planes of him and the weight of him has he shifted us both to the promise of the morning. His mouth covered mine greeting me, waking my body to the morning in a way that I loved. This time of day was always our own and it was the best part of the day for me.

There was no need to hurry and we now dallied at this time, staying in bed until well into the morning. Before our move north the demands of our days had seen us up and about early. Now we took the time to enjoy each other, to laugh and to love and then take the time to again rest before we rose to begin the day.

I loved the pattern of our lives here in Far North Queensland, and it was that which had made the thought of leaving so difficult, but I hoped that was some time away yet. As we moved about preparing for the day the memories of my dream returned to bother me.

Today Taipan had business to attend with John and a few of the other men so I made my way with him over to Marnie's where the men left us to ourselves. When they had business to attend to we didn't question them but I knew today Taipan would probably be seeing his father. They had met a few times in the past months and I could always tell when they were to meet again though he didn't say anything about it.

It was his mood which would tell me that a visit was planned. He would close in on himself, guard his thoughts and often carefully weigh his words almost as if he was in some way preparing.

I had not seen his father or any of his father's family since Taipan had stood with Sean and Andrew in the Bora ring an age ago. I knew that this was the way Ty preferred it to be. He had never overcome the challenge which the men, his father's people, had offered in regards to Jenna and he had once explained that if they felt they could offer such a challenge for Jen, then what would they do if they ever decided to draw me into question?

That was something that he would never tolerate. He had decided that they would not be allowed near enough to entertain such an idea. I was an unknown quantity to his father and their family and Ty had also decided that this wasn't yet the time to bring them into our lives.

However both Marnie and I knew there was something happening. It was unusual for the men to be gathering again, as it wasn't long since they had gathered to discuss matters, then not for the first time we both wondered what it was which kept them at their business..

Once we had discussed it again, neither of us any the wiser, we decided that it would be something which we would no doubt learn about in time if need be. So instead we moved onto more entertaining matters as we worked in the large utilitarian kitchen at the back of the house.

"How is it going with Alex finishing school this year? Does she know what it's she wants to do?" I asked, as I licked the sweet icing from the cake off my fingers, it was a delicious indulgence.

"Ahh… that girl!." Marnie said with a sweep of her hand, turning back to dampen the heat of the old stove as we settled with a cool drink. "Not a clue what she wants to do...just get into trouble I think. An' the boy… the one she is messing with now. No hoper' that one… I tell her but she's not listening. I know nothing…"

Grinning I understood Marnie's objections, though the tale of Alex and her friends was one that we often revisited. "Ty mentioned that Tom may be coming up soon. It will be good to have Denis back home I think. Maybe he can talk some sense into his sister."

"Yes having the two boys back up here would be good. John could use the help and it's time those boys were back before the wet season comes."

As I helped Marnie clear the kitchen thinking of the young men and the coming wet season I was slowly overtaken with a deep sense of disquiet. It made me restless. It was a restlessness that did not leave me even with the arrival of Alex and her friends as they collected in the bedroom.

I wanted to be back at our camp, but I didn't want to leave without Taipan who I knew should be back soon with the men. When the swift afternoon storm arrived I quickly accepted that I'd wait that out with Marnie so as we settled on the verandah with a mug of tea each, in anticipation of the men's arrival we chatted over the sound of the heavy rain on the roof we mused over the plans for the coming holiday season.

Hearing how John was planning on joining a camp for the men and the young initiates made me smile. Taipan had mentioned the camp, it was a strong tradition of the families here about and we had been invited to join the Elders and friends. It was very much a festive affair and I knew it had a great deal to do with arrangements Sean and Andrew had made, concerning the Shaman who were planning on travelling up to join the corroboree for the men.

The camp would draw together many of the family groups and the men felt it was beyond time that such a corroboree was enjoyed. It was a time for the young as well as the old and even the women would join the gathering before the important business of the men was addressed.

As women, we allowed the self important tasks of the men. Leaving them to their business was important for our sons and the men often had a need to feel their sense of authority. Women had the family to concern themselves with, we were nurturers and often the core of the family but men had lost the need to hunt along with much that had traditionally kept their place amongst their families. So now they concerned themselves with the welfare of the community on a whole, and the training of the young men to bring them into a proud and useful manhood. This worked well.

It caused us no worries, often giving added purpose to our own affairs. We could allow the men their authority, it was a sense they needed.

The families would gather not far from the ocean on the western side of the cape. The ocean was an important part of the ceremony and it was time to begin planning. It was something that I was very much looking forward to and even the tourists now came, though we had a special time for them to join us..

As the night fell I began to worry about the absence of the men. Even Marnie complained about their lateness. When Alex asked about dinner and was told to serve herself from the kitchen I knew that Marnie too was feeling my disquiet, so refusing to leave the verandah we tried instead to chatter about anything other than the late arrival of the men.

It was with a huge relief that we finally heard the sound of the truck along the track and the light cutting through the trees, it helped us to relax. The men were home at last, however as I watched John and then another of the men climb from the cab the absence of Ty soon had me on my feet.

Marnie too followed me to the edge of the verandah, not waiting for the men to reach us.

"You're late, what have you done with Ty?" she asked, immediately aware of where my own concerns lay.

"Never mind that woman, out of the way…" John demanded tersely as he sprung up the steps. "Is Alex home?"

"Alex..?" Marnie demanded irritated. "What do you want with Alex?"

We both followed the men into the house, fear filling my belly. I didn't like the look on Johns face and he wouldn't meet my eyes when he had tore past us and that had set every nerve on edge. "Alex..!" John bellowed, not waiting for her to join him as I heard the scrape of the kitchen chair against the floor.

"John. What the hell is going on…? You're scaring Aine… now stop this." Marnie demanded.

"He's missing. Taipan is missing. Now be quiet woman while I talk to Alex."

"Missing? How…?" The word echoed around my brain, bouncing it seemed like a shard that shattered my thoughts. "Missing…?" I repeated scared.

"Now Aine, I am sure it's alright…" Marnie tried to reassure me though I barely heard her.

"Missing?" I questioned again, as though unable to take in the idea

I watched frozen as John pulled Alex into the lounge and sat with her on the old sofa. "Alex girl… now think… you have to help us find him." John said, suddenly calm as his eyes searched those of his daughter.

"Dad I can't… it doesn't work like that."

"It does… you just have to concentrate… search for a sense girl." Impatient John glanced up at Marnie clearly irritated. "Haven't you been training her… for Lords sake Marnie…"

"What'chu doing?" Marnie demanded suddenly angry. "You don't do it that way… you don't know nuthin' you silly man." Reaching suddenly for her daughter she dragged her from the lounge. "Your scaring the girl," she said agitated, "here leave her to us… just tell us what is going on."

Marnie dragged Alex behind her, as though protecting her and I moved up to join them. The men were clearly not happy but neither was Marnie, and Alex was following her mother. All I could think of was that Ty wasn't here… he was somewhere..? But it wasn't here. I wanted to hear what had happened more than anything. I too wanted to know, but I had to force myself to breathe slowly in the face of the panic about me.

"Well old man?" Marnie demanded again growing impatient.

John suddenly looked across at me and slowly shook his head. "We don't know…we don't know where he is. He was scouting… on the plateau… looking for something, someone…?"

"Who…? What have you been doing? I tell you old man, if you want the women to help you have to tell us it all… the lot of it. None of this secret business!" Marnie demanded impatiently.

John stood, clearly torn by the demands of his woman, then as he looked across at me again; I knew he understood that he had to tell us what this was all about. I wanted to throttle him… tear it out of him and he must have seen the impatience and the growing anger in my eyes as he took a step back carefully as he considered what he might say to both of us, his glance shifting to the other men who had followed him into the house..

"Taipan's family came down a few weeks ago… wanting him to help. They have had trouble, quite a bit. It's been going on for a long time, for years… but it's getting worse and when they found the old bones, they knew they had to do something."

"Old bones? What old bones?"

"In one of the gorges up on the Palmer River, the old people buried them a long time ago though nobody has gone into the gorge, for a long time. There have been a few things that have been going on, a few accidents and the Cocky has asked the Elders if they could do something about it before someone is killed."

"And what has this to do with Taipan?" Marnie demanded, and I could have hugged her for her insistence.

"He was scouting, the area. We wanted to know what was about or if anything could be seen before we went in. He was going to pick a likely camp site maybe, check if there was something we should know about before we travelled so far, its difficult country there. We have to go in by foot." He protested inanely. "It's not clear country. It's old gold country woman, lots of old workings. Not country we would easily travel through."

"So he was flying?" I demanded suddenly and at Johns sharp look, I knew he understood my question.

Nodding he cast his glance around the company quickly. He was clearly uncertain about speaking about it, but I ignored his hesitancy. "Just where was he? Did you see him, where did he go?" I demanded again, impatiently.

John shook his head. "We found out later that there are shooters up that way, there were shots but we don't know where."

"Shots!" I demanded, suddenly shocked to my core. I had never considered such a thing. Though I knew it was something that I had heard Sean and Ty speak of. It was a risk they took, one they were aware of but the very thought of Taipan being shot while in flight was something I had never even considered. It was one of the reasons why they never took to flight in some areas. Ty would have known the risks, he would have been aware surely.

"Oh God!"

"Now Aine... I am sure he is alright." Marnie turned to me, I felt her arm around my shoulders as I considered what I had heard. How could this happen? How could this be? It wasn't possible surely.

"Alex. Come with us." Marnie said suddenly and turning from the group she led us outside. "John. Get into Cooktown or up to the Ranger and see if you can get onto Sean, sort something out. We need the family up here now."

"He's OK," I said more to myself than anyone, convinced I would know if he wasn't, "He can't be hurt seriously… I would know it. I would feel it… wouldn't I?" I demanded of the woman now trying to settle me on the verandah.

I watched as John and his friend strode past us and back to the truck. I listened as they fired it into gear and watched the lights as they moved through the trees… I watched them disappear in disbelief.

"Alex, sit here… take Aine's hands," Marnie said, moving aside for Alex to squat in front of me. "Alex can see Aine, she can see but she needs your help. She will feel if it's not good. You have to think of Taipan, draw him to mind… call to him Aine," she coaxed, her voice almost a whisper. The heat of Alex's hands gripped mine, they seemed so small… too small. How could she feel?" I wondered absently as Marnie's soft voice filled the air with a certainty that seemed to soothe me.

"I can do this… I did this once before," I added half fearful, half hopeful. It wasn't the same I knew but as I searched Alex's eyes, looking for any reassurance, it was the only thing I could think of saying. I wanted to reassure her and I needed her to listen for him, to tell me he was alright.

Alex nodded and closed her eyes, her hands gripped mine then she went deathly still. I heard the in drawn breath with a sudden heat and then steady breathing. I watched her, I couldn't have done other. Alex was breathing deep sure breaths and I felt her move subtly, almost stretching her limbs. Then she suddenly opened her eyes and they smiled at me.

I felt reassurance flood through me, I felt comfort in the deep brown of her eyes.

"He's sleeping," she said quietly. "He's hurt, but he's sleeping. There is someone there, they are looking after him. I can feel them."

"Oh God..!" I said suddenly and then I couldn't help myself, I almost collapsed to the floor of the verandah gathering Alex in my arms. "Are you sure?" I demanded, uncertain of what I was hearing and so afraid to believe it.

Alex nodded. "I am sure Aine. He's hurt." As Alex put her hand to her shoulder and ran it down her arm she again caught my eyes. "He's hurt, but the pain is worse than the wound. He felt I was there… he knows. God he is so angry," she added suddenly almost laughing in her own fear.

Also half laughing through my sudden tears I wanted to hug her. It was as though I could feel his anger and it reassured me, filled me with a confidence I wasn't sure I had reason to feel. I was suddenly certain he was OK, he was alive and that he would come back soon. It was just a matter of when… or how?

"How can we get to him?" I suddenly demanded. "Marnie… there must be a way."

"Calm down Aine… we will work out a way. The men will be back… we can't do anything in the dark. But we can figure it out… let's wait and see…"

"Wait! I can't wait!"

"Yes girl you can. We don't want two of you out there lost. Ty would not thank me if we lost you too."

Waiting for the men to return was impossible. Waiting to hear from Sean, from anyone was impossible. A dozen times I walked out to watch the night, a dozen times I made myself a cup of tea to try and calm myself and a dozen times I tipped it down the sink or tossed it on the ground. I even sipped it cold when Marnie tried to convince me to eat something.

The only time I felt any comfort was when Alex sat with me. Marnie had built up the campfire outside, more for something to do than any practical reason and while it was cooler outside than in the house, I knew I was more settled as I watched the dance of the flames. I saw the slow burning of the wood as though in some way it was helping. The constant activity of the flames seemed somehow to help the endless hours pass while we waited.

I knew what the men were doing, but that didn't help. They would need to cross the creeks, make their way through the tracks in the dark to where they could pick up phone reception. As much as I had come to love this forest, I now hated it. It had swallowed Ty; now all I wanted to be was safe at home, safe in the community. As a summer storm came and went it seemed to me that anywhere would be safer than here and yet I knew how ridiculous that thought was. I knew how much Ty loved the forest, how could I hate it?

When the men finally arrived back it was to a sudden flurry of activity. It was after midnight and I could see Marnie's relief that John was back. This was dangerous country to be travelling around at night and for the first time I realized that Marnie had suffered in his absence.

John though had a clear plan, a clear path and as Marnie told him of Alex's reassurance I could see that it was bringing him as much comfort as it had bought me.

"We are going to move the fire down by the creek. Give us a hand woman." John demanded gruffly, almost as soon as he had arrived..

Confused and uncertain about what was going on, I none the less gathered some of the smaller logs while John strode ahead with still burning fire sticks. Having immediately gone off in the general direction of the creek, his friend had dug out enough of a hole in the old fire pit by the bank to protect the fire. As we all worked at gathering the logs and building the fire John went on to explain, trying to answer Marnie's questions as she struggled to get information out of him, knowing I would soon be demanding answers if she didn't do it first.

"Did you get onto the community?"

"Yes, we got through to his mother, Dianne. I spoke to Sean, it took a while for them to get him down to the phone but they are travelling up to Brisbane tonight and catching a flight, they should be here tomorrow..."

"Well that is something old man."

"Moonggun is coming up ahead," John added and at the mention of that name I suddenly froze.

"What?" I demanded.

John looked up at me suddenly, and then looked away. "He will be here tonight."

Completely flummoxed I tried to make sense of what he was saying. "What… what do you mean he will be here…?"

John wouldn't meet my eyes; he ignored my words but looked across at me as I stood there.

"He will be here Aine, he will be able to find Ty in a way none of us can," John said steadily, looking as though he felt he had explained it all in those few words.

"How!" I demanded. "Where… where is he?"

"He's on his way."

"On his way…?" Suddenly it was just all too much. I didn't understand and I felt fear and the uncertainty overtake me. I couldn't see how someone I didn't even know could find Ty, he was hurt… he was hurting and there was nothing I could do about it except build up this stupid fire.

Dropping the small log I had been going to add to the flames I suddenly crumpled where I was standing and as I felt Marnie's arms come around me, trying desperately to soothe me, but I crumpled further into a heap.

"Aine… oh Darlin'. He will be alright, we'll find him," she cooed in my ear, trying to ease my pain and confusion.

I felt the support of John's arms, as he half carried me, half dragged me closer towards the fire and tried to settle me there, where the growing heat could warm the chill of my skin and ease the shock of my thoughts.

"Look there is no use in getting all upset. Give him a chance, he'll find Taipan."

"I don't care about him… I just want Ty home. He… he should never have gone." But even as I protested I knew the futility of such a thought. He was Ty, he went because he chose to, but I just wanted him back.

I was past voicing my fears, past thinking and past caring what others thought. Alex went back to the house and later brought out a doonah from her bed and gratefully I joined her, curling up into a ball to watch the fire.

When John began to beat a rhythmic clap on the sticks, I found at least that seemed to calm me.

I watched mesmerized as he beat a rhythm against a sturdy log he had dragged in front of him. The beating sticks I had seen used before, only they had not been used in the way John was now using them. Before they had beaten a rhythm against each other, now they beat their song against a larger partner. They were solid, carved and marked, having been patterned with fire. The sticks seemed to talk to the earth and being a listener to their conversation in some way helped ease my pain.

The sound was soothing, almost hypnotic and I found a solace in the rhythms of the night. I guess I slept. It seemed that way though I couldn't remember sleeping at all. I was aware when Alex stirred at my side and I felt the sudden change in the tempo of those around the camp fire and the tones of the beat against the earth in an endless tattoo.

It was like my dream, I was reliving the moment with an intense sense of déjà vu which immediately woke me so I was aware despite my confusion. It was like bringing to life the threads of dreams and after what had seemed like an eternity I suddenly felt a spectator to the sudden activity around me.

John stood slowly, leaving his song with the earth and stretching carefully, he moved around the fire while Marnie eased herself up from where she had slept nearby. The movement of the two men towards the creek alerted me. I knew… I understood what was happening even though I had not a clue and as the surface of the flow of the creek took on its own light directly in front of where the men stood I too… climbed to my feet to better see, to become part of what was happening around me.

It was in the quiet before the dawn, the star light was still reflected in the cold blue and black colours of the running water. The light of the fire hitting the moving water making it difficult to tell the difference between the reflection of the stars or the fire and a light that was born of the crystal stream and its deep still pools.

Then as the surface of the water broke, the shadow stood to be seen in the light. I was unsure if it was a reflection or a trick of the moonlight, or something born of the water but suddenly he was there, emerging from the river as though he was of the earth, born of the water and steadily he stepped towards the bank with water running from his hair and arms. Water clung to his body strangely and ran in rivulet's down his torso and legs, his simple hair belt and lap-lap his only adornment

In a sure movement he gained the bank then sweeping the water from his eyes he ran his hands through his hair, freeing the shower of droplets that fell about him as he shook his head. I watched stunned as his eyes caught mine, then he turned to meet John's steady gaze.

I was confused as he held out his hand, confused as I watched him take John's hand in what I knew to be a powerful grip, he stepped finally from the last of the water which seemed to hold him, and his eyes found mine again as I watched open mouthed.

"Andrew!" The words were more a question to myself than a greeting and it seemed to amuse him.

He gave me a sudden crooked smile as he released John and stepped towards me. "You took off the last time we met, I should have known they were trying to show me something," he said strangely as he moved in the shadowy dark and I wondered if I was awake or dreaming. I felt his support as he carefully gripped my arms. "You OK?"

"But... but I don't understand."

Andrew shook his head, agreeing with me strangely enough as I read the message in his glance. "It's not something I could tell you Aine; I knew you would learn when it was time. Taipan couldn't tell you of this Lore; it's not his to share. But I am here now and we can find him."

"But why? How... how are you here?"

"I have travelled up along the ancient paths with the Unggur Serpent. Where the water flows, even underground we can travel. It's the power of the Dreaming Serpent but I need a moment. I am still with the Spirit of the Serpent and she needs her freedom. Give me a minute to release her."

As Andrew let go of my arms I felt the loss of his heat, it was a strange heat which almost burnt and it had a deep resonant hum I could feel, it travelled through me yet held me. I watched as he drew deep breaths then I felt the slow cooling of the air around us. The tingling of my own body where he had gripped my arms shifted and faded. It reminded me of the sweep of the heat of the Serpent I had felt once before a lifetime ago.

It was so very still all around us as we waited, without knowing why, then the stillness broke slowly as I became aware of the bush noises intruding on our quiet.

"She is gone," he said softly, and then once more he smiled his reassurance with that crooked smile.

"How... I don't understand. How did you find us?" I said still confused.

"I only needed John's song. I can hear it in the earth, the clap of the sticks led me here. The sound of the bull-roarer does not travel so well in the ground water."

"The bull-roarer?" I repeated confused, and then I remembered Ty telling me once that it was the sound of the bull-roarer which could call to those with the ability to hear from a great distance.

"Hmm... you don't need to understand this. Tell me what you know instead." Andrew said with an open invitation to the company.

As John broke into my confusion, I hoped he would say something I'd not heard, something, anything new as I struggled to make sense of the things I'd just been told. I wondered if I was still dreaming. I could feel the air, taste the smoke as it drifted on the wind and I knew taste was never part of a dream.

"Ty has been gone since yesterday," John said in his careful explanation. "We lost him about noon up in the Palmer River area. We think he met with shooters up there. There are some rat bags up that way at the moment, some will shoot anything out of the skies. The others have headed across to the nearby homestead to see if they can organize an ultralight or chopper. They aim to search the gorges and gullies when it's light."

"Can you get a vehicle into that area?"

"No, not now. The track's in a bad way an getting worse, it hasn't seen a grader for a while. We can go as far as Lakeland an along the development road but from the turn off, the road is impassable. Which is why…"

"OK I can manage, but I need a few hours to build the strength I'll need. Has there been anything?" Andrew added cutting explanations off.

"Alex found him," Marnie cut in before the men could say anything. "We know he is alive, and there is someone… we're not sure of…"

"That has to be good. I need somewhere to rest, Marnie?" Andrew said.

"Yes… yes of course, come up to the house," she quickly apologised. "Aine, it will do you good to help. When will the men arrive?"

"Later today. Sean can organize a vehicle in Cairns but I need to find Ty before that in case he's seriously injured. I just need a few hours then I can get back out there. It depends on how badly he is hurt, it's likely that we will need the boys to help bring him out. Have you been able to reach them John? We will need them if he is in very rough terrain."

"We can head out to the nearest homestead then, I expect the others can meet us there. It will take a few hours but we can see how they're going with the chopper." John offered as the gathering turned to the feeble light of the house glowing through the bush. I followed still straining to hear all that was said in what was becoming a babble of voices.

I needed to talk to Andrew, I needed his reassurance and to hear how he planned to find Ty. The past year had bought changes in the man I had thought of as Sean's friend and close companion, though I had thought that he was still maturing. I could see I needed to introduce myself again to this man, who I now barely recognized. I struggled to equate him with the young man who I had once criticised in his relationships and thought to myself how I doubted I could speak to him in that way again.

I had watched him grow over the years but now, he was something very different and I could understand how Jen could say that he scared many of the women, making them careful around him. I didn't want to annoy or upset him now, he was here to find Ty and that was all that mattered.

Even Alex wasn't unaffected as we followed the men ahead of us. Andrew stood tall, broader in the shoulders than I remembered and I couldn't fail to note Alex's interest. For the first time I realized that she was without a ready opinion and she watched him carefully. I doubt he was even aware of this as we made our way back towards the house. She looked almost child-like as she dragged the tail of the doonah gathered in her arms then she vanished to her room almost as soon as we reached the verandah.

I had little time to wonder, or to thank her for her thoughtfulness as throughout the remainder of the night Taipan was all I wanted to concern myself with. While I knew I would have to give Andrew the time he needed to recover I was very impatient.

There were many questions that demanded answers immediately, so I waited for my opportunity my focus barely leaving Andrew as we tried to make him comfortable and I prepared one of the old couches on the verandah for him to rest for a few hours. I could wait; he wasn't going anywhere without my knowing, and I could count the hours as the men prepared to head back into the bush without me.

SHADOWS OF GOLD

Taipan:

The night was much cooler, a respite from the heat of the afternoon but down here, at least near the water it was a more temperate heat. Easing my side I tested the damage with movement and knew with relief that there were no breaks but still, the open gouge on my arm throbbed, the heat in the wound burnt like I had never felt before. It took a moment to find a more comfortable spot, the bruising and grazes around my hip and side were severe and would give me days of discomfit but at least the damage wasn't totally disabling.

My movement alerted the woman as she suddenly looked up from the fire where she sat with her partner and I knew she was going to join me. I watched as she rose then she walked steadily over to where I was resting against the trunk of a tree, well back from the warmth of the fire, she then dropped down on her haunches to carefully examine my injured side once again.

Her manner was odd, I hadn't been able to gauge who or what was happening here but I had my suspicions. Her touch was comforting as she took up the paste still wrapped in soft bark and again spread it onto the deepening bruise on my hip and into the deep scrapes down the side of my body. She said something softly in an attempt to reassure me but with words I didn't understand. She had said little to me at all and she was afraid to meet my eyes. I could tell that she didn't think I would hurt her, but it may have been that she recognized the markings of a Shaman across my body and she was unsure of me.

I had seen this before in other isolated communities. Women didn't question, it was their place to accept and allow their men to guide them in matters of life and their survival. I wondered if it was even that she was afraid of me. She was alone with this man who gave me cause to question their arrangement but he wasn't easy to get to know either. There was a great deal about this situation that kept me quiet. I needed to understand what was going on here. I had not expected to find such as these two so close to the towns and settlements of the eastern coast.

Struggling with my discomfit and the strange giddiness in my head I fought to keep my mind busy with the puzzles around me. I didn't want to slip back into the darkness which I felt nearby and the only way I knew to keep myself alert, awake, was to concentrate on what was about me.

I didn't expect them to show me any ill will, they had after all shared their meal with me and although they didn't invite me to the fire, they did tend to my needs in a way I had found unusual. The man didn't trust me but he was comfortable letting his woman tend my injuries and she had no hesitation in doing so. Her glance told me she knew what I was, if not who I was, which told me much of her life. A woman of the tribes even if she dressed in a bush shirt and canvas pants, an unusual mix in this day and I wished, not for the first time that I understood their conversation better.

As she left me and returned to the fire I took the opportunity to quietly study the man again. He wasn't of the tribes but he must have links to the Homesteads or Stations nearby, there weren't many around here. This was difficult land to live in but there was something about him I found disturbing and I hadn't quite worked out what it was.

He was Irish, his accent still distinct, though mellowed with a drawl like many country people. He had been in Australia a long time, most of his life I thought. He was nearing fifty I guessed though distinctly Irish, none the less for the deep red to his knot of hair which barely held a hint of the grey which would have marked his years. He wasn't a tall man, though he was solidly built. He reminded me of the old gougers of the opal fields though it wouldn't be opal that kept him here, it would be gold. He had about him the distinctive set of a gold miner of old, though with his woman, his manner was gentler than I would have thought. Perhaps it was she that kept him here as well, and I once more wondered about them.

I had said nothing, I knew enough not to speak until I understood what I was dealing with. The man's name was Francis that much I knew. I had heard her use his name with a tolerant yet tender affection, though I didn't know her name yet. He was gruffer in his manner. She understood and spoke English, though it was with an odd broken inflection which I also found unusual. She spoke in an old pidgin English which he understood and was obviously accustomed to. They had apparently been together for a long time.

He had said a few words to me when he had found me once I had woken to the harsh pain of my fall. He had asked what I was doing there and then almost immediately he had begun to answer his own questions in the manner of a man not often in the company of other men. I realized then that he thought I didn't understand him but listening to him, I learnt more than I would have learnt otherwise. It was an almost amusing running monologue he was entertaining himself with. He asked me a question and then answered it himself as he guessed at what I might say.

He figured I was a black heathen, his own words which were sprinkled with a fair amount of cursing but the words he used were almost of another world, another time and that had arrested anything I might have said. There was something going on that I didn't understand and the old colt revolver which he carried on his hip in its worn holster gave me reason to think that he wouldn't have hesitated to use it if he felt the need. It was an old piece, not what I would expect in modern days so I was going to find out what was going on before I made my ignorance obvious.

Not impressed with my nakedness he had thrown a dirty pair of canvas pants at me and with almost comic theatrics indicated that I should put them on. I knew now, this was more for his woman's benefit than mine though I doubt she would have cared. He had more sensitivities than she did which I also found somewhat unusual.

The pants he had tossed at me hung off my hips like a sack and rode high on my calf, but loose was good with my injuries, and it helped that I didn't need to stand, I couldn't have stood if I had wanted to at the moment., any suggestion of movement was still too painful. That much I had learnt when he had tried to help me walk to camp. It had been an excruciating move and I was only grateful that we had not gone far when he had decided we were going no further. Their camp must be nearby I realized as I watched when he had left me against the tree and disappeared down a track only to return some time later with some gear and food and those stiff canvas trousers which I now wore.

It had been after sunset that his woman had appeared and when she realized I was there, it was almost as though she was expecting me. It had been she who had cleaned and dressed my arm with carefully prepared bush dressings. She had also inspected the damage done to my side as I had scraped it badly in my fall when I had floundered against the side of this narrow rocky valley in a confused transition. I knew what had sent me into a spin, the heat of the bullet had gouged a path across my arm but I was mindful that it could have been much worse. I had been lucky and I knew to be grateful for small mercies. It worried me though that I had to struggle with my awareness, it would have been so easy to slip into the darkness that beckoned. It offered relief from the pain I was feeling.

The shooters, whoever they were would be miles away by now. My flight had taken me well away from them and in the air I had an easier escape than I would have had on land. At first I had hoped that the hunters hadn't had dogs with them and it would seem they didn't. Or if they did, the dogs had no drive to track me.

My first reaction had been a searing anger when I realized I had been shot without any warning. It had been an anger that had fed my transition when I knew I was losing height. It was an anger that had kept me silent when I had come around with Francis prodding me carelessly; he was almost as surprised as I was to find myself at the bottom of the gully. He had heard the shots and thought I was the target, though he hadn't realized I was airborne. All he had intended was to get me away from where ever the shooters might expect to find me.

What had been odd had been that he had so easily accepted that I was the target and that these men actually wanted to hunt me. His monologue told me he suspected that I was a thief, though he sympathized with me as it was apparent he was assuming it was food I was stealing. It wasn't until his woman turned up just after dusk that I understood where his sympathies had arisen from and I guessed this was why I was now kept at a distance. He in part understood the links that would bind people of Aboriginal descent, people of the tribes as he imagined I was, even if my skin was much fairer than hers, but he wasn't prepared to welcome me into his camp. His woman was his and he wanted me to know this.

The whole thing was a dilemma that kept me struggling to work it out, placing the pieces together as I watched them carefully throughout the evening. I had to continually force myself back from the edge of unconsciousness which was drawing me. I struggled through by reminding myself of things I had learnt in my research of the area in the past weeks and months. Things about the history of this area, the mood and tempers of the people from the past, and I didn't doubt that Francis was from the past. It became more and more obvious to me the more I observed them. In some way the past and present were linked in this place and while I recognized their place in the past, I wasn't sure if I was in their world, or they in mine. I had indeed found the haunted gorge, of that I was certain.

As I sat propped up against the tree my struggle with the looming darkness became more difficult, but I wasn't going to allow the darkness to win. I had to fight it.

This was the land of the Quinkan, my father's people and I tried to grasp at what strength the land could offer me. For the first time I wondered if the woman would be counted amongst that family. She was tall and her features were striking and showed the beauty of her people. As I watched her, I considered what opportunity I might have to talk with her and it was when her man Francis settled for the night, wrapped in his blanket, that I wondered if she too would sleep. That she didn't surprised me, she remained seated by the fire watching him, barely noting my existence. That alone gave me focus and I would have thanked her for that had I been able.

In my struggle to stay awake I wondered if Aine had been told of my plight. When I didn't return by nightfall the others would have been alarmed and I wondered what the men had decided to do once they realized I was in trouble. There were not many amongst them who could shape-shift, none that I knew who could take flight and even if anyone could, they would not do so with shooters about.

I had felt the presence of someone though and that had calmed me it was like the gentle spirit touch of a woman, I wondered who it was and thought perhaps it was Marnie, or even Alex. I knew they both shared Denis's gift of long sight though it was an unknown quality in the women. Whoever it was, I knew it was something of which Aine would be aware. Without Aine, they wouldn't have found me and this thought too helped settle me, despite the pain in my side making me restless but it was the darkness that calmed my mind for a while.

During the early hours I felt the presence of the woman again at my side. I was without a blanket and the coolness of the air was disturbing me.

Carefully I stretched my side, easing my weight towards the woman; my laboured look was one of enquiry and curiosity.

She offered me the water canister as I struggled to sit-up, somewhat relieved I reached for it. Tomorrow I would have to try for more mobility. I didn't know how long it would take for the others to locate me but exercise could only be a good thing.

"Thanks."

A simple word, but the shock on the woman's face was telling as she quickly moved away out of my reach and then as she considered my word I watched as her eyes examined mine for the first time, she was troubled with a look of confusion. Carefully she took in my features, my expression as she looked to test her own words and I waited.

"You speak'em Engl'n?" Her question was then followed by a small tirade of dialect and as I shook my head I broke into her flow of words.

"I speak." I said simply and waited for the impact of my words, which suddenly silenced her once more.

"You debil man?" she asked hesitant, indicating the scars across my chest.

"Spirit man," I corrected carefully, wondering now at her halting language. "You belong Francis?" I said trying to shift her focus from what I thought was her fear of me as once more I tried to find a spot on the hard ground that was comfortable for my injuries.

The woman glanced over toward the sleeping figure then looked back at me, her expression softened momentarily. "He good man. He sad man…"

The expression of her hands told me more than her words. Then as she went to leave I stalled her with a small movement.

"You?" Carefully easing myself up I tried to redirect my question making myself clear. Indicating myself I added. "Taipan, Bama people," and waited hopeful.

For a moment I didn't think she understood me and then she offered her name.

"Mayra, people in rock country my place." Turning in the next instant as though it was of little account, she however showed her respect in the wary set of her shoulders and gentle care in her step. She wanted not to disturb me in any way, she was here to serve me only and she left me to rejoin her partner as though to protect him while he still slept by the fire. Once more I carefully tried to resettle myself against the ground, still trying to avoid the dark shadow that I felt the lack of conscious thought offered.

It had been an oddly unsettling exchange and I wasn't sure what to make of it. I wondered if she would tell her partner Francis of the exchange but the question was lost to the shadows of the night as sleep finally claimed me.

It was the sound of the birds which woke me, the cacophony of the morning though at first I didn't know where I was. The growing half light of the bush brought back the sharp shift of a discomforting pain which truly woke me, my discomfit recalling to my mind where I was.

Then I realized, it was neither the birds nor the morning light which had disturbed me. The small glowing orb hovered, then it moved around exploring the camp as though gathering a knowledge of its whereabouts. Sitting up steadily and with some difficulty, I felt a flood of welcome relief despite my growing discomfit and then my eyes met those of the woman.

Mayra was awake also, she stopped frozen in fright as she too had noticed the arrival of the Koolrari light, the earth light of the desert, and she now looked across at me her face bathed in fear. I tried to reach towards her with my hand, in a futile gesture to calm her but she took flight.

But it wasn't so much her dash towards the shelter of the bush around us, but it was the wraith like passage of her movement which stilled the shout on my lips. The woman vanished, in a waver of light she was gone, before she had even reached the shelter of the bush and it was only then that I knew for certain that she had not been of this world.

With difficulty I struggled to my feet, using the tree that was my shelter to support me. The orb hovered, seemingly noting my movement and then it began to die. Moonggun would know now where I was and so I knew it would only be a matter of time before I would be found, but this wasn't what was driving me to my feet.

Seeking the support of anything I could, I reached for a thin branch buried in the sandy soil that had been my bed throughout the long night. It offered little enough support, but it steadied me and with difficulty I made my way painfully towards the small fire where Francis still slept.

The heat of the fire was still buried in its blanket of white ash and as I approached it I was careful to move in silence. Though I could see now that the blanket had no movement, I could also see that it didn't show the shape of a man beneath it

Gaining my balance, I used the stick to carefully drag back the dusty worn blanket and for some reason I wasn't at all surprised to find what I had thought to be a sleeping figure was in fact a rumpled old camp blanket which held nothing but dust. It was empty, Francis wasn't there. The camp was now empty of all but me and the slow dying fire. My companions, who or what they may have been had left.

There are many things that we may count as strange in this world, but when dealing with knowledge of what is not strange, all that is left are questions as to why what we have experienced or seen is here. The need to understand becomes the primary drive and as I searched my mind for understanding I glanced about the camp for clues. I was reluctant to move more than I absolutely had to.

There was little enough to find. All there was, was a blanket, a fire and a small collection of kindle left from the night. The foot prints about the camp told me more. My companions had substance, they were real and they existed still, but their reality had now changed as had mine.

Fear had driven Mayra into a safer place, a world which offered her a sense of well being. There were many things which linked the worlds and one of the only times control was lost was when there was fear. The instinct to survive surpassed rational thought and movement.

Sleep could also shift us between the worlds as it was when we were asleep that the Dreaming became our reality and this offered us a belief in that we could control our world. If you understood the Dreaming paths we could indeed control our world in learning and understanding much more about the things which made up the pattern of our lives.

Sleep I guessed had taken Francis to another place, probably one he shared with Mayra or perhaps it was she that had drawn him away. What concerned me more was the question of what it possibly could be that drew them back into our world against the order of the worlds. Could this be what had given these valleys and gorges the power they possessed over the mobs around here? Was their broken presence why this place had a reputation as somewhere the Spirits haunted the earth and the rocks?

As my side began to throb and my thoughts returned reluctantly to my situation. I needed to get off my feet, to give my body a chance the heal itself, so gingerly I looked about. The water offered a cool haven, it would ease the throb of my body and the swelling tightness I felt, so with care I made my way over to the pool to find a place in the slow flow of the creek.

Easing myself into the shock of cool water I watched as the full flush of day light began to fill the valley. I wondered how long it would be before the others found me. I didn't doubt that they would, the Koolrari light told me that Moonggun was seeking me, or at least another who could command the power of the Earth light. As I settled to wait, I wondered about the leeching I had witnessed between the worlds. It would have to be dealt with because such a bleed between the worlds bought nothing but ill, though first I would need to find the reason for these threads which linked the worlds before it could be dealt with properly.

It was perhaps an hour or so later that I noted the movement in the water surface, the subtle shift of light and change in the flow of current so sitting up with some difficulty, I struggled with the stiffness now overtaking my body, then I waited. I had hauled myself out of the cold flow of the stream earlier and had been enjoying the heat of the rocks as I waited; I watched the shadowy form announcing Moonggun's arrival. It never ceased to fascinate me, it was a Lore I was unfamiliar with but one that was now part of my own knowledge. Andrew's initiation into the Lore of the Mimi had given him not only his spirit name and placed him in touch with his spirit shadow, but also brought his unusual skill to the fore. It was a gift from his people.

It had surprised him as much as me, though Billy Black had looked for just such a skill. The Lore of the Banman had a blood history and Billy had the ability to discern the strengths of a man. I suspected that it hadn't so much been that Billy had found in Andrew a son, but that the son had found his family and his ancient lands. Drawn to its own, blood often found its rightful place, it was as strong as the pull of the Spirit.

I watched as Andrew emerged from the water and as he carefully shook off the binds of the Serpent, returning her to the water from where she had come. I acknowledged his place with some pride amongst the men of a high order; I had been rewarded in my judgment of him. He was growing accustomed to this transition, as accustomed almost as I was to the transition of a shape-shift and in time he would become stronger. As I watched I smiled in welcome, more than ready for some light relief and solid company to help me keep the darkness at bay still.

"What kept you?" I realised that words were becoming difficult to say. The sooner I got out of here the better.

Andrew grinned, and then pulled himself up slowly to settle beside me gathering his strength. He took a little time to regain his breath to re order his energies.

"Aine," he said with something of a challenge after a time, knowing he now had my full attention, he grinned ruefully. "She's not happy with you."

"Hmm…" I agreed suspecting as much. "Was it bad? I'm sorry about that."

Andrew's glance took in the valley, travelled the hills, the walls of the gorge, the river and then returned to me. There was something he found amusing. "I don't think I have ever seen her so angry at you," he added shaking his head, then drawing a breath carefully as he moved, still settling in his transition. "What is the damage here? Did you break anything?"

"No."

Moving around to my side he inspected my wounds, luckily they were mostly superficial soft tissue damage. Except for the deep gouge where the bullet had scored my arm and some of the deeper gashes on my hip. The wounds now exposed to the sun had dried and hardened.

"Looks like you'll live, though I'll be surprised if you don't end up with another scar," he concluded apparently satisfied, "Least it will make her happy that it isn't overly serious, it looks sore enough."

"You're not wrong. I know she'll be upset with me," I said, closing my eyes for a moment I struggled to find the level of ease I had felt earlier with the heat of the sun. "Moving about doesn't help. Any ideas about how we are going to get out of here?" I said softly, finding the earlier memory then mentally shaking myself as I felt the darkness loom again.

"Yeah…" Andrew answered. "I expect the ultra lights will be here sometime today, the locals seemed to know this place, once Aine found her sketches they knew it. I'll get a signal fire going soon and it shouldn't be too long."

"Her sketches?" The surprise in his words shook me from my lethargy for the moment, "What the devil are you on about?"

"Aine has walked this valley it's a place she knows well. She and Debbie have both been here. It seems it's something Alex also knew when the sketches hit the light of day. Aine has a series of sketches; apparently you don't know anything about them."

Shaking my head I frowned, "This is something I should know, why didn't she tell me about them?"

"Seems she did, months ago, before you headed north but you saw nothing in the early sketches she did with Deb. So I guess she just decided they were of little account."

"And just how is it you know about them?" I asked confused and irritated. Sketches and Debbie went together; they were so much part of Deb's young experience that the six year old, as with many of us, took them for granted. I knew it was likely that I had discounted them easily; I obviously hadn't paid enough attention to Aine's sketches either. I should have known better. It was easy now to find fault in my own actions in the light of what had happened. How much of this could have been avoided I wondered with irritation born of my obvious ignorance.

"I was drawn into her Dreaming only the other night," Andrew added almost apologetically. "I didn't realize it was Aine or I would have told you. I was called here by a woman, a woman of the Mimi who was using a very old song. I have been hearing her song for a while and I have just worked out how I could reach her in the Dreaming. It wasn't until I spoke with Aine that I realized that there has to be something else going on here."

As I considered what had been said I was left wondering at the ways we were being led. Life, our existence has purpose beyond our knowing and I recognized the relentless flow of the spirits work. What was it about this valley, this place that they had fought so hard to bring us here?

"I think I have met her," I added carefully as I eased my hip again, sitting hard up against the rock which offered some support.

"Who, the woman?"

"Hmm… she dressed my scrapes. I wondered at the time about her. Their camp is over on the rise somewhere. Did Aine mention a woman at all?"

Andrew's attention was for the moment drawn to where I had indicated then he frowned, and taking up my question he added. "Only in the terms of a Dreaming Spirit, she is a companion who draws her with a song. She was a little vague about that. You said 'their' camp though?"

"Yes… she has a companion. This must be the business of the women then, and for you to hear her song it must have something to do with the Mimi." I felt our conversation was keeping me back from the edge of darkness so I struggled to maintain it. "The woman said she was of the rock people. The Elders are looking to resolve some problems with the spirits of these valleys. They have had trouble here for some time and it's now intruding into their world. We need to find out more."

"We need to get you out'a here," Andrew corrected suddenly, perhaps growing aware of my struggle. "What happened to her, is she still about?" he asked almost as an afterthought.

"No, she's gone. It was the manner of her leaving that made me realize all wasn't as it seemed. She's a Mimi Spirit I think, but her companion..?" I shook my head unsure of my conclusions.

"What was he like?"

"Not sure if she was with him, or he with her. He wasn't of the Mimi though, that much I know."

"Quinkan?"

"No," I smiled, a little amused and glad for the sudden distraction. "Irish."

"Irish?" he repeated surprised.

"Yeah; an interesting type, much older than she. Odd manner about him though, I couldn't quite put my finger on it. I would have described him as an old prospector, his name is, or was Francis," I clarified, unsure of where he belonged. "He had this gun..., an unusual piece for modern days. Perhaps... perhaps something holds him here?"

"Hmm... you're right, that's what I would guess. We need to do some digging ... find out about the history this place, discover what has happened here."

"Well good luck with that," I said with some irony, feeling once more the exhaustion, the pull of a sweeping darkness. "I have a feeling Aine is not going to let me back here too soon with good reason."

Andrew's laugh was equally as ironic then he added. "Well let's get this signal fire going, or you'll be walking out of here and I don't fancy our pace if that's gunna be the case."

I envied him the ease of his movement and by the time I had retrieved the canvas trousers and donned them once more, then made my way over to the camp fire with some difficulty. Andrew had rebuilt the fire and had the smoke winding its way steadily down the valley on the tail of the light breeze.

It was some hours later, hours where I felt that at times I was losing my grip on reality, and long before it came into view we heard the annoying whine of the little ultra light as it wound its way up the valley. It was a compact and somewhat exposed little craft, but it served its owners well for mustering. Its range wasn't great, and being a tight two seater they could lift only one of us out of the valley along with the pilot but that wasn't the worry.

It was when the pilot started speaking into a handheld UHF radio, his booming voice echoing faintly against the sides of the valley that I realized there were two crafts working in tandem and the arrival of the second little machine soon bore this out as it spiralled up over the gorge..

By the time they had landed though, only one of the little planes were needed. Andrew had already left; he was on his way back home. His task had been completed and there was nothing to hold him here anymore. Convincing the pilot that he had been mistaken in seeing another man with me, was somewhat amusing and for a time it held at bay the darkness that threatened to engulf me.

The light told me that it was late into the afternoon when we finally arrived back at the homestead where there were a surprisingly large number of people waiting for us. Tom was amongst them with his mate Denis, both I discovered had been called in at about the same time as Andrew. They had both broken their walkabout to help out. John had decided it was time for them to return and he had travelled over the rough tracks in his truck to meet them at the homestead.

I was losing my battle with the darkness, it was as though I was being drawn away and I struggled with it silently. It was consuming me and I fought to find ways to keep my mind alert. I tried going over what had happened as I fought to maintain consciousness.

The local Cocky, a cattleman who held a Government lease abutting part of the Aboriginal reserve, had a longstanding arrangement with the family group; it was a working arrangement which served both the community and the homestead. He owned the ultra light aircraft and as a few of the men from the community often worked on the homestead, he had offered their use.

It was good to catch up with Tom again and momentarily this held me to a steady line of consciousness. I stubbornly elected to ride in the sheltered tray-back where I could stretch out rather than the cabin of the truck. It gave me the opportunity to attempt to talk to Tom even though the rough ride made me realize the stupidity of my decision. Also this left Denis to keep company with John in the front, I wondered if he was any more comfortable than I was. They had judged that my injuries weren't serious enough to call in the air ambulance or the Flying Doctor but that didn't help with the darkness that kept moving in on me.

The tracks were in a pretty bad way but it seemed my ordeal was nearly over. We would later look for explanations and work out just what it was that haunted the small gorge. I knew I had to reach Aine and that became a driving force which would not tolerate any interference.

For some reason, I knew my survival was dependent on Aine and that drove me. My companions were blind to my inner struggle, though I could see Tom seemed to be in some way aware of the conflict raging within me and I drew comfort from that for some reason. I could feel the threat of darkness all around me, it became my silent battle with a consciousness.

The thought of Aine helped me a great deal. She was going to be angry with me for a while and I was going to be sorry for a long time. But knowing that she would no longer be worrying about me at the moment, knowing that she would be watching me carefully for some time, way eased my concerns. I loved that woman, she wasn't just the closest anyone was to me or had ever been, she was part of who I was and that we would now have time to be together while my body mended bought me more comfort than anything else could have. I understood that now, she was the stronger of us at the moment and I knew I had to reach her.

It would be good to get back to her and while I absently dealt with Tom's concerns my mind stayed with Aine, desperately clinging to her. There would be time enough for figuring out what was happening in these lands and how we could deal with it. I thought that whatever it was had been going on for a long time. I kept my thoughts busy fighting the darkness that was enveloping me, it was drawing me into an abyss and I was afraid that it was because I had blood poisoning, or an infection of some type. I needed to get to Aine.

I had no doubt that Tom and Andrew could deal with things and with the guidance of John, it would be good for both of them. My part in this was done, and I could step back and leave it to those who had the strongest gifts amongst those that were needed, to handle what was happening here. They could work that out and knowing this was a release, and Aine once more filled my thoughts.

To distract myself from the discomfit of the ride back to John's place which seemed to take endless hours of jolting in the vibration of the road I closed my eyes and eased myself back against the hard sacking spread along the floor. Sacking cushioned only by an old foam mattress and an assortment of odds and ends and I occasionally took the moment to mark the differences the last few weeks had made in Tom. He had grown more confident, more accepting of his experiences in seeing things, experiencing the presence of the world of Spirit Men. He had grown much stronger.

He seemed to have grown taller too, though his solid bulk hid this well. Of all of us he was the most solid in build and the strength obvious in his arms and legs also told of his hard living these past months. Not for the first time I wondered about his father. I had never met the man other than in passing when I had called in to see our Mother, when Debbie was born. I expected that he now lived somewhere in Sydney moving about the community that seemed on the edge of the city, even if it was physically located within the heartbeat of the city itself.

I suspected that he had been lost to drinking. Our mother didn't talk about him much and we didn't ask. All I knew was that he had been a violent man, which made him less of a man and more of a creature of the night.

Tom had inherited his solid build from his dad; he was sturdier than either of his brothers Allan or Josh who looked to favour our side. Sean was the slightest amongst us and he had developed a powerful wiry strength which came from his talents and hard work more than from his father. Shape shifting did that to you and Sean's talents as a shape shifter had gone beyond mine.

To keep my mind busy and from falling into darkness and for a moment I wondered what Tom had learnt over the past months. His skills were unknown, untested. Even John had been unable to advise me of them. The Lore of the Featherfoot wasn't confined to physical skill, but included a spiritual strength. It was a gift that was difficult to measure.

It had taken two years for John to confirm that Tom belonged amongst the Featherfoot. The men of this Lore had held doubts amongst them and as such had delayed his training. It hadn't helped that he managed to get himself into all manner of trouble which wasn't uncommon at his age, but yet this shrouded his skills and potential.

I knew with some irritation that it had only been the apparent interest of the Spirit men and women in Tom's talents which had fired the Featherfoot into taking on Tom's training with anything bordering on seriousness. Andrew had told me that the Mimi would like to have seen to Tom's training; in fact they still hoped to capture his heart to this end.

This advice had fired John up enough to approach the Elders amongst the Featherfoot once Andrew had offered an alternative path. That had made John take Tom's training with more seriousness and I was pleased for that at least. I had begun to think that John wasn't the right mentor for my younger brother, his interest was keenly with his own son and more what Tom could bring to Denis's experience than in stretching Tom's skills, allowing him to learn.

That one of the Kadaitcha Men amongst them had come forward unexpectedly and offered to mentor Tom's skills had shocked everyone. As close as the Mimi and the Featherfoot were to each other, they competed fiercely for men of skill. The greatest difference between the two groups was that each lived in a different reality, a different world. These worlds were not open to everyone. They excluded those who didn't have knowledge of their existence or the strength of the Dreaming and they excluded the uninitiated.

It was odd what people accepted as their reality as they rationalized their existence, While I struggled with the darkness it was a inner battle and I fought for a grip on my thoughts, for mastery over my consciousness and drove my mind to cling to any rationalization.

The Kadaitcha Man, who both Tom and Denis had spent the last months with had not been known to me, but had been known to Andrew, or rather Andrew knew of him. He moved easily between the worlds and his reputation amongst both the Featherfoot and Mimi was strong in Far North Queensland and throughout Arnhem Land. He and his enclave were even known to the Central Desert mob and Billy Black had been able to tell Andrew a great deal about him. That was why I had agreed to allow the Kadaitcha Men to have so great an influence on Tom's training these past months, and on his future, I knew they would be testing him.

John had agreed to allow Denis to join Tom in the opportunity now presented to the boys. Both John and I knew that the Kadaitcha were the strongest sorcerers' of the Featherfoot Lore, indeed they were the very core of their society and it was a considerable honour for Tom and Denis to be offered this chance. Few were given such training and even now I wondered how the Kadaitcha Man had known of Tom and his talents. Such was the mystery of the Kadaitcha Men.

Like the strong and curious Emu, the Kadaitcha had been driven from their place in our lands and pushed back by the relentless spread of Western society and the cities and towns. Their Lore was unacceptable in a more modern world. People were unable to understand and grasp their strengths, their powers and as such their Lore, these men had been forced into what was almost a secret society of the most powerful of spiritual men. They were the cleverest of men.

The Kadaitcha Lore was largely drained from the consciousness of our own people, drained by the acceptance and exposure to other cultural influences and yet, I knew that the Kadaitcha was at the very core of our existence. They lived in the shadows of our world and time, a secret people and place.

It was a core, now largely ignored now by men throughout the land. None the less, it was a core that in this day survived in the thinning ranks of men of great skill and power. A core, a knowledge they guarded well, with reason.

The Kadaitcha nurtured the secrets of the Dreaming and the Dreamtime, our very history and culture. I wondered for a moment just how much had been lost, as so much had passed from the consciousness of societies. How much of this would Tom chance on?

I had felt often as men that we had largely lost our way and our place in our world, particularly as I considered the troubles I had seen within our society. Women seemed to have preserved this, but we as men no longer needed to hunt or fight for the security of our families. Instead we fought amongst ourselves and hunted for strange things, perhaps most of all for a reason to live.

I wondered if Tom had come to understand that yet. It wasn't something that could easily be explained. The Kadaitcha and the emu had a lot in common and it was in this way that their Lore could be understood. Tom would have been shown it. The Kadaitcha Man, his mentor would have explained or shown the boys in the very first instance. In their very first ceremony this would have become apparent.

To understand the emu, was to understand the Kadaitcha Lore. The emu man was the protector, the core of his society. The emu man was the one who carried messages, who guarded his people and carried warnings keeping them safe and it was he who fearlessly flew to the defence of all.

It's from here that the Featherfoot had drawn their name. It was the light tread of the Kadaitcha Men who was able to move swiftly and silently and with deadly accuracy, who wore the symbolic feathering on their feet and bodies in ceremony, which marked them as powerful and of a high order.

The emu male was the judge of life and the bearer of the consequence. It was his place to guard his family, to keep them safe and to make the decisions that would ensure this.

Many men had forgotten this quality. That which was the essential essence of man and it would eventually fall to Tom and to Denis, as it did to the Featherfoot and the Kadaitcha Men, to help remind others, seen in everything they did. They were to be a large part of what was the survival of our future, and the future of all.

This was the Kadaitcha Lore and it was little enough, the core of our humanity, and the essence of what was Man. My mind gripped the thought of the Kadaitcha, gripped and held tightly to their Lore and promise as I felt myself tumble over the edge of darkness into a strange existence… feathered by what I knew was happening around me.

Falling became a simple thing; it was like being drawn into a current and swept along into the darkness.

THE LORE OF THE FEATHERFOOT

Tom:

The trip back to Denis's place in the back of the truck was torturous for everyone and watching the jarring which hurt Taipan further, was difficult to accept. There was little we could do about it though and as we watched him wince in pain I found it particularly hard as I had never seen Taipan up against something which seemed to weaken him. He had always been strong, sure and a secure rock in a shifting world.

After a time though, he seemed to find himself a place in his thoughts to retreat to, this seemed to help not only him, but all of us.

I wondered how Sean had got on for a moment, in an attempt to distract myself from Taipan's suffering. Not knowing if we would be successful with the ultra lights as John had planned, Sean had gone in another direction and was working now with Taipan's Fathers people.

This mob had a less amiable relationship with the local landholders and as such they were trying other avenues in attempts to locate Taipan once they had heard he was missing. Sean had thought nothing of first seeking them out, then joining up with the men who had stood in judgement over the matter with Jenna. Though, outside the Bora Ring Sean was a powerful adversary, I knew they would accept him readily as did he accept their help under these circumstances. The only thing that mattered in this was Taipan; Sean would not allow what personal feeling he might have to stand in the way of achieving his goal in finding our brother.

We knew now that Ty was safe, and I wondered for a moment how we could get that message through to the others, and have Sean make his way back to Johns.

For a moment my thoughts flicked across to what the others would have thought of Sean's Spirit animal when he had arrived in their camp and that gave rise to a small smile of satisfaction. I hope it scared them. John had been very descriptive but he hadn't known what to call the spirit creature when he had seen Sean shift. The features he recalled most were the stripes across the hind legs and long powerful jaw. He wasn't so good at identifying animals and had not witnessed Sean's shape shift before, only Taipan's so he didn't know Sean could draw on some weird spirit animals from the kadimakara of the Dreamtime.

Although I pestered Sean at times, all he could tell me was that he drew on an ancient instinct, and often had little control over the animal spirits. In some ways they ruled his transition which was a bit disconcerting. He had told me that it was instinct and necessity which played the greatest part in drawing on the Dreamtime Spirits. He had given up worrying about the shape shift form, it was beyond his control but it always served his purpose.

I knew the others would not yet have heard that we had been successful in finding Ty. They also carried a large part of the responsibility for his predicament. They should have known there was a possibility of shooters about as it was their country after all. Taking to the skies wasn't a good idea in such a situation, even I understood that and I felt an edge of anger at their reckless ignorance. I had expected that they would surely have been aware of the risks and not for the first time I wondered at the skills they shared with each other. I guess I had become too accustomed to what most saw as paranormal stuff. Expecting it to control all and be all powerful. Even I had learnt the stupidity in such an opinion, it was an opinion marking ignorance.

The real world didn't really seem very real anymore to me, the world I had understood was really only as full as I had allowed. I had come a long way from the child I was, a short three years ago. Though to me now, my childhood in Sydney seemed a lifetime away. Had I really ever been so blind or unaware of what was around me?

For a brief moment my thoughts slipped back to the times I had watched my father talking to himself in his alcohol haze and weed fog that he often lived in, and I wondered if he had indeed even really been by himself? His demons were real I had no doubt of that now. I also had no doubt that they had delighted in tormenting him for his weakness, he was a marked man who was a mere shadow of what he should have been. Then I cut myself off from my memories, they were of another time, another world and I would not allow them to make me a lesser person, or weaken who I could be, or was. I didn't need the memory of the beatings which flicked through my thoughts occasionally. I was a different person now.

These past weeks had been something again. To be amongst a company of men who could see what I could see. Those who could talk to the Dreaming Spirits that often plagued my world, had affected me in a way that I had not expected. I wasn't strong enough to talk to these Spirits, but it was enough that I could see them for the time being. As I grew stronger, as my strength and knowledge grew it might be something I could do. I knew my skills would constantly change, flowing like a river and changing in strength and power, as long as I held the knowledge safely to myself.

Glancing across at Denis, I wondered how he now perceived me. He had known I could see Spirits and yet he had perhaps not understood how hard that was. For the first time he had felt the odd man out. He was one of the Featherfoot who could not see or hear the Spirits, his gifts were of another nature. They were as strong as my own in their own way, possibly they were even more useful, but they were different and I had learnt that in my time in the bush.

The Kadaitcha Men had explained how often the men of their creed were paired, even with the Featherfoot, each of their strengths complementing the other and together the pairs worked to make a whole. The strongest of the Kadaitcha Men worked together with others, it was their way. It was a structure built into their ceremony, their power as the men of the High Order of their skills. In this way, no man, no one man could claim to be the most powerful amongst them and as such destroy what had been built over time since the Dreaming Spirits had first walked, danced, and made love across the Earth, a time since they had bought order to our world.

Then there was the pairing of men and women, that was a talent apart from all others and while I had said nothing, I knew within myself that this was what now set Taipan and Aine apart. Perhaps even set Sean and Jenna apart and as they drew on each other's strengths they could achieve far beyond what others could achieve. That type of pairing was the essence of our world, not just its centre.

Denis and I had been through a lot together, mostly in the business of growing up and I wondered if his dad thought my company was truly a good idea for his son. We had managed to stay out of too much trouble, and what trouble we had got into, we had managed to keep from him. It was good to have a mate who understood your world, one with whom it was easy to talk to about things that other people found daunting. My training had seemed slow, but Denis was able to share a great deal with me once my first initiation was done. Perhaps this is what John had intended.

Den had a knowledge of our world that was much greater than mine and I understood that. It was a knowledge gifted from his fathers, and his grandfathers. My father had played no part in my life, at least no part that I would recognize. Taipan, John and even Andrew had been my fathers and for a moment I smiled as I wondered how they would accept such a thought. Particularly Andrew, he already had his hands full with the two young kids and yet he found time to help me to understand my world, the world of the Featherfoot which had now come to accept me as one of their own.

A man took on only what made him a better man, Ty had taught me that and it was perhaps the most relevant and meaningful of my lessons I had learnt over the years of growing and becoming a man.

I knew I still had a long way to go, a lot to learn and heaps to experience but I was a better person for having these men in my life.

None of this would have been possible if it wasn't for the man now stretched out on the old mattress. In this, what was happening now, I felt I could perhaps find a way to repay the gifts he had nurtured in me and the gift of knowledge he had given me despite the troubles I had caused him over the years. I guess I couldn't expect everything to be perfect, he would know that and that consolation made me smile wryly.

It was night by the time we finally arrived back, and I felt different when I at last climbed down from the truck tray, after helping Ty move off the tray himself. Something had changed in the time I had been away, and yet everything was the same as I remembered it. Then I realized it was perhaps I who had changed and as I settled that knowledge around me I began to observe what was going on.

Aine had run out from the house at our arrival and now as she reached Taipan, even I had to admit there was something grey about his appearance. She would not allow any of us help him but herself. She was so tiny up against him, it was almost comical.

"Damn it Taipan! Don't you ever… ever do that to me again!" she demanded of him, unsure whether to cry or scold.

Ty at first silently suffered her attempts to help him, but she was too small to offer any real physical support and as his eyes reached mine, I understood and stepped quickly up to his side to help, careful not to grip him where his injuries were.

"Kitten, OK. I promise for the time. You'll have to put up with me for a while anyway, I'm not going anywhere soon…" he almost whispered, his voice strained and gruff, laboured with a number of small gasps and I realized he has suffered much more than he had let on in the back of the truck, during the hours of driving.

As we helped him up onto the verandah, I noticed others about. Old Granny was back on the lounge but I knew not to greet her, but my eyes did it anyway and she smiled. I had come to accept her presence around John and Marnie's home, though I wouldn't mention it to anyone. She had with her a small child, a boy who was playing at her feet, he was perhaps three or four years of age built like a whippet but he had the most striking depth in his eyes and as we moved indoors the child followed silently.

I knew some children could see the Spirit people, Deb had taught me that but with no kids around I had no grounds for reference and as Aine fussed about Ty, trying to discover the extent of his injuries, she ignored the small child. This told me it was likely that she couldn't see him as he wasn't of their world.

The little boy stayed close to both Aine and Ty, curious about what was going on, though he looked very serious of nature and saying nothing at all he climbed up onto the back of the lounge, and perched high where Aine and John had settled Ty. Aine was busy still inspecting the different scrapes across his body and scolding him softly.

"You coming outside?" Denis asked quietly moving up behind me as I stood back watching the child, who was mostly focused on Ty, as was Aine. The two of them both seemed completely oblivious to everything else, though I could see Ty struggled to pay attention to Marnie's careful probing questions on the condition of his wounds. His skin colour definitely looked worse to me it was as though he was really not with us. Though I was reassured when they decided there were no bones broken, it was mostly soft tissue damage and bruising.

"Ahh.. yeah. Sure," I answered absently.

We left them quietly and made our way back out the door. The room had seemed overcrowded with us all there, even Marnie look flustered and there was little that could fluster Denis's Mum. Perhaps the prospect of Taipan being hurt more than any of us thought was a daunting concept for her and I wondered, sincerely hoping it was only the jarring of the long drive that was causing the problem.

"Well it's good to be back. I could sure use a feed, I wonder if Mum has anything in the kitchen?"

"Maybe we can check it out later, I think they're a bit busy. I'm going to heat up the donkey and take a good long shower."

As we made our way over towards the shed which was where Den slept, and that I shared when I was here, I was once more reminded of the changes I had felt when we had arrived. I knew there was nothing we could do while there were so many of the oldies around, so there was no use in getting underfoot. Taipan was in good hands now and it was a relief to let go of the worries which had travelled with me.

It had been a few months since we had been back in the shed. Denis had been down in the community with me before Andrew had told us we were required up here for ceremony. The Elders amongst the Kadaitcha Men had summoned us, it was a privilege, indeed a considerable honour and nothing would have prevented us from attending that initiation. John had been insistent as had Andrew and I was aware that it was indeed an honour to be called by these men.

Now, as we made our way into the dimness of the sheds interior, Denis hunted around for the lantern which usually stood just inside the door but it didn't come to hand.

"What the hell? Where is the damn thing?"

It was a few moments before our eyes properly adjusted, only to be blinded by the flash of the long match which Den used to light the lantern. Then as the light spread across the floor and our sight finally reached into the shadows and corners of the shed both of us stood there amazed.

The place had been transformed. The pool table was about the only thing that had remained the same. Denis's double bed had been decked out in rich colours and mosquito netting now graced its presence, but it was like no bug net I had ever seen, it was decorated in loose ribbons, glittery stuff and some crystals.

My big single bed, which had been brought in to replace the old hard cot I had at first used, was now covered neatly and strewn with pillows and magazines. The whole place had been redecorated in what was a very feminine style with filmy curtains and blowy stuff draped about and as Denis swore softly, I realized this had to be the work of Alex.

"I'm gunna kill her," he said softly with conviction as he set the lantern aside and moving to the door bellowed his sisters name.

This was gunna be good I thought, and moving easily into the shed, I made my way over to my bed now against the far wall and shifted some of the cushions and gear onto the floor and to the few crates Alex had arranged as a table decorated with a cloth. My bed had obviously become the lounge and as I settled myself I considered the added comfort of it. The table could stay as that was a good idea. I wasn't too sure about all the little cushions though, they seemed a bit pesky; then again I could thin them out.

I listened as I heard Alex obviously fly out of the house and meet Denis mid way between the two buildings. They both were in fine form and I grinned as the screaming match began.

"Don't you dare move any of my stuff! "Alex screeched.

"Your stuff! Get it out of my shed!"

"Mum said I could use it. You're never here... you haven't been here for months."

"I don't care... I'm here now and you ain't gunna be..."

The argument moved little from those parameters and it wasn't until Marnie came out to quieten them that I sat up, realizing they were bringing the argument into the shed now. Alex was the first to storm in through the doors and as she caught sight of me, she glared resentfully.

"Don't you mess up my lounge!" she spat as she marched over towards me and grabbed at the pillows I had dislodged from their artful arrangement. I just put up my hands in mock surrender, grinning at the fury in her eyes. As Marnie and Tom moved into the room, she tossed me a killing look before she turned back to them, still clutching the pillows like a shield in front of her.

"Mum… you said I could," she complained.

"I know luv, but you must see the boys are back. Look, you can share."

"I'm not sharing my bedroom!" Denis complained angrily. "You can't ask us to share with Alex and her friends, they have the house. No… no it's not on. We need our space… besides I built the shed."

"Denis you know that's not true," Marnie warned.

"It is. Dad and I built it for me and she isn't gunna get it while I am here. That's the end of it!" he warned, moving into what he clearly felt was his domain and throwing himself on the bed he struggled with the netting attempting to sweep it aside. "An' you can get rid of all this stuff hanging here," he added glaring impatiently at the decorations scattered over the netting.

"The table's good," I offered, only to get a quick warning to stay out of it.

"For goodness sake, we can work it all out in the morning," Marnie suddenly announced, her voice making the decision something of an edict as she began to firmly usher a complaining Alex out of the shed. "You have to give the boys some room Alex, you must see that."

"It's not fair…how am I going to study for my finals!"

"You will manage. Besides you… oh damn."

Suddenly Marnie appeared back at the door. "I have told Taipan and Aine to stay down here for the night, they are taking Alex's room…"

"Oh Mum you didn't!" Alex screeched in complaint.

"Alex, be quiet. Ty's pretty crook… it's done. You will just have to share with the boys for tonight, or you sleep in the lounge room." Turning back to us she spoke again to Denis. "You can share with your sister surely."

"Not bloody likely...she can sleep on the floor."

"Denis!"

"No its OK.. she can have my bed," I said suddenly. "I can share with Denis ore set up the swag on the floor. That's OK isn't it?" I asked, checking for his acceptance.

"Nup… she can sleep on the floor," he protested, but his small smile told me he was really kidding, and his Mum recognized it.

"Well that is settled then."

"I'm not sleeping on the floor!" Alex suddenly protested as she too stepped up to the door behind her Mum.

Marnie turned back to her. "Of course you're not… he's kidding. You should know your brother by now." Ushering her towards the house we listened to her protests which her Mum seemed to not hear. "It's only for a night Alex, surely you don't mind. You can sleep on the lounge if you like but I thought it might get noisy… Could you help me with dinner Darl'… "

"Mum…!" Alex's dying protest was half hearted and mostly accepting, so climbing to my feet I stretched my aching muscles and glanced at Denis.

"I'm going for that shower, the water should be ready in a half hour."

Den had begun ripping at the dainty decorations scattered about the mosquito netting, his friendly and somewhat triumphant glance dismissed me and I headed out from the shed leaving him to wreck what havoc he deemed necessary. Alex would be furious but what went down between sister and brother was their own affair.

As I built the fire under the old donkey water heater and sat back, enjoying the flicker and catch of the flame, I considered the sense of change I still felt. It had little to do with the shed; it was more a sense that stayed with me. It seemed more to do with the ceremonies I had been through. The Kadaitcha Men were strong and their Lore was the strongest I had witnessed. It was no wonder they were held with such regard and it was no wonder their Lore was so sensitive to any form of exposure.

It had been impressed on both Den and I that this wasn't a Lore spoken of amongst women, but neither was it spoken about readily amongst men. The greatest power of the Kadaitcha Men was nurtured within the enclaves; it was the business of no man, only the Men of the Lore. This was a trust given to us both and we understood it well and the consequences of breaching the trust were not to be considered lightly. It was a Lore I was forbidden to even discuss with Taipan, though they had said that he would know this, he would be shown what he needed to understand and given the consideration of a Father.

Somehow though I felt that this cut me off from him, from my brothers on whom I had come to depend so much and I wasn't sure that this was what I wanted. I had spent too many years as a kid without brothers, or older males of my family to depend on and it was a lonely existence in some ways. I was suddenly beginning to measure the value of brothers and I knew I had not paid it enough attention over the last three years.

Looking towards the house I wondered for the moment how Ty was getting on, sure he'd be sleeping. Aine would still be fussing and she wouldn't want me adding to her worries. I could check in the morning I decided.

Testing the heat in the forty four gallon drum, which was the donkey, I settled back down, it would be a few minutes yet. The shower was in a small enclosed space specifically built for its purpose though in reality it was a prefab aluminium garden shed built not far from the house, it offered the only hot showers but it worked well.

The small gas water heater they had in the kitchen was used for cooking and washing though I knew they sometimes used the hot water from the gas wall heater for basin bathing, but gas was a valued commodity as it had to be bought in from the Lions Den at Helenvale, or further afield at Cooktown and it was a labour-some task to fill the gas bottles, a real chore and one which fell to whoever used the gas usually, so that was something I avoided. Keeping the wood pile up was hard enough though I didn't mind chopping kindling and the petrol chainsaw made collecting it easy when I took my old ute along to bring the forest wood back.

A movement in the darkened shadows of the yard had me looking up and silently I watched Alex stride between the house and the shed, I grinned. Even from here I could see she was still in a spit. Her step had purpose and I didn't doubt Denis was gunna cop another ear full. Just as well I had left him to it I thought, she was a little firebrand and I usually tried to stay out of her way when she was on the rampage.

Alex was something of a problem for me. I found her as cute as a kitten but she was Denis's sister, not to mention John's daughter and that put her out of my reach as far as I was concerned. I wasn't about to malign myself in John's opinion, as one of her conquests. When it fell apart, it wouldn't work for any of us beyond that. I enjoyed seeing her fire up though and she did that regularly. I could think of a million ways to quieten her, distract her thinking and turn her ill-temper to laughter, but most of it had more to do with sex than friendship and I had decided long ago I wasn't going to go down that road with her.

It had been easy when she was younger, but now… now it was getting harder and I figured the best approach was to find another distraction for myself. With Taipan here, I planned on spending more time up this way rather than in the community near Nimbin. I had things to do that would keep me in the district. I would have to work something out this time. Maybe I could hunt around for some accommodation in the area or even build myself a shack somewhere in the forest. Then maybe I could work out how to stay close to family and friends. I wasn't keen to break out on my own just yet.

When the donkey finally reached the heat I knew I'd like, I grabbed my towel and gear and headed towards the small shower shed. I was going to enjoy the spill of heated water over my skin, and the chance to wash the dust out of my hair. I needed a haircut and a good clean-up. I had been able to manage the sparse chin growth but it would be nice to shave it off in a thorough fashion for a change. Yeah… I was looking forward to this.

When I got back to the shed, a towel draped around my hips and my gear in my hands, it immediately became apparent that there were going to be problems. I had forgotten about Alex and she had made over my old bed for herself and was lounging back under the covers, reading contentedly, settled for the night.

Denis grabbed his own gear and headed out towards the shower. "You leave me any hot water?"

"Yeah… some. You might have to give it a minute though to heat through, the fire's still good."

Headed for where I had dropped my duffle bag last, I ratted through what gear had been left and it was good to see that Marnie had thought to check the gear and had washed everything grotty in it. I had planned to sleep naked but this wasn't going to work with Alex about so I grabbed a pair of board shorts that had seen better days and keeping the towel about my hips hauled them over my butt, carefully conscious of Alex behind me.

As I made for Denis's much bigger bed which I figured he wouldn't mind that we could share, I considered an idea that had just occurred to me.

"You any good at cutting hair?" I asked, more out of something to say than any serious intent.

"You want a hair cut?" she asked sweetly, curious it seemed.

"Yeah. I'd ask your Mum only she seems a bit busy with us all about."

For a moment Alex considered me, as I climbed into the bed. It seemed she was giving it some thought which surprised me. It would solve my problem, though I had been half expecting a curt and impatient response.

"I haven't cut anyone's hair before, though my girlfriend would love to have a go, I know. She wants to be a hairdresser, she'd love it."

"She nice?" I asked partly teasing, partly out of curiosity.

Alex pulled a face and picked up her book again. "You'll probably like her… she's female."

I laughed as though to disabuse her of her opinion, but I was surprised at the tone of her voice. Then as I considered her words I decided her attitude was a good thing. "Yeah… you're probably right. I could do with some female company."

"Yeah well Julie could probably cut it. I can ask her tomorrow if you like?"

"Yeah thanks. If she makes a hash of it I will just shave it all off."

Again Alex pulled a face. "Thats a bit drastic don't you think?"

"Nah... makes it easy. I'd do it now only I don't have any shears, it's a bit thick."

"Oh well... I guess you can please yourself. Blokes are lucky like that. I suppose you want the lamp out?"

"No... no you read. Denis will sort that out, I'm beat. You don't mind if I just sleep?"

"Why should I mind? Go for it," she said, dropping her attention back to the book she had been reading.

I tried, I turned over keeping my back to her but sleep didn't come so easily despite the fact that I was tired. Eventually I did slip into a dreamless peace. I couldn't recall what time the others settled, so it must have worked for me in the end and when I woke to the morning it almost seemed all too soon, I had slept like a log. But in the bright light of the day I knew I had needed the time to recuperate. There was just so much that I had to assimilate, I had a lot to think about and napping often was the best way of dealing with things.

It was later than I wanted, but having slept well had its compensations. Both Denis and Alex had vanished when I eventually surfaced the next morning. Alex had gone to school but Denis? I guessed the place to find him was in the kitchen. As I made my way towards the house I wondered how Ty was getting on and as I headed towards the kitchen, I stopped into Alex's old room. I knew where it was, there weren't so many rooms in the house that it would be difficult but I knew from past experience, when I had been involved in Alex's bid to sneak out years ago, that her room was the one off to the right at the front of the house.

Ty was sleeping in the double bed there but Aine was nowhere to be seen, so instead of disturbing him, I moved on towards the kitchen where I could hear most of the family were still gathered.

Aine and Marnie were having a cuppa, with the remnant of a full morning scattered about the kitchen. Den was doing toast and poached eggs and that looked good, smelt even better so I added two more eggs to the pan and stood waiting for his toast to announce it was burnt enough before I slipped mine under the grill.

"How is Ty this morning?" I asked Aine, in a break in the conversation flowing around the room.

Aine chewed her lip; I could see she wasn't happy.

"Not as good as I hoped. I am wondering if we should get him into Cooktown or maybe even Cairns today."

"I really think we should wait till John gets back Darl'," Marnie broke in. "He knows where to find the others, he shouldn't be more than a few hours, not much longer Luv."

"What is the problem?"

Aine caught my eyes, hers troubled. "He didn't sleep very well, he is very lethargic Tom. I don't like it at all... there's something not right and I think he's got worse."

"Is Sean back?" I asked, wondering now at his absence.

"John has gone to get him," Marnie added. "He dropped Alex off and headed out to where the others are camped. He said he'd only be maybe four or five hours, he should be back by tonight for sure."

I had an invading sense that I had known about this, there was something familiar about the whole scenario and as I ate, I listened to the talk going on around me. The concern in Aine's voice and the seriousness of her expression worried me but I was unsure about what it could be. I felt that Marnie's reassurances were not meant for me and when I finally finished I simply stood and waited for my feet to take me where I knew I had to be.

Ty was still resting his back to the door so I moved in around the bed to better gauge his colour. There was enough room at the end for me to sit, so climbing onto the bed I sat cross-legged. I didn't feel the need to touch him, though his skin still had that pallor about it which concerned me.

Closing my eyes I found the place in my mind where I felt the most free, it allowed the world to slip away from me as I had been taught. I knew when the others arrived within reach of us, I knew when they left but I was unconcerned with their movement and they knew not to disturb me. Taipan was my only focus and I needed to allow the knowledge about me to become a part within my own.

Time had no meaning for me, but when I opened my eyes I knew there was something very wrong. What it was I didn't understand fully. Ty still slept, he looked almost dead and indeed I feared that this was what it was happening. It was only the slight movement of the blanket as he drew each breath that reassured me.

What I felt was his absence, even though his body was here in front of me. It seemed that his shadow had left him, deserted his body leaving only a shell and as the realization came to me I climbed off the bed. I could see him, I could touch him, but my brother wasn't here and suddenly I realized I had to find him. I wasn't sure how I could go about it. I needed the help of others more knowledgeable than me. I should have been able to reach him, to touch his shadow but it hadn't been there for me to reach.

I knew the slam of the front door would disturb everyone but I had no time to lose, containing my fear was struggle enough, I was driven by my fury. Despite hearing the others coming to find out what was going on I wasn't distracted, I didn't have the luxury of time. There were things in the shed I needed, tools I required and as I moved quickly that way with a single minded determination, it was as though I went without a volition of my own. I felt the alarm in the air, an alarm cast by others at my sudden action; they were confused by my actions. I heard things minutely, heard the foot fall that I knew was Denis strangely enough.

"What's going on?" he asked as he reached me, noting my scramble for the soft leather pouch in the bottom of my duffle bag.

"Ty... I know what's wrong," I said tersely. "I need to call the Kadaitcha Men; help me."

Uncaring if Denis followed me or not, I strode out of the shed, his help would be invaluable but I wasn't dependent on it, my anger would sustain me. I needed to find a place where Taipan could move to easily, a place he was drawn to and I knew exactly where that would be. I strode towards the track that led to his bush camp as I knew without a doubt that his Spirit or his Shadow would be drawn there. I was conscious of someone following me but I didn't care, I knew what to do. I heard the murmur of voices behind me, Aine was crying after being told something she didn't like hearing. Denis must have spoken to her, I hoped he had given her some explanation, it was beyond me, but as I reached the bush and moved into it I became lost to the people I loved, my friends.

I let the bush fill me; the noisy silence took me into its own world. I fought to cut myself off from the world of men, to become one with my surroundings as I moved quickly along the path, I was at one with the world which moved closer to another world, the world of the spirit men. I had a purpose and no one could distract me from it, there was no time to lose.

When I reached the bush shelter, I took a moment to decide where I would begin the ceremony. The fire place in front of the camp shelter would not suit my needs. I knew without hesitation what to do, so moving closer to the quiet shelter of the trees I began to prepare a place.

Scooping out a hollow and clearing the area quickly I set a small fire to help me concentrate, gathering the timber within easy reach. Focusing, I once more tried to find the place within me where I could work from. My fingers wrapped around the large, carefully shaped bull-roarer, feeling its weight and its strength, understanding its call. Its strong, fine cord tangled my fingers as it became the message stick I would need to summon help.

When Denis joined me around the fire, my concentration wavered little. I had expected him. His strong sight would be a help, his mind was able to cast thought abroad great distances and these thoughts would find his father. He also would be summoned to return soon.

When I knew I was ready I stood, I found a place in the clearing then I was aware that Aine had also joined us but I ignored her and she knew enough not to distract me. The other women had left us earlier seeing that I was intent on some ceremony as they had not wanted to distract me from what was clearly men's business, but Aine had felt the need to return. Holding the cord of the bull-roarer in a strong grip I began its wind up, I listened to the low hum build of its song. The deep tones of the bull-roarer began to fill the air, filling the silence with a deep resonance that was difficult to ignore as it vibrated through the forest.

The deep thrum of the sound carried far, it travelled out over the forest calling to those who I intended to hear. The forest became silent within the echo of its roar, it sounded amongst the trees vibrating the air, the sound moving smoothly through the gullies and up the small rise to where the camp nestled. The sound travelled on the tide of its own momentum.

I sustained the roar, fed it with my anger, my determination with the twist of cord in my fingers biting my skin; it was rubbing my finger raw but I ignored that, it was nothing. When the breeze caught and gave a twist to the spinning lead, the tone began to die then it was reborn. Even my hand began to vibrate in tune with the song of the bull-roarer and its sound fed my Spirit. It settled my drive and I felt the power about me even as my wrist felt the strain of the movement that gave birth to the bull-roarers song.

Over the following few hours Den and I took turns, but we did have some breaks which gave the forest life some relief from the deep hum before we once more threw the message to the winds again. In the end, Marnie came up from the house.

"I am sure you don't need to keep calling," she said carefully, reluctant to be criticising. "Those you are calling would have heard, and each time you call, Taipan becomes restless and Aine gets upset."

That stopped us. It was only then that we considered we might have overdone it, but I felt reassurance in that we had reached those who needed to hear. Den and I took a break and raided the supplies Aine had left in the kitchen looking for something to eat that the possum hadn't found, saying little. It was only then I realized that it was past noon, John was expected back soon and he would be able to advise us. It was time to wait.

Sean was the first to arrive up from the house and the relief I felt when he stepped into the clearing was tangible.

"Hey," he said greeting us. "You've been causing something of a racket, what's it all about?" Moving over to the fire where Den and I had been waiting, he settled quickly.

"I'm glad you're here," I said ignoring his question for the moment as I considered how to answer him. "How's Ty?"

Sean shook his head. "He looks sick as a dog, his father wants to take him into Cooktown when we saw him, he feels there is something ill about Alex's room but when I had heard the bull-roarer earlier, I realized…"

"No!" I said quickly. "I have called the Kadaitcha Men, it's a sickness of the Spirit Sean, I am sure of it."

"How do you mean?"

"I can't feel him. I mean I can usually feel people about me, but I can't feel Taipan even though he's in front of me. I can't explain it. I can even feel the Spirit children, the young ones. But not Ty this time, it's like he is not here. The healer checked him over at the homestead yesterday, no broken bone, just superficial stuff. Some of it's deep but there didn't seem to be infection either. They all considered him quite lucky not to have broken something. I mean he was even well enough for Andrew to leave, he headed back yesterday."

Sean's face grew serious. "How about here, can you feel him in the camp?"

I shook my head. "I mean the sense of him is stronger here, but he isn't here."

He considered what I said and then looked up. "That was what the racket was about, you realize you over did it. The district will be in an uproar over the sound, there will be questions."

"Yeah…well I didn't know. I mean I knew… but I didn't think. I wanted to be sure…"

He grinned, "Fair enough, I'm glad of it. We will just ignore any questions, we can blame each other. His grin was fleeting and dismissive. Well I guess we will just wait for them to get here, they can't be far away, the Kadaitcha Men travel swiftly when they want to."

For a moment we watched the flicker of the fire, it was comforting. Then thoughtfully Sean looked up. "You mentioned you have seen Spirit Children about?"

"Yeah, cute little one. He is down at the house mostly. Why?"

Sean grinned, "They can hang around when they're looking for a birth mother, only one child?"

"Yeah."

"Then it's a good thing Jen isn't here," he added. "I wonder if Aine...?"

"What... a baby?" I said surprised then I thought about it. "God... what if Ty's really not going to pull through this?"

Sean scowled impatiently, "He'll pull through," he said quietly, with as much determination as I felt. "We'll have to find out how... who... has done this? Maybe his father has some idea. I can't think of anyone else..."

"Where is he?" Struggling to follow Sean's line of thought, I tried to remember Ty's father amongst those at the Bora grounds an age ago.

"He's down at the house... he came back with me when he heard Ty was hurt. I've spent some time with him and he was keen to hear anything I can tell him about Taipan. He has a lot of pride and he knows that business with Jen cost him dearly. It sits heavily with him and I think he's hoping too make amends somehow."

"Are you sure it isn't just a ploy... his interest?"

Sean shook his head. But I could see he wasn't sure.

"Well my experience with my Dad isn't so hot. They usually look after number one." As the words were born, I resented them. None of us, not even Sean had solid memories of a father he could rely on. It seemed to be a trait of a generation of men, or perhaps it stretched back further and I was being naïve.

Denis interrupted, I had forgotten about him in the emotion of the moment. "Sorry guys, but... "Shaking his head he continued. "He could be serious? I mean... my dad is great. You gotta give him a chance. Dad's a fair judge of character and he agreed to bring him to see Taipan. I mean he hasn't actually done anything... has he? He didn't even get involved with the payback really. That was all Ty's brother... what's-his-name and his mates"

"Yeah well they can all be awful," I said resentfully, then regretted my words. "Not your Dad, or even Taipan. He would be a great dad," I clarified. "An' Andrew..." I gave up before I exempted the lot of them. But I knew my criticism was more of my own experience. I had wanted my experience to be normal but I had to accept at some point that it wasn't. "OK. That was a bit harsh," I finished almost with apology.

Sean shot me a conciliatory smile. "So we give him the benefit of the doubt. That doesn't mean we give him carte blanche though." Standing suddenly he continued. "I'm getting back down there let me know when your lot turn up. I'm gunna keep an eye on the old bloke for Taipan's sake."

With that I watched him go, wondering if perhaps it was Ty's father who was responsible for Taipan's state. It bought home to me that it had to be someone who had done it, someone with enough strength to draw the shadow from a man weakened by accident. Someone who was intending that Ty should die of his injuries. The thought angered me afresh and I felt the frustration of ignorance and inexperience. I should have thought of that earlier, I might have been able to help him, or even protect him, damn!

The afternoon stretched out and seemed to become interminable. I was tempted to go down to the house and see how Ty was, but I knew the Kadaitcha Men would seek us out first so they wouldn't be pleased about a crowd. There would be explaining to do, and we would best do that alone. I felt in part I was flying blind here and I wasn't entirely sure what was going to happen or even if the Kadaitcha Men could help us. I didn't know enough about this whole business.

THE BLOOD LORE OF THE KADAITCHA MEN

Aine:

I wasn't sure whether to leave Ty with his Dad, thinking that perhaps they needed a moment? Ty looked so ill and he said very little. He didn't seem to appreciate that his Dad was here which I thought was a shame, yet each time I moved as though to leave, his fingers would tighten about mine.

The man was obviously concerned about his son, even I could see that and he sat quietly in the corner watching him. I thought he might have nodded off at one point but he was sitting so straight, so still, that I became convinced he was more lost in thought. He reminded me of Ty in some ways, his forehead and the depth in his eyes, but the set of his mouth was very different, not as kind perhaps.

At first he had been surprised at my presence, as surprised as I was to hear that he hadn't known about me. Even now he would occasionally glance my way as though I was still something of a surprise and there had been a conversation going on between John and Ty's father which I couldn't understand. That was until John had switched to English to answer a question and I had realized that those questions had been about me.

That had silenced Ty's Dad and now he glanced at me warily. I couldn't be bothered with him, not at the expense of looking after Ty.

He didn't have a fever, yet he sweated, and his skin was clammy, that worried me. He would have bouts of restlessness; much like he had suffered during the night. I was beginning to think that I preferred these bouts to the quiet, almost deathly stillness which inevitably followed.

I had to take a break after a while so when Marnie had come in and insisted that I stretch my legs, it had been good to do so, even the worried tears had helped but I couldn't take those back to the house.

That I could get Taipan to eat and drink, reassured me. His limbs were sound, I agreed with the healer in that and his gashes were beginning to heal. The bruising was worrisome but it was expected that it would worsen before it actually began to fade. It was just that he was so sleepy and listless that I couldn't be convinced that he was on the mend properly.

We had been at the point of taking him into Cooktown, but then Sean had arrived back from seeing Tom up at our camp and had said that they had sent for a spirit doctor. It was a sickness of the Spirit which he had probably bought back from the valley and that everyone agreed on this, helped me to accept what I found difficult. However if he was no better by tomorrow I wasn't going to allow him to stay here. If I had to drive him myself to the hospital I would.

It helped me when I felt Taipan slip into sleep. I could tell, his hold on my hand would soften and his breathing would become slow and rhythmic. His sleep only lasted for an hour at the most though and then he would begin again with the restless movements which troubled me more and more. It was as though he was fighting something and I wished I could understand what it was. It seemed in these bouts his father would sleep, and it confused me when I realized that. I wanted to say something, to ask about it but there never seemed to be the opportunity. I don't think he would have answered me anyway.

It was late in the afternoon while I was taking a break outside on the verandah, not far from the window of the room where I could wander down the verandah to check on how Ty was. His father was still with him and Sean had returned from talking to Tom who was sitting again with Taipan now. I didn't know what Tom was up to up at our camp but I understood that it in some way was helping, even Sean seemed confident in that and as far as I was concerned, any help was a good thing.

As I sat on the step, I watched Alex and her friends arrive home from school and head off towards the shed, which spared me the relief of a smile. She waved, and then veered my way, waving her friends on. The last few steps taken almost in a dance as she reached me.

"How is hubby?" she asked. The first cheery voice I had heard all day and it was hard to stop my suddenly watery eyes.

"Still not good. I want to take him to town to the hospital, but we are waiting on a healer or something."

"Oh... I thought he would be better. Did you hear the bull-roarer this morning?" Then with a moment's thought she frowned and queried me.

"That wasn't...?"

I nodded. "It was the boys, they were calling the healer."

"They called in the Kadaitcha Men?" she almost squeaked. "God! We thought someone was playing around. The school was in an uproar..."

"You could hear it from the school grounds? But that is miles..."

"Yeah. God I wonder if I should tell the girls?" Glancing over towards the shed she swung back, obviously expecting an answer from me.

I shrugged at first and then shook my head. "I wouldn't. The men won't like us talking about it."

"No not about the bull-roarer..." Then she grinned, "Though I could, Den owes me... he'd probably find it funny. Hmmm... maybe not. Anyway. I mean about the Kadaitcha Men. They sorta creep me out, if you know what I mean. I can't believe Den and Tom have taken their initiation with them. I mean I know I'm not supposed to talk about it but I heard Dad..."

"Well I don't think so. You know what the men are like," I said cutting her off, more to bring an end to the prattle than any other intent.

At the sound of a footfall behind us, I turned to see who was joining us. Warren had been in the lounge room earlier and as he approached now, I shot him a half hearted smile and turned back to Alex.

"You know Warren, Ty's half brother?" I asked of her quietly.

Alex considered him. Though her look wasn't entirely friendly.

"Yeah... you're the brother who tried to spear Sean, and Ty..., and Andrew," she said curtly.

Warren gave her something of a lopsided grin as I sat in surprise. I wouldn't have been so blunt, but I wished I could have been. I didn't much like Warren, but I was apparently more tolerant than Alex.

"Yep, you're right. It wasn't my spear that injured Sean though. I was over it by the time payback came about," he said carefully.

"Yeah sure. Easy to say when it's over. I was there! I didn't see you back down." Alex challenged.

"I couldn't," he explained. "Anyway it's done with, that was ages ago. Sean and I have found a common ground and I accept Jenna and he are..." Shrugging he looked for the word he would use but managed to make it sound something of a slight. "...together. An' Sean and I aren't really brothers you know."

"Oh... I thought..."

"No. There's no blood between us, though I actually like him," Warren added as he sat down, joining me on the stairs.

"Yeah well whatever... I've got company. So if you will excuse me," swinging away I watched as she left us, making her way towards the shed. Both Warren and I watched her, there was something about her attitude that made me want to apologize, but then I squashed the thought. I didn't want to apologize as she had only said what I wished I could've said, if I hadn't been so distracted with Ty.

With that thought I stood up, I wanted to get back to be with Ty. I shot a quick apologetic smile Warren's way, and left him on the step.

He had arrived with Taipan's father though Ty barely acknowledged the presence of his half brother, or his father for that matter. In fact every time Warren came into the bedroom I had noticed Ty's sudden restlessness. John had explained that they hoped to make amends with Taipan and were both wanting to make things right. Warren obviously felt that there was no real reason for this but my guess was that his father had insisted. I personally felt Warren didn't really want to be here but was here only because his father wanted it to be so.

I didn't much care either way about Warren, while I had compassion for Ty's Dad, I had little for his half brother. I also couldn't forget the sight of him throwing his spears at Taipan, who had also stood unarmed in the Bora ring that day. I even found it hard to be polite. Something in me rejoiced at Alex's bravado and I decided I would have to make a point of letting her know that, when this was all over.

I heard Alex come into the house soon afterwards and ask her Mum, about Tom and Denis. Marnie explained how they were up at our camp and that they would be staying up there tonight but when Alex announced she was headed up that way, Marnie tried to stop her. Alex would have none of it and offered instead to take up some food for the boys.

From the other room I had to smile, it was easy to see how Alex manipulated her mum when it suited her purpose and I wondered if Marnie realized it. Outside the afternoon was growing late, though there were a few hours left of daylight, as for me, I yearned for the simple peace of our bush camp. Sweeping my hand gently through Ty's ruffled hair I wondered where it was his thoughts were taking him. He was so restless, so lost at times to what was happening about him and I just wanted him back and well. It seemed however there was nothing for me to do about it.

I settled myself to wait on the healers, knowing that if things didn't improve I would be driving to Cooktown or Cairns with Ty tomorrow. Of that I was certain.

THE SPIT-FIRE

Alex:

The house was tense and had that sort of worried atmosphere which comes when someone is ill and no one is quite sure if it's a physical thing or something that pervades the spirit. I had felt that feeling before around people who were ill and I didn't like it. For this reason, I didn't bring my friends inside. Instead we stayed out in the shed but it too, didn't have the same atmosphere since Den had changed the decor that I had taken so many pains with. I wasn't too happy about losing my retreat to the guys but... well I guessed there wasn't a lot I could do about it.

Julie insisted on coming up to see Den and Tom with me and I wasn't sure I was too keen on the idea. I had told the girls that we were expecting the Kadaitcha Men to see to my uncle who was ill. They had accepted that easily and that had been enough reason for them to leave.

Only Julie hadn't understood the power of these men and had decided to stay. I liked Julie, she was uncomplicated but she didn't understand our culture and hadn't asked. I even had to explain who the Kadaitcha Men were for her. She was from Melbourne and didn't have much of a clue really. She would have had little to do with Aboriginal Lore.

Julie had grown up in suburbia, a place I didn't know much about but I did know it existed and that was at least something. I had often wondered what it would be like to live in a suburb somewhere with a million other kids around, to not be so isolated. Here we only had the tourists to deal with and they were easy to avoid as long as you understood what it was they were looking for and where they would be. Plus they only came around in droves in the tourist season, the wet season was all our own and that in itself isolated us up here.

What she had trouble understanding was that our Lore was part of us; it wasn't something we elected to believe in. That would be like electing to believe in life, it simply was.

Julie was a good friend to have, but because she didn't understand our ways it was difficult at times to include her. She had only been at the school this year and had found it hard to settle in. She had a gregarious nature though and that had helped when she had been drawn into our group. When she had started dating one of the boys we had all wondered how she would fit in, it hadn't lasted long but she had by then made friends amongst us girls. I knew that a few of the other girls were a bit resentful of her affluence, though it wasn't something she knowingly flaunted often.

Her dad worked out on the islands as a chef or something like that, he was only home on rotation for what were mid week, weekends. She lived with her mum just out of Cooktown near one of the beaches. I had been there once and it had taken me some time to get around to inviting her back to our place. It had made no difference to her though, the difference in our life styles and that was great. I think she thought of living in the forest as some sort of adventure. We had slipped into an easy friendship after that.

It had only been Julie who had volunteered to help bring the meat up to the camp with me; the others had said they wanted to get home before night fall. I knew that was an excuse. I had seen the reluctance in their faces to stay and understood the reason for it, but since Julie had the car the dark didn't faze her, she had decided to stay on and I was hoping she would be able to stay the night, perhaps even for the weekend.

If the boys were staying in Taipan and Aine's camp, then it would work out well. Julie had stayed over the weekend before and Julie's mum didn't seem to care much. She left Julie to make her own decisions. I wished sometimes that my parents would be as liberal, I was after all nearly eighteen now. Dad wasn't so easy going and at least expected me to let him know where I was headed and what plans I had. I guess as long as I lived under his roof then there wasn't a lot I could do about it.

Julie was keen to meet Tom. She had met Denis and she was a bit of a flirt, but Den didn't mind that. When I had asked her if she would like to have a go at cutting Tom's hair for him, she had really been keen, especially after I had described him to her. She had even bought along this fancy bag that held all the hair stuff she had, we had tried some of the stuff out before and it had been a lot of fun. Maybe it would be something we could get into later, it was always fun to try out different things and the opportunity didn't arise all that often.

We found the boys around the camp fire, they had built another fire aside from the main one and I wondered why, but I didn't question it. Maybe they had wanted to set a demarcation between the others. I knew Mum was intending to send both Warren and Taipan's dad up to stay in this camp overnight if they didn't leave soon, and it didn't look as though they planned on leaving tonight. With the arrival of Sean the house was now full and I knew Mum wasn't keen to have Warren and his Dad sleeping in the same quarters as Sean, she didn't trust them much either it seemed and she knew Sean wanted to stay close by Taipan.

"Hi you two, Mum sent us up with some food," I said by way of greeting to the guys as they watched us approach from the camp track. I could see the interest immediately in their eyes when they caught sight of us and I knew it had more to do with Julie's presence than mine, which served to irritate me somewhat. I wished Tom didn't have to be so blatant in his interest, as for Denis, I didn't care. In fact I hoped he would find Julie amusing.

I enjoyed a playful banter with Tom. I liked nothing more than to annoy him which was really quite difficult to do at times. He gave in so easily and yet I knew he could give as good as he got. I had seen him and Denis battle it out in a joking sort of manner and he never gave in with Denis. Occasionally I could get him to argue with me and those times I really enjoyed.

"Hey thanks," Tom said, standing to reach for the bread and snags we carried, passing them on to Den to deal with. "Grab a seat, there are some drinks still in the water barrel; I suppose you want a cup?"

"Yeah... thanks," I answered with a small grimace, though normally I wouldn't have cared but I figured Julie might not be so easy going. "This is Julie by the way, I told you about her."

"Hi there." Den countered, and Tom tossed her a smile. Den wasn't content to be left out of the conversation and as I listened to the two of them swap light banter, I considered how she might find the guys.

Den wasn't so bad looking, and she had shown an interest in him before. I know he was keen on her but then he was keen on a lot of my girlfriends. Tom too, had a string of girls and I didn't doubt that he still had someone down at Nimbin; he seemed always to have someone. He came across as really nice in a big masculine sort of way though he had never picked up any of my girlfriends before. Sure he had flirted with them on the rare occasion we had been in the same place at the same time, but normally I didn't see much of Tom and Denis, particularly since they had both finished school a year ago.

I had watched Tom grow up over the last year or two and it had been interesting. He had taken on a physical strength that had only been a promise when I first met him. I rather liked the growing shadow of his whiskers and the power and breadth of his shoulders, there was something attractive about that. Though he was Tom, very like a brother to me in many ways and he treated me like a sister. I wasn't sure if I liked that or whether it annoyed me. I did like the easy friendship we had even if he irritated me as often as he did. At least I felt I could tell him he was irritating, something that made him laugh as though he enjoyed the thought.

We had celebrated our school formal two months ago and since then, I hadn't seen much of my old boyfriend. At least I figured he was by now 'old' which made me smile too. I can't say I was upset over the idea but I had been fairly keen on him before the formal, though now I had decided that he was too much hard work, a little too moody for my tastes so it was easy for us to just drift apart. Though school was nearly over for good, then I didn't really want to see that much of him anymore. The effort seemed really not worth it.

As Tom handed me the cups, and then the bottle of soft drink I thanked him and began to organize the drinks. "Any sign of them yet? Do you know when they will get here?"

Tom frowned slightly, "The Kadaitcha Men?"

"Mmm..."

He shrugged, "Who knows, they could be here now for all I know," he said seriously. "Your Dad was here earlier, he'll take them straight to Ty I would think. He knows them better than us."

"Oh good. Then we might stay up here then," I suggested somewhat relieved.

Tom grinned. "You don't like them much... that's strange," and he found that amusing for some reason.

"Why? They creep me out."

Julie looked up, obviously interested and amused, "What do they look like? I mean... they are sort of like medicine men aren't they?"

"No... and yes. They are more like sorcerers with problems, they can deal with the cause rather than the effect," Denis answered, "Sorta like a psychologist only they actually do something rather than talk about it."

Julie shrugged; confused still but then it was hard to explain to someone who grew up with no experience of the spirit people. I was accustomed to scepticism not only in city people but even in our own people. The Kadaitcha Men were not as common as they once had been and it seemed fewer and fewer people had come up against their strengths. We didn't dwell on it, there was no resolution to scepticism other than to allow people time to learn and accept by experience.

Tom however attempted an explanation of a sort. "They are normal men, they just do things differently. They're aware of more things than others might be. An' they get together sometimes to train and learn with others with the same skills."

"Do you and Denis do that?" Julie asked curious.

"Yeah sure, so do you. Get together with others I mean. What do you think school is? Are you going on to college next year? That's the same thing only ours is an old lore. We don't need buildings and computers and so on."

Julie's answering giggle was light and amused. "It's not the same," she protested.

"It's the same," he countered. "Only we have been going to these learning camps for years, our growing up begins when we begin to grow up."

"No it's not the same." Laughing she eased back against her arm, making herself comfortable, flirting with Tom. Neither of the boys was unappreciative and while it was entertaining to watch them I wanted it to stop.

"Are you staying up here tonight?" I asked. It was more in an attempt to change the subject than anything else. "Julie has her hair kit with her and she can cut your hair if you want."

"Do you mind?" Tom asked her.

"Not at all. I can't promise anything, I'm not too bad but I'm not a hairdresser. I want to study hairdressing next year. Have you thought of something different maybe? I could dye your hair, or maybe a mohawk. We could have some fun with that."

Tom laughed at the thought but I could see even Denis was amused by the suggestion.

"We could do a spiky thing, shave the sides... turn it purple maybe," he teased laughing at Tom.

Strangely though, I could see Tom wasn't rejecting the idea out of hand. While he too laughed, he also still considered the suggestion.

"I've always wanted to try those dreads," he said suddenly.

"We could do dreads... though it's a really strong chemical and I don't have any at the moment. Your hair is long enough, but we would need to go into Cairns."

"How about plaits," I suggested. "Those really fine ones... that would suit you." My suggestion was more about being part of the conversation really. Though as I said it, I realized that it would suit him and it would certainly be different.

"Let me think on it," Tom offered as he sat up.

We all heard the approach of footsteps along the path and when dad, Ty's father and Warren emerged into the clearing I was surprised to hear Tom's soft exclamation.

"Ty?"

 The surprise in Tom's voice had us all looking for whatever it was he had meant in his quiet expression. Denis though grabbed at Tom's arm suddenly, as though to hold him back but both of them looked startled as he whispered softly but with urgency under his breath, his words short and low to Tom,

"He's not with them."

Tom climbed to his feet quickly while Denis struggled to follow trying to maintain the restraining grip, seemingly not wanting to let him go. Both Julie and I looked in the direction of the others then we scrambled up more slowly, wondering what it was that was alarming the boys.

Tom looked strangely angry for some reason, it was enough to make us both step back and out of the now very obvious line of fire between Warren and Tom, that we could easily see. For some reason there was going to be a confrontation, that was obvious to us all and while we struggled to understand it, the two men glared at each other. Tom's fists were balling as though to fight as he struggled to contain a building anger but still I couldn't see any reason for the antagonism.

"It's you!" Tom spat harshly, but his look seemed to move about the group, it wasn't steadily on Warren as I would have expected. "What have you done?" he demanded harshly confusing us. He had no thought for anyone other than Warren, who was looking as startled as everyone else bar Tom and Denis.

The expression which fled acrossed Warrens face was half fear and half panic but as Tom struggled with Denis's grip, finally breaking free and still furiously angry, he took the first long steps towards him. Warren swung back, and shocked I watched as he reached for something in his back pocket.

The flick knife startled us all and I heard Julie squeal, though I wasn't sure whether it was because of the threat in Warren's stance or because she had seen the quick light flash of the blade as I had.

Tom stopped in his advance suddenly and then braced himself like an animal in a subtle crouching attack, only a few bare footsteps from Warren. It was then I realized that he was going to take Warren on and they were going to fight, as his shoulders curled into an attack stance and his eyes hardened taking on a threat as he prepared in his own way for any blows while his muscles tightened like tense bands ready to spring.

For a scarce moment I couldn't believe that he would attempt to face off with a flick knife but he held his arms akimbo as though to offer a target in either direction. We could see the tenseness in his body, his muscles were now held taut ready to move in an instant. We knew that nothing would have persuaded him to back down and my thoughts sought a reason for his anger, it seemed inexplicable to me. But it was the low short laugh that surprised me. He looked like he knew what he was doing, he even looked like he was going to enjoy it and as the two of them began to circle each other, it was the shock on dad's face and Ty's father's face that registered with me.

Out of the corner of my eye I saw Julie scramble further backwards then as Warren moved towards us, as he circled in to face-off with Tom; I felt my stomach tighten in fear.

With barely a thought I dived lightly towards the small pile of timber the boys had set aside for the fire. There was no way I was going to get anywhere near that flick knife, or let it anywhere near me. I grabbed at a longer solid branch, one balanced amongst the wood pile, then I lurched towards Warren and swung it wildly aiming for his head.

The crack when it hit him from behind shocked me as equally as the reality that I had actually hit him. What I didn't expect was for him to crumple as he was flung to the side by the force of my blow.

For a moment we all stood there in disbelief, Warren was crumpled on the ground and blood had begun to ooze from his head. I heard the shocked expletive come from Tom and I looked up to see the utter surprise and disbelief on his face as he looked at me.

"Geezus Alex... What the hell...!" but his words froze as the low chant hit the air.

Completely taken by surprise we all swung towards the forest, towards the deep masculine chant and watched as a Kadaitcha Man steadily emerged from the bush. He was coated in ceremonial markings of soft white down, which travelled a decorative stripe plastered across his shoulders. Running deep into his chest and down along his legs and feet were the circles that I knew marked him a Kadaitcha Man of strength. Mesmerized I watched as he approached us slowly with a carefully measured step.

I couldn't believe what I was seeing yet the Spirit Man was there and his eyes were fixed on Warren's prostrate form, it was so close to where both Tom and I now stood as though frozen to the spot. That I felt the compulsion to move but I couldn't for some reason.

My deeply drawn breath held traces of fear; he looked as though he was coming towards me and I was terrified that he was. I shuffled back in a silent fright and out of the corner of my eye I saw Tom move too, he moved quickly, and in my direction. Just when I thought we were both about to launch into flight I felt Tom grab my arm. He was swinging me, stalling me, then suddenly he pulled my weight into his body, upsetting my centre of balance. As he towered over me, the hard constraining bars of his tense arms were quickly around me, holding me still, stopping me. He held me fast and for a horrible moment I felt he was offering me to the Kadaitcha Man. He was preventing my escape so I squealed, struggling to fight him off.

"Shhh... quiet..." he said in quickly whispering. "He isn't after you. Don't try an' run," he added tersely which was enough to make me freeze in fear once again, I was mesmerised by the sorcerers approach.

I watched horrified as the Kadaitcha Man came nearer to us both with a measured step that was in time with the growing chant. It was then that I could see that his focus was on Warren's prostrate body. Only then did it occurred to me that I might have killed him and with that frightful thought, I felt myself go almost limp in Tom's hold.

The Kadaitcha Man bent towards Warren in the oddest way; almost as if it was part of a dance. and reaching he eased his fingers and then his hands into the now bloody matt that was Warren's hair. Then in a strangely paced dance he slowly circled the prostrate form as though gathering something in his arms and pulling it to him while he sang his low melodic song. Then he began a slow stepping dance as he chanted and backed towards the small smouldering fire in that same strangely measured step and I found myself, although scared, I was worrying that he might step into the hot embers.

I caught my breath in a horrible anticipation as I could see his steps took him into the fire and if it wasn't for Tom's hand which clamped about my mouth quickly I would have screamed in warning, although I heard Julie scream then I saw Denis move quickly to quieten her.

"He won't get hurt," Tom said urgently in a whispered explanation. "He's drawing Taipan with him."

"What?" I tried to say, but Tom must have heard or felt my muffled breath.

"He has Ty's Shadow, he has taken it from Warren and is drawing him into the fire with him," He countered in a low voice and amazed I watched the Kadaitcha Man seemed to do just that. As he stepped into the bed of low flame and ash, disturbing a fine puff of white ash that had gathered over the past few hours, I watched shocked as the fire seemed to haze then flare and suddenly they were gone, or rather he was gone.

Unable to believe what I had just seen I watched stunned as the haze of smoke cleared and the ash settled where the Kadaitcha Man had stepped.

As Tom's grip about me eased, Ty's father moved quickly towards the now unsettled figure of his younger son who lay as though burrowing into the dirt with his face and chest. Warren had stirred and begun to groan while his father broke into a tirade of language that I did not understand. It was obvious though that he was angry, furiously angry.

Dad just stood back and watched for a moment and then with eyes on me he nodded.

"We need to get to the house, the Kadaitcha Man should be there now," and with that he turned as though to leave, completely ignoring Warren and his father. "Alex!" Dad bellowed suddenly shaking me from my shock. "You better bring everyone, the lot of you. Leave them!" he ordered without thought to any protest we might make.

Tom let me go and I turned ready to obey my dad without question, as I struggled to gather my wits. Denis had Julie ahead of him and he was ushering her after dad, in the same way that Tom was pushing me with his hand in the small of my back. Only then did I notice the others, there were other men around us standing back watching. They had emerged from the trees and were dressed in the same manner as the Kadaitcha Man. They had obviously been prepared for ceremony or perhaps in ceremony when they had joined us, or found us. I wasn't sure which.

"Come on Alex, move quickly," Tom said under his breath as he urged me along. "The Men have a purpose and it's not a place for women now."

"What... what are they going to do?" I asked half afraid to hear, realizing that Warren was now left to the Kadaitcha Men, all of them. "What is it?"

"Warren had Taipan harnessed, he had harnessed his spirit. I could see him... Ty was tied to him in some way. He could have done Ty a great deal of harm; it was a black sorcery of some kind."

"What are they going to do to him?" I whispered as we walked, Tom wasn't letting us lag behind, he kept up a steady pace..

"They can deal with the blackness of what he's doing. They won't kill him just take the power from him. Though that blow you gave him might just kill him."

"Oh God... you don't think so?" I said suddenly horrified at the possible consequence of what I had done with so little thought. I hadn't meant to cause such damage, I had just meant to protect myself, protect Julie and me.

Tom grinned suddenly and in disbelief I stared at him. Then he noticed my attention and tried to hide his smirk. "Do you really want me to answer that? The bastard nearly killed my brother. Do you realize that this is the second time he has had a go at my family."

"I thought he was going to kill you," I said suddenly, remembering the flash of the blade.

"Mmm... you're right. That is the third time then," he said.

"Tom! That's not what I meant!" I protested at his attitude. But as we approached the house we both heard the soft chant and at the sound of it, quite suddenly Julie froze ahead of us.

"I'm not going in there," she said fearfully. "That bloke is in there...The Kadji guy. You've got to be kidding if you want me to go in there!" she warned and the extent of her fear was more than apparent.

In a dilemma I heard her and although Denis obviously was of two minds in how to go about dealing with her, I stepped in quickly. "We can go back to the shed," I suggested with some reassurance, as though I too understood her, which quite frankly I did. "I'm not too keen on going in either.... I can't... I mean I don't need to do I?"

The question was aimed at Tom and for some reason I really expected him to know the answer. Dad had moved ahead of us and had already entered the house. He had wasted no time, as he obviously wanted to ensure that things were going as he had expected them to.

"OK then, you can take Julie back to the shed." Tom answered, having considered the question. It was then that I realized he was assessing our level of fear and the shock on our faces. "Den and I need to go in. We'll come and get you if we need you but I can't see that we should. You should be OK."

Taking Julie's hand I wasted no time retreating to the shed. It was frozen and she looked clearly to be in some sort of state. Drawing her towards the shed I watched as the two boys moved into the house. I was incredibly relieved that we were not required to be there. We could still hear the soft chant and I knew it was coming from my bedroom. Dad had been right, the Kadaitcha Man was still in there and while my curiosity was rampant my fear kept it at bay.

Despite the warmth of the evening we settled ourselves and sitting together on the lounge we waited. Watching as the dusk fell, then the night claimed the corners of the shed first and the darkness arrived. Once I had the lantern lit it wasn't so bad, but the only thing that filled our thoughts was the soft chant we could hear coming from the house. The song had been strengthened by other voices and a steady beat was keeping the pace of it.

"What do you think they are doing?" Julie asked after some time, as we waited to see if the boys would come back for us. Curled up on the lounge we both seemed to be hiding from that possibility.

"I don't know. Singing my Uncle I expect."

"What does that do?" she countered almost tersely, and irritated that she had difficulty in understanding. It sounded as though she was afraid of the answer she might get and I searched for a way to tell her, give her an answer that would soothe her.

"It will calm him, help him to heal. I think he had some sort of death wish he was fighting. That is what Warren did. He must have done it somehow."

I felt Julies eyes on me, she was frowning and I wondered how else to answer her. "Ok... a death wish. I didn't realize you could do that."

"Yeah... you can, if you know how."

"How... how did Tom know... about it I mean?"

That was harder, I couldn't think of what to say. I knew Tom was sensitive to spirit men, he would never have been accepted into the Featherfoot Lore if he wasn't, but I didn't know the extent of his sensitivity. It could be like Den's where he could sometimes feel the spirit men about him, or hear them. I had never been told all of it.

"I don't know. You will have to ask him." I said finally.

I moved closer towards Julie, more to help still the slight shivers we were both experiencing and it was a comfort. Both of us stayed curled up, waiting, half expecting the boys to turn up at the door, dreading that they might ask us to join them. It was a terrible wait, one that seemed to go on forever.

BACK WITH THE LIVING

Tom:

Taipan lay resting, his colour was much better and he had life in his eyes as he looked at Aine beside him which was more reward than I had ever felt before. The Kadaitcha Man sat still in the corner, his mind and his Spirit guides still at work ensuring all was well. It would take time but the danger had passed.

Witness to this was the blood still streaked across Ty's chest, blood which we couldn't yet allow Aine to wash away even though she had prepared to do so. It was Warren's blood, it was now smeared everywhere even on the bedding, the hand prints of the Kadaitcha Man still could be seen on Ty's skin at his side. It was necessary I knew, it had been required to return Ty's Shadow, to bind it soundly to his body once more and Alex, even though I was sure she didn't know it, had ensured not only Taipan's health but preserved Warren's life for him. Warren would thank her for that in time I was sure and for a moment I wondered what she would make of his thanks.

The Kadaitcha Men would now deal with Warren, it was out of our hands, it would take time, days at the very least to take from him the black power he had practiced. I wondered also, what shell would be left of the man when they were through with him.

It had been hard to understand why he had attacked Taipan in such a way. Who knew the workings of such a mind but I didn't doubt that it had something to do with the respect Ty held in both communities. It couldn't have been because of his want to own what had been his brothers, not even Ty's dad had known of Aine and the happiness they had found together and for just a moment I wondered what could have come about if either Warren or his father had been aware of the treasures Ty enjoyed in his life. Perhaps Warren really had thought that by dimming the shadow cast by such a strong brother, he would instead stand more surely in the sun. The Kadaitcha Man, who knew the thoughts of other's had said as much. That attitude surprised me, I couldn't understand why anyone would choose to stand revealed in the sun light. I much preferred the half light of uncertainty where I could move more freely. It was a half light where I knew Ty moved at times, shadowed by his own reputation.

Taipan had shown me the value of the shadows and I had absolutely no intention of ever stepping into the sun light, exposed to all. I could think of nothing worse and this was a sentiment I knew Sean and nearly all Shaman shared with me.

As I stood to leave, Taipan turned his attention to me. He was at ease and happy to be truly on the mend.

"Tom thanks. I am indebted to you and it isn't a debt I will dismiss lightly."

Grinning, I glanced at Aine. "I couldn't let you go you know," I said by way of explanation. "What would we do with the coming..." stopping myself suddenly, I shrugged. I had been going to say, with the coming baby. The Spirit Child who even now slept at the end of the bed.

Taipan grinned, "I know, I feel it also. It's like the brush of air, the movement of a breath across my shoulders. I have felt it for a while now."

In the one moment we both glanced towards Aine, both hoping we had not pre-empted the news that was hers alone to give and then realizing what we were both doing, Taipan chuckled and I too dropped my glance ruefully.

"What?" she said suddenly, looking between us both alert to something we weren't sharing.

"Nothing Kitten," Ty said contentedly. "It's nothing now. I'll tell you what I meant later."

"OK then," I added, still smiling and keen to get out of the room now. "I'll... I'll let you get back to it," as I moved to make a quick exit, Taipan again forestalled me.

"We will have to talk about what we are going to do about the haunting in the gorge. While the Kadaitcha Men are here, they can help us. They will be here for a few days yet. It's something I feel we need to sort out."

Even though we both looked towards the Kadaitcha Man, he wasn't disturbed by our question and knowing that it wasn't perhaps the time, I nodded and began moving towards the door.

Taipan was right... though I couldn't believe that he was jumping straight back into this. The Men could advise us if this was something given to us to resolve. If this was what we could do for the community here, then it was best to organize it while we had the benefit of their advice and I knew Taipan would not let it go. He was a Karadji and his sense of responsibility to his people and family was his life.

"Well that can wait till you're at least on your feet," I suggested with some irony, as I went to leave. I didn't suggest that he should let it go, as I knew that this same sense of responsibility was what had drawn me from the life I had led in Sydney. I understood how this drive in him had given me so much. Asking Ty to turn his back on this was like asking a dancer, not to dance. Or a poet not to dream... it wasn't possible.

"Not at all, we can talk as I mend, though we will need to wait till the wet season is over before we head back into that area. What makes you think it isn't your problem? This business is right up your alley, it would be good training for you as a Shaman. It would give you a sense of the manner and strength in skills you have Tom. You're maybe the only one that can confidently follow this through, no matter where they go Tom, you can see what or who haunts the gorge and perhaps with the help of the Kadaitcha, follow where ever it's that they go. That much is more than obvious to me.

We need to take advantage of what tools we have around us and there is a fine gathering of useful men at hand who can help."

"Yeah well, a couple of days and then we can talk about it. I need to wind down a bit." I said, knowing I needed to take a few days at least to get my head back together after my recent time with the Kadaitcha Men. "And you need to get some strength back."

In the kitchen, Denis was helping his mum with the clean up after something of a haphazard meal an hour or so ago. I noticed that there were still two covered plates on the table and when Marnie saw me she turned from the sink, then wiped her hands absently on the tea towel before she set it aside.

"Well, you two can take this out to the girls. They haven't been in yet and I'm thinking while... well they won't be in a hurry to come up to the house. Do you mind?"

"No... that's OK. I should check on them anyway... I think we spooked them out a bit."

"Yeah... well I think so," Marnie said a little apologetically. "Julie will probably stay the night. It's getting too late for her to go anyway and she mentioned her mum was away for the weekend again. Don't let her go home will you, I don't want her on her own not with no one at home at this hour."

"Yeah sure," moving towards the door Den picked up the two plates wrapped in foil which kept them warm, I took one from him and headed out to the girls.

Out in the shed it was quiet. I had expected some noise, a radio or some music but all was still and when we stepped inside the door it was immediately apparent why. Both the girls were curled up on my bed against each other, sleeping, though Julie perhaps wasn't sleeping so soundly because when Den set the plates down she immediately opened her eyes and moved to sit up.

"Your dinner..." Den said softly, "It's still warm."

Attempting to sit up, Julie suddenly became aware of Alex who was curled into her side she stopped not wanting to wake her. Moving towards them and taking the weight of Alex against my arm I carefully allowed Julie the freedom to move, letting her climb to her feet as I eased Alex into a more comfortable position against the pillows, sending Julie a quick smile as she moved off.

Alex stirred as the others stepped outside where I knew they intended to stir up the camp fire as was often our custom and as I watched her stretch into the comfort of the lounge she opened her eyes, closed them again but then almost immediately opened them, frowning as she caught the sight of me squatting beside the bed.

"Sleepy head," I said softly, smiling. "There's some dinner here if you want it I'm going out to the fire with the others."

Almost immediately Alex moved to prop herself up, gathering her wits. "Have they gone?"

"The Kadaitcha Men..? No, they'll be here a few days up at the camp I think."

Watching as she mentally shook herself, she then suddenly frowned once more, struggling to sit up properly. "Is he dead?" she questioned and I realized she meant Warren.

"No. Your Dad went up to check on him earlier, he's fine. A bit sore from when you brained him, but he'll survive. Believe me he has more to worry about than a head ache."

"Mmm... I had this horrible dream where he was dead, and they... the men came to get me. It was horrible, I was sorta taken but you found me, protected me for some reason."

"Yeah well... it's OK. They aren't going to come and get you," I smiled at the thought, knowing that the Kadaitcha men were something that parents often threatened kids with if they misbehaved. "I guess I should thank you, you saved us all a lot of trouble by hitting him although it wasn't what we intended."

"He was going to kill you," she countered still put out. "He had a knife, didn't you see it?"

"Yeah I saw it. It's not the first time someone's pulled a knife on me you know." I said smiling. "I grew up in Sydney. My dad used to take me into Redfern with him when I was just a kid and he wanted to go drinking an' catch up with mates. I've seen a lot of fights Alex. Sometimes you run, sometimes you don't."

"You could have been hurt!"

"Yeah... it was a little knife. You just don't let it get too close to you is all. Your idea worked better in the long run anyway."

For a moment she considered me and I suddenly grew uncertain under the onslaught of her eyes.

"You've never spoken about your dad before?"

I grinned, in an attempt to mask my surprise at her comment. "Don't wait for it to happen again," I said softly as I stood. "The others are out by the fire, but you and Julie can have the shed tonight. I'm thinking I would rather sleep around the fire and I think I would rather stay away from Ty's camp for a few days."

"Thanks, we didn't mean to put you out, but I appreciate it." Reaching for the plate on the table she stood unsteadily, but soon had her balance. "How's Julie?" she asked as we moved towards the door.

"Looks fine; Den's with her."

The two of them were settled around the fire pit within the glow of the flame and as we joined them we moved into what was a comfortable and easy going evening.

I don't know what it's about a camp fire, but it settles you, eases your mind as you watch the dance of the flame, occasionally tending to the life of the fire and its warmth and comfort. Living so close to the bush and nature wouldn't be half as attractive without the life around the camp fire. It offered everything that was wanted within the range of its light. It was far more entertaining than the screen of a telly, which in comparison seemed repetitive and sterile, and there was nothing that could compare with the companionship of friends around a campfire at night.

We, the four of us, didn't talk of the events of that afternoon again. It was a mutual agreement between the girls. I don't think they wanted to hear about something they knew we wouldn't explain ultimately. Ty continued to mend but we heard little from the upper camp though John would often be missing, and I knew Ty's father also spent his time up there. It was a business beyond our experience and neither I, nor Den expected to be included in the ceremony that we knew was going on.

The following afternoon the girls decided that it was time to work out what it was I wanted done with my hair and after much discussion I elected to take the opportunity to have it plaited into the fine plaits Alex had suggested. This was an intricate process, which took both Alex and Julie a great deal of time though I can't say I found the experience an unpleasant one. They soon got into the flow of things and Alex took to adding small colourful beads to the end of some of the plaits. I felt like something of a play doll which the girls were amusing themselves with. I enjoyed it and it certainly seemed to afford them a great deal of amusement.

The result was rewarding, though I wondered what others would make of the colourful play of beads when I moved my head. It was a fun exercise, one that was to stay with me for some weeks.

When Ty was finally up and about I knew he wasn't very impressed with my new look but he said little. Aine liked it, it seemed the style was something that appealed to the women, and I thought that this could only be a good thing.

Julie had been around a few times since the girls had done my hair, always in the company of Alex and both Den and I enjoyed her company but we hadn't yet decided if she was interested in either of us. Having Alex around certainly had its benefits as she had a wide circle of friends who were constantly about and I got to know a few of them over the following weeks.

The business of the haunting had been set aside for the moment. The wet season had arrived proper and the regular torrid drenching of the afternoons and evenings was a welcome respite from the humid heat in the height of summer. Sean had left to return home with the arrival of the Wet and as I settled in to sit out the season, Den and I were given the time to explore all that we had learnt in the past months.

Travelling around the old goldfields was an impossible task in the Wet season. The rivers and creeks were swollen and with the crocodiles lurking in the estuaries and mangroves and the snakes on the move, it wasn't a good idea to try to move across such challenging country. Instead I learnt more about surviving in the far north Queensland tropics from both Denis and his dad John while Taipan fussed over Aine enjoying the prospect of the new baby to fill their lives.

It would be April before we would head out into the country again and in the mean time there were many other things to keep us busy preparing for when the Wet season had passed. Settling into the leisure of this season had its advantages though the humidity was something that was difficult to get used to.

We spent much of our days fooling about in the river and keeping tabs on where the croc's were. We could smell them I discovered, though it paid to be wary of them and constantly aware of where they were setting up nests or hanging out waiting for a feed.

It was in this season that we honed our skills, there was plenty of food about and hunting became an enjoyable pastime. We couldn't venture far, but if we headed into the mountains and deep rainforests we could find more than enough to feed everyone. The cleanskin cattle were often the game we hoped for, they had run wild in the rainforests after they had escaped from branding and now were game for anyone on Aboriginal Traditional lands who was given the right to hunt, including those from the cattle stations adjoining the land boundaries.

Living without commodities that most people took from granted was a reality up here, there simply wasn't anything that could be supplied readily. So we had to do for ourselves and in some ways that was more rewarding and challenging than trying to live where supplies could be easily accessed.

The people who made their lives in the forest didn't have an address, let alone electricity or any other service. It was a challenging life which bred a particular type of outlook on life. It was a life I could get used to I decided as I settled in with Taipan and Aine nearby and shared my time between the two camps.

It was a life that was truly going to teach me new skills, show me new outlooks and take me down a path I would never have dreamt of before I left the city.

Life was good.

The End

CAVERNS OF THE DREAMTIME

Book 4
The Dreaming Series

Preview:

Tom:

The various crossroads you come to in life always present problems. You think that you will make the right choices, because who in their right mind is going to deliberately take the wrong choice? Then the road becomes rough and you are left wondering about the path you could have taken.

They say there are alternate, parallel realities where perhaps you or your spirit shadow took another path and perhaps they aren't now experiencing the same problems and decisions you are labouring over? It's an interesting thought and I don't know the answer to this but it would be a comfort if it were true. You could always try to swap places when things got a bit tough.

I can't go back easily even if I wanted to and I don't, but when the path ahead looks difficult it's easy to think about the other choices you could have made. I was becoming to realize that I would have to deal with the same difficulties which my brothers dealt with. My life was to be different from so many of my friends, mainly because of who I was and what I was trying to achieve.

I knew Taipan had made choices, and these choices mapped his path in life. It was a path he chose, and one I know he has no regrets about. In Aine he had found a woman who was willing to travel this path with him and I wondered, perhaps if one day this would need to be my choice also. Unless I found something that would cause me to leave the path I am choosing. It didn't seem likely.

Women were the most intractable things on Earth I thought as I looked around the company, knowing it was probably a woman who would most affect my choices. I didn't know if there was one out there for me, I doubted it and it wasn't even something that hovered in my mind much. There was too much else going on in my life now and I had to bring some order to it somehow. I wanted to be sure of the path I could plot for a future, a decision about where my future would be.

I knew Ty and Aine had spoken about moving south again and I needed to decide if I was going to follow or if I would stay and if I chose to stay, then once again just what was I staying for?

I had a lot to think on and this was the perfect night, the perfect place to chew things over in my mind. There was enough distraction here to stop me from obsessing, but not enough to stop me from finding my way in all this.

Denis and I had talked about this life, so many times in the last months, seen so many things and been welcomed in so many places. The experience of living with people, staying for days or weeks, bound as we had been by the transitions between the season and watching the movement of water across the land had opened my eyes to so many possibilities. It had been a huge learning curve in so many ways.

www.ingramcontent.com/pod-product-compliance
Lightning Source LLC
Chambersburg PA
CBHW071629260626

47170CB00001B/24